Marie Sexton

...an intriguing mystery romance...a remarkable saga.
~ *Literary Nymphs Reviews*

...a beautiful love story...scorching hot sex...an interesting read and something very different from any of Marie Sexton's previous books. I can't wait to see what she offers us next.
~ *Fiction Vixen Book Reviews*

...I was beyond excited to read a new book by this writer...so very well-written...really great chemistry going and the sex scenes were really hot... ~ *Jessewave Reviews*

...a tale that is woven together from several threads... At its heart, however, this novel is the story of two men who find their way to each other from different paths in life...it was so well worth the trip... ~ *Top 2 Bottom Reviews*

SONG OF OESTEND

MARIE SEXTON

Song of Oestend
ISBN # 978-0-85715-747-8
©Copyright Marie Sexton 2011
Cover Art by Posh Gosh ©Copyright 2011
Interior text design by Claire Siemaszkiewicz
Total-E-Bound Publishing

Published in 2011 by Total-E-Bound Publishing, Think Tank, Ruston Way, Lincoln, LN6 7FL, United Kingdom.

SONG OF OESTEND

Author's Note

On the pronunciation of Oestend — it's not as hard as you might think. I actually took it from the Spanish word for west. Just say oh-EST (if you say it really fast, it sounds like "west"). Now, add the "end".
Oh-EST-end.
~Marie

Chapter One

Aren had heard of the wraiths, of course. Everyone had.

The thing was, nobody believed the stories were real. Not where he came from, anyway.

But on his first night in the town of Milton, as the wind howled outside and beat against the shuttered windows of his room, Aren Montrell lay awake and trembling in his bed. He began to remember every story he'd ever heard about the wraiths.

Every nanny—and probably every parent, too, although Aren wouldn't know about that—told stories of children found cold and lifeless in the morning because some spiteful adult had left the window open after tucking the kids into bed. It was said that wraiths came on the darkest of nights, stealing the breath from any person fool enough not to be inside, behind closed doors. Even back home, across the sea, in the bustling cities of Lanstead, many houses had signs of protection over their front doors. Still, Aren had never had reason to believe the stories were true. He'd always believed the signs were more decorative than anything. But he'd quickly discovered upon his arrival in Oestend that every building had the signs, not just over the front door, but over every door, and the windows as well. Even the barn where weary travellers boarded their horses had been warded against the wraiths.

He'd seen the way the hostel-keeper and his wife had systematically checked each and every window in each and every room. He'd made note of the double bars on both the front and back doors. Then, as he was finishing his dinner, the wife had stopped next to him. Her hand on his shoulder was rough and calloused and her face was grim. "Don't open your window once the generator goes on," she'd said. "I don't care how hot you get."

Aren wasn't even sure what she meant by the word 'generator', but she'd moved on then, before Aren could ask questions. He'd nearly jumped out of his skin when the generator had kicked on a few minutes later – not that he would have known that was what it was if the woman hadn't warned him. It made a nagging, low-pitched drone that Aren didn't so much hear as feel, low in the base of his skull. He found it nerve-racking, but it was obvious the locals were used to it. He'd gone to his room feeling less than confident.

Maybe this had been a mistake. Maybe he shouldn't have come here, to the pitiful, dusty edge of the world. But after the incident at the university, running to Oestend had seemed so logical. So obvious. A suddenly sympathetic Professor Sheldon had helped Aren secure a job at one of the large ranches on the Oestend prairie. At the time, Aren had thought Sheldon had done it out of pity. Now, as he faced the realisation that this was a life he did not know how to live, Aren began to also realise he'd been duped. No doubt Sheldon and Professor Dean Birmingham, the man Aren had thought of as his lover for the past four years, were laughing together over their brandy, pleased they'd manage to rid themselves of him.

"Fuck you," Aren said. His voice was loud in the small room. He sounded strong, and it gave him courage. "Fuck you!" he said again, louder this time, feeling more sure of himself. "I'm not scared."

He jumped as somebody pounded on the wall of his room. Not one of the wraiths that may or may not have been outside in the wind. It came from the room next to Aren's. "People trying to sleep in here!" the man on the other side of the wall yelled.

Aren couldn't believe anybody could sleep through the buzz of the generator and the racket of the wind and yet be kept awake by somebody talking, but he didn't want to cause trouble, so he resolved to stop cussing at people who were halfway across the world. Still, his outburst had given him the strength he needed to examine his situation rationally.

There was no point in being scared. If there really were wraiths in Oestend, it was obvious the locals knew how to handle them. The man who'd hired him had directed him to this particular hostel for the night. Presumably he wouldn't have sent Aren to a place that was known for allowing its tenants to be killed in their sleep. Although the shutters on windows rattled, they seemed solid enough, and Aren would have bet his last coin there was a warding sign over the window as well. He had to trust those things would be enough to keep him safe.

He pulled the blanket over his head and snuggled down under the covers. At least the bed was soft and the sheets were clean. Tomorrow, a man from the ranch would arrive to take him to his new home. Whatever this backwater land wanted to throw at him, Aren was sure he was ready.

* * * *

He was right on most counts. He was ready for the dust. He was ready for the wind. He was ready for the two-day trip to the ranch.

What he wasn't ready for was Deacon.

Deacon was the man who arrived to take Aren to the BarChi Ranch. Deacon had come into town the night before, but had apparently elected to spend the night elsewhere — in the stables or at the whorehouse or at another inn, Aren didn't know, and didn't care. Deacon arrived at the hostel the next morning driving a wooden wagon drawn by a pair of sturdy draught horses.

The first thing Aren noticed about him was the deep colour of his skin. Back on the continent, skin-tones ran from white to pink to golden, but one rarely saw anybody darker than the sun could make them. Deacon, on the other hand, had skin that was a rich, dark reddish-brown. He wore a straw cowboy hat, and his pitch-black hair hung in a queue down his back. Aren supposed him to be around thirty years old. He was tall and broad and muscular and rough and everything Aren might have expected from a man who'd spent his entire life doing hard labour on a remote Oestend ranch. He was exactly the kind of man who usually managed to make Aren feel small and insignificant simply by being there. He looked at Aren's pile of luggage with barely disguised amusement.

"You got an awful lot of stuff," he said, turning his mocking gaze onto Aren. "What's in all those?"

Deacon's scrutiny made him uncomfortable. Aren tried to smooth his light brown hair down—it had grown out longer than he'd ever had it, which was still short by Oestend standards. It was too short to pull into a queue like Deacon's, and though Aren tried to keep it straight, it seemed determined to form soft curls around his ears. He had a hard enough time getting men to take him seriously because of his small stature. Having hair that curled like a girl's wasn't going to help.

"Well?" Deacon asked, still waiting for an answer. "What's in the bags?"

Aren forced himself to stop fidgeting, although he couldn't quite meet Deacon's eyes. "My clothes. Books. Art supplies."

"Art supplies?" Deacon asked, as if the words held no meaning for him.

"Yes," Aren said, and for some reason, Deacon's absurd question gave him the strength he needed to stand up straight and face the rough cowboy in front of him. "Canvas and paint."

Deacon's eyebrows went up, and although he didn't laugh, it was clear he wanted to. "Good thing. Barn's needed a new coat of paint for a while now."

Aren felt his cheeks turning red, and he hid it by turning to pick up the nearest suitcase. It had seemed perfectly reasonable to bring his art supplies with him, especially since he feared both paint and canvas might be hard to come by on the ranch. It bothered him that Deacon had managed to make him feel foolish for it. The fact that he'd done it within moments of meeting him only made it sting more.

One by one, he loaded his many suitcases into the wagon. He could feel Deacon's gaze upon him the entire time. He moved quickly because he knew they had other things to do in town before they left. When his last bag was in the wagon, he turned to face Deacon again, ready for the mockery he'd seen in Deacon's eyes before. He was surprised to see Deacon was no longer laughing at him. He was watching him appraisingly, and Aren thought he even saw a hint of approval in his dark eyes.

"Would have done that for you, you know," he said.

Then why didn't you? Of course, if he'd wanted help, he could have asked, but this was obviously a world where physical strength earned more respect than education or refinement. Aren hated to give other men a reason to think he was weak. Just because he wasn't made of muscle like Deacon didn't mean he couldn't handle his own luggage. A familiar feeling of angry rebellion bloomed in Aren's chest. "I'm not helpless," he snapped.

Deacon's look of puzzled amusement returned. He shook his head. "Why're you mad?" he asked.

It was a good question. Why *was* he mad? Because Deacon was laughing at him? Because he hadn't helped with the bags? Or because he seemed surprised that Aren hadn't asked for help with them? Or was it only because here, just as at the university, he was bound to be seen as less than a man by all the other men around him?

"I'm just tired," Aren said, which wasn't exactly a lie. He'd been travelling for more than a month to reach this point—four weeks on the small, stinky ship from Lanstead to Francshire, Oestend's eastern port, being seasick most of the way, followed by two nights straight on the noisy, rickety train from Francshire to Milton, the western-most point of what could loosely be termed 'civilisation' in Oestend. Although he'd managed to get a few hours of sleep at the hostel the night before, he still felt terribly out of sorts. "I feel I've barely slept in ages."

The smile that spread across Deacon's face this time wasn't mocking. It was friendly, and a little bit mischievous. "Don't worry. Pretty sure you'll sleep good tonight."

"Why is that?" Aren asked.

"Staying at the McAllen farm," Deacon said. "Lots of maids and daughters there." He winked at Aren. "One of them's bound to tuck you in."

Aren hoped the sinking feeling those words caused wasn't apparent on his face. He fought to keep his voice steady. "I see."

"We best get moving if we want to get there before the wraiths get us."

"Of course," Aren said, although at that moment, he would have preferred to take his chances with the wraiths.

They made a few quick stops for supplies before heading out into the prairie. Aren hadn't seen much of Milton when he'd arrived. The hostel he'd stayed at was near the outskirts of the east side. They had to drive west all the way through town before leaving.

Although the cities back in Lanstead had their slums too, the parts Aren had been familiar with were filled with upscale shops and brightly-painted town homes. Stained glass windows had recently become a fad, and nearly every home sported at least one, usually as prominent and garish as it could be. Glancing around the dusty town of Milton, Aren saw nothing of the sort. The walkways fronting the businesses were bare wooden planks. The buildings he saw looked as if they'd never seen a single coat of paint. The few painted signs he saw were faded to the point of being practically useless.

"Some of these buildings don't even have windows," Aren said.

Deacon shrugged. "Glass is expensive. Plus, it's damn hard to patch the hole in the wall if it breaks."

Everywhere he looked, it seemed Aren saw no colour at all—only varying shades of brown and grey. He found it a bit depressing.

In the town's centre lay a large wooden platform. It almost looked like a stage. Aren might have thought it was for executions, except there was no sign of a gallows.

"What's that for?" he asked Deacon.

Deacon's jaw clenched, as if the question angered him. He didn't look at Aren. "That's where they used to sell the slaves."

"Slaves?" Aren asked, alarmed. "They still have slavery here?"

"Not anymore," Deacon said, "but it lasted longer than you'd probably think."

Once they'd passed the last building, Deacon drove onto a rutted trail that led into the long, golden-green grass of the Oestend prairie. They were headed due west, presumably towards the BarChi Ranch, where Aren had managed to secure a job as a bookkeeper. As the bustle of the town fell behind them, Aren found himself feeling simultaneously liberated and scared to death. In leaving Milton, he was abandoning all vestiges of the civilised society he'd grown up in. Ahead of him, Oestend held only ranches, mines, buffalo, and mile after mile of prairie. He was leaving behind the trappings of luxury. Back home in Lanstead, most homes had running water. A few even had electricity. He would find none of that here in Oestend.

Lanstead had first colonised Oestend a hundred and fifty years earlier, but shipping goods back and forth had proved to be more trouble and more expense than it was worth. Since that time, the empire had long since lost interest in the remote land, and the colonies had become more or less independent. The eastern seaboard was where the majority of the population resided, living off what the sea provided. Further inland, most of Oestend's limited prosperity came from the many mines to the south and fur and fishing in the north. Of course, everybody in Oestend, from miners and trappers to the inn-keepers and blacksmiths, had to eat, and that was where the ranches came in. By accepting a position at one of them, Aren had committed himself to a life that was considered downright primitive by most of his colleagues.

Ex-colleagues, he reminded himself. It was time he stopped thinking of himself as a bourgeois university student from the most cosmopolitan city on the continent. He was now a bookkeeper for an Oestend rancher.

"You work for Jeremiah?" Aren asked Deacon.

Deacon frowned at the question. "Guess so."

"Are you his son?"

"Nope."

"Are you the foreman?"

Deacon tipped his head a bit to the side, squinting as if the question confused him. "Guess I'm the closest thing we got." He glanced over at Aren, looking him up and down in an appraising way — though not as if he were interested in Aren sexually. Aren thought it was probably closer to the way he might have examined a cow he was taking to market. "You're not married, are you?" Deacon asked.

It seemed like such a strange question, completely out of nowhere, and it surprised Aren. "No," he said. "Why?"

"Possible Fred McAllen'll be throwing one of his daughters at you tonight."

Aren found that alarming. It was bad enough he might have to face women who wanted sex, but if his host was expecting it for some reason, things were going to be even more uncomfortable than he'd imagined. "You mean he encourages his daughters to 'tuck in' the guests?"

Deacon laughed. "Hell, no! He catches one of them doing that, he might take a shotgun to you."

That was something of a relief. "Then what—?"

"I mean a bride."

Any fleeting sense of relief Aren had felt disappeared. "A *what?*"

"The McAllens have a lot of daughters, and not many eligible sons around here to marry them off to."

"I'm not getting married!"

Deacon laughed. "No, not tonight you ain't. I'm just saying, they'll likely be sizing you up as a possible husband."

"Holy Saints, that's the last thing I need."

"It's possible they'll hold off. Wait to see if you pan out before letting one of their girls marry you."

"Is there anything I can do to discourage them?"

Deacon laughed, and somehow the look he turned on Aren seemed far more congenial than it had been before. "Make yourself look like bad husband material, I guess."

"How do I do that?"

"I don't know. Never thought about it before. I suppose act stupid. Or mean."

Nobody in the world would believe Aren if he tried to act mean. Stupid, though? Stupid he thought he could do.

Chapter Two

A couple of hours before sunset they rode over a ridge and the McAllen farm appeared below them. There was a house, a barn, and a few small outbuildings. Lined up behind the barn were pen after pen of pigs. Rising high above it all, casting its long shadow over the house, was the biggest windmill Aren had ever seen. It was also the strangest. It obviously wasn't part of any mill. Its base ended in a giant contraption that looked like an engine that had fallen off a passing train.

"What is that?" Aren asked.

Deacon laughed. "Ain't you ever seen a windmill before?" he asked.

"Not one like that."

"Runs the generators," Deacon said. "That transformer at the bottom stores the energy so we still have juice even if the wind stops. Not that it does that too often out here."

"There weren't any windmills in town."

"Generators run on different things. Most people in town use coal. These will burn coal too, if they need to, but hauling wagonloads of it out into the prairie ain't exactly efficient."

They were getting closer to the farm. Aren could hear the pigs now, and even worse, he could smell them. The stench was horrendous.

"Hog farm," Deacon said when he saw Aren covering his nose with the sleeve of his shirt. "Good news is, no hogs on the BarChi. Cows and horses shit too, but somehow, it don't smell near as bad."

"Thank the Saints for small favours," Aren mumbled.

They were greeted outside the barn by six young women. Four of them wore rough-spun trousers and blouses, and Aren noticed all four of them had opened the top few buttons of their shirts. Their necks were tanned, but the soft swells of flesh below their temptingly gaping necklines were pale and creamy, and the girls seemed completely unashamed as they jockeyed for the best position to display them to Deacon.

The other two girls stood apart. They wore ankle-length dresses covered by long white aprons and had lace kerchiefs over their neatly-braided hair. And every single button was done up tightly. They ignored Deacon and came straight to Aren.

"Hello," the taller one said to him, shaking his hand. "I'm Beth. This is my sister, Alissa. We're so pleased you're here."

Aren felt himself blushing. He could have sworn his throat was closing up, blocking off any words he might wish to speak. He'd spent most of his life in all-male boarding schools, and the rest of it at the all-male university. The only woman he'd ever known at all had been his nanny, but that had been twenty years before, when he was only a child. He'd avoided the society parties his father had thrown and had never gone to the red-light district with his classmates. Whether they were whores or maids or true ladies didn't matter — Aren had no idea how to behave around women. He looked over at Deacon, hoping for some help, but Deacon was lost amongst giggling maids.

"You'll join us at the house for dinner, I hope?" Beth asked. She had golden hair and blue eyes, and Aren supposed she was pretty.

"Ummm..." He looked to Deacon again but couldn't even manage to meet his eyes. Beth followed the direction of his gaze and seemed to think she understood his thoughts.

"Don't worry," she said. "The maids will make sure he gets dinner in the barn."

Next to her, Alissa snorted. "Dinner — plus dessert, I'm sure."

Beth glared at her. "Alissa, don't be crude."

Alissa blushed deep red and ducked her head. She was shorter than her sister and skinnier, with none of her sister's alluring curves. Her hair was darker than Beth's, and she had freckles across her long nose. She glanced sideways at Beth, then glared with open hostility at the maids surrounding Deacon.

Poor Alissa, Aren found himself thinking. Lost in her sister's shadow when potential suitors arrived, held hostage by the rules of her class, not allowed to unhook her top button and try for Deacon's attention either.

"Come on," Beth said to him, turning towards the house, obviously expecting him to follow. "I'll show you to the guest room."

"What about Deacon?" Aren asked. He knew it was foolish, but he wasn't about to let himself be led like a lamb to slaughter by Beth and Alissa. "Shouldn't you show him to his room, too?"

Beth seemed at a loss for words, but Alissa wasn't. "He sleeps in the barn," she said.

The rigidity of the social structure was starting to become clear. Back in Lanstead, society was also stratified by position and income, but for some reason, he hadn't expected to find the same type of issues here in Oestend.

"I'll sleep with Deacon in the barn," he said, then felt himself blush when he realised how that might sound.

"Don't be silly," Beth said. "We have a bed for you at the house."

"W—well…" he stammered, unsure what to say. He was saved by Deacon, who walked up behind him and clapped him on the back.

"Listen, ladies," he said, and he seemed to include all six women in that statement, "Aren and I have to get these horses unhitched and brushed and fed, and there's not much daylight left. If you'll just bring us a bite to eat, we'll be happy enough."

It was obvious the maids were thrilled and the daughters less so, but they all left, and Aren did his best to help Deacon unhook the team, although he felt he probably got in the way more than anything. Eventually, Deacon handed him a brush and pointed him towards one of the horses. The beast stared at him with black eyes, its ears back, and Aren could have sworn it was daring him to step within kicking range.

"I don't know how," he said to Deacon.

The big cowboy rolled his eyes. "You never used a brush before?"

"Not on a horse."

"Not much to it," Deacon said. "Just go in the direction of the hair."

Aren wasn't exactly reassured. He was afraid the big mare would suddenly decide she didn't want to be tended to after all, but he didn't want to look too craven in front of Deacon, so he slowly approached the horse and started to brush. Deacon was in the next stall, brushing down the other horse. He'd taken his hat off, and one of the maids had obviously undone his queue while flirting with him, because his thick, black hair hung loose down his back.

"Can I ask a question without you laughing at me?" Aren asked.

"Probably not." But his tone was friendly, so Aren asked anyway.

"The wraiths are real?"

Deacon didn't seem surprised by the question. "Yup. They're real. You boys from the continent never believe the stories, but you wander out after dark, you'll find out they're true right quick."

"They only come when there's no moon?"

Deacon laughed. "That's another story you boys always have in your heads." He shook his head. "If it's dark, the wraiths can come. Only a fool relies on the moon to protect him."

"But we're safe as long as we're indoors?"

"Might be safe enough if everything's locked down tight, but the only way to be sure is to be inside the net."

"What net?"

"You seen the wards, right? Over the doors and windows?"

"Yes."

"Used to be the wards was enough. But over the years, they stopped working. Don't ask why," he said, glancing at Aren. Aren snapped his mouth shut on the words, which had already been halfway out of his mouth. "Nobody rightly knows. But then along came a man figured out how to fix it."

"By making a generator?"

"Exactly. The generator connects them all. Makes a net the wraiths can't get through."

"Like a fishing net?"

"Well, you can't actually *see* the damn thing, but I guess it's the same idea."

"So as long as the generator's on, it's safe to walk outside between the buildings?"

"Wouldn't recommend it," Deacon said. "They say wraiths can get through the net if they want to. They just don't like it. Long as we're all indoors, they got no reason to bother. But you go walking around in the dark, they may just decide it's worth a try."

"What do the wraiths look like?"

"Can't really say. Never seen one. If you watch out a window, you can't see much. Things blowing around in the wind, dust devils. Some people think they're in the wind. Some people say they're invisible." He shrugged. "I only know they're there. Seen enough people they've killed to know it ain't a story."

"How do they kill you?"

"Can't really say that, either. Never any blood or wounds. Bodies are blue, like they suffocated, or froze to death."

"What about animals?"

"What about them?"

"How do you keep the cattle safe? Do you have to bring them all in each night?"

"Wraiths only kill people."

"Why?"

"Saints, I don't know!" Deacon said, although there was something in his voice that made Aren wonder if he was telling him the truth. "That's just the way it is."

The maids returned with cold ham sandwiches and a jug of milk. Once Deacon and Aren had eaten, the flirting recommenced. Aren quickly realised he would have been better off taking his chances with Beth and Alissa. Now that he had effectively classified himself as closer to Deacon in social standing, and the daughters were out of sight, the maids seemed to have decided he was fair game. Deacon was still their first choice, he could tell, but the two who seemed to be getting the least attention from the tall, handsome ranch hand had turned their efforts towards Aren. And they were frighteningly aggressive.

"Really," Aren tried to tell them, "I can't do this."

"Sure you can," the bolder of the two said. She was unbuttoning his pants, and the other was undoing yet another button on her own shirt.

"No, honestly, I'd rather just go to sleep." He was trying to block their wandering hands, but between the two of them, he couldn't seem to fend them off fast enough. "Ladies, I think—"

"The 'ladies' went inside," the other girl told him, as he blocked yet another attempt at his groin. "It's just us here now."

"Lacy and I can do it together, if you want," the first one said.

"No. I can't—"

He gasped as he felt bare fingers push into his pants and fondle his mostly limp cock. Lacy looked up at him in surprise. "Don't you like us?" she asked.

"Of course!" Although he wasn't sure that was entirely true. "But I can't do this—"

"I thought you meant you'd taken an oath or something," Lacy said, still trying to coax his penis to life. Of course, now that their attention was on it, it seemed to be shrinking. Aren wasn't sure if he was relieved or dismayed. "Did you have some kind of accident?"

"Yes!" he said, suddenly seeing a way clear of them. "Yes, a horrible accident. It's really embarrassing—"

"You poor thing!" the other cooed, kissing his neck. "Maybe if we try a bit harder—"

"No!" he said, then worried he'd sounded a bit too relieved. "No," he repeated, this time with more solemnity. He did his best to look sad and embarrassed. "It's a terrible reminder of what I'm missing. It's depressing, really, and I'm very tired."

"Well," Lacy said, and both girls looked over to where Deacon was still flirting with one of the maids. The other had apparently given him up as a lost cause. "If you're sure…"

"Very sure!" he assured her. "Thank you, really, but it's not a possibility. You understand."

As ridiculous as the ploy had been, it worked. The girls had obviously lost interest in him already. They let him go, returning to Deacon's side, much to the obvious annoyance of the girl who thought she'd secured her prize. Aren sighed with relief and took himself as far away as he could get within the confines of the McAllen barn.

He fell asleep quickly, but was awakened some time later, although at first he couldn't figure out why. The night before, the wind had been howling like crazy, but tonight there was only the low whine of the generator, and Aren quickly started to wish the wind would start to blow again.

A few stalls down, Deacon was obviously being entertained by one of the maids. Aren could hear them. He could hear their heavy breathing, Deacon's moans and the girl's little gasps of pleasure. He tried for a while to ignore them. He didn't want to eavesdrop. He didn't want to be aroused by the sounds of their lovemaking. But it seemed the more he strained to *not* hear, the more he *did* hear, and whether he wanted it or not, the sounds were turning him on. His cock was hard, aching, straining against his pants. Aren tried not to think about the last time he'd had sex, at university nearly two months before. He tried not to think about being blindfolded, bent over a table, having one man's saltiness shooting into his throat as another man pounded into him from behind. He tried not to think about the shame of going to classes the next week, wondering which of the professors had been there, wondering how many of them had used him.

It seemed it had always been that way—men using him, and him letting himself be used. At boarding school, the boys who were so inclined had quickly discovered Aren's proclivities. In the light of day, in the crowded hallways of the school, those boys had always scorned him. But in the black of night they'd be there, groping their way into his bed. Once he was at the university, it had been the same. It hadn't taken Professor Dean Birmingham long to learn the same thing those boarding-school boys had known—Aren was an easy lay.

But Aren didn't want to think about university. He didn't want to think about how many times he'd lain there with his legs over some man's shoulders, loving it, yet hating himself at the same time. He especially didn't want to think about Dean.

Aren thought instead of Deacon. He listened to the deep moans coming from the other stall as he released his cock from his pants and stroked himself. He tried not to think about whichever maid Deacon was with or whether she had her legs wrapped around him. He thought only of Deacon's body, and his cock, and the way his dark eyes probably looked when he climaxed. Aren turned onto his stomach, thrusting into his own hand against the clean straw. The straw was rough and itchy, but his hand was warm and soft. The sensation of pushing through his own fist into the cool straw was a new one, and Aren revelled in it.

"Harder," Deacon's maid called out, and although she wasn't talking to him, Aren obliged her. He thrust harder into his fist, imagining Deacon underneath him, imagining as he so often did what it must feel like to be on the giving end instead. And when he heard Deacon's cry of release, Aren spent himself into the straw, breathing hard.

It wasn't until long afterwards that he stopped to wonder if Deacon and the maid had been able to hear him, too.

* * * *

They left early the next morning, mostly because Aren hounded a very amused Deacon each step of the way.

"Why you in such a hurry to get away?" Deacon asked. "That Daughter didn't propose already, did she?"

"No!" Aren said. "And I'd just as soon not give her another chance, if you don't mind!"

"Maids'll be around later, too," Deacon said with a wink. "Seems like you changed your mind about one of them last night. Sure you don't want to take one more roll before we go?"

"Quite sure!" Aren said, and even though he knew he was blushing, he didn't turn away. "Will you please finish hooking up those damn horses already?"

"Keep your pants on!" Deacon said, then laughed at his own joke. "Guess that's the point of cutting out so early, isn't it?"

Aren bit back a sigh of frustration. "If you're so desperate to lift one of their skirts again—"

"Calm down!" Deacon pushed his hat further down on his head and turned away. Was he actually embarrassed? Aren was surprised and more than a little pleased that he'd somehow managed to make Deacon uncomfortable. "We'll be set to go in no time, if you quit nagging me."

Aren breathed a sigh of relief when they finally left the McAllen ranch behind. He'd never in his life imagined finding himself in a place where he had to fend off women.

"Is the BarChi like that, too?" he asked Deacon.

Deacon shook his head. "BarChi's a male ranch."

The phrase made Aren think of corrals full of young men, and he laughed out loud. He could never hope to be *that* lucky. But the thought bloomed in his imagination, as thoughts often did, turning into a picture on canvas—buff, tanned cowhands like Deacon, standing naked in the corral, chewing on straw. Was there a market for cattle like that? Aren laughed again and Deacon turned to him in surprise, causing him to quickly bite back his laughter. "I'm sorry," he said, making an effort to compose himself. "I'm afraid I don't understand."

"McAllens have daughters. Five of them total, but one died and one they got married off to one of Jeremiah's Sons at the BarChi, and the third one's still awful young, which is why she wasn't out courting you last night like the other two were. With daughters around like that, a man'd be a fool to keep too many ranch hands around. One of those daughters would be bound to end up in a bad way. Ranch hand can't afford to keep a family, but a father can't marry her off to any respectable son after she's proved to not be pure. Best she could do is convince the man who knocked her up to run off to the mines with her, and that ain't much of a life, from what I hear. So a man with daughters hires maids to work the ranch. They can't work as hard as men, but they don't get as much pay either, so he can afford to hire more of them. And that way, he sure don't have to worry about any unwanted grandchildren to feed, either."

"But the BarChi is different?"

"Jeremiah's got all sons. Not many men with that kind of luck. 'Course, they're all married now, and their wives are there with them at the BarChi, and Jeremiah got nice dowries for them all, I'm sure."

"But you're not married?"

"I don't own any part of the BarChi. I'm just a ranch hand, and hands don't marry daughters."

"But you can marry the maids?"

Deacon shrugged, which Aren was realising was one of his primary forms of communication. "I suppose," he said. "But can't afford to support a family on what Jeremiah pays me and don't have a house to keep a wife." Another shrug. "Marrying a maid would be more trouble than anything."

"So the maids at the BarChi —"

"You don't listen." Deacon pushed his hat back to glare at Aren. "There's no maids at the BarChi. Just like a man with daughters is better off with no hands around, a man with sons is better off with no maids around. 'Cause if one of his sons gets a maid in a bad way, father's got an extra mouth to feed and no dowry to make it worthwhile. Only women at the BarChi are the son's wives, and old Olsa." He shook his head and chuckled. "A man'd have to be in a pretty bad spot to roll with Olsa. She must be near eighty years old by now."

"What if a man has both sons and daughters?"

Deacon laughed. "I guess he's in a world of trouble, then," he said. "Have to weigh pregnant maids against pregnant daughters." He shook his head. "I'm no father, so I can't say which is worse." Deacon looked over at Aren appraisingly. "Every man with a daughter to marry off will be looking at you, waiting to see what happens."

"What do you mean?"

"Like I told you yesterday—waiting to see if you last. 'Cause if you do, good chance Jeremiah's paying you enough you could build a house eventually. A father may help you build one as part of the dowry. You stick around and don't go running off scared, you'll be the most eligible bachelor around."

"Holy Saints, that sounds like hell."

Deacon laughed. "I suppose," he said. "Still, a man can get pretty lonely. A few months with no women, you might be surprised what you'll decide to do."

"I'll be fine."

"What's that mean?" Deacon asked.

"I've managed on my own this long. I think I can take care of myself a bit longer. My hand doesn't pay me a dowry, but I don't have to build a house for it, either." He was surprised to find he could say those words to Deacon without blushing, and he was pleased when Deacon laughed. Deacon was handsome enough normally, but he was absolutely gorgeous when he laughed. His eyes crinkled and his teeth flashed white against his dark skin. And sitting there next to him, bumping down a rutted dirt farce of a road in a creaky old wagon, Aren realised he felt good. More than that—he felt *free*. He wasn't sure he'd ever felt so light before. It made him laugh out loud. He felt giddy, almost drunk. He couldn't remember the last time he'd felt so *present*, or been so pleased to be wherever he was, doing exactly what he was doing. The prairie stretched out endlessly on every side. The sky somehow seemed bigger and bluer than it ever had before. The sun was bright and felt warm on his face. For the first time, Aren started to think maybe he'd made the right decision after all.

Next to him, Deacon was still laughing. He pushed his hat back and looked over at Aren with mischievous eyes.

"You better watch out for the wives at BarChi. Just 'cause they're married don't mean they won't be after you. Especially Daisy. Seems Dante don't pay her much attention. But take my advice, friend—don't go there. Dante or Jeremiah find out, they'll throw you to the wraiths, and I ain't joking."

"Don't worry," Aren said. "I'll keep my hands off the wives."

"Not your hands I'm talking about," Deacon said, and Aren found himself laughing. "We got nine hands at the BarChi, not counting me," Deacon went on. "Nearest women are at the ranch we just left behind. Next nearest is the Austin ranch up north, and that's a two day trip each way."

"What about the whorehouse in Milton?"

"Only a fool would go there." Deacon shook his head. "You'll be glad you had a chance last night. All the way back to the McAllens' is a blessed long way to go for a roll."

"Must make for some rather uptight ranch hands," Aren said, and this time it was Deacon who laughed.

"They're young," he said. "Stiff breeze'd be enough to make them 'uptight'."

"So," he said to Deacon, "three sons and nine hands. And you."

"And you now, too."

"Plus three wives. Any children?"

"Yeah, couple of the sons have kids, but you don't gotta worry about them."

"Is that everybody at the ranch?"

"And Jeremiah."

"And Olsa?"

"And Olsa," Deacon confirmed. "But Olsa's been around so long, she's not treated quite like a maid or a hand. She stays in the house."

"Where do the hands stay?"

"In the barracks."

"Where will I stay?"

"You'll be in the barracks, too."

"With the hands?"

"Yup."

"What are they like?"

"Hands come and go. They're almost all city boys like you, but younger."

Aren was only twenty-four. If the hands were younger, it meant they were boys who hadn't gone to a university, and maybe hadn't even finished their basic schooling, either. Young men who had no skills to offer except the strength of their bodies. "Is it hard work?"

"Hard enough, I guess. Some go home after a season. Some decide the mines pay better. Some decide to try a different ranch, or forget this ain't the city and wander off at night and the wraiths get them. Or maybe they get gored by a bull or shot by an angry son for lifting the wrong skirt." He shrugged. "Most of them aren't men yet, no matter what they think," he said. "They're only boys."

"You don't like them?"

"Not that I don't like them. I just don't care. Hands are all the same in the end."

"Including you?"

"Not anymore."

"Including me?"

Deacon looked over at him, and Aren was glad to see that, for once, he didn't seem to be mocking him. His smile was open and friendly. "No. I haven't quite decided where you fit in."

"I don't know, either."

"I know you don't. But don't you worry, Aren. Soon as I figure it out, I'll be sure to clue you in."

"You do that," Aren said. They both laughed. Aren wasn't really sure why, but he was pretty sure he didn't care.

Chapter Three

They arrived at the BarChi shortly after dinner time. It was bigger than the McAllen ranch in every way. There was a large house, flanked by the biggest barn Aren had ever seen. Then again, being from the city, that wasn't saying a lot. Corrals surrounded the barn. Yapping dogs ran in excited circles around the wagon as they drove up, although the only people Aren saw were four young boys playing tag in the yard. Other than the dogs and the laughter of children, he could hear nothing but the swishing of the long grass blowing in the wind and the distant lowing of cows. Aren wasn't sure if it was peaceful or spooky.

The buildings formed a rough circle around an open courtyard. Across the courtyard, opposite the house, was another building, long and low.

"That's the barracks?" he asked Deacon.

"Yup. Your new home."

There were two large windmills, one near the house and the other by the barracks. Another house with its own small windmill stood farther off, past the corrals, roughly two hundred yards from the main buildings.

"Who lives there?"

Deacon frowned. "Nobody, anymore."

"Why not?"

"Haunted."

Aren looked at Deacon in surprise. He thought the big cowboy was pulling his leg, but Deacon's expression was earnest. "You can't be serious."

"Swear I am. Used to belong to Jeremiah's brother, but he died thirty years ago. Since then, nobody's been able to live there. Few people've tried over the years. Had a foreman back when I was a kid, then a bookkeeper a few years later. Both went crazy, I guess. Went running outside in the dark."

"And the wraiths got them?"

"Yup. Last person tried to live there was Jeremiah's middle son, back when he first got married. They lived there one month, and his wife told him she wouldn't stay another damn night. Told him if they didn't move back to the main house, she was packing up and going back to her daddy's house, and taking her dowry with her."

There was nothing outwardly frightening about the house. It had once been white, like the main house, but had long since faded. It was two stories tall, but very small, with a covered, wrap-around porch. Aren couldn't help but think it was a waste to leave a house like that vacant.

They pulled up to the barn and Deacon stopped the wagon. "You go on in the house," he told Aren. "Jeremiah'll be wanting to talk to you."

"What about my things?"

"I'll take care of it. Don't worry," Deacon said, winking at him. "I won't steal your paint."

A young lady wearing a long dress and a lace kerchief on her head was waiting for him at the front door of the main house. She led him silently to an office. It contained a giant desk and two straight-backed wooden chairs, one on each side of the desk. The only other thing in the room was Jeremiah Pane himself.

"Have a seat," he said, after shaking Aren's hand. "Let's talk a bit." Like most men, Jeremiah was taller than Aren, and his hands were hardened with calluses. Although he was probably closing in on sixty, he was fit and lean. Not a soft man, like Aren's father or his father's rich friends. Not like the professors at the University who'd never done a hard day's work in their boring lives. Jeremiah may have had three sons and ten hands to work his ranch and mine, counting Deacon, but it was clear he did plenty of work himself as well.

"Here's what Gordon left behind," Jeremiah said, handing Aren a stack of ledgers he pulled from one of his desk drawers.

"Gordon was the previous bookkeeper?"

"He was." Jeremiah cleared his throat and fidgeted nervously with the kerchief around his neck. "Gordon had a room here in the house, but there was some" —he stopped and looked pointedly at Aren—"*trouble* with one of my daughters-in-law. I don't want to tempt fate a second time, so I've put you in the barracks with the hands."

"I'm sure that will be sufficient."

"Nights down there can be awful rowdy, but during the day they'll all be working, so that should give you the peace and quiet to get your work done." He fidgeted some more with his collar. "Did Deacon warn you about the wives?"

"He recommended I keep my hands to myself," Aren said.

"Do us both a favour, son, and take his advice."

"I promise you sir, it won't be a problem."

Jeremiah snorted. "That's what they all say."

That was probably true, but those other men obviously hadn't been men like Aren. He doubted he could bed a woman even if he tried. Still, there wasn't much else he could say to reassure the man, besides spilling his secret, and he didn't think that would be wise.

"There's always plenty of extra work around the ranch," Jeremiah told him. "I hired you on as a bookkeeper, and that's the only job you're required to do, but if you want to earn the respect of the hands, you'll help them out when you're able. Having the respect of that bunch of fool boys may not seem like much, but if you don't have it, they'll do what they can to make your life hell, especially if you're living out there with them."

"That makes sense."

"Good." Jeremiah stood up from behind his desk, indicating the interview was over. Aren stood up, too, gathering up the ledgers. "Go on downstairs now. Kitchen's in the back of the house. You boys missed supper, but Olsa will make sure you don't go to bed hungry."

Aren found his way to the kitchen and a woman who could only be Olsa. Her slightly stooped back was to him, but she turned at the sound of his footsteps. Aren was surprised to see her eyes were clouded white.

"You smell like the city," she said. "You must be the new boy."

"Yes, ma'am."

"Well, sit, sit!" she commanded. "I saved some supper for you and Deacon. Not easy to do with those greedy hands eating everything in sight!"

Aren watched her make her way around the kitchen, her movements as sure as if she'd had two good eyes. She gave him a bowl of thick stew and the crusty end of a loaf of bread, then sat down across the table from him. He found the unwavering gaze of her sightless eyes unnerving.

"Deacon warn you not to roll with the wives?" she asked.

"Yes," he said. "He warned me."

"Good." Her face was dark brown and deeply-lined, and her long, braided hair was as white as her eyes. "Keep it in your pants and you'll do fine."

Aren was glad she couldn't see him blush. He wasn't sure how to respond but was thankfully saved from having to answer by Deacon's arrival.

"There you are!" Olsa said, and Aren couldn't help but wonder how she'd known it was Deacon. "I saved supper for you."

"I knew you would," he said. "Thanks, Olsa." He leaned in as if to kiss her on the cheek, but she pushed him away.

"Get away!" she snapped. "You smell like cheap perfume. Don't you come near me till you've washed it off. You know better than to roll with a maid that covers herself in that filth."

"Sorry, Olsa," Deacon said, although the smile he gave Aren didn't look sorry at all.

"You're not sorry now," she said. "I can hear it in your voice. But you will be when you're coming to me with your pecker oozing 'cause some damn girl gave you the rot."

"Yes, Olsa," Deacon said, although he didn't look any more apologetic than he had the first time.

"She leave a mark on you?"

"Nothing that won't fade."

"Fool! How many times do I have to tell you that marks are symbols, and symbols have power?"

"It ain't that kind of mark."

"Bah." She waved her hand dismissively at him. "Ungrateful brat. Don't know why I waste my time on you." Deacon seemed to be used to such insults. He grinned as he sat down and started eating his stew.

Olsa turned back to Aren. "Fred McAllen shove that daughter of his under your nose?"

"He did," Deacon answered for him.

"You be careful, now," she said, still apparently watching Aren with her cloudy eyes. "That girl looks sweet enough, but you marry her, there won't be any blood on your sheets the next day, I promise you that."

"Oh, blessed Saints," Aren swore, ducking his head to hide the blush on his cheeks. Even as he did it, he realised it was pointless. Her eyes might have been sightless, but he had a feeling Olsa could see his embarrassment just the same.

"Now that younger one," Olsa went on, "she's probably pure, but only because she don't like men as much as her sisters. You could marry her, but you'd find your bed awful cold at night."

Aren covered his face with his hands, willing himself to stop blushing.

"Olsa," Deacon teased, "stop. You're embarrassing him."

"I'm doing him a favour! Those girls are trouble."

"You'll scare him away before they do."

"Fine!" She jumped up from the table with a speed and agility that was surprising and snatched the bowls of stew away from them. "Go on with you, then, if you're so damn smart."

"Come on, Olsa," Deacon groaned. "Don't be like that."

"I'll be any way I like. That's the privilege of being old."

"We'll be good —"

"Bah!" she said as she set the bowls down on the floor for the dogs. "Get out of my kitchen."

Deacon sighed heavily. Aren had managed to finish most of his stew before Olsa had snatched it away, but he was fairly sure Deacon hadn't had more than a bite or two. "Come on," Deacon said to him. "There'll be no changing her mind now."

Chapter Four

"Crotchety old woman," Deacon griped as he led Aren across the lawn, although he sounded more amused than angry. "I swear I go to bed hungry more often than not."

"Is she always like that?"

"Most days."

Deacon was walking fast, and Aren had to hurry to keep up with him. The armload of ledgers he was carrying wasn't making it any easier. "Would you really go to her if you caught the rot?"

"Probably, although she'd never let me hear the end of it."

"Is she a doctor or something?"

"'Or something', I guess. She knows things most folks don't, about plants and how to use them to heal people."

"But she's not a doctor?"

"No. She's one of the Old People."

That puzzled Aren. "What does being old have to do with it?"

They'd reached the barn, and Deacon stopped at the door and turned to look at Aren, obviously amused by the question. "Not because she's *old*. I said, she's one of the Old People." Aren's confusion must have shown on his face, because Deacon sighed. "Didn't you go to some big, fancy school back east? Didn't they teach you this shit?"

"Shit about old people?" Aren asked.

"*The* Old People! The people who lived here before the settlers showed up and found the coal and the silver and the iron and started making the place their own."

"Oh!" Aren said. "Sure! The natives. They were incorporated into our society and—"

"Yeah," Deacon said, turning away. "'Incorporated.' Let me give you some advice, Aren. Don't go spouting that shit to Olsa. You won't eat for a week. Now," he said, finally opening the door and leading Aren into the barn where his many suitcases were piled in a corner, "you won't have room for all these in the barracks. Take the things you really need, and you can leave the rest here for now."

Aren picked out the bags that had his clothes and toiletries. He still had the stack of ledgers, too, so Deacon carried one of his suitcases and led him across the courtyard to the long, low building that served as a barracks for the ranch hands. There was a mark burnt into the wood of the door. It was a circle, with a line segmenting it diagonally, more than midway down. Had it been a watch face, the line would have crossed from the nine to the six, although it continued out of the circle on both sides for about an inch.

"Is that a ward, too?" Aren asked.

"Nope. It's the BarChi brand," Deacon said as he pushed the door open and led Aren inside.

Nine sets of eyes turned their way when they entered, and Aren did his best to appear confident under the scrutiny.

"Vacation's over, boys," Deacon announced, looking around the room. "I'm sure Jay took it easy on y'all while I was gone, but tomorrow it's back to work."

This was met by groans from a few, laughter from some of the others.

"This is Aren," Deacon told them. "He's the new bookkeeper. That means he's the one who tells Jeremiah whether or not he can afford to give y'all a raise, so you might want to be nice." Most of the boys looked spectacularly unimpressed.

Deacon dropped Aren's bag unceremoniously on the floor. "See you tomorrow," he said as he turned to leave.

"You're leaving?" Aren asked, and immediately regretted it, because he knew he sounded inexplicably desperate. Deacon turned back to him, once again looking rather amused. Aren thought he was fast becoming Deacon's primary source of entertainment. The other men were still watching them, and Aren lowered his voice so only Deacon could hear him. "Where are you going?"

"I don't sleep in the barracks."

"You have a room in the house?"

"No. I sleep in the barn."

"Oh," Aren said. He looked again at the group of young men. Some were still watching, but a few had gone back to whatever they'd been doing when he and Deacon had walked in. It reminded Aren far too much of his years at the boarding school. He knew the games boys played, the alliances they made, the way he'd be shunned because he was small, yet sought out by one or two who were willing to put their scorn aside once the lights went out. He hadn't had sex in far longer than he liked to admit, and for better or worse, he knew when one of the boys found him in the night, or alone behind the shed, he'd do what he always did — he'd give in to his lust, he'd let himself be used, he'd even enjoy it while it lasted. But later would come the snickers and the embarrassment, especially if the boy he gave in to was the type to brag. Or, even worse, if he was the type who thought he was doing Aren a favour instead of the other way around. Aren would once again be weighing his sexual desires against his pride.

He swallowed the fear that was trying to bloom in his chest. He was being ridiculous. This wasn't school. He was older than the boys here by several years. He didn't have to play their games.

"You all right?" Deacon asked.

"Fine," Aren said. He didn't know if he was lying or not.

Deacon left and Aren stood there wondering what exactly to do next. The ranch hands were mostly ignoring him. He glanced around, hoping one of them would decide to take pity on him. Four were playing poker, two were playing backgammon, two more seemed to be drinking for the sole purpose of getting drunk. The last one sat alone on his bunk with a book in his hand. He wasn't reading it, though. He was actually the only person in the room who was looking back at Aren.

"That bunk's open," he said, pointing to the cot closest to the front door.

"Thanks," Aren said. He unpacked quickly. There was a wooden trunk at the foot of the bed, and what didn't fit in there he left in his suitcases and stuffed under the bed. When he was done, he turned to find the farm hand still watching him. He was smaller than all the other men in the room except Aren, and he looked unbelievably young. Aren wondered if he was even seventeen yet.

"What's your name?" Aren asked.

He saw the heartbeat of hesitation and the way the boy glanced towards the other men before he answered. "Frances."

"*Frances*," one of the poker players mocked in a sing-song voice, and his friends snickered. The backgammon players glared at them but said nothing. The drinkers ignored them all.

Frances' face turned red but he didn't respond. He continued to stare at Aren, some kind of mute plea in his eyes.

Frances had obviously been deemed the weak link in the group. There was always one. It was a role in which Aren had found himself many times before, and he was overwhelmingly relieved that in this case one had already been singled out. It might save him a great deal of pain.

On the heels of his relief, though, came shame. He knew what it felt like to be Frances. Lines had already been drawn, alliances made, as they always were in situations like this. All that remained was for Aren's place in that hierarchy to be established.

He put on his biggest smile. He walked over and reached out to shake Frances' hand. "It's good to meet you," he said, his voice loud and clear, and he saw the gratitude in Frances' eyes. He then lowered his voice to ask, "Can you perhaps tell me where the facilities are?"

Most of the building was taken up by the room they were in. It held rows of cots against the wall, and a few tables near the back. Frances led him past it all and through a door at the back of the building. It led to a washroom of sorts. There were more tables, a few dishes, and two large hand pumps for water. Frances used one to fill a tin cup. He held it out to Aren with a pleased smile. "You can drink it here," he said. "Not like in Lanstead. This comes straight from the well in the ground."

Nobody drank the water back home. It was said to be unhealthy, and if its smell was any indication, the rumours were true. Aren sniffed the cup of water Frances had handed him. It smelt fresh. Still, Aren was hesitant. He looked over the rim of the cup at Frances. If it had been any of the other hands, Aren might have suspected a prank, but there was no trickery in Frances' eyes. Aren tipped the cup up and took a drink. The water was shocking against his tongue, ice-cold and sweet with a slightly metallic tang that probably came from the cup. It was surprisingly refreshing. Somehow, it tasted bright. It tasted like spring. He found himself wishing he could paint it.

Aren drank it all and smiled as he handed the empty cup back to Frances. "It's good."

"Glad you think so," Frances said. "Unless you use your wages to buy alcohol in town, the only things we get are this or milk."

Another door led them into a small, square space with doors on all four sides. Frances pointed at the one straight ahead. "That goes outside. These two" — pointing to the ones on the side — "are the privies."

Aren opened one and was pleased to discover they had their own version of flushing toilets. A pull chain above the seat released water into the bowl while opening a flap at the bottom, effectively washing the filth away.

"The privy water comes from rain barrels on the roof," Frances told him. "Only use it if you have to, and don't use more than you need. They tell me it gets pretty nasty when we run out."

He led Aren back into the wash room, but stopped short before going back into the bunk room. He turned and looked at Aren, chewing his lip nervously, seemingly debating something. Finally, he sighed. "You want the run-down?" he asked.

"On what?"

"On the guys." He flicked his head towards the sleeping room.

The guys. Frances was offering to fill him on the social politics of the group. "I'd appreciate that," Aren said.

"The two guys drinking? That's Ronin and Red."

The drinkers were large and burly, clearly the roughest men in the room. "I assume Red's the one with red hair?"

"Right. You can't tell by looking at them, but they're twin brothers. They're born and raised in Oestend, and they've worked about every ranch around. That means they think they're better than all of us from the continent, or even than the men from Lancshire. They don't talk to me at all, but they don't talk to Sawyer and his lackeys either. Now" —he pointed to the backgammon players— "that's Simon and Garrett."

Simon and Garrett were the only men in the room who were older than Aren. Aren guessed them to be twenty-six or twenty-seven. No one else in the room was more than twenty-one. It went a long way towards explaining why they held themselves apart from the others.

"Simon and Garret are decent," Frances said. "Came here together a couple of years ago. They've been here longer than any of the rest of us, and they don't take any shit from Sawyer. Can't say they're exactly my friends, but they're not assholes either."

"Which one's Sawyer?" Aren asked, although he thought he already knew.

"The one you saw make fun of me," Frances said without embarrassment. "He's been here almost a year. Thinks he's pretty hot shit. The two on either side of him are Calin and Aubry. They've been here a few months, and when Sawyer says 'boo', they jump. The one opposite Sawyer's only been here a few weeks. His name's Miron. Still not sure what to think of him. I don't think he likes Sawyer any better than I do, but he knows better than to cross him, too."

"They sound like such a lovely bunch," Aren muttered.

"Yeah," Frances said, looking away. "Lovely."

"How long have you been here?"

"Two weeks."

So he was the new guy—or had been, at any rate, until Aren had showed up.

"Listen." Frances dropped his voice so low that Aren had to step closer to hear. "About Sawyer—you see how he is when everybody's around. But don't let him get you alone." Frances' cheeks turned red as he talked, and his voice shook, but his gaze was level and steady. "He'll do nasty things to you if you let him get you alone." He paused for a moment, and when Aren didn't answer, he asked, "You know what I'm saying?"

Aren felt his own cheeks turning red. He had the horribly uncanny feeling he was looking in a mirror, somehow facing his own psyche, having a conversation with a younger version of himself. He half expected to wake up and find it was all a dream, nothing more than a trick his all-too perceptive subconscious had played on him. But no. This was real. This young boy with the bright blue eyes that suddenly seemed full of damaged innocence was staring back at him, waiting for an answer.

"Yes," Aren said, although his voice didn't sound like his own. "I know what you're saying."

He saw the relief on Frances' face. "All right." He turned to head back into the room, but Aren stopped him.

"What about after everybody else is asleep?" he asked.

"No," Frances said, shaking his head. "He'd never risk the others finding out."

Just like boarding school.

Aren eyed Sawyer. He wouldn't have called him attractive, although he seemed to be well-built. He probably had a great body. Aren felt his heart begin to race when he thought about the possibility of having sex again. It had been far too long. Masturbating the night before had helped, of course, but facing weeks or even months with no other option was bound to get old. Aren had sacrificed his dignity to his own lust before. Still, as he watched Sawyer, as he listened to him laugh and boast, a cold knot of dread formed in his stomach, overriding any sense of arousal he might have felt. He'd met guys like Sawyer before. He'd been used by them and abused by them, sometimes willingly, sometimes not. He hoped he would never be that desperate again.

Frances went to bed soon afterwards, and Aren followed suit, for all the good it did him. The hands kept him awake far into the night. It wasn't that they were mean, or even that they particularly cared that he was there. But they were young and obviously a somewhat rowdy bunch. The poker players and the drinkers seemed to be having some kind of contest to see who could be the most obnoxious.

Eventually, the backgammon players, Simon and Garrett, went to bed. Ronin and Red passed out. The poker game devolved into an argument, which quickly turned into a fistfight between Calin and Aubry, which awoke the entire barracks. The other boys pulled the combatants apart amidst much cussing and yelling. Red and Ronin drunkenly threatened to kick "all you fuckers' arses". More arguing and general chest-thumping commenced. Eventually, they all went sullenly to their beds, and Aren breathed a mental sigh of relief. He felt as if he'd barely fallen asleep when he heard a distant bell ringing. What followed was the tumultuous chaos of nine boys cursing and swearing and yawning and, in the case of one of the drinkers, vomiting. Finally, they all filed out of the door, slamming it shut behind them.

Aren pulled the blanket over his head and went back to sleep.

Chapter Five

"You want to eat, you best get up."

The voice was rough and slowed by a heavy drawl, and it took Aren's sleep-addled brain a moment to connect it to a person — Deacon.

"Go away," Aren mumbled, burrowing further down into the bed.

Deacon laughed. "Hands're finishing up now," he said. "You want to eat before dinner, now's the time."

Dinner? There was no meal between breakfast and dinner? That thought was enough to wake him up in a hurry.

"I'm coming," he said, and he tried not to be annoyed at Deacon for laughing at him as he stumbled around, taking care of his morning toilet, then finally getting dressed.

"You don't have lunch?" Aren asked as he followed Deacon around the barracks to the back of the house where the kitchen was.

"'Lunch'?" Deacon asked with obvious amusement. "I always forget you boys from the continent call it that."

"What do you call it?"

"Dinner."

"So what's dinner?" Aren asked, confused.

Deacon laughed. "Well, if you mean what do we eat at the end of the day, it's 'supper'." He laughed again, shaking his head. "No wonder you jumped out of bed so fast!"

Aren did his best not to be annoyed, which would have been easier if he felt like he'd had more than two hours of sleep.

"More often than not, for dinner — or 'lunch', I guess" — Deacon winked at Aren as he said it — "me and the boys are out in the field somewhere. Olsa sends food with us. So most days, there won't be a bell. You can probably go by whenever and she'll feed you. Unless she's ornery, of course, then you'll go hungry like me. For breakfast and supper, you'll hear the bell. You can eat with the hands if you want. I usually wait till they're done, so you're welcome to do that, too."

That statement sounded a bit like an invitation. It seemed like a gesture of friendship, and Aren was pleasantly surprised.

"Sundays, we all have dinner together at the house," Deacon went on, "family and hands, too. You're expected to be there, unless you got someplace better to be."

"Like where?" Aren asked.

Deacon laughed. "Exactly."

They'd reached the door to the kitchen, and there, sitting on the ground leaning against the wall, was Red.

"Why the hell ain't you out feeding with the rest?" Deacon asked, nudging him in the thigh with the toe of his boot.

Red looked up at them with bloodshot eyes. "Don't feel so good."

Deacon shook his head. "Maybe one day you'll learn not to drink so much when there's work to be done the next day."

"Saints, Deacon, give it a rest," Red said, holding his head with both hands like he thought it might fall off if he didn't. "There's enough hands to do the work. Can't you let me take the day off?"

"I don't pay you to take days off, and if I let you sit on your ass every time you're hanging from the booze, we won't get a day's labour out of you."

Red didn't answer. He bent over his knees with his head still in his hands.

"You got till the others get back," Deacon told him. "Drink some water. Have some hair of the dog if you got to, but you ain't getting out of chores."

"Fine," Red groaned, and Aren followed Deacon into the kitchen.

"Jay always takes it easy on them when I'm gone," Deacon said. "He don't know how to be hard ass, which means I got to be the asshole every time I get home."

They found Jeremiah in the kitchen. It seemed he'd been waiting there to talk to Deacon.

"Trip into town went fine?" he asked, while Olsa bustled about, handing them both bowls of lumpy, lukewarm oatmeal.

"Yup."

"Hands out feeding right now?" he asked Deacon.

"All but Red," Deacon said. "He's sitting out the back door sweating out the booze."

"Typical," Jeremiah said. "What you got them doing today?"

"Got to move those cattle from the west pasture to the other side of the river. Probably take four of those boys most the day to do it. Might put two with that cow in the barn. She's going to be birthing that calf right soon." Deacon shrugged. "One man could handle it, unless something goes wrong."

"Play it safe," Jeremiah said. "Worth letting a couple of them be lazy to keep from losing her."

"Other than that, it's usual stuff. Muck out the barn, chop wood. Time to do the maintenance on the generators. Got to clear the northeast pasture if you want to use it for planting in the spring. Plus have to send a couple out to mend the fence by that watering hole. Damn bull keeps pushing his way through, and don't seem to care he cuts himself to hell in the process." He shook his head. "Lot to get done in one day, but we'll do our best."

Jeremiah nodded. He gestured towards the back door. "Red causing you trouble?"

"Nothing I can't handle." Deacon shrugged. "There's always one."

"Should I let him go?"

"No. His brother's a good worker. Makes up for it."

"How's the new kid?"

"Small," Deacon said. "Skittish." And even though they weren't talking about him, Aren felt himself bristle at the comment. "Don't know if he'll last or not."

"He'll be fine," Aren said.

Deacon turned to look at him in surprise, and Aren felt his face turning red. Jeremiah didn't seem to notice his outburst. "All right," he said. "I'll take those sons of mine and move them cattle. You have your boys cover the generators. Wraiths get us, it won't much matter where the cows are."

"They're gonna bitch," Deacon told him, although he didn't seem to be bothered by it. It was more like saying kids were going to make noise — a simple statement of fact.

Jeremiah laughed. "They always do."

He left, and Deacon and Aren finished their breakfast in silence. Afterwards, Aren followed Deacon out into the courtyard, where the men were gathering. While they waited, Aren looked around. Behind him was the barn. Next to it was a corral, and in the corral was...

"What the hell is *that?*" Aren asked.

Deacon's laugh was so deep and so loud, it startled Aren almost as much as the creature had.

"It's a cow."

"That's *not* a cow!" Aren said. He may have been a city boy, but he'd seen cows, and they bore only a faint resemblance to the thing he saw in front of him.

"May not be what cattle in Lanstead look like," Deacon said, "but I promise you, here in Oestend, that there's a cow."

The overall shape of the animal in question was cow-like, but its size was all wrong. It was huge, nearly as tall as a horse and twice as wide. It had long, menacingly curved horns on its head. "Why's it so big?"

"Used to be there were two kinds of buffalo in Oestend. There's the normal ones you see now. Ranchers were crossing their biggest cattle with them as soon as they settled here. Then back when Jeremiah's daddy was only a boy, they found a new breed way down south. Twice the size the ones you see now. Hard to domesticate. They're all dead now, mostly killed by the trappers for their pelts, but before that happened, they got mixed in, too." He gestured to the animal in question. "That's the result. That's what Oestend cows mostly look like, now."

Looking at the thing, Aren felt the need to back up. He could have sworn it had murder in its eyes.

"It looks angry," Aren said.

Deacon laughed. "They castrated that one yesterday, so he might be."

"They're not dangerous?"

"Well, I wouldn't mess with the bulls, or the ones like him who just got cut. Sometimes they come down with the froth, too, then they'll kill you if they get the chance. Those horns'll end you right quick, and their hooves are sharp as knives." He shrugged as if it was barely worth mentioning. "Not really anything to worry about, though, most of the time."

Aren didn't exactly feel reassured as he eyed the beast in the corral. He was glad he didn't have to deal with the 'cows'.

The ranch hands had all arrived and were obviously waiting for Deacon to tell them what to do. "Hope you boys are all rested," Deacon said to them, "'cause we got our work cut out for us this week. We got some maintenance to do today, and tomorrow we start clearing the northeast pasture.

"Ronin, Red, Calin and Aubry—it's your turn on the generators." All four of the men moaned, but Deacon ignored them. "You know what to do. Get the ladders and the harnesses from the shed. Open them up—"

"Simon and Garrett did that last month!" Aubry whined, and Red and Calin nodded. "They're fine! They don't need to be cleaned again already!"

"It ain't a question of whether or not they're 'fine'. Generators don't get good maintenance, they stop working. Or you feel like getting friendly with a wraith?"

"It's a waste of time," Red said. His brother Ronin looked unhappy with his outburst. He elbowed him in the ribs and whispered something low to him, but Red ignored him. "I ain't doing it!"

"You want to keep your job, you'll do what I say, and I say you're cleaning the generators."

"The three of them can handle it," Red said, gesturing at Calin, Ronin and Aubry, who all looked less than pleased that he was trying to get himself out of the work, leaving them with more.

"Takes at least two men," Deacon told him. "Three won't do no good. With four, you can split into two teams. Each of you take one mill, you'll be done by supper."

"It ain't gonna kill you to let me take a day off."

"No, don't suppose it would kill me," Deacon said. "But I still ain't doing it. You get your ass out with the others-"

"Fuck you!"

Deacon grinned. It wasn't a nice grin, either. It gave him a mean, feral look. He broadened his stance and squared his shoulders. "Come on up here and say that again, if you got the balls," he said.

"I will!"

"No!" Ronin said, grabbing his brother's arm. "Don't be stupid! It's just cleaning gears. It ain't worth losing our jobs over!"

But Red ignored him. He shook his brother off and walked through the cluster of men to stand in front of Deacon. He wasn't as big as Deacon, but somehow, he looked meaner. He stood toe-to-toe with Deacon, his shoulders back. Aren noticed that the other men all backed up a bit.

"Now," Deacon said, without moving a muscle. "Say it again."

"I said fu —"

Deacon's fist slammed into Red's face so hard and so fast, it made Aren jump. He'd expected there to be more talk. More posturing. More insults. Apparently Red had expected the same, but Deacon didn't seem inclined to waste time with such testosterone-laden banter. He had apparently decided to cut right to the chase. Or, in this case, the ass-kicking.

He punched Red again, knocking him down. The man landed clumsily on his ass. Deacon's third punch knocked him flat on his back.

Deacon straightened up again to his full height. He wasn't even breathing hard. Aren wondered if his own pulse was pounding faster than Deacon's, and all he'd done was watch.

"Now," Deacon said, "you got anything else to say, or are you ready to clean some gears?"

"Mmmpphhh," Red said.

It didn't sound like much of anything to Aren, but it seemed to satisfy Deacon. "Good," he said. He looked over at Ronin. "That's the second time he's crossed me," he said. "One more time and he's out."

"I know," Ronin said with sad resignation. He was staring down at his brother, who had managed to sit up but didn't appear to be standing any time soon.

"You're a good man," Deacon said. "You can still stay-"

"Wherever we go," Ronin said, "we go together."

Deacon shrugged. "Your choice." He turned to the rest of the men. "Simon, you and Miron stay with that

57

pregnant cow in the barn. Hard to say when she'll start birthing. Take turns watching her. Easy enough to clean the stalls while you're there, maybe get some wood chopped."

"You bet," Simon said.

"Garrett, you and me are going to walk the northeast pasture, check the fences and mark what needs to be cleared."

"Sure, boss."

"Sawyer, you go out to the watering hole and restring the barbed wire on that fence. Take Frances with you—"

"*No!*" The word was out of Aren's mouth before he knew he was going to speak. Suddenly every hand in the courtyard was looking at him, including Deacon.

"What the hell did you say?" Deacon asked. Aren couldn't tell if he was amused or annoyed. He had a feeling Deacon wasn't sure either.

"I just..." Aren looked at Frances. The boy's eyes were huge, and while Aren imagined he could see hope and maybe even a silent thanks in them, he also saw Frances shake his head, just barely. He didn't want Aren saying anything in front of all the other men, and Aren couldn't blame him.

Aren felt his cheeks turn red. He hated to back down, but he wasn't going to spill Frances' secret to everybody. "Nothing," Aren said to Deacon. "I'm sorry I interrupted."

Deacon had apparently already decided to ignore him. He turned back to the men. "Y'all know where to find me if you need me."

The men didn't exactly hurry, but they didn't dawdle either. Ronin helped his brother up off the ground, and Aren could hear him saying, "I told you not to push him!" as they walked away.

"Garrett, you go on in the barn and find some markers to use. I'll catch you on your way back."

"Sure, boss," Garrett said.

The moment he was gone, Deacon turned on Aren. He grabbed his arm so hard that Aren yelped a bit. "What the hell's your problem?" Deacon asked.

Aren felt his cheeks turning red again, but now that he was alone with Deacon, there was no reason not to tell him. "I don't want you sending Sawyer and Frances off alone together."

Deacon's grip on his arm loosened and some of the anger left his face. "I can't protect him all the time," he said. "He's got to learn to handle a bit of bullying."

"It's more than bullying," Aren said, looking into Deacon's eyes, willing him to understand.

"You're saying he takes advantage of the boy?"

It annoyed Aren. Deacon made it sound as if what was being done was no worse than if Sawyer cheated Frances out of his wages at cards, or bullied him into shining his boots. "If by 'takes advantage of' you mean 'rapes', then yes," he snapped.

"You know this after spending one night here?"

"Frances told me. He warned me so I'd know not to let Sawyer do the same to me."

Deacon sighed in frustration, but he let Aren go. "Sawyer came to me before I left for town. Told me he wanted to help the boy toughen up. I thought he wanted to help."

"Help himself, maybe."

"Shit!" Deacon swore, turning away. "I actually believed that son of a bitch, too." He shook his head, pushing his hat up to rub his forehead. "Means I'm slipping."

He actually cared. Aren was surprised to realise that.

"Hey, boss," Garrett called, as he came jogging back from the barn with a burlap sack over his shoulder. "You ready to go?"

Deacon sighed again. He looked exhausted, but by the time he'd turned to face Garrett, he seemed to have regained every ounce of his composure. "Change of plans," he said. "Run down the new kid. Take him with you instead."

"Frances?" Garrett asked with obvious distaste. "He won't even know what to look for."

"I know it," Deacon said. "But guess he's got to learn some time."

Garrett seemed to consider for a second before shrugging good-naturedly. "Sure thing."

"Tell Sawyer I'll be along shortly to help him string the wire."

"Got it." He started to turn away, but Deacon stopped him.

"Garrett?"

"Yeah, boss?"

"You and Simon keep an eye on the kid, will you?"

"You think he's trouble?" Garrett asked in confusion.

"Saints, no, but somebody else may be making trouble for him. And I don't mean you got to be the kid's best friend, neither. But watch Sawyer, and make sure he ain't going to any great lengths to get the kid alone. You know what I mean."

Aren watched as understanding slowly appeared on Garrett's face. He nodded. "There's always one," he said. "We'll take care of it."

He turned and left Aren and Deacon standing alone. "Simon and Garrett are good men," Deacon said. "They'll know what to do."

"Thank you," Aren said.

"I'm glad you told me." Deacon turned to Aren with an expression that was part amusement, but part warning. "You got any other problems with the way I run this ranch, you best learn to tell me in private. You question me in front of my men again, I'll knock your ass in the dirt so fast you won't know which way is up. We clear?"

The thought of being on the receiving end of one of Deacon's punches was enough to make his heart pound. Aren had to try twice to make his voice work. "Clear."

"Good," Deacon said. "See you at supper."

* * * *

The subsequent nights in the barracks were the same as the first had been. Men argued and drank and boasted until the wee hours of the morn. They teased and mocked and harassed each other. They seemed to do their best to make each other miserable. Aren hated it. It reminded him too much of his years in boarding school. He found himself looking over his shoulder when he went to the latrine. He steeled himself for the night one of them would grope their way into his bed.

He wished more than anything that Jeremiah would allow him to stay in the main house. He wished there was a way to convince him he wouldn't roll with any of the wives. More than once, he considered going to him and confessing just how little he liked women, but in the cool, wind-blown light of day, he always thought better of it. He had no idea how men with his particular sexual preference were viewed in Oestend. Back in Lanstead, men like him were frowned upon by the lower classes, but among the university crowd they were grudgingly accepted, albeit often ridiculed. His relationship with Professor Dean Birmingham hadn't been much of a secret.

The first time Aren had heard the word 'catamite' whispered behind his back, he'd nearly cried. Likewise the first time somebody had referred to him as a 'kept boy'. But over the last four years, he'd grown used to the crude comments, especially with regards to his relationship with Professor Birmingham. He'd also come to accept the fact that 'kept boy' wasn't actually so very far from the truth.

Yes, in Lanstead it had been possible to be somewhat open about his lifestyle. But here in Oestend, he had no idea if his proclivities would be accepted or not, so no matter how bad things in the barracks sometimes seemed, Aren did his best to bear it.

The nights might have been bad, but his days were his own. No matter how late they'd been up or how much they'd had to drink, the morning bell called the ranch hands to work bright and early each morning. With the men gone, he had the barracks to himself, just as Jeremiah had predicted. First, Aren would eat breakfast with Deacon, then he would go back to his bunk. He would sit on his bed with Gordon's ledgers spread out in front of him. As he sharpened his pencil with his penknife, he always wished he could spend the time drawing, but art would have to wait. He had work to do.

It took him the better part of four days to sort out what Gordon had done. The man had obviously been less than meticulous. There were notes scratched in margins where there should have been numbers written in columns. There were scribbles and lines crossed out and arrows pointing across pages. And to make things worse, every bit of it was written in the sloppiest penmanship Aren had ever seen.

But Aren persisted.

By noon on the fifth day, he'd finally sorted them out as well as he could hope. He was reasonably sure he knew what went where and how much money was held in reserve. He found the ledger book that had the most blank pages left. He ripped the used pages out of it, and he started anew.

When he was done, he sat back to examine his work. His back and neck hurt from bending over the books. His eyes were tired from squinting at the print in the low light of the barracks. His hand was cramped from holding the pencil for so long. But when he looked at what he had accomplished, he felt proud.

He put down his pencil with a smile. It was a bit like art, after all.

He wandered outside into the bright, warm sunlight. The wind was blowing as it usually did, making a song in the grass and the branches of the trees. In the yard on the far side of the house, two of the wives were hanging out laundry to dry. He knew their names, although not which of them was which. Deacon had pointed out Jeremiah's sons to him — Jay, the youngest, who was friendly enough, but seldom spoke; Brighton, the middle child, who lived up to his name, smiling and laughing more often than not; and Dante, the oldest, whose eyes were angry and temper quick. He seemed to suspect that every man on the ranch was rolling with his wife. Aren didn't know if his suspicions were grounded in reality or not, but he did his best to steer clear of him.

There were a few kids, too. All boys. Two belonged to Brighton, and two were Jay's. Aren didn't know which were which. He knew none of their names. None of them was older than eight. Aren saw them in the mornings as they went about their chores and in the evenings as they ran playing in the fields. But other than that, he ignored them.

"You're outside!" Deacon called from the side yard, where he was chopping wood. "I was starting to think you were afraid of sunlight."

Aren was growing used to Deacon. They ate breakfast and dinner — or 'supper' — together every single day. Other than that, he'd barely seen the man, but those few hours had been enough to teach Aren not to rise to Deacon's teasing. "I've been working on the accounts," Aren told him as he drew closer.

"Forgot to tell you this morning that Brighton and Garrett are heading into town in a few days. You want to go with them?"

There was a bench against the side of the barn and Aren sat down on it to watch Deacon work. "Why would I?" he asked.

Deacon stopped his axe mid-swing and looked at him surprise. "Got to stop at the McAllen ranch on the way there and again on the way home. Every hand here's begging me to let them go."

Women. That's what he was referring to. "No, thanks," Aren said.

Deacon shrugged and swung his axe back into motion. "Suit yourself. You got anything you need from town, let one of them know."

Was there anything he needed? Other than a place to sleep that wasn't in the barracks, Aren couldn't think of anything.

"Tell me about the money," Deacon said as he chopped through another log. "Is there enough income to hire a tenth man?"

"Yes," Aren said. Although he knew it was wrong, he couldn't help but admire Deacon's body as he watched him work. The man was huge and appeared to be made of solid muscle. Aren counted it as both a blessing and a curse that Deacon had his shirt on. "Is that what you need?"

Deacon somehow managed to shrug as he swung the axe back around. He wasn't even winded, although Aren knew he would have been out of breath if he'd been the one chopping wood. "Need a lot of things. Tenth man, new baler, another bull."

"Another bull? If you needed a bull, why did you castrate that other one?"

"No good," Deacon said, tossing the split wood into a pile and starting on a new log. "Genetics. Got to mix up the blood. Traded one with the Austins a few months ago, but he came down with the froth. Had to be put down."

"The Austins live north of here?"

Deacon stopped swinging his axe long enough to point at a battered wagon trail that climbed the hill to the north. "Up there. Two days from here."

"Why so far away?"

"Bad land between here and there. Rock and clay. Can't grow nothing on it."

"If it takes two days to get there, how do you stay safe from the wraiths on the way?"

"There's a shack at the halfway mark," Deacon said. "Small generator."

"So you swapped bulls with them, but the one he gave you was sick?"

"Not like Zed cheated us or nothing. No way he could've known. But yeah, it got sick a few weeks later. Got a few cows fat with him, but then he started swaying like they do, swinging his head. 'Course that don't always mean the froth, but you got to isolate them, keep your eye on them. Day or two later, they turn mean. They'll bust their way right out of the barn if you let them. Ram anything they see—horses, other cows, men."

"So what do you do?"

"Have to put them down." Deacon stopped chopping wood to look at Aren. "You ever shot a gun?"

"No."

"You ever seen one?"

"In a store once."

"But have you seen one used?"

"No."

"Not as useful as you probably think. Not accurate at all. Saw a guy try to shoot a bull once and hit his own brother instead." He shook his head. "Even if you hit the damn thing, if you're too far off, you're likely to just piss it off more."

"So what do you do?"

"Got to surround it. Lasso it without being gored. Rope its legs and head, pull it down to the ground. Once it's secure, someone's got to get right up next to the blessed thing." He touched his temple with the tips of his first two fingers. "Got to put the barrel right against its head."

"Sounds dangerous."

"Yup." Deacon picked up his axe again and went back to chopping. "Seen men killed more than once."

"So you need a new hand, a new bull, a new baler…" Aren thought about the books and how much money he thought they had. "Anything else?"

"Sure wouldn't mind a damn bottle of whisky."

Aren laughed. "Well, *that* I think we can afford."

Chapter Six

The next day, after breakfast, Aren found himself with a whole day of free time. For the first time since arriving in Oestend, he took out his sketchpad and the leather bundle that held his penknife and pencils. He tucked them under his arm and walked out of the barracks, into the courtyard. Now that he actually had time to devote to drawing, he realised that outside the courtyard, he didn't know his way around the ranch. He had no idea where to go. He looked around. Nobody was in the courtyard except the kids and some dogs. His eyes landed on the abandoned house.

The house seemed to call to him. It sat away from the hustle of the courtyard, on top of a small hill, its windows dark. It looked forlorn.

Aren climbed the gentle slope to the bottom of the porch steps. The steps themselves were grey and sagging in the middle. The entire structure was in need of paint. Still, Aren imagined it was lonely.

He climbed the steps. The front door had a long, narrow window next to it, and Aren peered inside. The glass was thick and cloudy, but he could see a narrow entryway. There was a doorway on the left and a staircase against the wall on the right, and between them, a corridor leading towards the back of the house. There was one other window on the front of the house, and Aren peeked into it as well. It showed him a room with a bare wooden floor and one wall taken up by a large fireplace. There appeared to be furniture in the room, too, hidden under tattered horse blankets and dusty sheets.

He thought again of what Deacon had said about it— that it was haunted. It seemed absurd. He couldn't help but think it really had been a prank. And yet, why else would it be sitting here vacant while the inhabitants of the BarChi crowded themselves into the other buildings?

The main house was off-limits to Aren. He was reluctant to intrude on Deacon's privacy in the barn. He thought about having to go back to the barracks, where boisterous boys played their ridiculous games. Why should he sleep with them when there was a perfectly good house available?

It took some searching, but he finally located Jeremiah mucking out stalls in the barn.

"Don't you have hands to do that?" Aren asked.

Jeremiah didn't stop what he was doing. "Lots of chores to be done," he said. "Since I'm the boss, I get first choice."

"And *this* is your first choice?"

"Today, it is." Jeremiah shrugged. "Simple. Something I've done a thousand times in my life. Lets me think of other things." He tossed another pitchfork full of soiled straw out of the door. "What's on your mind?"

"I'd like your permission to move into the empty house."

Jeremiah finally stopped what he was doing. He planted the tines of his pitchfork in the floor and turned to look at Aren, leaning on the handle. "Deacon tell you why it's vacant?"

"He said it's haunted."

"But you want to live there?"

Aren did his best not to squirm under Jeremiah's scrutiny. "I thought maybe I could rent it? We could negotiate a fee from my salary—"

"Not mine to rent," Jeremiah said, yanking his pitchfork free and turning back to his task.

"It's not?" Aren asked. "Whose is it?"

"Deacon's."

Nothing could have surprised Aren more than that. "But he said he didn't own any part of the BarChi," he said. "He told me—"

"Look, son, what he told you ain't none of my business. Up to him what he wants you to know and what he don't. All I'm saying is, that house ain't mine to rent. You get his permission, that's good enough for me."

It wasn't hard to find Deacon. He and some of the other hands were branding cattle, and Aren could hear him yelling out orders from the other side of the courtyard. One glance at the men going about their task told him it wasn't a good time to ask Deacon for anything, and he decided supper—the late day meal Aren still thought of as dinner—would be soon enough.

He arrived at the kitchen as the hands were leaving. Deacon was nowhere in sight.

"Sit!" Olsa commanded him. "Those damn boys ate all the ham, but there's still beans and cornbread, and I saved you a bit of cheese."

Cheese was something of a treat. He wasn't sure what he'd done to warrant special treatment from Olsa, but he wasn't about to complain. "Thank you," he said as she put the food in front of him.

"I hear you don't want to go to town with Brighton and Garrett," she said.

"No need to," he told her.

"Those women at the McAllen Ranch aren't motivation enough for you?" she asked.

He ducked his head and ate more beans. If there was one thing he'd learnt from Deacon and Olsa, it was to keep his mouth shut and eat while she was still happy, because there was no telling when she'd snatch the food away. He glanced at the doorway, hoping Deacon would arrive soon.

"He's coming," she said. Her blank white eyes seemed to give her an uncanny ability to see through walls and into minds. He wondered if he'd ever get used to it. "You be careful what you say," she said. "It's a touchy subject."

"How do you know —?"

But Deacon arrived at that moment, cutting off Aren's question. "What's a touchy subject?" he asked as he sat down next to Aren.

"Aren has something to ask you." She stood and shuffled to the other side of the room to get Deacon's supper.

Aren felt his cheeks turning red. He turned to look at Deacon, who was watching him with his eyebrows up and laughter in his eyes. "You change your mind about going to town?" he asked.

"No," Aren said. "It's not that. It's about the house."

"What about it?"

"Well, I hate the barracks. I'd really prefer to not sleep with the hands, and—"

"I don't know why you're talking to me," Deacon said as Olsa put his plate down in front of him. "Hey!" he said to her. "How come Aren gets cheese and I don't?"

"I'm not wasting my cheese on you. Not tonight."

"What'd I do?"

"Nothing," she said. "Yet."

He sighed and turned back to Aren. "Look, you want to stay in the house, you got to prove to Jeremiah you'll keep your hands off the wives. It's of no matter to me—"

"Not this house," Aren said, interrupting him. "I mean the other house. Your house."

Deacon froze, his eyes on his plate. There was a stiffness to his posture that hinted at danger, and Aren found himself wishing he was sitting farther away. "Who told it was my house?" he asked, looking up at Olsa with obvious suspicion.

"Don't go blaming me," she said.

"It was Jeremiah," Aren said. "I asked if I could rent it and he said—"

"I don't care what he said." Deacon's strange stillness was gone, although he didn't turn to face Aren. He picked up his spoon. "It ain't my house," he said.

Olsa moved fast, faster than Aren ever would have believed of somebody her age. She had a long, wooden spoon in her hand and she brought it down hard on the back of Deacon's hand, knocking his own spoon onto the floor.

"Ow! Saints, Olsa, what you have to go and do that for?"

"'Same reason I took my spoon to you when you was a boy," she said, shaking it in his direction. "You lie—"

"It's not a lie!"

"You shame your family—"

"Don't start!"

"Everything I taught you—"

"I never asked you for none of it!"

"You refuse to accept—"

"*Enough!*" Deacon's voice cut through her accusations with a thunderous finality, and she fell silent. Deacon took a deep breath, obviously trying to calm himself. He turned to Aren, and when he spoke his voice was quieter, but still tight with suppressed anger. "Even if it were my house, it ain't fit to live in. I told you that."

"You told me it was haunted—"

"I wasn't lying."

"With your permission," Aren said, "I'd like to try. I'll pay you—"

"Aren!" Deacon snapped. "Listen to me—it ain't safe!"

"It could be made safe enough," Olsa said. "You know the song."

The song?

Deacon turned on her, his body rigid, almost vibrating with rage. "Don't start—"

She smacked him again with the spoon, not as hard this time but hard enough to get his attention. Then she opened her mouth and started to...sing?

It took Aren a minute to figure out what was happening. Her voice rose and fell. It was melodious and yet harsh. Not quite music. It had stops and starts, strange hitches in the middle of extended vowel sounds.

She was talking! It was a language, although no language Aren had ever heard. She finished with a flourish, her long wooden spoon pointed at Deacon's face.

And Deacon answered her.

It sounded different when it came from him — less like a song, more like chant — and Aren stared back and forth between them in stunned silence. He could make out no distinct words, only sounds, but there was no mistaking the anger in Deacon's face.

Back and forth they went, faster and louder, until Deacon suddenly lapsed back into the common tongue. "No!" he yelled, slamming his hand down on the table for emphasis.

Olsa stared at him for moment, then she jumped forwards, snatching his plate from in front of him. "Ungrateful brat!" She pointed towards the door. "Get out!"

It was proof of his anger that Deacon didn't try to argue. He swept his hat off the table and stalked out of the room without a backwards glance.

Aren sat very still, wondering what in the world he'd just witnessed. He wondered how long Deacon would be angry and if there was any chance of changing his mind. He looked over at Olsa, wondering if she'd offer some kind of explanation.

"Well," she said, as she sat down again across from him, "that went better than I expected."

* * * *

Deacon didn't come to breakfast the next day, and Aren sat there with only Olsa for company, eating lukewarm porridge. Olsa hummed absent-mindedly and didn't say a word.

Afterwards, Aren took his sketchpad and his penknife and pencils, and he walked. He went past the empty house with its sagging boards and vacant eyes. He walked out into the long grass of the prairie until he found a place where he could sit. He had a view of the cattle grazing in the field, lazy and stupid and yet serene at the same time. A big bull stood near the fence, staring at absolutely nothing.

Aren sharpened his pencil and he started to draw.

His art took him away, as it so often did. He lost all sense of space and time. He barely noticed the soreness in his backside from sitting on the ground, or the pain in his shoulder from his hunched position. He knew only shapes and lines, reflections and light. It was a calm place inside him that occupied him, yet left some remote corner of his mind free and clear to think of other things. Today, he thought only of the sun and the grass and how surprisingly good it felt to be there. He had worried he wouldn't fit in here, and maybe he didn't, but he found it suited him all the same.

He didn't see or hear Deacon approaching. It wasn't until he sat down next to Aren in the grass that he noticed him at all. Aren looked over at him in surprise.

Deacon didn't look at him. He didn't say anything, either. He sat there, his knees up and his forearms draped over them, staring out into the field, and Aren waited, wondering what in the world was on the man's mind.

Deacon finally looked over at him and he seemed startled to find Aren watching him. "Am I bothering you?" he asked.

"Not at all," Aren said. "I missed you at breakfast."

Deacon shrugged uncomfortably, obviously disconcerted by such a frank statement. He looked down at Aren's sketchpad. "What're you drawing?"

Aren hesitated, afraid Deacon would make fun of him for his art as he had the first day they'd met, back in Milton, but he saw no mockery in his eyes. Only friendly curiosity.

He held his sketchbook out and Deacon took it.

He didn't say anything for the longest time. He looked at the drawing, then up at the bull in the field, then down again at the drawing. He seemed puzzled. "I don't get it," he said at last. "I can see it's the bull, but it's not the same at all."

Aren's heart fell at the words. "I guess it's not very good," he said, reaching to take the pad back.

Deacon pulled it out of his reach, still looking at it. "That ain't what I said. It's just..." he looked up at the bull again, then down at the sketchpad, his brows furrowed as he tried to find the words. "When I look at your picture, he looks... Well, I guess he looks strong. And proud. He looks special, like he's something way more than all the other cattle." He looked back up at the bull standing in the grass, lazily chewing his cud. "But he's just a bull," he said, pointing out at him. "Nothing special at all."

It was such awkward praise, and yet Aren found himself smiling. He felt something inside him swell with pride. "That means I did it right," he said.

He reached for the pad again, and this time Deacon let him take it. The big cowboy sat staring at the ground, nervously tugging at the grass. "I don't want you to be mad at me about the house," he said at last, his voice quieter than before.

That surprised Aren. It hadn't occurred to him Deacon would care how he felt. "I'm not mad. But I do wish you'd reconsider."

"It ain't safe."

"Olsa said it could be made safe…"

Deacon was already shaking his head, and Aren let his words trail away. "Folk tales," Deacon said. "Nothing more than that. Olsa's stories won't do nothing against the dark."

Aren looked back out over the field, and the cattle grazing there. He wasn't sure what else to say. He was glad Deacon wanted to make peace, but he wished there was some chance of changing his mind.

"Is it so bad out there with the men?" Deacon asked.

"Yes and no." Aren looked over at the big cowboy. "You've lived out there," he said. "You know how it is."

"That's different," Deacon said, still not looking up at him. "I'm their boss. I have to set myself apart."

Aren thought about that. It *was* different for Deacon. And in some ways, living with the men wasn't so bad. They didn't see him as one of them, which meant he was mostly excluded from most of their petty games. It was the fact that it reminded him too much of his past, all those years in boarding school. It made him forget he was an adult. It made him lose his confidence.

And the distinct lack of privacy was getting old, too.

"I'd like to have my own space," he said, and although that wasn't the whole truth, it wasn't a lie either. "I miss being able to paint."

Deacon frowned, but he nodded. "Guess I can understand that. Thing is, I'd hate for something to happen to you. You move into that house and something goes wrong, it'll be my fault."

"How would it be your fault?"

"It's my job to take care of the men," Deacon said. "I'm the one responsible—"

"Deacon," Aren interrupted him, "I'm not one of the hands." Deacon turned to him, looking both confused and surprised. "I know you take responsibility for those boys in the barracks, but I'm not one of them. Jeremiah's my boss, not you. And the only person responsible for me is me."

Deacon pondered that, and as he did, Aren saw his expression go from thoughtful to amused. A slow grin spread across his face. Finally, he said, "Don't know if that makes me feel better or worse. Not quite sure I can trust your judgement."

Aren laughed. "Me neither, to tell you the truth."

Deacon laughed, too, and Aren couldn't help but think how much different he looked out here in the grass, when the burden of leadership wasn't weighing him down. With his men, he always seemed angry and menacing, but sitting in the sunshine next to Aren, he was somebody else completely.

"It could be a place for you, too, you know," Aren said before he could think better of it. "Wouldn't you like to be able to relax and have a drink once in a while?" He smiled at Deacon, half-teasing but half-serious, too. "Think about it—a nice soft chair in front of the fire instead of a bale of hay in a draughty barn. A place where none of the ranch hands could find you."

Deacon smiled and shook his head in wry amusement. "I knew soon as I saw all those damn bags of yours you was going to be trouble."

"Does that mean 'no'?" Aren asked.

"Blessed Saints," Deacon swore, looking up at the sky in exasperation, and Aren knew then that he'd won.

"Does that mean 'yes'?" he asked, trying not to smile.

"Come on," Deacon said, unfolding his long legs and standing "Let's go see your new house."

Chapter Seven

Aren followed Deacon back through the grass. He was pleased that Deacon had changed his mind. The idea of having his own space—and more specifically, of having a place to paint—thrilled him. He followed Deacon up the porch steps. At the front door, Deacon turned to him. He pulled something out of his pocket and held it out to Aren.

It was a key.

"You had it with you?" Aren asked. It surprised him. It meant Deacon had already been wavering when he'd walked out to find Aren in the grass.

Deacon seemed embarrassed by the question. He was still holding the key out to Aren, and he used his other hand to push his hat further down onto his head. "Are you gonna take it or not?"

Aren bit back his smile and took the key. It was heavy, and the metal was warm from being close to Deacon's body. It felt like the greatest gift he'd ever received. "Thank you," he said.

"Just open the blessed door," Deacon said, ducking his head so the broad brim of his hat hid his face. "I don't got all day."

Turning to unlock the front door allowed Aren to hide his grin from Deacon. He liked that something as simple as a "thank you" could disarm the big cowboy so completely.

It was colder in the house than he'd expected. Aren hugged his arms around himself as they explored the tiny living room.

"Don't start a fire yet," Deacon said. "I'll send one of the boys out to clean the chimney and the generator. Have them bring those bags of yours, too. They're taking up half my damn barn. Had to make the horses sleep double."

"You did not," Aren laughed. He lifted a couple of the dust covers. There was a high, long table—more bar than anything—against one wall, and a small end table. Wooden chairs without cushions seemed to be the only seating in the room.

"Most of the good furniture got moved to the main house," Deacon told him. "Not sure exactly what's left."

"Whatever's here will be fine," Aren said, and he meant it.

Deacon followed him down the hallway to the back of the house. The room at the back was too small to be called a kitchen—whoever had built the place had obviously planned on eating meals at the main house. It was more like a large pantry with a hand pump for water. An old rag rug covered the floor.

"We put the pump in a few years ago," Deacon said, "when Brighton and his wife thought to live here." He nodded towards the door at the back of the room. "Privy, too."

Having his own privy seemed like an unbelievable luxury.

Deacon led him onto the back porch, where the generator sat. He opened it up, revealing more gears and cables and wheels than Aren had ever seen. "How much you want to know?" Deacon asked.

"Only as much as I need to."

Deacon laughed. "Smart man." He showed Aren how to turn it off and on, and where the coal went if they ever had to resort to that. "If they ever make one we can turn off and on from inside, we'll be sitting pretty, but till then, make sure you don't wait till the last minute. Always turn it on before the sun sets."

"I will," Aren assured him.

They went back into the house and up the stairs. The back bedroom was small and dark and held a dilapidated armoire, a four-poster canopy bed that no longer had a canopy cover, and a lone ottoman. That was nice, but it was the other bedroom that made Aren's heart soar. It held no furniture but had a large, east-facing window. The room was bright with sunlight, and although the glass in the window was thick and cloudy with bubbles that distorted the view, Aren thought it was perfect. He felt some forgotten place inside him open up. The artist in him was truly awakening, stirred by the golden opportunity of having a space dedicated to painting, and Aren couldn't help but grin from ear to ear.

"Thank you!" he said again to Deacon. "You have no idea how much this means to me."

As before, the words "thank you" seemed to unnerve Deacon. He pushed his hat down low and shoved his hands deep in his pockets. "Don't thank me yet," he said. "Might not work out."

"Still, I really apprecia—"

"Got to get back," Deacon interrupted him, keeping his head down so Aren couldn't see his face.

"I understand," Aren said. "We haven't discussed the lease yet—"

"I don't want your money."

"It's only fair—"

"Don't argue with me, or I'll take it back," Deacon said, finally glancing up at Aren past the brim of his hat.

"Fine." Aren was trying not to smile at Deacon's prickliness. "You don't want my money. Is there anything you do want in return?"

And finally, Deacon smiled. It was a shy smile, and it seemed out of place on such a big, hard man. "After supper," he said, "guess I wouldn't mind that drink you mentioned."

Aren felt a grin spread across his face. He didn't actually have any whisky, but he vowed to himself he'd find some by supper. "It's a deal."

Ten minutes after Deacon left, the parade of people began. First there were ranch hands bringing his bags, cleaning the chimney and chopping firewood.

"I can do that myself," Aren protested. In truth, he'd never chopped wood in his life, but he didn't want to be known as the only man on the ranch who couldn't do his share of the work.

"Don't worry," Simon said with a friendly smile as he tossed the split boards into a pile. "You'll be doing it yourself after today."

Aren caught Red as he was dumping two of Aren's suitcases in the bedroom. After some haggling, he bought a bottle of the ranch hand's whisky for what he was sure was an exorbitant price. He didn't mind. No matter how much Red had overcharged him, Aren felt quite sure it would be worth it.

Behind the hands came the wives, sent by Olsa. They set about gathering up the furniture covers, beating the rugs, dusting everything in sight and putting clean linens on the bed. Aren was trying to cram his clothes into the creaky armoire when he heard somebody behind him.

It was a nervous cough, unmistakably feminine, and Aren turned to find one of the wives behind him, her dress buttoned up to her neck and a lace kerchief on her head. He didn't know which one she was. He knew them by name, but not by sight.

"Mr Montrell," she said. "I'm Tama."

Tama, he remembered, was Jay's wife. As always when confronted by a woman, Aren found himself inexplicably uneasy. "Hello," he said. He glanced nervously towards the bedroom door. It was still open, so presumably she wasn't planning any kind of attack. Or a seduction, which would have been worse.

"I believe you met my sisters when Deacon brought you here?" she asked. Her cheeks were red, and her fingers fidgeted with the hem of her apron. "Beth and Alissa?"

The McAllen farm! He remembered Deacon saying that Fred McAllen had married one of his daughters to one of Jeremiah's sons. Now that he looked at her, he noticed her resemblance to Beth. "Yes," he said. "I met them."

"And did you like them?" she asked.

"Of course," he said, wondering where the conversation was going and hoping against hope it would be over soon. "They seemed very nice."

"Mr Montrell—"

That name made him think of his father, and he interrupted her to say, "My name is Aren."

"Aren," she said. She couldn't quite meet his eyes, and her cheeks were turning an alarming shade of red. "I was wondering if you might like either of them enough to marry."

"To *what?*" he asked, and immediately felt like a fool. It was, after all, a simple word. "I mean, I barely know them. We only spoke for a minute—"

"I just thought," she said, interrupting him, "now that you have a house, you might need somebody to help you, and—"

"I really don't—"

"I know the Austins still have a daughter to marry off, too, and Shay will probably suggest you marry her sister, Rynna. And I don't want to speak ill of Rynna, but—"

"Tama—"

"—she's awfully bossy and spoilt, too. She'd spend all your money. And my sister Alissa—"

"Stop—"

"—would really love to come here and be with me. She's much smarter than Rynna, and I know she's not as pretty as Beth, but—"

"That's not the poi—"

"—she'd be a really great wife. Better than Beth. Alissa can sew and cook, and she's not afraid to work—"

"Wait—"

"—and I'd be so happy if she could come here and be with me because I miss my family so much and my daddy can give you a nice dowry I think and—"

"*Stop!*"

She did. She looked down at the ground, nervously twisting her apron into balls in her hands. She almost reminded him of Deacon and the way he shoved his hands into his pockets and looked down at his boots when he was uncomfortable.

Aren took a deep breath. He ran his fingers through his hair, wishing it was long enough to tie back so he didn't have curls hanging loose like a girl's.

"Tama," he said, "I'm sure Alissa's very nice. And whether or not she's as pretty as Beth isn't the issue."

She glanced up at him, confused. "Do you doubt she's pure?" she asked. "I give you my word, she's not been with a man—"

"No!" he said, covering his eyes rather than face her while she spoke of such things. "That's not it. I just..." He dropped his hand and met her gaze. "I just don't want a wife."

She looked confused by that. She looked around the room as if she might find an explanation. "Well," she said at last, "if you change your mind..."

"If I change my mind," he said, "I promise Alissa will be at the top of my list."

One might have thought he'd promised her all the gold in Oestend. Her face broke into a smile so bright, he found himself thinking she was rather pretty. Prettier than her sister Beth. "Thank you!" she said. "Thank you, thank you, thank you!"

"I said 'if'," he said, but he was relieved they seemed to have reached the end of their conversation.

"I understand," she said.

But somehow, Aren had his doubts.

* * * *

Aren was surprised when Deacon came back that afternoon with Olsa at his side.

"Get your paint, boy," she told him as he let them through the door. "Red. And a brush. We'll be in the pantry."

Aren knew better than to argue with her. The suitcase that held his paints hadn't been unpacked yet, and he dug in it until he found the things she needed and took them to her at the back of the house.

"What are you doing?" Aren asked her.

"We're going to sing the ai'huara."

As if that meant anything to Aren. He looked at Deacon for explanation. Deacon rolled his eyes. "Folk tales," he said.

"You know better than that!" Olsa snapped.

Deacon crossed his arms across his chest and clenched his jaw, but didn't answer her.

"Don't let him fool you," Olsa said to Aren. "He knows all the songs. All the ones that matter, anyway. He knows the marriage song—"

"Fat lot of use I have for it, too."

"—and the birth song, and the warding song, and the death song—"

"Only 'cause you made me learn them before I was old enough to know better!"

"Is it so horrible I wanted somebody who could sing the death song for me when I go? Will you deny me a proper end?"

"I told you I'd do it, and I will," he said, his cheeks red under the darkness of his skin. "Now can we get on with this? I got work to do."

"Ungrateful brat." She grabbed on to Aren's arm. "Help me down, boy." Aren supported her as she slowly lowered herself to her knees. She pushed the rug out of the way to reveal a door cut into the floor.

"A cellar!" Aren said.

"Don't you go down there," Olsa said. "It's a bad place." She looked up at Deacon. "Well, get the paint and get over here."

Deacon gritted his teeth, clearly biting back an angry retort. He grabbed the paint and the brush out of Aren's hands and held them out to her. "Here."

"What good are they to me?" she snapped. "Get down here on the floor!"

"Why?"

"'Cause you're the one's got to paint the sign!"

"Why me?"

"'Cause I'm blind, you blessed fool! Why do you think? Now get down here before I take a switch to you!"

Aren almost had to clamp a hand over his mouth to keep from laughing out loud at the image of tiny little Olsa chasing Deacon around the courtyard with a switch in her hand. The look Deacon gave him should have burnt him to ash there on the spot. But Deacon didn't argue. He got down on his knees next to Olsa, close enough that he could wrap one arm around her.

Seeing them there, side by side, Aren saw something he'd failed to notice before. The realisation hit him so hard, he wondered how he'd missed it.

Deacon was one of the Old People too.

He had marvelled at Deacon's deep, dark skin tone, and yet he hadn't quite noticed that Olsa's was the same. Maybe it was the many, many wrinkles in her old face that had thrown him. Maybe he'd been distracted by her strange, sightless eyes, or the fact that her hair was silver-white instead of pitch black like Deacon's. He couldn't say why he hadn't noticed, but there was no doubt in his mind it was true.

He wondered if they were related. Olsa was far too old to be Deacon's mother, but she might be his grandmother, or even his great-grandmother. He wondered just how long Deacon had been living on the ranch. He wondered—

"Aren," Olsa said, "your brain's making too much noise."

Her words spooked Aren, as the things she said so often did. Could she hear his thoughts? Next to her, Deacon smiled at him as if to say, "See what I have to live with?"

"Sorry," Aren said. "I'll try to make it quiet down."

"See that you do."

Deacon ducked his head, hiding his smile. He dipped the tip of the brush into the paint and held it ready over the wood. Olsa's wrinkled old hand came down on top of his.

"You ready?" Deacon asked her.

She nodded. "I'll sing it. Best it comes from me since your heart's turned away."

Deacon nodded. He put the brush on the floor and he started to paint. He went slowly, his lines thick and sure, stopping occasionally to re-wet the brush, and, as he did it, Olsa sang.

Their language sounded musical even when it was spoken, but there was no doubt that what came from her now was a true song. It seemed to be only a few words, sung over and over as they made the mark on the ground.

It didn't look like much—a circle with some lines in it—but when it was done, she sat back with a smile. "You done good," she said to Deacon. "It's strong."

"How would you know?" he asked. "You're blind, remember?" But there was no missing the hint of pride in his voice, or the fondness in his eyes when he looked at her.

"Bah!" She waved her hand dismissively at him as she so often did. It was different this time, though. There was no real exasperation in her voice, and looking at them there on the floor, Aren realised this was probably a scene from their past. He wondered how many times they'd sat together as she'd taught Deacon the songs.

And yet now, Deacon pretended he knew none of them. He acted as if what he did know, he didn't want. He didn't want to be what she was. Aren found it puzzling.

Deacon stood up and helped Olsa get slowly to her feet. "Go on," she said to him. "Go do your work. Aren will get me home."

Deacon hesitated for a moment, looking at her. He glanced nervously at Aren, as if daring him to laugh, then he leaned in and kissed her on the cheek. "Thanks, Olsa."

She watched him go with her cloudy eyes, and Aren could have sworn he felt her love for the big ranch hand pouring out of her.

"His whole life," she said once Deacon was gone.

"What?" Aren asked, puzzled.

"You wondered how long he'd been here, and how long I'd been watching over him. The answer is, his whole life. Since he was a babe."

"Are you—" He was going to ask if she was his grandmother, but she cut off his words before he could finish.

"I won't tell you no more right now, boy." She pointed down at the mark on the floor. "Let the paint dry before you put the rug back. Check it every so often. Make sure the paint's not rubbed away."

"I will."

Olsa turned and started down the hall towards the front of the house, her arm held out in front of her as she groped for the wall. He rushed over to her side to help her. "Is it like the wards on the doors?" he asked as he took her arm.

"The wards are to keep things out. The ai'huara is to keep things in."

"Will it be part of the net?"

"The net!" she said with obvious distaste. "Bah! The net's a load of dung, boy."

"But Deacon said—"

"Deacon don't say half of what he knows, and what he *does* say is stuff other people *think* they know, but most the time get wrong."

Aren tried to puzzle that out as they moved slowly towards the door. "I don't understand," he confessed at last.

They were in the entryway now. Olsa stopped and turned to look at him with her clouded eyes.

"What did Deacon tell you?"

"He said the wards used to work, but now they don't."

"Not all wards quit working," she said. "Just the ones against the wraiths."

"Deacon told me somebody learnt how to make a generator to make the wards stronger—"

"The generators got nothing to do with it." She sighed in exasperation, shaking her head. "Symbols have power, but only so long as people know it."

"So the generators don't do any good?"

"That's not what I said, boy. They do their part keeping the wraiths away, but it ain't got nothing to do with the wards, despite what people think."

"But the house is safe now, right?"

"Hard to say," she said.

"Whatever's here, it's in the cellar?"

"I think so."

"How do you know?"

"I don't. It's a guess."

"Was it somebody who lived here?"

"Might be."

"Was it—?"

"Son, it's Deacon's house. It's Deacon's tale. He wants you to know, he'll tell you. Until then, best you can do is keep that cellar door closed and hope for the best."

Chapter Eight

An hour after supper, Deacon was knocking on his front door.

"This is for you," he said, as soon as Aren opened up. He shoved a giant, rolled bundle into Aren's arms before ducking his head and turning away, obviously embarrassed.

"You brought me a housewarming gift?" Aren asked, trying to figure out what it was. It seemed to be a roll of thick leather.

"No," Deacon said, despite the obvious evidence to the contrary. "Just seems like there should be a rug or something in front of the fire. Bear or wolf skin would be better, but since this is a cattle ranch, all we got is cowhide."

Aren unrolled it. It was surprisingly big. Then again, so were the Oestend cows. The side that had been rolled in still had hair. It was thick and unexpectedly soft, almost woolly. "This doesn't feel like cow fur."

"Not a normal cow, no. It's a breed from way up north. Few years ago, Brighton got into his head to try raising a herd, 'cause the pelts would be worth more."

"It didn't work out?" Aren asked as he spread the hide in front of the fire. It did make the room feel homier.

"Turns out they can't much take the heat. Summer came and they were dropping like flies."

"It's really nice," Aren said. "Thank you."

The sentiment seemed to make Deacon uncomfortable, just as it had earlier that day. He pushed his hat down low, looking down at his boots so the brim hid his face. Aren bit his lip to keep from laughing. "How about that drink?" Aren asked.

It was lucky that Brighton and Garrett were leaving the next day for a run into town. Aren had entrusted Garrett with a bag of coin and a list of things he needed for the house, including glasses and some better whisky than Red had given him. He'd managed to beg two glasses from Olsa to use until then, and he poured a generous amount of whisky into each. By the time he turned around again, Deacon was over his embarrassment. He was in one of the hard, wooden chairs with his long legs stretched out towards the fire. His hat hung on the arm of his chair.

Aren handed him the glass. Deacon took a sip and winced. "Holy Saints! Are you sure that's whisky?"

"Bad, isn't it?"

"Where'd you get it?"

"From Red."

Deacon laughed, and Aren found himself thinking once again how different he seemed when he was away from his men. "Guess I know now why he's so hungover all the time," Deacon said, but he took another drink.

Aren settled into the other chair. "Olsa said you've lived at the BarChi your whole life?"

Deacon sighed, leaning back to stare up at the ceiling. "Olsa talks too much."

"She says she raised you?"

Deacon didn't answer.

"And you own this house?"

"I told you, it ain't my house."

"But Olsa and Jeremiah said—"

"Blessed Saints, you can't let it rest, can you?"

Aren found Deacon's prickliness amusing, but he hid his smile by taking another drink. He waited, and his patience paid off.

"I was born here," Deacon said, still not meeting Aren's eyes. "In this house. My parents died when I was only a babe."

"How did they die?"

"Depends on which one you mean," Deacon said, and the tone of his voice made it clear he wasn't going to talk any more about that. He sat up and finished the rest of his whisky in one swallow. He sat looking down at his empty glass as if he might find the words he needed at the bottom. "Jeremiah wanted to take me in. Olsa, too, of course. Old Man Pane ran the BarChi back then, and he wasn't too keen on the idea, but they talked him into it. So I lived there in the house in Olsa's room, until..." He smiled, "Well, until I reached the age where sharing a room with her was causing me some serious discomfort." He laughed, shaking his head. "That old woman knows too much, and I was leaving too many stains on the sheets, if you know what I mean."

Aren laughed. He'd always thought there couldn't be anything worse than waking up in a room full of boisterous boys, but he realised he'd actually had it fairly well. At least all the boys had been in the same predicament, especially once puberty started. They were somewhat understanding and willing to ignore the muffled moans as boys handled themselves after the lights went out or in the early hours of the morning. Aren couldn't imagine having to deal with such things in Olsa's presence.

"So what did you do?"

"Moved into the barn," he said, "until I was old enough to move in with the hands."

"But then you moved back to the barn again?"

Whatever laughter had been in Deacon's eyes suddenly burnt away. He stood up and walked over to the table to set down his glass. "Old Man Pane hated me. And I ain't just saying that. He wanted me gone, and if he'd lived much longer, I probably wouldn't be here now. Jeremiah did the job I do now. I was just another hand back then. But once the Old Man died, Jeremiah put me in charge of the men." He turned to look at Aren, leaning back against the table. "Can't be one of them and be in charge of them, too," he said.

"Do you miss being one of them?"

Deacon ducked his head. He put his hand on top of his head, and Aren realised the movement was to push his hat further down on his head, although his hat was still hanging on the arm of his chair. He didn't answer.

Aren found himself smiling. He almost wanted to laugh. He could not remember ever being so genuinely happy. Here, in a house that was not quite his, in the middle of the back end of nowhere, he was free. The wind blew outside. The fire crackled in the hearth. The cheap whisky warmed his gut, and Deacon's hesitant friendship made him feel lighter than he had in a long time. He found himself thanking whatever Saint had sent him to Oestend…and whatever Saint had sent him Deacon.

"Pour yourself another drink," he said to Deacon, and he loved the smile he got in return.

* * * *

Away from the barracks, in the sanctuary of Deacon's unwanted house, Aren's days began to take form.

In the morning, while the ranch hands ate their breakfast, he did chores. First and foremost, he had to learn how to chop wood. He was relieved he was behind the house when he did it, out of site of the rest of the ranch, because his first few efforts were clumsy at best. By his third day, his arms and shoulders were so sore he could barely move. Olsa, with her amazing ability to see everything despite her blind eyes, gave him a jar of salve to rub on them at night.

He couldn't help but notice the salve might have other, more intimate uses as well, if only he had a partner.

He persisted with the firewood and after a week or so was starting to get the hang of it. He came embarrassingly close to chopping his own foot in half on more than one occasion, but he was determined not to ask for help. He didn't want to give anybody on the BarChi reason to think he was weak.

Every morning, after the hands had finished their meal, Aren walked over to the main house and had breakfast with Deacon. Generally, Olsa was there, too. Occasionally, Jeremiah or one of his sons might be as well. Every day after breakfast, Deacon would go to work with his men, and Aren would go back to the house. He split his time there between painting and working on Jeremiah's books. On nice days, he took the ledgers or his sketchpad outside. He'd walk out to the south pasture and sit in the sun. He loved the way the grass swayed in the wind, and the way the warm light seemed to caress the back of his neck as he bent over his work. He loved that sometimes there would be men in the field, herding or feeding or mending the fence or doing any number of chores Deacon assigned to them. Some of them would wave or stop to chat. Some of them ignored him. Either way, he didn't mind. He missed lunch — *dinner* — most days, not because he meant to, but because he always seemed to be lost in whatever it was he was doing.

In the afternoons, as the men were returning from the fields, Aren would walk over to the main house. He never volunteered to help the men with their more strenuous chores, but he found that something as simple as offering to unsaddle and brush down the horses for them when they came home went a long way towards fostering friendship.

After that, he and Deacon would eat 'supper', although Aren still couldn't bring himself to use that word. Shortly after supper, Deacon always arrived at his door, and they'd sit in front of the fire.

And Deacon would talk.

Sometimes he told Aren about his day, or about the men, or about the cows, or about how they didn't have the right tools for the job they needed to do. Sometimes he talked about branding the cattle, or birthing a colt, or the fact that the irrigation ditch in the north pasture seemed to be running dry. He never said anything personal. It was never deep. But Aren began to realise how very, very lonely Deacon had been before Aren had arrived. He held himself apart—apart from the sons, apart from the hands, certainly apart from the women—and although he would never have put any of it into words, Aren knew Deacon was relieved and grateful to finally find *somebody* he did not have to hold at a distance. Sitting there by the fire, listening to Deacon talk, Aren realised he was the first friend Deacon had had in a very long time.

It made him feel good. It made him feel like his presence on the ranch truly served a purpose. Yes, he did the books. Yes, he helped care for the horses and occasionally mucked out their stalls. But if he'd turned his back on the ranch, simply walked away or been taken by the wraiths, those things would go on. They would be picked up by other people. Life on the ranch would carry on without a hitch.

But Aren knew beyond any doubt that Deacon would miss him, and Deacon was the heart of the BarChi. Jeremiah ran the ranch in theory, and his sons helped, but it was Deacon who was truly the driving force behind the entire operation. He knew where everybody was at any given time. He knew where the cattle were and if any of them were sick and if and when they'd have to be moved. He knew the horses—this one spooked at rivers and that one liked to bite and the other was as stubborn as a mule. He kept track of which ones had been ridden each day so they'd not be used again the next. He knew every inch of the land, past the fences, into the places Aren had never been. He knew the roads—the one back to the McAllen Ranch, and the one that went past the BarChi, into the wild and on to the Austin place. He knew the sky and the clouds and could predict with startling accuracy when it would be clear or when it was going to rain. He was, in every way, the person who kept the ranch on its feet.

And no matter what happened, no matter if things went right or wrong, he would be there at the end of each day, standing on Aren's porch, waiting for a chance to leave it all outside.

Of course, they only had an hour or two, then the sun would be falling in the sky and Deacon would have to leave in order to get back to the barn before dark. Aren would start his generator and climb the stairs to his bedroom. He would go to bed alone…

In the house.

His first couple of nights there he'd lain awake, wondering if anything would happen, but nothing had. After the third night, he stopped worrying. By the time he'd been there two weeks, he was beginning to wonder if the whole 'haunted' thing was a prank after all.

Of course, that was when the ghost decided to prove him wrong.

Chapter Nine

He woke to the sound of knocking. He'd been deep in slumber, and he woke only enough to register the sound.

Knocking.

On his door.

Must be Deacon.

That was as much as his sleep-addled brain managed. After all, Deacon was the only person who *ever* knocked on his door.

He was on the top landing when it occurred to him he was naked. He stumbled back into the room, grabbed his pants and made a clumsy effort to insert himself into them as he made his way down the stairs.

Still the knocking continued.

"I'm coming!" he yelled, and the knocking stopped.

He was halfway down when it dawned on him that it was the middle of the night. The fire in his hearth had long since reduced to coals. It was full dark out. Nobody in their right mind should have been outside. The thought helped jump his brain into wakefulness. If somebody was knocking on his front door at this time of night, it meant something was very, very wrong.

He got his pants on and even got them buttoned. He had the door unlatched and was about to open it when he realised he should look out through the window first, and when he did, his blood suddenly ran cold in his veins. His heart began to pound.

There was nobody outside.

He re-latched the door with shaking fingers, thinking of how close he'd come to opening it.

Had he imagined the knocking? He'd been asleep. Maybe it had all been a dream?

He turned and leaned against the door and willed himself to think. It had to have been a dream. There was simply no other explanation.

Boom, boom, boom!

Aren jumped at the noise. It no longer sounded like somebody knocking. It sounded like somebody *pounding* with all their strength. And it wasn't coming from the front door at all. It was coming from the back of the house. Was it possible somebody was at the back door?

Somehow, he didn't think so.

Aren pushed himself away from the door. He made himself put one foot in front of the other. He forced himself to walk down the short hallway to the back of the house.

He stepped into the small back room. He was struck immediately by the cold. It was freezing in the pantry, far colder than anywhere else in the house. It was also pitch dark. There were no windows in the room and no hint of light penetrated the blackness. It was the kind of dark that seemed to breathe on its own. Aren could feel it all around him, bearing down on him, cutting off his air and making it hard to breathe. The only thing that kept him from truly panicking at that moment was the fact that he was still in the doorway, hanging on to the wall. He felt certain if he'd taken even one step into the small room, he'd have lost his way back.

Boom, boom, boom! The noise came again, louder than before.

Aren slowly back-tracked to the living room. It was dark there, too, but not so dark that he couldn't find the lantern on the table. He used one of his few matches to light it and turned the wick up as high as it would go.

Light flooded the familiar space and, as the darkness abated, Aren took a deep breath, willing his heart to stop pounding inside his chest.

Boom, boom, boom, boom, boom!

He picked up the lantern and walked back down the hall into the back room. The pantry was still freezing. Aren swore he could see his breath. The light helped, but even its comforting glow seemed to waver and dim in the oppressive darkness.

The pounding continued.

It was *not* coming from the back door.

Now that he could see, it took only a second for Aren to determine the real source of the noise—the cellar. He reached down with a shaking hand and grabbed the edge of the rug. He slowly pulled it away from the cellar door. The symbol Deacon had painted was still there. The paint hadn't faded or chipped.

The pounding came again, and the cellar door shook with the impact. The hinges rattled. Aren backed up fast, running into the wall behind him.

There was *something* in the cellar, just as Olsa had suspected. Aren wondered what he would see if he opened the door—a person, or a ghost, or something else? Not that he had any intention of doing such a thing. The pounding continued.

"Who's there?" Aren called. His voice was shaking and his heart was pounding, and he wasn't sure if he expected an answer or not, but he asked anyway.

The pounding stopped. Aren's heart laboured on. He could have sworn that whatever it was behind the cellar door, it was listening. It was waiting. "Are you there?" Aren asked.

A piercing shriek shattered the silence. Aren's lantern sputtered. The temperature seemed to plummet.

Aren ran.

He wanted to leave. He wanted to get out of the house, and he knew suddenly why the foreman had run out into the night. But somewhere underneath his terror, the rational part of his brain stopped him from opening the front door. He bolted up the stairs and into his bedroom as fast as he could go, slamming the door behind him. He nearly dropped his lamp, and he thought how disastrous it would be if it shattered on the floor, igniting the fuel. He'd have to choose between being inside a burning house or being outside with the wraiths.

He forced himself to breathe. He forced himself to slow down. His hands shook as he put the lamp down on his bedside table. He pushed his dresser in front of his bedroom door.

Downstairs, the shrieking went on.

He climbed onto his bed, but he couldn't make himself lie down. Instead, he sat huddled against the headboard with his arms around his knees and his eyes on the door. He wondered what in the world he would do if it moved.

Eventually, the shrieking seemed to wind down. Eventually, whatever was in the cellar lapsed instead into tears. Even all the way upstairs, Aren could hear the bitter, wrenching sobs of whatever was on the other side of the door.

There was no way for him to judge the passage of time. There was no window in the bedroom. He hadn't carried his pocket watch in weeks. He didn't need it on the ranch, where life was dictated by bells and the sun. He didn't know where it was, and he had no intention of getting out of bed to look for it. He stayed where he was, huddled against his headboard. After some indeterminable amount of time, the crying stopped, and Aren sighed in relief.

All the fear and the tension and the adrenaline drained away, leaving him limp and exhausted. He was finally drifting off to sleep with his head on his knees when the pounding started again.

Aren started awake, terror welling up again inside his chest. He wanted to cry. He curled into a ball, fighting back the fear and the rage inside him. He wasn't sure he could handle it if the thing in the basement started shrieking again.

"Aren?" he heard a voice call.

Deacon!

It wasn't the ghost at all. Aren almost sobbed with relief. He dragged himself off the bed, wincing at the cramps in his back and neck from spending so many hours huddled in such a tense, awkward position. He struggled to push his dresser from in front of the door.

"Aren?" Deacon called again, and Aren could tell from his voice he was getting worried.

"I'm coming," he called.

He remembered the last time he'd said that, when the knocking had first started. How many hours ago? Was it morning now? It had to be, if Deacon was on his front porch.

He opened the door to his bedroom. He could tell immediately it was daytime. Sunlight filtered through the window in his studio and the one by the front door. He stumbled down the stairs, and after fumbling for far too long, he managed to get the door open.

"You all right?" Deacon asked. "You missed breakfast."

Aren wondered how he'd missed the morning bell. "I did?" he asked. But his voice came out all wrong. It was much closer to a squeak than normal.

Deacon's eyebrows went down, his eyes suddenly suspicious. "Something happened last night, didn't it?" he asked. "I told you this house wasn't fit to live in!"

Despite everything that had happened, despite the terror he'd felt mere hours before, the idea of losing the house kicked Aren into gear. He thought about his studio, and his privacy, and his own privy. He thought about evenings spent with Deacon in front of the fire. Standing there in the bright light of day, Aren suddenly couldn't quite remember how afraid he'd been. The sun was warm, the wind blew his hair, reviving him, blowing his mental cobwebs away.

He loved the house. He didn't care how bad it was at night. He'd bolt himself in his room every night, if that's what he had to do.

He smoothed down his hair. He stood up straight. He did his absolute best to look like somebody who hadn't spent the last several hours huddled into a ball on his bed trying not to cry.

He made himself smile.

"I'm fine," he said to Deacon. "I guess I just slept late."

He could tell Deacon didn't believe him. Deacon waited for him to dress, and as they walked across the clearing to the main house, the big cowboy kept looking at him sideways.

"You look like shit," Deacon said.

"Thanks for telling me."

"You sure everything's all right?"

"Of course," Aren said, although deep in his coat pockets, his hands were still shaking.

"I told you that house ain't fit to live in."

"It's fine."

"Maybe you should move back to the barracks."

"No!" Anything seemed preferable to that. "Besides, there's only one empty bed and if you're going to hire another hand next time you go to town, he'll need it."

Deacon sighed, but he stopped arguing.

After eating a late breakfast, Aren couldn't quite face going back to the house. He went to the barn, where he found Garrett and Simon mucking out stalls. "You look like shit," Garrett said to him.

"So I hear," Aren said as he grabbed a pitchfork and went to the next stall.

He saw the way the two friends glanced at each other, as if trying to determine which of them would pursue the matter. It turned out to be Simon. "House haunted like they say?" he asked.

Aren debated how to answer. He didn't want to admit to Deacon that anything was awry, but could he trust Simon and Garrett? "If you'd asked me yesterday, I would have said no."

"What happened?"

It wasn't exactly that he'd decided to tell them but once he started talking, the words kept coming out, and before he knew it, he'd told them the whole story of the night before. When he'd finished, he looked up to find them both staring at him with wide eyes.

Garrett shook his head and whistled. "You're a braver man than me."

That surprised Aren. He'd just finished telling them in embarrassing detail how scared he'd been. "I doubt it," Aren said.

"No fucking way I would have stayed in the house," Garrett said. "You must have the biggest set of balls in Oestend."

Aren felt his cheeks turning red at the comment, but he felt oddly flattered by it, too. Strength and bravery weren't things he'd ever been accused of before.

"You know," Simon said, looking thoughtful, "way I heard it, nobody's died inside the house. They all got scared and ran into the night. But Brighton and that wife of his lived there a month and they survived. Brighton said Shay near left him over it, and vowed to never step foot in there again. But they weren't harmed."

"Small comfort that is," Garrett said, and the three men all bent back to their work.

Despite Garrett's quick dismissal of Simon's statement, Aren found himself pondering it for the rest of the day. Nobody had been harmed in the house. Standing in the sunshine with the cool Oestend wind blowing his hair, Aren found the terror of the night before harder to remember.

He finally climbed the porch steps to his front door. Inside the house, there was nothing to hint at the chaos of the night before. The house was the same as always—

slightly chilly because the fire had burnt out sometime in the night and Aren had never stoked it back to life—but other than that, there was nothing at all out of the ordinary.

Aren went into the pantry. As always, it seemed to be a few degrees colder than the living room, but otherwise, it was only a room like any other. Aren looked down at the mark on the floor. Olsa had said it was good. The paint was not chipped or faded. He felt sure it would keep him safe. The rug was lying in a heap where he'd dropped it the night before. He spread it back over the door.

Yes, something was in the house, but it was trapped in the cellar. Olsa and Deacon had sung their song over it. As long as he didn't let it out, and as long as he didn't let his fear drive him outside into the night, he'd be fine.

He felt good as he walked back to the house to eat dinner with Deacon.

"I don't think you should stay in that house," Deacon said, predictably.

"I'll be fine," Aren assured him, and he must have been more convincing than he'd been earlier that day, because Deacon let the subject drop long enough for them both to eat. After dinner, he followed Aren back to the house, and Aren poured them both drinks as he did almost every night.

"I know something happened last night," Deacon said, looking down at the whisky in his glass. "You were spooked this morning. You can't tell me you weren't."

Aren sighed, contemplating the amber liquid in his own glass. He didn't want to lie to Deacon. On the other hand, he feared Deacon would insist he move out. "I heard some noises," he relented. "That's all."

"Only noises?"

"*Only* noises," Aren confirmed, telling himself it wasn't exactly a lie. "It was probably just the wind."

In the cellar.

Right.

Deacon looked sceptical. "I wish you weren't alone out here. Anything could happen."

"What, you want me to invite one of the hands to stay with me?" Aren asked, joking. "Do you really think that would make any difference?"

Deacon shrugged. "I could stay."

It was a tempting offer. Aren thought he might feel better if Deacon were with him. But then he considered what a wreck he'd been the night before, huddled on his bed, trying desperately not to cry. He didn't want Deacon to see him like that. He didn't want Deacon to know he was weak.

"It was probably just the wind," he said again.

Deacon didn't exactly look convinced.

"Where would you sleep, anyway?" Aren teased. "On the floor?"

Deacon eyed the hard boards at his feet. Aren knew what he was thinking. Even sleeping on the cow pelt in front of the fire was bound to be exceedingly uncomfortable.

"I'll be fine," he told Deacon. "And you'll sleep better in your own bed."

That was all easy enough to say while Deacon was there, but once he'd left and Aren had bolted the door behind him, his courage began to fade. He turned on the generator, then checked every lock twice. He checked the cellar door three times. He dragged his heaviest chair from the living room to put on top of it. He drank two more shots of whisky.

In the end, he climbed the stairs to his room and closed himself in. After some debate, he pushed the dresser in front of it again. He undressed and climbed into bed.

Midway through the night, the pounding started. On and on it went, and Aren's heart pounded faster and louder each time. But eventually it stopped. Eventually, he heard only sobbing. He lay in his bed, and finally, he drifted off to sleep.

When he awoke the next day, he knew — he was as safe in the house as in the barracks, where some fool hand might open a door and let in the wraiths. Or grope their way into his bed. He missed sex, but not enough to debase himself again.

Not yet, anyway.

Whoever's ghost was in the cellar, Aren decided it was of no concern to him.

Chapter Ten

The next few nights were still rough, but each morning that he awoke safe and sound in his bed seemed to prove there was nothing to fear. After a week the sounds stopped and the house again fell silent. Aren was relieved, but not such a fool as to think it was over.

It took another week for Deacon to stop asking him constantly if everything was all right, and Aren was relieved when the big cowboy finally let the subject drop. Aren hated lying to his only real friend, but he wasn't going to risk being sent back to the barracks, either.

A few days later, he walked across the grassy expanse from the house to the courtyard to meet Deacon for breakfast as he did every morning. The wind was blowing, as it ever did in Oestend. Sometimes it was quiet. Sometimes it was loud. Often it built to a crescendo in the deep of night. But this morning, it was faint and soothing, heard only in the soft rustle of the long, swaying grass that Aren walked through. A path was beginning to form through it from his many trips back and forth. Seeing it made him smile. It somehow solidified his place at the BarChi, and his place in the world as a whole. It seemed like proof that he belonged. The fact the track through the grass was two men wide was the best part of all. It meant that he wasn't alone.

He went to the kitchen first, but he knew before he entered that Deacon wasn't there. He could hear raised voices coming from inside.

"I know what you're doing!" It was a man's voice, although Aren couldn't place it right away. "I know you were with him last night!"

"What do you care?" The second voice was female.

"I won't have you lifting your skirt all over the blessed ranch!"

Aren stopped outside the door. He had no business listening—he knew that—but he couldn't quite resist the entertainment.

"My skirts are none of your business," the woman said.

"You're my *wife!* How can you say it's not my business who you fuck?"

It could only be Daisy and Dante. He didn't think either Tama or Shay ever slept with the hands, and if they did, they were smart enough to not argue about it where anybody could hear.

"We both know you don't care," she said, her voice like ice. "We both know you've never had any interest whatsoever in what's between my legs!"

"That doesn't give you the right—"

"It gives me every right! Why should you care, anyway? You've never pretended to love me."

"I won't have the hands snickering behind my back because my wife acts like a common whore! At least a whore has the brains to ask for money in exchange, rather than giving it away for free!"

"You'd do the same, if the one you wanted would have you."

A heartbeat of stony silence, then, "What do you mean?" Dante's tone was no longer confrontational. He sounded alarmed.

"You think I don't know?" she asked, and there was no missing the gloating tone in her voice now that she had him on the defensive. "You think I'm blind? You think I don't see you watching—"

Her words were cut off by the unmistakable sound of a slap. Aren started forwards through the door, thinking he should intervene, but a voice behind him said, "Aren, don't!" He turned to find Tama, a bucket of fresh milk in each hand, looking at him with wide eyes. "Trust me," she said. "You'll only make it worse."

Dante's voice was tense with suppressed rage. "I won't be the laughing stock of this ranch just because you can't keep your skirts down. It better *stop*. I find out it's happened again, I'll take my daddy's gun and put a bullet in his skull."

A muffled sob, then the sound of running feet—only one set of footsteps, and too light to be Dante's. Daisy had fled the room.

Dante cursed, and Aren heard a crash that he guessed was a chair thrown against the wall.

"Excuse me," Tama said, pushing past him with the milk to walk into the kitchen. *Braver than I am*, Aren thought. He had no desire to have to face Dante. He turned instead towards the barn, hoping to find Deacon. The big ranch hand wasn't inside, but when Aren walked around to the far side of the building, he found him. Deacon was leaning on the wooden gate of the corral, staring at the bull inside.

"Hey," he said as Aren leaned on the gate next to him. "Daisy and Dante done fighting yet?"

"For now, it seems," Aren said.

"Good." Deacon pointed towards the bull. "He's not acting right. Worried he's got the froth, like the last one."

"Is that why he's here, in the corral?"

"Yup. Got to watch him." He shook his head. "He's the last bull we got, too."

Aren wasn't thinking about the bull, though. He couldn't stop thinking about the argument he'd overheard. "Daisy's sleeping with one of the hands?"

"More than likely." Deacon turned to look at him. He ducked his head a bit to look Aren in the eyes, his expression grave. "Is it you?"

"No!"

"Good," Deacon said, standing up to his full height again. "Lifting that skirt will buy you more trouble than it's worth, I promise you that."

"Who do you think it is?"

Deacon shrugged, turning back towards the bull, obviously uninterested. "Don't rightly know," he said. "Don't rightly care, either. I do my best not to get involved."

The bull suddenly let out a bellow, swinging its head from side to side. It stepped forwards and knocked its head again the side of the barn.

"Son of a bitch," Deacon swore under his breath.

"Is that bad?" Aren asked.

"It sure ain't good."

"Do you have to put him down?"

"We'll see." Deacon pushed his hat back on his head. "Could still be a fever, in which case he'll come out of it in a day or two."

"There's no way to check for sure?"

Deacon grinned over at him. "There is, if you want to get close enough to him to put the thermometer where it needs to go."

"Ha!" Aren laughed. "No thanks!"

"Smart man," Deacon said. He clapped Aren on the back. "Come on. Us standing here starving ain't gonna solve anything."

As always, Deacon had chores to do with his men as soon as they had finished eating. Aren walked back to the house alone. It was a beautiful day. The breeze was light. The sun was shining overhead. He had no intention of wasting it indoors.

He headed for his bedroom, where he'd left his sketchpad and the leather satchel that held his pencils and penknives. But when he walked through the door, he stopped dead in his tracks.

The ghost had been there! He'd learnt over the course of the previous weeks that her presence was sporadic, although he'd only ever heard her at night. He wasn't sure how she'd found her way out of the cellar, but there was no other explanation for what he saw.

There was paper everywhere. Almost every page had been torn from his sketchpad and tossed onto the floor. His satchel was on the floor, too, but it was empty. All around it lay pieces of pencil.

"Oh, no," Aren groaned. He fell to his knees and started picking up pieces. "Stupid ghost," he mumbled as he did. "Guess you don't like art."

The pencils were all broken in half. That wasn't the end of the world. Short pencils worked as well as long ones. But when he found his penknife, his heart fell. "Son of a bitch!" he cursed.

The knife was ruined. The handle was little more than splinters. The small blade was bent, and the tip broken.

Having pencils did him no good if he couldn't sharpen them.

He gathered up the pencils and put them back in the satchel. He wrapped the pieces of his penknife in his handkerchief and stuffed it into his pocket. He collected the pages of his sketchbook. Some of the drawings had been torn in half, but most of the pages were still intact, if slightly crumpled. He smoothed them out as well as he could and tucked them back between the covers of the book. A few drawings had escaped the ghost's wrath, including the one of the bull he'd been drawing the day Deacon had given him permission to move into the house.

Looking at the drawing, he realised it actually was pretty good, considering it was only of a bull. He also realised it was probably the bull that was now contained in the corral, sick with either the fever or the froth. Somehow, that seemed ominous.

Once the pages were all put away, Aren put the pad back on the armoire and headed for the courtyard in search of Deacon. It took some hunting, but he finally found him in the barn. He was in a stall, examining the leg of one of the horses.

"Is something wrong with him?" Aren asked.

"*Her*," Deacon corrected. "She's been limping a bit, but I ain't sure yet why." He came out of the stall, smiling at Aren. "You looking for work?"

"Not today," Aren said. "I was wondering if there's a trip to town any time soon?"

"As a matter of fact, there is. We're leaving day after tomorrow. Gotta drive some cattle into market. Hire that new hand you said I could have. Put out word we're looking to buy a bull. Why?" Deacon grinned at him. "You want to come along? Feeling lonely out there in your house?"

Women. It always came back to women. "No," Aren said. "But I need a knife."

"You don't need to buy one. I got plenty of knives." Deacon reached into his boot and pulled out a bone-handled blade at least eight inches long. He offered it handle-first to Aren.

Aren eyed the monstrous thing. He pictured himself trying to sharpen his pencils with it. He'd probably sever a finger or three in the process. "I'm sure that's very effective for… something." What, he wasn't exactly sure and probably didn't want to know. "All I need is a penknife. Something like this." He pulled his handkerchief out of his pocket and showed Deacon the pieces.

"What the hell happened to it?" Deacon asked as he re-sheathed his giant knife.

"Uh…" Aren realised too late he'd led himself into a trap. He didn't want to tell Deacon it was the ghost, because he knew Deacon would want him to move out of the house. "I dropped it."

Deacon's eyebrows went up. "You *dropped* it? Then what? Rolled a boulder on top of it for good measure?"

It *had* been a stupid excuse. Dropping it wouldn't explain the many pieces it was in. "I mean, I dropped it, then I stepped on it. But, you know, not on purpose or anything. It was an accident." He knew he was babbling, and he forced himself to stop. Deacon's eyebrows rose a bit higher. His eyes were full of good-natured laughter, and Aren found himself becoming annoyed. Not least of all at himself. "Look, can you get me a new one or not?"

"'Course I can," Deacon said, but that was as far as he got. He was interrupted by a commotion in the courtyard — what sounded like a giant crash, followed by men yelling.

Simon burst through the barn door. "Deacon, get out here! That bull just busted right through the gate."

"Son of a bitch!" Deacon swore. He turned to Aren. "Go to Jeremiah's office and get his gun. Top right drawer of his desk."

He didn't wait for confirmation. He and Simon were grabbing lengths of rope off the hooks on the wall of the barn.

The courtyard was chaos. The bull was in the centre, waving its head back and forth, snorting. Men were coming out of the barracks and the outbuildings with ropes, trying to surround it. Garrett was already swinging a lasso over his head.

Aren stayed close to the buildings, glad that in the chaos nobody would be looking at him. Nobody would see how much the thing scared him. He ran quickly up to Jeremiah's office and found the gun where Deacon had said it would be. It was a large pistol, and it was far heavier than he expected. He had no idea how touchy the trigger was, and he kept it pointed away from him. There was a box of bullets next to it, and he grabbed those, too.

Back in the courtyard, some of the men had managed to rope the bull. One rope was around its neck, another around one of its huge horns. More were around its front feet. It had been pulled to the ground, but it was far from being secure. It was kicking and bellowing. Red, Ronin and Sawyer were already holding ropes, leaning back to put as much weight on them as possible. Garrett, Deacon and Simon held the others. The rest of the men were standing back a bit, waiting for instruction.

"Frances," Deacon yelled, "take Simon's rope! Calin, take Garrett's."

Neither Calin nor Frances looked too sure of themselves, but they both stepped forwards and took the ropes they'd been ordered to. Garrett immediately grabbed another length of rope, holding the loop loose in his hand.

"Hold those tight!" he yelled. "I'm going in close to try to get those back feet."

"Simon," Deacon called, "Aren's got the gun. You want to do it, or want me to?"

"I'm faster than you, old man," Simon said. Aren suspected it was supposed to be a joke, although it came out a bit flat.

"Aren," Deacon said, "give Simon the gun."

Aren's hands were shaking, and he wasn't even one of the men fighting to secure the animal. He watched as Simon checked the pistol. It must have been loaded already, because Simon handed the box of ammo back to Aren and tucked the gun in his belt before grabbing another rope. Garrett had managed to wrap another rope around one of the bull's hind legs, and was handing the other end to Miron. The bull had less room to move now, and Aren watched with his heart in his throat as Simon darted closer to throw another length of rope over the beast's horns.

They were out of men, not counting Aren, but the bull still wasn't secure. It suddenly seemed to find its second wind. It bucked hard, kicking out with its feet, tossing its head, and a few men were pulled to the ground.

"Hold tight!" Deacon yelled.

It lurched to its feet, but the ropes tripped it up. The men who were still standing pulled, and it toppled back to the earth with a crash and an angry bellow. Men were trying to get up, trying to get farther away while still holding the ropes.

All but one.

Frances was frozen. He stood in wide-eyed fear, his rope slack in his hands, staring at the raging bull.

"Hold that line, Frances!" Deacon yelled.

But it seemed Frances couldn't hear him. He was staring at the bull with mute horror in his eyes. The men next to him were obviously straining to keep their lines tight.

"I said, *hold that fucking line!*"

Frances didn't drop the line, but he didn't snap out of his daze, either. He was frozen, his mouth open, his eyes fixed on the bull. The bull lurched to its hind feet again, bucking against the rope. Miron, whose rope was around one of the beast's hind legs, was pulled closer to the bull.

"Deacon," Miron yelled, "I'm losing it!"

"God damn it!" Deacon yelled. He looked next to him at Ronin, who was holding his own line without obvious strain.

"Go," Ronin told him. "I'm fine."

Deacon tossed his line to Ronin and ran for Frances, not bothering to verify that Ronin had caught the rope.

The bull tossed its giant head around, kicking out with its front legs, trying to get them free of the rope so it could stand. Calin and Sawyer had the ropes that held its front feet, and they both pulled backwards, trying to pull the bull off its feet.

"Don't—" Miron started to yell, but his words were cut short. As the bull fell forwards, it kicked out with its one free hind leg, hitting him hard in the gut and knocking him backwards out of the circle of hands. He landed a few feet away. He wasn't moving, and his entire front seemed suddenly to be covered in blood.

Deacon pushed Frances out of the way. He grabbed his line, pulling it tight. "Aren, grab Miron's line," he yelled, and although his heart pounded in his chest and his knees felt like rubber, Aren dropped the box of bullets he was holding and did as he was told. He knew he wasn't as strong as the other men, but he grabbed it and pulled, leaning back in order to put his weight into it.

The ropes went tight, and the huge animal again crashed to the ground.

"Tighter!" Deacon yelled, and all the men leaned into their lines, pulling hard. The bull stopped thrashing. It was breathing hard, and Aren was sure it was only catching its breath before trying again.

"Now!" Deacon yelled to Simon.

Simon handed his rope to Garrett, taking only a moment to make sure his friend had a firm grip. Then he pulled the giant pistol from his belt. He ran into the circle and placed the muzzle against the side of the beast's head. He pulled the trigger, and the bull at last lay still.

The shot was still ringing in the air when Deacon turned on Frances. Before Aren was even able to drop his own rope, Deacon punched Frances hard in the face. Frances' head ricocheted back, his face covered in blood. Deacon didn't stop. He hit him again, hard, knocking him to the ground.

It was so sudden and so horrifically violent that Aren felt his bile rise. He couldn't stand to see such brutality. It reminded him of all the other times he'd seen bigger men beating up weaker ones. He wouldn't let it happen to Frances! He started to move towards them, thinking to stop Deacon, but Simon grabbed him.

"Don't interfere."

"Let me go!" he said, trying to pull away, but Simon was too strong.

"Stay out of it," he said, his voice low and threatening.

Frances' face was covered in blood. He tried to roll away from Deacon, but Deacon leaned over and grabbed his shirt. He pulled him part of the way up off the ground and punched him again.

"He'll kill him," Aren said.

"No, he won't," Simon said, and it seemed he knew what he was talking about, because right at that moment, Deacon released Frances, letting him fall roughly to the ground.

Deacon leaned over him, pointing his finger menacingly in his face. "Wagon leaves day after tomorrow," he said. "You got till then to decide if you got the balls to do this job or not. 'Cause I'm telling you here and now, if you ever fail me like that again, I'll beat your fucking head in, and I won't blink an eye about doing it, either. Do you understand me?"

Frances covered his face with his hands, moaning. "I'm sorry," he cried, although it was barely intelligible through his bloody hands. He tried to roll away, but Deacon grabbed him. He lifted him up, drawing his other fist back to punch him again.

"I said, *do you fucking understand me?*"

"Yes!" Frances sobbed. "Yes! I understand! I'm sorry!"

Deacon dropped him, backing away, and Simon finally let Aren go. Aren went to Frances, who was curled in a ball, sobbing quietly. When Aren tried to touch him, he flinched away.

The brutality was more than Aren could stand. Deacon was so big and so strong, and just like every other big man, he thought it was acceptable to bully other men who happened to be smaller than him.

"You didn't have to hurt him!" Aren yelled, standing up and turning on Deacon. He pushed him hard in the chest, although the big cowboy barely budged. "You didn't have to humiliate him like that!"

Deacon's jaw clenched. His hands balled into fists at his side, and for a moment, Aren thought Deacon was going to punch him. "I didn't have to *hurt* him?" Deacon asked, his voice like ice. "Is that what you said?"

The threat in his voice was clear, but Aren wasn't going to back down. "You heard me!"

Deacon moved so fast Aren barely saw his fist coming. He didn't punch him, but he grabbed him by his upper arm hard enough that Aren yelped in spite of himself. "Come here," Deacon said, dragging him bodily towards where Miron lay on the ground, surrounded by Olsa, Daisy and Shay. "Look at him," Deacon said, shoving Aren forwards.

Aren didn't want to look. He could see blood. He could smell...something. Something he couldn't quite identify. Whatever it was, every instinct he had was to look away. He dug in his heels, tried to turn away from the bleeding, moaning body on the ground, but Deacon was too strong. He pushed him forwards again, harder this time. "I said, *look at him!*" he yelled, and Aren obeyed.

It was horrific. Even looking, Aren couldn't quite tell what it was he saw. Everything from Miron's chest to his groin seemed to be red. And wet. He was covered with shredded pieces of something that might have been clothing or might have been skin or might have been something else.

"His bowel is torn," Deacon said. Aren turned to look at him — anything was better than seeing Miron's broken body on the ground — and he realised there was more in Deacon's eyes than anger. There was pain there, too. "Even if the women could sew his guts back together, there's no amount of medicine in the world that can keep the infection away." His voice was quieter now but no less intense. "No morphine on hand, either, so we can't even make him comfortable. Only Olsa's tea, and that will barely touch this kind of pain."

"In town—" Aren started to say, knowing even as he said it that it was foolish.

"That's two days from here. Even if we left right now, we couldn't make it to the McAllen farm before nightfall. Soonest we could leave is tomorrow. He'd never make it anyway."

"But—"

Aren's words were cut off by a horrible, heart-wrenching sound from Miron. It was a sound of pain — a wet sound, more than a moan, not quite a scream.

"This is all that's left," Deacon said. "One of two things will happen now. Either he spends the rest of the night crying and begging and screaming while we lie to him and tell him everything will be fine, or he'll realise what's happened and ask for mercy." Deacon's gaze was piercing, his grip on Aren's arm still painfully tight, and Aren wished he could escape. He wished he could run away. He wished he could erase the entire day from his life. Anything but face what Deacon was saying. "If that happens," Deacon said, "who do you think has to do it?"

The full impact of what those words meant hit him hard. It was too much. Aren felt his eyes filling with tears, felt his whole body start to shake. He didn't want to cry in front of Deacon, but he couldn't handle what he was being told. "There must be a way," he said weakly, his words breaking on the lump in his throat. "There must be..."

But there wasn't. He knew that. He blinked hard, trying to make the tears stop, but they only came faster.

He looked up into Deacon's eyes, expecting to see disgust now on top of the anger, but he saw only sadness. All of Deacon's rage seemed to have drained away. "Go home, Aren," he said, finally letting go of his arm. "Go back to your paint."

Chapter Eleven

Aren didn't go straight to the house. He stopped first to help Frances up from the ground.

"Come on," he said gently. "You can come home with me."

The kid was a mess. There was no other way to put it— in physical pain from the beating Deacon had given him but also racked by guilt. Twice on the way to Aren's house, they had to stop while Frances vomited into the grass.

"I'm sorry," he sobbed over and over. "I'm so sorry!"

Aren couldn't tell him that everything was all right. A man was dying, and it was largely Frances' fault. But he couldn't muster any anger towards the boy, either, and berating him more would do no good. So Aren didn't say a word. He waited silently at Frances' side until he was ready to start walking again.

Once they were inside, Aren poured a hefty shot of whisky into a glass and handed it to Frances. He wondered if they at least had that much to give to Miron. Ronin and Red always had plenty of alcohol. He hoped they'd spare some for the dying man. Maybe that mixed with Olsa's tea would help numb the pain, a little at least.

Aren fetched a rag and a pail of water, and while Frances sat on one of his hard wooden chairs, hiccoughing as he tried to stifle his tears, Aren began to clean his wounds.

Frances' nose was broken. Aren didn't know how to set it right and feared any attempt would only cause Frances unnecessary pain. It was going to be crooked, but not badly so. Frances' lip and eyebrow were both split and swollen, but the bleeding had stopped. The bruises were starting to form. As violent as the attack had been, Aren realised Deacon could have hurt him much, much worse.

Aren sighed. He wasn't sure if he understood Deacon's rage or not. He wasn't sure if he could forgive him or not.

Frances' face would heal. That was the important part. That was what Aren tried to keep in his mind as he wiped away blood and tears.

"I can't go back to the barracks," Frances whispered as Aren worked.

"Sure you can."

"No." He shook his head. "I can't face them."

"Will you go home?"

"I can't go there, either."

Aren didn't ask why. He knew the reason didn't matter. There was no going back for him, either. This was his home now. He tried to imagine what he'd do if he suddenly had to leave the BarChi.

Frances' blue eyes were huge, filling again with tears. The left side of his face was quickly turning an ugly shade of purple. He was so young. Aren reached up and wiped the tears away. He brushed his finger over Frances' swollen lip. He heard Frances' breath catch in his throat. "We'll figure something out," Aren told him.

He saw the glint of hope in Frances' eyes, the way he suddenly lowered his lashes, biting on his already-split lip. He recognised the signs, and although his cock jumped to life at the thought, something in his chest rebelled. Some small piece of his heart turned cold at the thought.

"I could stay with you," Frances said, his voice barely a whisper.

"I only have one bed," Aren said, deliberately refusing to acknowledge the kid's point.

Frances smiled, although the effort obviously pained him. He put his hand on Aren's chest. "I'll sleep with you," he said as his hand started to migrate south. "I'll take care of you. Just let me stay."

It was a tempting offer. Aren's heart was pounding in his chest. His cock was hard and straining against his pants. The thought of having sex again almost made him dizzy. But still, there was that piece of him, that tiny part of his heart screaming at him that this was wrong.

Frances' hand moved lower. His fingers brushed the bulge in Aren's pants, and Aren moaned despite himself. He felt his resolve slipping. His hips seemed to push towards Frances' hand of their own accord.

"I'll do whatever you ask."

Aren couldn't help but imagine Frances bent over in front of him. He thought about how good it would feel to grab hold of his ass and push into him from behind. He felt a surge of excitement at the prospect of finally being the one in the control.

"Anything you want to do to me," Frances said, and that might have been the turning point—that might have been the moment when Aren's body won its battle with his conscience, finally ending his long streak of celibacy—if only he hadn't been watching Frances' face when he said his next words. "I'll let you," he said, and as he did, his eyes filled with tears.

Aren's heart ached for him. He was young, and lost, and horribly confused. Aren remembered men from his own past, men who had taken advantage of him when he was at his weakest. He didn't want to be one of those men. Taking Frances to his bed would be the worst thing he could possibly do to him.

Aren reached down and gently removed the boy's hand from his groin. "Don't turn your body into a commodity," he told him. "That's a hard place to come back from."

Frances' tears began to fall again, coming faster this time. "It's the only thing I have to give you."

"Frances, you don't owe me anything—"

"You're the only friend I have. I know I'm a mess right now," he said, tentatively touching the bruised side of his face, "but I won't always be. Maybe once the cuts heal—"

"This isn't about the way you look," Aren said.

"Then what's wrong with me?"

"Absolutely nothing," Aren told him. "But I know what it's like to feel as if your body is the only thing you have to offer. I've traded my own for far less, and I remember very clearly the way I always felt the next morning."

Frances' eyes started to fill with tears again. He nodded, looking down at his lap. "I wouldn't feel that way with you." But the tremor in his voice hinted otherwise.

"Maybe not," Aren said, because it wasn't a point worth arguing, "but I don't want to take that chance."

"I'm afraid to go back there."

"You can stay here tonight," Aren told him. "But I don't want you to think you have to spread your legs for me in return."

They were interrupted by a knock on the door and although Aren was a bit relieved to be given an escape from their awkward conversation, he was tempted to not answer it. Deacon was the only person who ever came to the house and Aren wasn't sure he was ready to face the ranch hand yet. The knock came again, and Aren sighed, realising his folly. Deacon wasn't the type to be easily dissuaded.

He was both surprised and relieved to find it wasn't Deacon at the door after all. It was Daisy.

"Olsa told me to bring you some food," she said without preamble as soon as he opened the door. She was carrying a basket, and she pushed past him into the house. She barely glanced at Frances as she set it down on the table. She reached inside and pulled out three small packets— they looked like tiny brown pillows. "She sent these, too. She said to soak them in cold water for fifteen minutes, then put them on his face. She said it would help with the swelling." She tossed them down on the table and turned to leave.

"How's Miron?" Frances asked.

"Not dead yet," she said, before the door slammed shut behind her.

* * * *

The rest of the afternoon passed in awkward silence. Aren helped Frances put Olsa's packets on his face, and later they shared a cold supper from Olsa's basket.

Afterwards, Aren tried to convince Frances to sleep in his bed while he slept on the floor, but the boy curled up on the rug in front of the fire instead, and before Aren could argue, he was fast asleep. Aren hadn't even thought to warn him about the ghost, and he hoped she'd be quiet for the night.

"Everything's going to be fine," he said to Frances' sleeping form as he spread a blanket over him. He was glad Frances couldn't hear him, though. He wasn't sure his words were true.

There was enough food left in the basket to eat for breakfast the next morning, too, but not for lunch or dinner. Frances wasn't ready to face the other hands yet. Aren wasn't sure he was, either. He was debating walking across the lawn to the main house and begging Olsa for another hamper of food when someone knocked on his door.

He feared it was Deacon. He hoped it would be Daisy with more food. Instead, he found Simon on his front porch, his hat pushed down and his jacket collar turned up against the wind.

"I need to see him," he said.

Aren couldn't imagine any good could come from making Frances face one of the ranch hands. He stood in the doorway, refusing to let Simon enter. "He feels guilty enough already," he said. "The last thing he needs is a lecture from you."

Simon sighed in obvious frustration. "That's not why I'm here."

"I don't think—"

"Let him in," Frances called from the living room.

Aren still hesitated. It was one thing to defy Simon while he stood outside in the wind and Aren was inside, but somehow, allowing him into the house felt like letting his guard down. But he also knew he and Frances couldn't hide forever. He opened the door and stood aside to allow Simon to enter. He followed him into the living room, where Frances sat staring into the fire, unable to meet anyone's eyes.

"How you doing?" Simon asked.

Frances shrugged but didn't speak.

Simon sat in the empty chair that Aren thought of as Deacon's, opposite Frances in front of the fireplace. He took his hat off and put it on the table next to him. He put his elbows on his knees and leaned towards Frances. Frances continued to stare into the fire. He was chewing on his lower lip. His chin trembled a bit, and Aren felt sure he was fighting back tears.

"Look, kid," Simon said, "I know you think what happened was your fault—"

"It was."

"Maybe," Simon said. "Maybe not."

"How can you say that? You saw what happened. I was scared. I dropped the line—"

"I saw. The thing is, this a rough job. It's a rough country. People die out here every day."

"Maybe," Frances said, "but it's not the same."

Simon didn't answer at first. The room was silent except for the soft crackle of the fire and Frances' quiet sniffles. Frances continued to stare at the fire, and Simon stared at Frances, seemingly looking for the words he wanted to say. Finally, he took a deep breath and began.

"Here's the thing, Frances. I been in Oestend ten years now. I worked the mines a couple of years. I did some trappin'. I been a hand on four different ranches. And every single job I worked, I saw men die. Lots of 'em.

Sometimes it was their own fault. Sometimes an accident like what happened yesterday. But no matter how it happens, there's one thing the same — there's always someone left behind to carry the guilt."

Frances still wasn't looking at Simon. He still wasn't responding. But he was listening. Aren could see the words were sinking in. He no longer appeared to be on the verge of tears.

"First year I knew Garrett was on a ranch. Foreman sent him and two other hands up into the hills with a herd of sheep. Had a shack up there, should've held them all safe for a month while the sheep got fat. Second week there, those boys got drinking. Middle of the night, Garrett wandered out to the outhouse like a fool. Walked right through the night and not a wraith touched him. Locked himself in the outhouse and passed out cold sitting on the hole. Didn't realise till morning he'd left the door to the shack open. Found both other hands dead on the floor. Wraith-killed."

Frances finally raised his eyes to look at Simon.

Simon kept talking, his voice low and calm and steady. "Guilt's a hard thing. Garrett buried those men. Told me later he spent the next three days trying to get up enough courage to kill himself. But in the end, he couldn't do it. He finished his month on the hill and drove those sheep back down the trail alone. He feels guilty to this day. And maybe he should. Thing is though, Frances, he learnt from it. Garrett hasn't had a drop to drink since that night. He knows, now, he's got to be stronger than the alcohol. It's the same with you, kid. You gotta learn to be stronger than your fear."

"Everybody will hate me," Frances said. "And I don't blame them."

Simon shrugged. He leant back in his chair, letting his long legs stretch towards the fire as he did. He seemed to be relaxing now that Frances was talking. "Some of them," he said. "Maybe. Thing is, most men in that barracks probably got a story too. I got one of my own, but you notice I told you Garrett's and not mine. The men that can't forgive you, they're probably the ones still haven't forgiven themselves. And if any man out there doesn't have his own tale like yours yet, trust me when I say, they will. It's only a matter of time." He shrugged. "It's a hard land, kid. It's a hard job. But you don't got to let it beat you."

"You're saying I should stay?"

"You got anyplace else to go?" Simon asked, and it was clear he already knew the answer. "I'll tell you what. You stay here with Aren again tonight. I think that's wise. Tomorrow morning, Deacon's headed into town. If you go, it'll be me, Calin, and Red going with him. But if you stay on here at the ranch, it'll be Sawyer, Calin, Aubry and Garrett. They'll be gone near a week. That means if you stay, it'll just be me and you and the twins here at the ranch. The twins won't be no nicer to you than they were before, but they won't be no worse either. Miron's death don't mean squat to them. Several days on the trail, Deacon and Garret can put those other boys in their place while you get your feet back under you here. By the time they get back, things will have shifted." The doubt in Frances' face was mirrored by the doubt in Aren's heart, but Simon nodded at him. "Trust me," he said.

Frances looked at Aren, and Aren shrugged. "It's up to you," he said.

Frances looked back at Simon, but Simon had apparently said all he felt he needed to. He stood up, putting his hat back on his head as he did. "You think about it," he said. "Tomorrow morning, you can either go back to town with Deacon, or you can stay here with me. You got to learn to live with what you did," he said. "My feeling is, you may as well do that here as someplace else."

Aren followed Simon to the door and out onto the front porch, closing the door behind him so that Frances couldn't hear. The day was bright and windy, dust flying through the air like it had somewhere to go.

"Miron won't last more than another hour," Simon said, turning towards him. "We'll bury him this afternoon. Best if you can make Frances be there. I know he won't want to, but men will respect him more if he faces it, even if he's crying like a babe while he does. It's turning his back that'll bring him trouble."

"I'll make sure he goes," Aren said.

"Good." Simon pushed his hat farther down onto his head and hunched his shoulders into the wind. He was halfway down the steps when Aren called after him.

"Does Deacon know you came?"

Simon glanced back at him with a grin. "Deacon's the one who sent me."

Chapter Twelve

The burial wasn't as bad as Aren had anticipated. Although Sawyer and Calin glared at Frances, the rest of the attendants were stoical. And although tears continued to stream down Frances' bruised and battered face, he didn't blubber. He didn't try to hide it by wiping them away, either. He stood stiff and silent next to Aren, the wind drying his tears nearly as fast as they came.

After it was over, Aren steered Frances back towards the house, deliberately avoiding Deacon even though he saw the wary look the big man gave him. He stopped in the kitchen long enough to beg more food from Olsa before taking Frances back home.

It was nearly dark when the knock he'd been dreading finally came. He left Frances in the living room, and rather than allowing Deacon into the house, he joined him on the front porch, hugging his thin jacket tightly around him against the wind. He refused to look at Deacon. He stared instead at the swiftly-falling sun, bright against the horizon. He concentrated on the gentle song of the wind — the rustle of the swaying grass and creaking of the trees.

"I know you're mad," Deacon said, then stopped short, as if he didn't know what else to say.

Aren didn't answer.

"I'm glad you're helping him."

Still, Aren kept his silence.

"Is he gonna go or stay?"

Aren sighed. He'd hoped to put off dealing with Deacon until after he'd returned from his trip to town, but it seemed Deacon wasn't going to accommodate him, and Aren supposed giving the man the silent treatment wouldn't solve anything, either. "He's decided to stay."

"That's good," Deacon said. "I'm glad."

"You're *glad?*" Aren said, finally turning to face Deacon. "You beat him up, you humiliated him in front of everybody, you made him feel weak and worthless and pathetic, and you're *glad* he's decided to stay?"

Deacon's cheeks turned red at Aren's words, but he didn't turn away. "Look, Aren, I know you think I was harsh —"

"Ha!" Aren laughed bitterly at the understatement. He turned back to the sunset, turning his back on Deacon.

"The thing is, I'm their boss. I have to be like that. It's my job to make sure they toe the line. I need them to be more afraid of me than of some damn bull."

"You need to prove you're strong, and the best way to do that is to make men like me and Frances look weak."

Deacon was silent for a moment, and Aren wished he could see his expression, but it was easier to have this conversation if he didn't have to face him.

"You're not weak, Aren," he finally said, his voice quiet and strained. "Maybe he is, but you're not. You're nothing like him."

"I'm exactly like him."

"I don't..." His voice trailed away, and Aren forced himself to turn around again and face him. The confusion on Deacon's face was clear. "I don't know why you think that," he said.

Aren couldn't answer. He couldn't tell him the one thing that really made him and Frances the same.

"Aren," Deacon said again, and Aren was surprised at the grief he heard in his voice. "I've seen a hundred hands come and go. Maybe more. Every one of them needs to fear me. Every one of them needs to respect me. But not one of them needs to like me."

"Good thing," Aren said, "because none of them do."

Deacon winced at that. He shoved his hands deep in his pockets and looked down at the grey boards of the porch, allowing the wide brim of his hat to hide his face. "I don't have the luxury of being their friend," he said quietly. "Only person I have that luxury with is you."

The words hit Aren hard, not least of all because he knew how hard it had been for Deacon to say them. He closed his eyes, trying to hang on to his anger. He wanted to keep his indignation. He wanted to make Deacon pay for what he'd done. And yet, deep down inside, he wasn't sure why. It wasn't all about Frances. Aren recognised he was taking a great deal of his own anger at himself and his past and men like Professor Birmingham, and he was trying to make Deacon pay for it all. Although it pained him to admit it, he knew he wasn't being entirely fair.

Still, he couldn't quite let it all go yet, either.

"You're asking me if we're still friends?" he said at last.

He wasn't surprised it took Deacon a moment to answer. He wasn't surprised at the way he kept his head down and his face hidden. Friendship and loneliness weren't things men like Deacon discussed. When he finally responded, his voice was so low, Aren barely heard him over the sound of the wind. "Yes."

Aren turned again to the sunset. It was now only a blush of light on the distant plain. It was nearly dark, and Aren knew they'd both be wise to get back inside. He crossed the porch to his front door, but he stopped short of going inside.

"How long will you be gone?" he asked.

"Five or six days."

"I used most of my good whisky on Frances," he said. "You bring me more, and maybe I'll forgive you."

"I'll bring you the best they sell," Deacon said. Aren could hear the relief in his voice. He finally risked another look back over his shoulder. Deacon was looking at him again, almost smiling, and despite everything, Aren almost smiled back.

* * * *

The men left early the next morning, driving a herd of cattle ahead of them. Shortly afterwards, Simon was knocking on Aren's front door.

"Come on, kid," he said to Frances. "Time to face the world. There's plenty of work to be done with them others gone."

Frances didn't exactly look confident, but he followed Simon out of Aren's front door and back towards the barracks. Aren watched them go. The house suddenly felt emptier than it ever had before. He thought about breakfast, and the fact that Deacon wouldn't be there. He had a sudden, irrational urge to call Simon and Frances back, but he knew it was foolish. They had chores to do.

He went inside and closed his door, and for the first time since his arrival at the BarChi, he felt completely and utterly alone.

He walked over to the main house and into the kitchen. It seemed strange to sit there by himself, without Deacon at his side. Olsa puttered around, humming to herself and ignoring him except to hand him his food. He found it was hard to remember what being angry with Deacon felt like.

He wandered back to the house, and after a few hours of working on the books — and confirming for the tenth time that yes, they could afford to hire a tenth ranch hand — he found himself upstairs in his studio.

He'd stretched a new canvas a few days before and it sat on his easel, awaiting his attention. He hadn't known at the time what he was going to paint. He stared at the canvas and realised he still didn't.

He had no idea what to do with himself. Eventually, he made his way back to the barn where he helped Simon and Frances with chores until it was time for supper. Since there were only the five of them, he ate with the hands. Ronin and Red talked only to each other and ignored everybody else. Frances kept his head down and didn't talk to anybody. Aren attempted to make small talk with Simon, but in the end, his awkward attempts at conversation seemed to only make the rest of them uncomfortable, so he lapsed into silence, lost in his thoughts.

He missed Deacon.

He told himself he was a fool. He told himself to grow up. But that evening, as he sat alone in his tiny living room in front of a roaring fire, he could not deny he missed the big cowboy's company.

Finally, he built the fire up to help keep the house warm through the night. He went out to the back and started the generator, and he climbed the stairs to his bedroom.

The pounding on the cellar door started, and Aren lay in his bed, thinking.

He found himself wondering about the men going into town. He hoped they'd made it safely to the McAllen farm. He wondered what they were doing.

Then, he realised he *knew* what they were doing.

They were at the McAllen farm, where the only women who were to be found for miles around lived. Undoubtedly they were each being 'tucked in' by one of the maids tonight.

And that, of course, made him think of Deacon. He thought of when they'd been there together, of listening to Deacon a few stalls down as he rolled with a maid. He thought of the things he'd heard and of masturbating alone in his stall to the sounds of their pleasure.

And suddenly, he had a raging hard-on.

It had been far too long since he'd had sex. Not since the onset of puberty had Aren gone so long without a partner. During his years in boarding school, there'd always been *somebody* to alleviate his sexual frustrations with. He'd never loved any of them, except perhaps Professor Birmingham later on at university. He hadn't even liked a great many of them. But when they'd found their way into his bed in the quiet of night, he'd almost always enjoyed it. He might have been ashamed later. He might have had regrets. But when it came down to choosing between his pride and his sexual desire, his pride never did win.

He no longer tried to chastise himself for it. He liked sex. He liked to be fucked. He longed for the freedom to do more, to have time with a man to really explore what pleasure could be. He wanted to know how it felt to be the one with his cock inside another man, instead of always being the one with his legs in the air.

He could have had it. With a groan, he thought about Frances and the proposition the boy had made. The logical part of Aren's brain knew he'd done the right thing by telling Frances no, but his throbbing cock certainly didn't care. He could not help but wish he'd taken what Frances had offered. He missed sex. He missed the release and the sated laziness that came after. And yes, he could masturbate—he had masturbated, in fact, far more in the past few months than at any other time in his life—but the satisfaction was nowhere near the same.

He wondered how long he could go on without a sexual partner without losing his mind.

Chapter Thirteen

The next few days were much the same. Aren watched Simon and Frances together, and he could not deny that Frances was doing better. The swelling was gone. The bruises had begun to fade. And just as Simon had predicted, Frances was starting to regain his confidence. He still kept quiet far more often than not. He still had a hard time looking most people in the eye. But on a few occasions, as Simon helped him, Aren thought he even saw a hint of a smile on the boy's face.

"He'll be fine," Simon told Aren when they had a few minutes alone. "He's stronger than he knows."

For the first time, Aren believed him.

It was the fourth day with the other men gone. The sun was shining, but the wind was blowing in hard, cold gusts from the north, and Aren wrapped his coat tightly around himself as he walked back to his empty house.

Inside, it was cosy and warm. The fire he'd left burning was down to smouldering coals, and he stoked it back to a blaze. He was caught up with the books. The weather was too nasty to take his sketchpad outside. He poured himself a drink — the very last of his whisky until Deacon came back — and he wandered upstairs to his studio.

The light coming through the cloudy, bubbled glass of the window was golden. Outside, the wind robbed it of its heat, but here, in the comfort of the house, he could feel its warmth. He positioned his easel so he could stand in the glowing rectangle it made across the floor. He put his drink down in the corner of the room where he wouldn't spill it while lost in his art. And he began to paint.

He couldn't have said when he'd decided what his subject would be. It was as if some secret part of his brain had made that call for him. But as he mixed colours, as his brush moved with its own purpose over the canvas, the picture began to take form.

Deacon.

It wasn't a scene he'd actually witnessed. Not exactly. Yes, it was Deacon as he'd seen him many times, standing in the barn, hanging up tack as he teased Aren about some foolish thing he'd said. It was different, though, too.

He painted him bare from the waist up. He'd never actually seen Deacon shirtless, but that didn't bother him. He knew the shape of Deacon's body, the way his broad shoulders sloped, the way his torso narrowed to his waist. He knew the way his ass curved in his work pants and the way his pitch-black hair hung down his back. But there was more to it than capturing the man's physical form. He also knew the spark in Deacon's eye when he laughed, and the way his eyebrows went up slightly when he was amused. He knew the way he squared his shoulders when he was facing down his men, and the way he let them finally fall when he walked through Aren's front door.

He painted for hours. He lost all track of time, as he often did when he was involved in his art. In the end he didn't finish, but when he finally broke from his artistic trance, the sun had long since passed over the house and its golden light no longer graced his windowsill. He noticed, too, that he was getting cold. The fire in the living room must have gone out. He retrieved his mostly-full drink from the corner of the room and stepped back to admire his work.

He liked it. He couldn't say it was the best painting he'd ever done, but he thought he'd captured a little of what he'd been aiming for. Deacon looked strong and sure, mildly amused as he so often was in Aren's presence. He looked alluring. He looked...

Way too damn sexy.

Aren sighed, shaking his head and turning away from the canvas. He drained his whisky in one swallow, although it was a rather poor substitute for what he really needed.

He would not think about Deacon that way.

* * * *

That was an easy enough resolution to make in the light of day, but once he was asleep, he had little choice. His subconscious took over, and it was obsessed with exactly one thing — sex.

When he awoke the next morning he couldn't remember the details of his dreams, but he knew they'd been sexual and that Deacon had been involved. What he could remember was nothing more than fleetingly sensual images — dark skin and callused hands and shared breath — and the overwhelming urge to come. The dreams left him feeling disoriented, and a bit off balance. And unbelievably horny.

He went to the barn again to help Frances and Simon with the chores, thinking a bit of good old-fashioned physical labour would keep his mind off sex, but he found it difficult to concentrate. He couldn't stop thinking about the dreams. He couldn't quite ignore the nagging ache in his groin. He found himself staring at Frances, watching the way his hips moved. He watched Simon, noting how the muscles in his shoulders bunched under his shirt as he worked. He even eyed Red and Ronin when they all ate supper together. He imagined getting them drunk and offering to go down on them. He'd learnt from experience that, especially in a place with a distinct shortage of women, there were plenty of men who couldn't say no to such a thing, whether they actually preferred men or not.

He shifted in his seat, squirming in pants that suddenly felt way too tight. He gritted his teeth and did his best to think about anything besides sex.

He failed.

It was a good thing Frances didn't notice his twitchiness, or if he did, he didn't recognise the signs. If he'd made his offer again, Aren would not have been able to say no, whether he thought it was wise to fuck the kid or not. In truth, at that moment he would have begged any one of the ranch hands to touch him, to use him, to take him any way they pleased. He would have thrown away his dignity to even be allowed to suck one of them while he jacked himself off. *Anything* to alleviate the terrible pressure in his groin.

That night, he took out the salve Olsa had given him. He lay naked in front of the fire on the cowhide rug Deacon had given him. He greased both of his hands well. And he gave himself over to self-gratification.

He fucked himself with the fingers of one hand while stroking his cock with the other. He resisted the urge to rush right for his orgasm. Instead, he did his best to make it last, taking himself to the edge, then backing off to make it last longer. He thought about Frances. He thought about Simon. He thought about being shared by the twins in every conceivable way.

He thought about Deacon. He thought about his dark hair and his laughing eyes and his big, strong, work-worn hands. He thought about how good it would feel if the fingers moving in and out of him were Deacon's instead of his own. He imagined what Deacon's cock looked like, and the heat that might burn in his eyes when he came.

When Aren finally let go, when he finally pumped his shaft hard, letting his orgasm release him from the tension he'd been living with over the last few days, he cried out with the sheer relief of it. And yet, afterwards, even as he lay catching his breath from the strength of his climax, he felt a lingering sense of disappointment.

He could no longer deny himself the pleasure of a partner. Once the men came back, he'd do whatever he had to do. Whether that meant Frances, or whether it meant sacrificing his pride to one of the other men, he did not care. One way or another, he was going to get laid.

* * * *

He felt better the next day for having indulged himself. But only a little.

His resolution to find a willing sexual partner did not change. He spent the morning debating which of the men to approach.

On one hand, Frances was the obvious choice. He'd already made an offer. Taking him up on it would have been the easiest solution. The thing was, Aren was pretty sure that in this case, the easiest path was also the worst. The kid was fragile. He might develop a dependence upon Aren which Aren did not want to foster. He did not want to do to Frances what so many men in his own past had done to him. Also, Frances' position with the other hands was going to be precarious at best. If they suspected he was willingly sleeping with another man, it was likely to make things worse.

Having ruled out Frances, the next logical choice was Sawyer. Although he didn't like the man, there were benefits to be had. For one, he knew Sawyer was willing to fuck men, and as crude as it was, that simple fact was critical. Second, he knew Sawyer didn't want the other hands to know about that particular habit. That meant he wouldn't tell anybody. And third, it occurred to him that if Sawyer had a willing victim, he might stop forcing himself on an unwilling one. By having sex with Sawyer, Aren might actually be helping Frances in a round-about way. Yes, he found the man despicable. But he knew from experience that with the right motivation, he could forget such things for a while. Specifically, for as long as it took him to come.

There were other men he would have preferred — Simon or Garrett, who were both kind; Calin, whom he knew from his days in the barracks was particularly well-hung; or Deacon, who…

He couldn't think about Deacon.

The logical choice was Sawyer.

That decision made, he moved on to debating his approach.

He could choose to eat with the hands, sit next to Sawyer at supper, initiate some unnecessary physical contact and see if the man took the hint. He doubted he would, though. Sawyer didn't seem overly bright.

He could invite him to his house some night, ply him with whisky and take him by surprise. Of course, that course of action would be made more difficult by the fact that Deacon was usually at his house in the evenings. That was a problem he could solve when the time came. But inviting Sawyer to his house invited a certain intimacy Aren did not want. He did not want the man invading his space. He certainly did not want to give him any reason to think he could use their relationship to gain anything, like more pay or lighter chore duty. It was best to keep things as impersonal as possible.

What he needed to do was get Sawyer alone some time during the day, outside, while doing chores. He wondered what Deacon would say if Aren asked him to put Sawyer on duty mucking out stalls with him one day. The two of them would be alone in the barn. It would be unbelievably easy after that. But such a request was bound to make Deacon suspicious. Most of the other chores were done in pairs or teams. They wouldn't provide a means for him to get Sawyer alone unless he offered to help with some of the harder duties, like stringing barbed wire. But again, that would mean asking Deacon. And Deacon would want to know why.

He was still debating it when he was startled by a knock on his door. He was so lost in his thoughts that he was a bit surprised to open it and find Deacon standing on the other side. There was a blush under the dark skin of Deacon's cheeks, and he smiled nervously. "Brought your whisky," he said, holding a bottle out to Aren. "You ready to quit being mad?"

"I..." Aren's sentence died away, because he had no idea what he'd intended to say. He couldn't think at all. Every rational thought he might have had was eclipsed by Deacon.

The man was gorgeous. He was sexy. He was big and strong and the very image of masculinity. All the half-remembered images from Aren's dream two nights before came back to him in a heartbeat—the feeling of callused hands on his skin, the sensation of a weight against his back, fingers groping between his legs.

"Aren?"

Holy Saints, stop!

Aren shook himself, trying to shake the dream memory from his brain, trying to regain his composure. He felt his cheeks turning red and was glad for it. Better the blood flow there than where it had been headed a few seconds earlier. Deacon, his one and only real friend, was apparently back at the BarChi, ready to resume the comfortable, easy friendship they'd shared before the incident. It was something Aren wanted, too, but it certainly wasn't going to work if his cock grew hard every time Deacon looked at him. He had to get a grip on himself.

It'll be better when I finally get laid, he thought to himself. Sexual frustration had him tied in knots, but once it had been alleviated, he'd be back to normal.

Deacon was still watching him with obvious confusion. "I'm sorry," Aren said. "I just wasn't expecting you. I lost track of the days."

Deacon's hesitant smile faded. He looked sceptical and more unsure of himself than Aren had ever seen him. "You *are* still mad, aren't you?"

Deacon was so strong with everybody else, but the insecurity he seemed to feel with Aren was endearing. Aren felt a smile spread across his face. "No," he said, and he was pleased to realise he was telling the truth. He opened the door wider and stepped aside, inviting Deacon in. "I'm glad you're home." The words clearly made Deacon uncomfortable. He was suddenly shoving his empty hand in his pocket and looking down at the floor, and the shyness of the gesture made Aren laugh out loud.

"Come on," he said to his friend. "Let's have some of that whisky."

Chapter Fourteen

It felt unbelievably good to pour a drink for them both and sit down in front of the fireplace with Deacon once again.

"I brought you two more bottles, too," Deacon said as Aren handed him his glass. "Left them in the barn, but I'll bring them tomorrow."

"Are you making up for future transgressions?" Aren asked, smiling.

Deacon smiled back. "Wasn't sure how mad you were."

How could something so simple feel so good? Aren found he couldn't stop smiling. Even the sexual frustration of the last few days paled next to the pure happiness he felt at having Deacon home. "How was the trip?" he asked as he sat down in his usual chair across from the big cowboy.

"Fine," Deacon said. "Hired two more hands. New one you said I could hire and one to replace Miron." He looked down into his glass, swirling the amber liquid in circles, avoiding Aren's eyes. "How's Frances?"

"He's good," Aren said. "He's doing better."

"Simon's helping him?"

"He is."

Deacon nodded, finally taking a sip of his drink, and for the first time Aren thought about everything Deacon had done for Frances since the incident. Yes, he'd beaten him up. And as far as Frances knew, that was it. But Aren knew better. Deacon was the one who had arranged for Simon to talk to him. Deacon was the one who had carefully planned who would go to town and who would stay behind, depending on whether or not Frances decided to stay. Despite playing the role of the bully — of the *boss*, Aren corrected himself — he had done everything in his power not only to make sure Frances stayed, but to make sure things went well.

"Thank you," Aren said, "for helping him."

Deacon shook his head, uncomfortable with the sentiment as he always was. "Just doing my job. I'm sorry that..." he stopped, letting his words trail away.

"That what?" Aren prompted him.

Deacon shrugged heavily and drained the whisky from his glass.

"Sorry you always have to be the bad guy?" Aren asked.

Deacon shrugged again, looking sad, and Aren decided to change the subject. He was happy Deacon was back. He didn't want to ruin the evening.

"How was the McAllen ranch?" he asked, teasing. "Those maids take good care of you?"

Deacon grinned at him. "Good enough, I guess." His grin grew mischievous. "Brought something back for you, too."

"Something better than the whisky?" he asked.

"Suppose that depends on who you ask."

"Where is it?"

"Back at the house, far's I know."

"When do I get to see it?"

"Right soon, I guess. Jeremiah told me to invite you to the house for supper."

"You brought something for me, and I have to go to supper at the house to see it?"

"Yup," Deacon said, looking sheepish. "Want you to know right now it ain't my fault, either. I don't want you getting mad at me again."

"What?" Aren asked, laughing. "Did you bring me a maid looking for a roll?"

"No," Deacon said. "Brought you a couple of daughters, looking for a spouse."

It took a moment for those words to register. The enjoyment Aren had been feeling as he bantered with Deacon was quickly replaced by alarm. "You *what?*" he asked, jumping up from his chair. His eyes flew to the front door, as if a girl might suddenly appear there. He had a sudden and irrational urge to run.

Deacon laughed. "I knew you were gonna fly off the handle."

"Are you insane? Why would you do that to me?"

Deacon held up his hands as if in surrender, but Aren noticed he couldn't keep the smile off his face, either. He was having great fun. "I told you," he said. "It ain't my fault."

"Then whose fault is it?" Aren asked.

"Tama's, I guess."

"What? *How?*"

"She had me take a letter back to her daddy, and she must have told him all about you living in this house, and how much you needed a wife, 'cause when we came back through on our way home, he'd already decided he and his daughters was coming with us to the BarChi to meet you."

"Holy Saints!" Aren swore. "What do I do?"

"Well, seems to me like you go on over to the house and have supper and wait for Fred McAllen to offer you a bride. I'm sure he's got a dowry in mind. You can bet it's a lowball offer, too, so don't take it without talking him up some first."

"I don't want a dowry! I don't want a wife!"

Deacon cocked his head at him, looking puzzled. "Why you so set against it?" he asked. "Is it the money? Brighton's always joking about how much it costs to keep one. Jeremiah not paying you enough?"

"It's not the money! It's that—"

I don't like women.

He couldn't say that. Not to Deacon. He swallowed all the whisky left in his glass and went to the table to pour some more.

"You think if you show up drunk, they'll change their mind?" Deacon asked.

"It's worth a try," Aren said, swallowing the shot.

"Well," Deacon said, standing up, "you best start getting ready. Don't want to show up in your work clothes."

"What about you?" Aren asked.

And although Deacon tried to hide it, Aren did not miss the hint of pain those words caused him. "I ain't invited," he said.

"Wait a minute!" Aren said with sudden realisation. "You told me when we first met that you didn't make enough money to support a wife and didn't have a house to keep one in." Deacon turned away, looking extremely uncomfortable, but Aren went on. "This house is yours, and I do the books, so I know you lied about the money, too! You're paid more than anybody on this ranch!" And he earned every bit of it, too.

"So?"

"'So'? Why aren't you the one going to supper?"

"Ranch hands don't marry daughters."

"But—"

"Aren, stop!" Deacon said, turning to face him, and Aren was surprised at how upset he looked. "It don't matter why!"

It seemed they both had their secrets. He might have wondered if they were the same if he hadn't seen Deacon's ready response to the McAllen maids. "All right," Aren relented. "I'm sorry." He was still curious, but he didn't want to fight. He didn't want to go to dinner with the family, either, but it seemed he had no choice. He looked out of the window, checking the position of the sun in the sky. "I probably do need to get ready."

"I got work to do, anyway," Deacon said. "Too many chores left undone with all of us gone. Two new hands to see to. They're probably branding them now."

"Branding the ranch hands?"

"Yup. That's how they show what ranches they been on." Aren had noticed some of the brands when he'd lived in the barracks but hadn't ever thought to ask what they meant. "New boys like Frances have to earn theirs," Deacon said, "but these new men been on ranches before. They'll want to do it right away. It's their way of proving to the other men that they're committed."

"Or that they need to be committed," Aren mumbled.

Deacon laughed. "You been here long enough. You could run on down there and get your brand too," he teased. "Show that wife-to-be that you're tough."

Aren didn't much want to impress any 'wife-to-be', and having some drunk ranch hand brand him like he was a blessed cow seemed like way too much pain to try to prove he was macho. "No thanks."

Deacon laughed. "Turns out you're smarter than you look."

Aren laughed. He couldn't believe how something as simple as having Deacon tease him could feel so good. "Will I see you tonight after supper?" Aren asked.

Deacon shook his head. "No time." Aren's heart sank at the words. He thought he could have handled supper better if he could have come home to a drink with Deacon. "See you tomorrow at breakfast," Deacon said, then he grinned wickedly and winked at Aren. "Unless you're too busy with your new wife."

"Holy Saints," Aren said, laughing, "not a chance in this blessed world."

He followed the big cowboy to the door, leaning against the door jamb to watch him leave, but Deacon paused on the porch. He turned around again, and Aren was surprised at the blush on his cheeks. He let his gaze fall and pushed his hat down so its wide brim hid his face. He pulled a small, burlap-wrapped bundle from the pocket of his coat. "Brought you this, too," he said, shoving it into Aren's hand.

He turned and walked away before Aren had even recovered from the surprise. "Thank you," he called to Deacon's back. Deacon didn't look back, but Aren knew he'd heard from the way he ducked his head.

Aren opened the bundle and stared down at what was inside.

It was a penknife. The ghost had broken his old one more than a week before, on the day of Miron's death. After the accident and everything that had followed, Aren had forgotten all about it.

But Deacon had remembered.

* * * *

If there was anything worse than being seated at supper between two women who thought they wanted to marry him, it was having their father try to negotiate a dowry right in front of them as if they were cattle instead of women.

"Jay didn't ask for any of the farm when he married Tama," Fred said, "so best I can offer right now is a third of it, with the possibility of more once the other girls is married off."

"I appreciate the offer," Aren said, forcing himself to smile, "but I'm really not interested in running a ranch. I don't know the first thing about hogs."

They were in the Pane's formal dining room, seated around a table that was way too big for such a small group. On his left, Alissa sat with her head down. She seemed miserable, and Aren couldn't blame her. On his right sat Beth, doing her absolute best to impress him. She was nothing but smiles and compliments, and she laughed at everything Aren said as if she found him fabulously amusing.

"Daddy," she said, "Aren has a house here at the BarChi. Of course he doesn't want to move all the way to our land!"

"Well, son, let's not beat around the bush! Daylight's burning! Tell me what you think is a fair price."

Alissa covered her face with her hands. Was she crying?

"Sir, with all due respect, I don't think it's polite to discuss such things in the presence of your daughters—"

"We can send them out of the room. Beth, Alissa, run on down to the kitchen to finish your supper."

"Daddy!" Beth protested.

Alissa actually started to stand up, but Aren stopped her with a hand on her wrist. She sat slowly back down, looking at him with such heartfelt gratitude in her eyes, it made him blush. "Mr McAllen, I've not yet agreed to marry anybody. I'm only here because Mr Pane was kind enough to invite me for dinn—I mean, supper."

"But, son," Fred said, "certainly—"

"Fred," Jeremiah said, "ya'll will still be here tomorrow, and so will Aren." Aren's heart sank at those words. He'd hoped they were leaving the next day. "No need to rush into things."

"No need to stall, either!"

"Brighton, Shay and their two sons are up at the Austin place right now, visiting Shay's parents," Jeremiah said. "Austins have a daughter to marry off, too. Shay was going to bring Rynna back here for a few days so Aren could meet her before he makes a decision."

Aren barely stopped himself from groaning out loud at the prospect of having yet another potential bride to deal with.

Fred slammed his hand down on the table. "All the more reason I should lay all my cards on the table now!"

"Daddy!" Tama hissed. "You're being rude!"

"Pumpkin, I'm only—"

"Mr McAllen," Aren said, doing his best to sound calm and reasonable rather than disgusted and annoyed, "what I'd prefer is if you'd give me your offer in writing. I'm a bookkeeper, after all, and that way I'll have time to properly contemplate your offer."

Fred seemed to consider that for a moment. He nodded. "Yeah, I can see how that makes sense," he said.

After that, the awkward subject of dowries was dropped, and Aren breathed a mental sigh of relief. But his torment was far from over.

"Aren," Tama said, "Alissa is a fabulous cook! If there anything you've been craving, she could make it for you tomorrow."

Alissa blushed at the compliment, but she turned to him with a shy smile. "I'm really good at pancakes," she told him, "and desserts. I could make you a cake."

The idea of cake did make Aren's mouth water—Olsa didn't often bother with desserts—but he didn't want to give Alissa false hope.

"That's very kind," he said, "but—"

A hand suddenly landed on his right thigh. Aren jumped. His knees hit the underside of the table so hard that the glassware on its top rattled. Everybody at the table turned his way. Aren felt his cheeks turning red as he pushed Beth's hand away. "Excuse me," he said, standing up. "I just realised I forgot to…umm…take something, ummm, to…" They were all staring at him. The women looked alarmed. Fred McAllen looked confused. Jeremiah looked downright amused. "I have to go," Aren finally said. "Thank you for a lovely evening."

It was all he could do to keep from running as he left the room. As he crossed the grass to his house, he found himself looking over his shoulder, hoping against hope that nobody from the disastrous supper had decided to follow him.

Once inside his house, he bolted the doors. He poured himself a very large drink. He retreated to his bedroom so that anybody who came looking for him wouldn't be able to look through his window and see him inside.

One more day, he thought. *I have to avoid them for one more day, then they'll be gone.* Of course, then Shay would be back with her sister, Rynna.

He sighed. Was it so odd for him to not want to marry? Deacon was older than him, and liked women, but he wasn't married. Why should Aren be any different?

Deacon obviously had his reasons.

Aren was startled by the sound of a knock on his front door. It wasn't the ghost in the cellar—he knew that sound well enough. Besides, the ghost only knocked on the door at night, and although the sun was low in the sky, it wasn't nightfall yet.

He also knew the knock wasn't Deacon. He'd grown just as used to the big cowboy's window-rattling knock as he had to the ghost's. The timid tap on his front door wasn't him.

Aren groaned. He sank lower in his chair, as if whoever it was might otherwise be able to see him through the door and the walls and the floor.

He was *not* getting married. If he said no long enough, surely they'd give up.

Eventually.

He hoped.

Chapter Fifteen

He was awake early the next morning. He always met Deacon for breakfast, but after what had happened at supper, he was reluctant to venture outside. He pictured Tama, Beth and Alissa crouched in the grass, waiting to pounce on him as soon as he emerged. He pictured Fred McAllen showing up in the kitchen with his dowry offers written like auction bids on paper.

They leave tomorrow morning. I just have to get through this one day.

He was surprised, again, by a knock on his door. It was the thunderous pounding that could only be Deacon, but Deacon never came to the house before breakfast.

Aren opened the door a crack and peeked outside. Deacon was standing on his front porch, grinning at him. He was holding a bundle wrapped in cloth.

"If there's a girl in that package, I'll never forgive you."

Deacon laughed. "No girl," he said. "Only breakfast."

"Thank the Saints," Aren said, letting him in. "I was wondering if I could survive without food until they leave tomorrow."

"Not sure such drastic measures are necessary," Deacon said as he put the bundle on the table and opened it. "But I thought you might prefer to stay in." Inside the cloth were biscuits, a piece of ham, and some of Olsa's cheese.

"Cheese, too?" Aren asked. "Olsa must have been in a good mood."

"She said to tell you you'd be happy about it in the end."

"About what? Having those girls here? Or having cheese for breakfast?"

Deacon shrugged, smiling. "You think I ever know what she's talking about?"

He turned to leave, and Aren resisted the urge to beg him to stay. He fully expected one of the McAllens to show up at his house eventually, and he thought he could have handled it better with Deacon at his side. "Is there anything I can help with today?" he asked hopefully.

Deacon didn't laugh, but the amused look he turned on Aren told him he knew exactly why he was asking. "You could do the barn, but I'm sure those gals will find you there as easy as here."

"Anything else?"

"The rest are herding, and you can't ride a horse."

Aren sighed. "It was worth asking."

Deacon shook his head at him, smiling. "I never seen anybody so dead set against having a wife."

"Hello, pot? It's me, kettle."

Deacon laughed, shaking his head as he turned to leave. "Nice thanks I get for bringing you breakfast."

Aren's next visitor was Jeremiah, who arrived barely an hour after Deacon had left.

"Fred sent these," he said, handing Aren two pieces of paper that had barely intelligible scribbles on them.

"Great," Aren muttered, hoping he sounded less sarcastic than he felt. "Thanks a lot."

"I take it you'd just as soon not have another supper like last night?"

"I'd rather be thrown to the wraiths."

Jeremiah laughed. "I don't blame you," he said. "That was damn awkward. Still, marriage ain't so bad. I'd give anything to still have my Caspa with me."

It had never occurred to Aren to ask about Jeremiah's wife. "I'm sorry," he said, for lack of anything better.

"I would have had a daughter, too," Jeremiah said. "But Caspa died birthing her. Baby died, too." He turned to look out of the window at his ranch. "Can't imagine having a daughter here, with all these randy hands running around. Especially if she'd been as pretty as her momma. I imagine I would have had my hands full."

Aren didn't say anything. He wasn't sure Jeremiah expected an answer at all.

"A man sometimes feels better knowing he has a legacy," Jeremiah said, turning to look at him again. "You might worry less about the girl, and think more about what it means to have a son." He shrugged. "Or a daughter."

Aren didn't want kids. He was absolutely sure of that. All he wanted was time to spend his own way, a space to spend it in. A chance to paint. Maybe somebody to share it all with. But whoever that somebody was, he was sure it wasn't Beth or Alissa McAllen.

"I appreciate your advice," Aren said, smiling in an attempt to lighten the mood. "I appreciate even more your willingness to allow me to avoid another supper like last night's."

His attempt at banter worked. Jeremiah laughed. "I'd prefer not spend any more time with Fred than I have to, either."

Shortly after midday, his next guest arrived. This time, it was Alissa. Although he didn't want to marry either of them, Aren found Alissa far less threatening than her sister.

"I'm sorry about supper last night," she said as he let her in. "I know my father can be..." She stopped, fumbling for a word.

"Disconcerting?" he asked her.

She blinked at him, obviously unfamiliar with the term. "I suppose," she said. She looked down at the floor. She took a deep breath, and Aren braced himself for her onslaught. "I know I'm not pretty like Beth," she said, and when Aren opened his mouth to protest that her looks weren't an issue, she held up her hand to stop him. "It's fine," she said. "I know what men like."

Not men like me.

"The thing is, I'd be a good wife. I can cook for you. I can sew. I can keep your house. I can..." She seemed to have run out of things she thought she could do, and she bit her lower lip nervously, looking around the room as if she might find something else to offer.

Aren couldn't help but think the entire thing was insane. They'd now met exactly three times. How could she be so willing to throw herself on the mercy of a man she barely knew?

"Why do you want to get married?" he asked her.

She looked up at him, her eyes wide. She twisted her hands together, as if she might be able to wring an answer out of them. "Nobody's asked me that before."

"Well, I'm asking you now. Why do you think you want to marry *me*? Be honest. This isn't me fishing for compliments. I truly want to know why you think you want this."

"I want to leave home," she said. "I want to be away from my daddy, and away from the hogs, and away from Be—" She stopped short.

"Away from Beth?"

She nodded. "Tama's always been my best friend. I just want to be here with her."

"And if being married to me is the price, then it's a price you're willing to pay?"

"You seem nice."

He laughed, hiding his eyes behind his hand. "I'm not the marrying type."

"I don't know that I am, either," she said quietly. "But maybe that would work in our favour."

It was perhaps the most honest thing she'd said since walking through his door. He dropped his hand, looking over at her, trying to really see her. She looked less nervous than before.

"You don't have to love me," she said. "Maybe we could be friends."

"But still be married?"

She hesitated, then gave him a slight nod.

He liked her. He liked that she was honest. He liked that she wasn't trying to use her body to change his mind. He felt as if he understood her.

But he still didn't want to marry her.

"I'll tell you what," he said. "I can't promise I'll marry you. But I promise if I choose a wife, it won't be your sister."

She smiled. It was a mischievous smile, almost childlike, and he couldn't help but smile back. "I must be petty," she said, "because I think that's good enough for me."

* * * *

It was just after supper time when the visitor he'd been dreading most of all arrived.

He saw Beth coming across the grass. Her hips swayed. The sun shone on her golden hair. Red, Ronin and Calin, who were chopping wood near the barn, all stopped what they were doing to watch her pass. She was extremely attractive.

Beth was all smiles when he let her inside. He noticed her bodice seemed a bit too tight. The apron that daughters and wives so often wore was gone. Her dress accentuated the soft curves of her body.

She was pulling out all the stops.

"We'll be leaving early, but I wanted to see you before we go."

"I hope you had a pleasant visit," Aren said. He knew it was a mundane nicety, but he truly had nothing else to say. "May your journey home be safe."

She smiled. "You're so polite," she said. She edged closer to him. "You don't have to be."

"I'm sorry. You'd prefer I be rude?"

She took another step closer, and Aren instinctively took a step back. "When you were at our farm, you chose to stay in the barn," she said. "There's only one reason a man does that."

"It's not what you think. I just didn't know the Oestend customs yet, and—"

"You don't have to lie." She stepped closer still. Aren tried to back up, but ran into the wall behind him. "I know what men like."

Not men like me, he thought for the second time that day. *You're so, so wrong.*

Her soft, white fingers landed on his chest, fingering the top button of his shirt. "I can be like them," she said, her voice soft and sultry. "I can do what they do."

"Beth, this isn't a good idea."

"Are you worried I'm not pure?" she asked. "Because I am." She smiled, inching closer. Her breasts pushed against his chest. "Pure enough." Her hand began to slide towards his groin. "You could be my first."

Aren blocked her hand as it reached his belt. "I think you should go," he said, although it came out as more of a squeak. "Really, this is a bad idea."

She pressed harder against him. She smelt like vanilla. One pale arm snaked around his neck. They were almost the same height. "Close your eyes," she said, and he did. He didn't know why. It was partly the irrational hope that when he opened them again, she'd be gone. "That's right," she whispered.

He felt his pants being untied, then he felt her hand slide inside. He was tense. He was opposed to the whole idea. He was sure it was the most awkward moment of his entire life.

But more than anything, he was so undeniably horny.

After months of feeling nobody's touch but his own, even Beth's soft, feminine fingers felt like heaven. He moaned, and she gripped him tighter. "See?" she said. "Don't you like that?"

Don't talk, he thought. *Don't ruin it.* Because he did like it. It was a warm hand on his cock, and it felt unbelievably good. But he didn't want her talking, because as her hand moved on him, he wasn't thinking about her at all. He was thinking about men—not any one man in particular, but a parade of men. Men he'd known, men he'd seen, men who only lived in his dreams. Men who would suck him, or fuck him, or beg him to fuck them instead. He thought of Frances. He thought of Deacon. He even thought of Dean. He thought of rough hands and stubbly cheeks, the smell of their musk and the taste of their cum. "Oh, Saints," he breathed as the hand on his cock squeezed his tip. "Yes!"

He thought of strong, muscular thighs and hairy chest. Heavy, pendulous scrotums, and thick, hard cocks. He thought of men bent over in front of him, their entrance greased and ready for him to push inside. He thought of—

His erotic fantasy was interrupted by lips brushing over his. Soft, smooth lips, and a tiny, feminine moan.

The illusion shattered. Beth's hand still moved on him, but his reaction began to reverse. His eyes snapped open, and he noticed she'd undone her top button. She let go of his cock long enough to take his hand and place it on her breast, and he felt his erection start to fail.

Why? he thought. *Why can't I enjoy this?*

Of all the men on the ranch who would have killed to be where he was, men who would have given anything to have a woman as attractive as Beth touch them at all, let alone jerk them off, why was he different? Why couldn't he just relax and enjoy it?

Her hand was moving on his cock again, but he was barely half-erect. "What's wrong?" she asked.

Everything.

Everything was wrong. She was soft and smooth and smelt like vanilla. She was creamy and curvy and everything most men would want in a woman. But of course, that was just it—she was a woman.

"I can't do this," he said, trying to push her off. "I need you to leave."

"You're doing great," she purred, pushing harder against him. "Just relax. I know what to do."

"No! Please!"

"You can undo my blouse."

"No—"

"You can touch me anywhere you want."

"Oh, Saints—"

"You can lift my skirt whenever you're ready."

"I don't want—"

"Or I can finish for you like this."

Her hand moved again on his now-limp cock, and Aren wavered. Could he close his eyes like before? Could he pretend she was a man?

Boom, boom, boom!

Aren almost jumped out of his skin, and Beth looked with alarm towards the door.

It was Deacon! Aren knew the knock. It was, he realised, about the time Deacon usually arrived at his house after supper.

"Thank the Saints," he said in relief, before he could help himself. He didn't miss the hurt look on her face, but he didn't care. "I need you to leave."

He saw the series of emotions in her eyes—first confusion, then anger, then the guise of complacency. "I understand," she said. "It's noble that you want me to come to our marriage bed—"

Aren didn't bother to listen. He went to the front door and pulled it open. "Thank the Saints you're here," he hissed as he pulled Deacon inside. "I was almost eaten alive."

He pushed Deacon into the living room, where Beth stood with her skirts rumpled, her top button undone, and her mouth hanging open.

"Goodbye, Beth," Aren said. "Have a safe journey home."

Her mouth opened and closed once, then again, as she fumbled for something to say. It seemed she found nothing, because on the third time, it snapped closed, and she turned and stalked out of the room, slamming the front door behind her.

Aren's heart still pounded. His hands shook. He hated that Beth had unnerved him so much.

"Did I interrupt something?" Deacon asked in amusement.

"Yes!" Aren snapped. He went to the bar and grabbed a glass. He poured a hefty shot of whisky into it and slammed it back in one swallow. The warm liquor hit his empty stomach, and he poured himself another. "Thank the Saints you *interrupted!* Why couldn't you have *interrupted* ten minutes sooner?"

He turned to look at Deacon, and Deacon suddenly looked away. "Your pants," he said.

"Fuck!" Aren put down his glass and turned away to tuck everything back in place, but he didn't bother tying his pants back up. His shirt hung down low enough to cover him. He picked his glass back up with a hand that still shook and drank the second shot of whisky.

"She had your pants undone and her skirt up, from the looks of her, and you're *glad* I interrupted?"

171

"Extremely." He poured another shot. After a moment of deliberation, he doubled it. With no food in his stomach, he knew he was flirting with trouble. He knew he'd regret it in the morning. But he found he didn't care. Getting drunk suddenly seemed like the best idea he'd ever had.

"Did she offer?"

Aren snorted at the sheer inadequacy of that question as he took another drink. "Yeah," he said. "She offered."

"And you said no?"

"Yes."

"Why?"

"Because."

"Do you not like sex?"

"Good grief, of course I like sex!" Aren said, glancing over his shoulder at Deacon. "What do you think?"

"Then why did you tell her no?"

"Saints, why the hell do you care?"

"I'm surprised, that's all. Are you worried about her dad?"

"Fred has nothing to do with it."

"Then what—?"

"Why can't you let this drop?"

"Why can't you answer the question?"

"For fuck's sake, Deacon! Because I don't like women, all right? I like men!"

The words were out of his mouth before he knew it, and Aren was sure his heart stopped beating when he realised what he'd said. Still, there was no taking it back. On one hand, he was relieved to finally have the truth known. He was tired of hiding. But more than anything, he was angry at himself for the way he'd let the conversation get away from him. He'd been so flustered by Beth, he hadn't thought about what he should or shouldn't say to Deacon. Afraid of Deacon's response, he braced himself for what might come—the questions, or the derision, or the disgust from his one and only friend. The judgement from the one man on the BarChi whose opinion he valued.

But the only response was silence.

He swallowed the last of his whisky in one gulp and put the glass down on the bar in front of him. His hands were shaking. Deacon's unnatural silence was made worse by the fact that Aren couldn't see his face. Aren splashed a tiny bit more whisky into his glass. He steeled himself for what he might see—confusion, mockery or disgust—and he turned to face Deacon.

What he saw surprised him. Deacon didn't appear to be upset at all. He looked nervous. But not only that. He looked...

Intrigued.

When Deacon finally spoke, his voice was low and husky. "You have sex with men?"

Aren felt his pulse speed up, but this time from excitement. Was he reading Deacon wrong? Was his judgement skewed? He quickly considered how much whisky he'd slammed in only a few short minutes, but he didn't think that was to blame.

"Yes," he said, watching closely for Deacon's reaction. "I like to fuck men."

Deacon's breath caught for only a moment. His cheeks flushed. His fists clenched around the hat he held, almost twisting it in two.

"Oh, Deacon," Aren breathed, feeling something that was part hope and part sheer elation flare to life in his chest. "Tell me I'm not imagining this. Tell me you like men, too."

"I don't..." But Deacon's words trailed away. He seemed unable to meet Aren's eyes. His gaze darted nervously around the room and his cheeks turned an even deeper shade of red. He twisted the hat in his hands again. The crackling of the straw seemed unbelievably loud in the otherwise silent room. Aren couldn't help but think he'd regret having ruined the thing tomorrow. He was debating asking Deacon again, but then he saw something that gave him the answer — the growing bulge in Deacon's pants.

"Oh, thank the blessed Saints," he said. And in the very next moment, he lost all sense of himself.

Chapter Sixteen

Aren's not-quite-empty glass shattered on the floor behind him, but he didn't give it a second thought. All he could think about was getting his clothes off and Deacon's, too. Not necessarily in that order. "I can't believe you didn't tell me," he said as he ripped Deacon's shirt open and started to push it off him. "I can't believe I didn't figure it out."

Deacon's chest was broad and scarred, and Aren put his nose against Deacon's dark skin and breathed deeply. It was intoxicating. After Beth and her soft, pale skin, her vanilla scent, her undeniable femininity, Deacon seemed like absolute perfection. He was strong and big and not soft at all. He smelt like hay and horses and something that was so unbelievably *masculine*, it made Aren moan. His hands moved to the buttons on Deacon's pants.

"Aren, wait!" Deacon said. "I can't..."

Aren flicked his tongue over Deacon's nipple as he slid his hand into his pants, caressing Deacon's cock. The feel of it in his hand made him weak at the knees. It was thick and hard, and Deacon's words died, trailing away into a deep moan.

"You can," Aren said, as he started to stroke him. *Please. Please!*

"No," Deacon whispered, but it was a weak protest at best.

"Have you ever been with a man before?"

A heartbeat of hesitation, and Deacon shook his head. "No."

"I can make it so good for you." He tongued Deacon's nipple again as his fingers played over his foreskin. *Please don't say no.*

"No," Deacon said again, but his body said otherwise. His hips began to move and he thrust into Aren's hand.

"I haven't had sex in months," Aren told him. "You can't say no now."

"Oh, Saints, Aren…"

Right or wrong, Aren's patience was at an end. He wasn't interested in Deacon's protests. He wasn't interested in talking him into it. He didn't want to waste time persuading Deacon it would be all right. The only thing he wanted was to finally alleviate the terrible pressure in his groin. He pushed Deacon roughly back against the wall. He dropped to his knees, pulling Deacon's pants out of the way as he did, and he swallowed Deacon's cock all the way down to his root, because he knew it would put an end to Deacon's half-hearted protests.

"Ohh," Deacon moaned, and just as Aren had expected, all the fight went out of him. He arched his back against the wall, pushing his hips out and his cock deeper into Aren's mouth.

Sucking a man's cock was an act Aren had always had mixed feelings about. On one hand, he liked it. It turned him on more than he could say. He liked the feel of another man's hard shaft against his tongue. He liked the musky smell that clung to their hair. He even liked the taste when they came. He liked the moans, and the way he could make them fall apart using nothing more than his mouth.

What he didn't like, with Birmingham at least, was the way Dean had gripped his head and fucked hard into his mouth, whether he was ready for it or not. He didn't like the way, when it was over, Dean would pat him on the head and say, "Good boy." He didn't like the fact that Dean never returned the favour.

But doing it for Deacon was something else entirely. Aren pulled back up his length, sliding his tongue into the pocket of Deacon's foreskin as he sucked hard on his tip. Deacon gasped and grabbed Aren's head, and although his fingers tangled in Aren's hair, he seemed only to be hanging on, not taking over. Aren released Deacon's tip and swallowed his length again, caressing the underside of his shaft with his tongue, and the moan it elicited from Deacon was almost enough to make Aren come.

He continued to move on Deacon. His own pants were still undone and it was easy to pull his erection free. His own hand had never felt so good as it did at that moment. He moaned against Deacon's flesh as he stroked himself, and he sensed more than saw Deacon looking down at him.

"Aren," Deacon gasped, and the urgency in his voice was unmistakable.

A little longer, Aren thought, as he stroked himself fast. *Just a little longer, please!*

He sped up, both his hand on his own cock and his mouth on Deacon's. He loved the way Deacon smelt. He loved his deep-throated moans, and the feel of his strong, muscular thigh under Aren's free hand. He loved that he was a *man*, and not just any man, but one who was strong and virile and sexy and the very image of what masculinity could be.

He wished he had more time. He wished he could undress Deacon and see every piece of him. He wished he could explore every inch of his body. He wished he could push him down on the bed and spread his legs. He wanted to prove to him how good sex with a man could be. He wanted, more than anything, to fuck him. To grip his hips and drive into him and hear him cry out from the pleasure of Aren's cock inside him.

Aren's orgasm hit him fast. He closed his eyes, leaning into Deacon's body, still sucking him as he worked his own cock with his hand, stroking his climax free. Deacon looked down at him and moaned.

"Aren!" Deacon gasped, and his fingers clenched in Aren's hair just as his first shot filled Aren's mouth. Aren sucked hard, swallowing fast, loving the desperate sounds Deacon made as he did.

When Deacon was done, Aren lay back on the floor, breathing hard, almost laughing with relief. "Blessed Saints, you have no idea how much I needed that!" He closed his eyes and breathed deeply. He knew he was smiling like a fool, but he didn't care. He revelled in the sated, heavy feeling he hadn't felt in far too long. He laughed out loud at the sheer joy of it.

He heard Deacon leave his place against the wall. He heard his footsteps as he crossed the room, and the sound of him collapsing onto one of Aren's wooden chairs. But Deacon didn't say a word.

Aren cracked his eyes open and glanced over at Deacon...and his heart fell. Deacon was bent over, his elbows on his knees and his head in his hands. "Aren," he whispered, "that shouldn't have happened."

"Shit," Aren mumbled, mostly to himself, trying not to be annoyed that his post-coital bliss was apparently going to be cut dreadfully short. "It's fine," he said to Deacon. "You don't need to freak out."

Deacon didn't answer. He only shook his head.

Aren sighed, pushing himself up off the floor. He did up his pants. He pulled his kerchief out of his pocket and used it to wipe up the mess he'd made. He was stalling, hoping Deacon would pull himself together, but when he turned to look at him again, he still hadn't moved. Aren stood up and went to the bar. He poured a generous shot of whisky into a glass. "Here," he said, handing it to Deacon. "Drink this."

Deacon's hands were shaking when he took the glass, but he obeyed, tossing the alcohol back in one shot.

"Better?" Aren asked.

"No." Deacon shook his head. "Oh, Saints," he moaned. "I should go."

He tried to stand up, but Aren put his hand on his shoulder and pushed him back down. "No," he said. "Not yet." He wasn't exactly sure what he hoped to gain by keeping Deacon there. He only knew that it seemed like a bad idea to let him leave when he was so out of sorts. And it felt selfish not to try to help. He poured another drink for Deacon and handed it to him. This time, Deacon only swallowed half the glassful before leaning back in the chair with his eyes closed. He sighed heavily.

"You all right?" Aren asked.

"Yes," Deacon said, although he didn't sound very convincing.

Aren was beginning to feel guilty for having pushed Deacon. It was a new feeling for him. He'd felt guilty many times for allowing *himself* to be persuaded into sex that he later regretted, but he'd never been the one on the other side of the equation before. "I'm sorry," he said.

Deacon shook his head. "Don't be." He sat up straight. He rubbed his hands roughly over his face. "I really should go," he said again, but he didn't attempt to stand up.

"Finish your drink."

Deacon sighed, but he swallowed the rest of the whisky and handed the glass to Aren. "More?" Aren asked, and Deacon nodded.

"I don't know what happens now," Deacon said as Aren handed him the glass again.

Aren thought about that as Deacon sipped his third drink. He wasn't sure what would happen, either. He didn't know if they'd become lovers, or if it had been a one-time thing. He didn't know if tomorrow they'd have breakfast together like they always did, or if Deacon would suddenly avoid him. Those things, it seemed, were up to Deacon, and Aren couldn't change them. What he did know was it was possible that, starting tomorrow, he'd be right back where he'd been before, with no sexual partner except his own hand. And if that was the case, he didn't want to let Deacon walk away quite yet.

He got down on his knees in front of Deacon, so that he could look up into his eyes. Deacon's cheeks turned red, and he looked half-scared, but he met his gaze.

"Stay with me tonight." He saw the near-panic in Deacon's eyes, and he rushed on before Deacon could interrupt. "Just one night. That's all I ask."

"Then what?" Deacon asked as he set his empty glass down on the floor next to his chair.

"What happens tomorrow is up to you. We can do it again, or we can pretend it never happened. Or anything in between. I'll leave it completely up to you. I won't tell anyone. I won't chase you or pressure you. I won't ever mention it again, if that's what you want." He was getting through to him. He could see that Deacon was thinking about it. "Please, Deacon," he begged, looking up into Deacon's dark eyes. "Please don't leave me yet. Please, just give me tonight."

He saw the hesitation in Deacon's eyes. He knew he was considering it, and his heart skipped a beat at the thought. "I don't know how it works," Deacon said, his voice so quiet that Aren had to strain to hear him, even though he was only inches away. "Not with a man."

"I do." Aren tried to fight back his hope, lest he be disappointed. He tried to fight back his arousal, because following it had ever led him astray. He tried to concentrate on the reassurance he knew Deacon needed to get past this moment. "I can make it so good for you. I promise you won't regret it."

He waited, watching Deacon while Deacon watched him. His heart was pounding in his chest. He was excited, and a bit scared, unsure what Deacon would decide.

He saw the change when it happened. He saw in Deacon's eyes the very moment he stopped fighting and decided to take a chance. Still, he hesitated, waiting for Deacon to say the words.

But Deacon didn't say anything. Instead, he reached up and slowly brushed Aren's hair out of his eyes. Aren smiled at the gentle sensuality of the gesture. Then Deacon hooked his hand behind Aren's neck, and he kissed him.

Kissing was the one thing Aren had very little experience with. It was something the boarding school boys avoided. Even Birmingham had never truly kissed him. It was such a simple thing, something he'd never thought much about, but when Deacon's mouth claimed his, it seemed as if every nerve in his body responded. Deacon's lips were soft and warm. Deacon's tongue seemed to ask for permission to enter, and Aren granted it. His tongue pushed gently into Aren's mouth, tasting of whisky, and Aren heard himself whimper. He'd let his body be invaded many times, but somehow this felt different.

Aren wrapped his arms around Deacon's neck and let himself be drawn in deeper. The pure sensuality of being kissed amazed him. He wondered how an act which involved only their mouths could be so unbelievably arousing. It didn't matter that he'd spent himself less than half an hour before. His cock was already growing hard again. Every part of him ached to feel Deacon's hands, or his mouth, or his skin. He wanted to own Deacon, or be owned by him. He hardly cared which. He only wanted it to be soon.

Aren found the queue of Deacon's hair, tied with thin strips of leather. One by one, he pulled them out until Deacon's hair flowed through his fingers, thick and coarse in his hands. One of Deacon's hands was still on the back of his neck. He used his other hand to lift Aren's shirt. He caressed the small of his back, and Aren heard himself moan. He marvelled at how good that simple touch felt.

Deacon pulled him tighter against his body as his kiss became more urgent. The hand on Deacon's back slid down to explore what lay below and Aren whimpered again.

Aren's hand travelled down Deacon's broad chest. Deacon moaned as Aren's fingers slid over his stomach. But when Aren began to slide his hand into Deacon's still-unbuttoned pants, Deacon stopped him, grabbing his hand as he broke their kiss.

Aren moaned in frustration. He didn't want to stop. He knew at that moment he'd do anything Deacon asked just to keep the cowboy there. There was no limit to how much he'd debase himself simply to be allowed the pleasure of one night with him.

He looked up at Deacon. They were both breathing hard, and Aren imagined he could see the conflict raging in Deacon's eyes again. "Please," Aren begged. He didn't care if Deacon thought he was weak or pathetic for it. His desire was, now as it had ever been, far stronger than his pride. "*Please*, Deacon," he said again.

Deacon smiled but didn't release his hand. "Can we go in the bedroom?"

"Is that what you want?"

Deacon hesitated, then nodded slowly. "I want to undress you."

Aren had no argument with that at all. He didn't care where they were, as long as Deacon kept touching him and allowed Aren to touch him back. He took a moment first to go out to the back porch and start the generator so they wouldn't have to worry about it later, then he took Deacon's hand and led him upstairs. While Deacon lit a lamp and turned the wick down low, Aren dug in a drawer and found the salve Olsa had given him weeks before.

When he turned around, he found Deacon staring at him. He'd removed his boots and his shirt. Only his pants remained, still unbuttoned, his erection peeking through the open fly. His long hair hung loose and dishevelled around his shoulders. Lamplight seemed to caress the muscles of his chest. It accentuated his deep, dark skin. Aren could see the scars more clearly now — two thin lines stretched across his ribs on the right, and another reached from his left collarbone almost to his navel.

"Blessed Saints," Aren breathed, "you're amazing." He tossed the salve onto the bed for later. He reached out and traced a fingertip over one of Deacon's scars, and Deacon's breath caught. "What happened?" he asked.

Deacon shrugged. "Just ranching."

Aren circled him, trailing his fingers over Deacon's dark skin. There were more scars on his back. Two were smooth, thin lines. One was wide and mottled with scar tissue. The one scar he expected to see was missing, though.

"No brand?" he asked.

"Not for me."

It was ironic that so many hands would wear the mark, but the one person who seemed to belong to the BarChi through and through didn't.

Aren circled to stand in front of Deacon. The tip of Deacon's erect cock seemed to tease Aren from inside the flaps of his open fly. Aren wanted to see more of it.

"Take off your pants." Aren didn't realise until the words were spoken that they sounded like an order, but Deacon didn't hesitate. He pushed them off, kicking them out of the way, and stood naked for Aren's inspection.

He was big. Looking at his engorged cock, Aren was a bit surprised he'd managed to swallow it all. He wanted to do a great deal more with it now. He started to slide his hand down the cowboy's stomach, wanting to feel it again in his hand, but Deacon grabbed his wrist, stopping his caress. Aren looked up into his dark eyes. "Now you," he said.

Aren couldn't help but feel a bit inadequate next to Deacon, but he did as Deacon asked, slowly pulling his own shirt off over his head and removing his pants. Deacon watched him with naked desire in his eyes. It surprised Aren how quickly Deacon had shed his reservations about being with another man, but it seemed now he'd made the decision, he was determined not to waste time looking back.

Aren found himself smiling as he turned to face Deacon again. "Can I touch you now?" he asked.

Deacon reached out and took his hand. "Yes," he said as he pulled Aren into his strong arms and kissed him hungrily, pulling him down onto the bed.

If kissing Deacon before had been good, it was nothing compared to the way it felt to kiss him now, while every inch of their bodies was in contact. The simple pleasure of feeling skin against skin was so sensual, so wonderfully erotic, it made Aren breathless. Still, as much as he loved it, he was ready for more, and as they kissed, it became increasingly clear that if he waited for Deacon to make a move, he'd be waiting half the night.

Aren broke their kiss, rolling them over so he was on top. He grabbed the jar of salve. Having never been with another man before, he knew there was no way Deacon was ready to be entered. He spread the salve on Deacon's shaft and smiled as Deacon moaned, pushing himself into

Aren's hand. He groaned in frustration when Aren released him. Aren could see the impatience in Deacon's eyes as he straddled him, but Deacon didn't grab him. He didn't try to make him hurry. He lay there, breathing hard, his eyes half-lidded as Aren moved into position atop him.

Deacon was large—larger by far than Birmingham had been—and Aren took his time as he pushed down onto him, slowly allowing Deacon's cock to fill him, slowly allowing his body to adjust. Deacon's eyes closed, and he moaned deep in his chest. His hands gripped Aren's thighs, his strong fingers digging into the muscles. But Deacon didn't push. He let Aren go at his own pace, slowly sinking down until Deacon's cock was buried in him to the hilt.

He stopped there, and Deacon's eyes snapped open. He grabbed Aren's arm and pulled him down so he could kiss him again, his lips gentle but insistent. "Aren," he said. He sounded desperate, and Aren knew the word was a question. He could see it in Deacon's eyes.

"What do you want?" Aren asked him.

"To be on top."

Aren tried not to be disappointed. This was how it always was, men wanting to fuck him their way. But he wasn't about to tell Deacon no and risk having him leave. "That's fine."

Deacon smiled. He pulled Aren down and kissed him again, slow and deep, his tongue gently tasting Aren's. Deacon rolled them over, kissing Aren's neck as he did, their bodies still locked together.

It wasn't at all what Aren was expecting. Deacon didn't stop kissing him. He didn't push Aren's legs into the air so he could fuck him. Instead he continued to hold him close.

"You're so beautiful," he whispered in Aren's ear as he began to move in and out of his body. "You have no idea how beautiful you are."

At any other time, from any other man, Aren might have been offended. "Beautiful" was a word he likened to femininity, and femininity was something he hated to be associated with. But somehow, when Deacon said it, the word didn't bother him. Maybe it was the note of awe he detected in Deacon's voice. Maybe it was the way he caressed him. Maybe it was nothing more than the fact that being fucked by him felt so unbelievably good.

Deacon's thrusts were long and exquisitely slow, and as he moved on top of Aren, he never stopped kissing him. He kissed Aren's lips and his neck and his shoulders. Deacon's hands were everywhere, stroking and exploring, and Aren couldn't believe how good it felt. Deacon's fingers were hard and work-worn, but his touch was soft and very gentle.

Aren had wanted to be Deacon's guide, to show him something new, but he realised Deacon was doing the same thing for him. Aren had been fucked many, many times in his life, but nobody had ever made love to him with the slow deliberateness Deacon was showing him now.

This is what it feels like to be a woman, Aren thought. Not the penetration — that had nothing to do with it. It was the way Deacon touched him and seemed to cherish him. It was the way Deacon whispered his name as they moved together. And in the end, although Aren had expected to lead, he gave up. He wrapped his arms and his legs around Deacon's strong body and let the tide carry him where it would. And when they crashed upon the shore, both of them spent, still Deacon held him close, caressing him and kissing him.

Aren wrapped his arms around Deacon and held him tight, wondering if, when morning came, he'd be expected to let him go.

Chapter Seventeen

"What's that?"

He recognised the voice, but it took Aren a moment to claw his way up out of his perfect, sated sleep into consciousness. Next to him, Deacon was sitting straight up in bed, his eyes wide.

"What's wrong?" Aren mumbled, or tried to. He still wasn't awake enough to form completely coherent words.

"I heard something," Deacon said. "There's somebody knocking on the front door."

"There's not," Aren assured him with a yawn. "It's just—"

The pounding started again, louder than before. Aren hadn't realised how used to it he'd become. It rarely woke him anymore.

"Who could it be?" Deacon asked.

"It's only the house," Aren told him.

Deacon looked over at him. "You mean it really is haunted?"

"I guess so. It's just noises. It can't hurt you."

"How do you know?"

Aren shrugged. "It hasn't hurt me yet."

"You told me there'd never been any trouble."

"I lied."

Deacon shook his head in amusement. "I'm not surprised."

"She'll start crying next," Aren told him.

That seemed to trouble Deacon. "It's a woman?"

Aren shrugged. "I think so. It sounds like a woman."

"What else is there besides the noise?"

"Not much," Aren said. "Not when I'm here, anyway."

"What you mean, 'not when you're here'?" Deacon asked. He seemed confused, and Aren couldn't figure out why.

"I mean, sometimes she does stuff during the day when I'm not here. Breaks glasses or moves things around. Remember the penknife?"

"Yes."

"That was her. I came home and found it smashed to pieces."

"But," Deacon said, seemingly even more confused than before, "that doesn't make any sense."

Aren wasn't sure what about it didn't make sense—it was a ghost, after all, and as far as he knew there weren't rules dictating their behaviour—but he wasn't interested in discussing the house any more. "I get you all night, right?" he asked, teasing.

Deacon's confusion was replaced by a slow smile. "I'm sure not leaving in the dark."

"Good." Aren pushed Deacon back down onto the bed, straddling his hips. "How about if I distract you from the noise?"

It was different the second time. Not quite as gentle. Not quite as much like making love. Still, it wasn't the type of sex Aren had grown used to over the years. It was fun, almost playful, and although Aren found himself once again taking Deacon into his body, he found he didn't resent him for it at all. Maybe it was because Deacon let him lead. Maybe it was because he knew that whatever happened, whether tomorrow they were lovers or friends or nothing at all, Deacon wouldn't laugh at him. He knew he wouldn't mock him. How Deacon chose to deal with it in the end would be his own business, but Aren felt secure in the knowledge that Deacon knew him now in every way, and he wouldn't have to hide. He wouldn't have to be ashamed.

He pushed Deacon back onto the bed and rode him hard, giving himself up to pure sexual pleasure.

When he awoke the next morning, Deacon was already gone. Aren took it as a sign. Deacon had given him his one night, but he hadn't stuck around for the morning after. He hadn't even waited so they could walk to breakfast together.

Aren had promised not to pursue him. He debated whether meeting Deacon for breakfast as if nothing had happened would seem like pressure. In his experience, if men wanted to have sex again, they would find him. He decided the best thing to do was to give Deacon his space until he made up his mind. Besides, the longer he stayed in his house, the more likely the McAllens would be gone by the time he emerged.

He skipped breakfast completely and didn't go to the main house until dinner, while the men were in the field. He rarely visited the kitchen at that time of day, and he was surprised to find the wives sitting around the table together — all but Shay, of course, who had taken her sons and Brighton to visit her family.

"They should have been back by now," Tama said. "Shay said they were only staying three nights, which means they should have been back two days ago."

Daisy waved her hand dismissively. "So they changed their minds," she said.

"What if it's something worse?" Tama asked.

"Like what?" Aren asked as he sat down next to them with his plate.

"Wraiths," Tama said.

"Don't the Austins have a generator?"

"Of course, but sometimes things happen."

"Like what?" he asked again.

It was Daisy who answered. "I heard a story," she said, and there was no missing the relish in her voice at getting to tell him a good tale. "Several years ago, before Jeremiah ran the BarChi, Old Man Pane sent some men up to the Austin ranch, and they didn't come home. So after a few days, he sent two more, and they didn't come home either. And he sent another. And he didn't come home. So finally, he sent his sons." She stopped, savouring her moment. "Now, you know it takes two days to get there, right? And there's a shack in between?"

"Yes."

"The shack's at the halfway point, and once you get there, you have to stay. Never enough daylight left to turn around and come back or to push on to the Austin ranch. That time, turned out a storm had blown the roof off the shack. And each group of men that went up had tried to fix it, but couldn't get it done in time for dark. Jeremiah said they found all those men dead inside."

"Holy Saints," Aren swore. "That's awful."

"Exactly," Tama said. She clearly didn't find the story as entertaining as Daisy. Her face had gone ashen. "Shay and Brighton could be dead up there at the shack with their sons."

"You're being over-dramatic," Daisy chided. "You know how Shay is! It's not like they've never stayed a few extra nights before. We were worried then, too, and it turned out to be nothing."

"I know," Tama said, chewing her lip. "But it's not only that. It's also what Olsa said."

Daisy rolled her eyes, flicking her hand at Tama dismissively. "It's bull dung."

"What did Olsa say?" Aren asked.

"Well..." Tama's cheeks turned red. "I said something about Alissa being a better wife for you than Rynna. I said Rynna was..."

Her words trailed away, but Daisy finished for her. "A spoilt-rotten bitch."

Tama's cheeks turned an even deeper shade of red. "Something like that, yes. And Olsa said I'd feel bad later for having spoken ill of the dead."

"That old woman's crazy," Daisy said. "You know better than to listen to her."

Tama didn't look convinced, but it seemed she didn't want to argue about it, either. She glanced nervously at Aren. Although Aren couldn't deny Olsa was sometimes odd, there was also no denying she had an uncanny knack for knowing things nobody else did. He didn't blame Tama for being concerned.

"So what happens?" he asked.

"Jeremiah will give them a few more days," Daisy said, "but eventually, somebody has to go investigate."

"Who?"

"Probably Deacon," Tama said.

That alarmed him. Why couldn't somebody else do it?

Of course he knew why. Because Deacon was the best man for the job. He was the best man for any job.

The next few days were the same. Aren made every effort to give Deacon his space. He ate his breakfasts late and his suppers early, so as not to force the big ranch hand to see him before he was ready. Those things he could handle. But every evening after supper, as he sat alone his house, he found himself depressed.

He missed Deacon. He only wished Deacon missed him, too.

Many times, he passed him on the ranch. He felt Deacon's eyes on him. The one time he bumped into him in the kitchen, they exchanged awkward pleasantries. Although Aren did his best to act casual, to act as if nothing had happened between them, he noticed Deacon could not meet his eyes. His cheeks remained red until Aren gave up and left the room.

He'd hoped Deacon would come for him. He'd hoped he'd want more. But as the days went by, it became more and more clear that Deacon wanted nothing of the sort. Aren felt guilty and alone. He wished he could undo what he had done. He'd been so determined to have a lover for even one night.

He wished that one night hadn't cost him his friend.

* * * *

"He'll be leaving soon," Olsa said to Aren on Saturday afternoon, as he sat eating supper alone. Aren didn't have to ask who 'he' was. She could only mean Deacon.

"To check on the Austins?"

"Yes."

Aren's heart sank. He hated the thought of Deacon going off into the wild. What if the roof had been blown off the shack again? What if something went wrong?

"You're worried about him."

"Of course." Although he was reluctant to confess how much it mattered. "He's the heart of the BarChi. It would be impossible to replace him."

"So, you two boys are going to keep circling each other forever, pretending like you don't know what you want?"

Aren stared at her, trying to determine if there was judgement in her tone. Her sightless eyes gave nothing away. "I don't know what you're talking about," he finally said.

"Bull dung. You two were peas in a pod one day, and the next day you show up separate, but covered in each other's smells. Ever since then, you've been giving him a wide berth, and he's been moping around like a damn fool. I may be old, but I'm not stupid. I can put two and two together."

Aren resisted the urge to laugh. He'd been foolish to think anything would get past Olsa. "I told him he could decide what happened between us."

"And do you think he's decided?"

"Well, he seems to be keeping his distance, so I guess that's a decision of some sort."

"Bah!" She waved her hand at him. "You're as much a fool as him! You deserve each other!"

"Are you saying I'm wrong?"

"Of course you're wrong, you stupid boy! You think he's keeping his distance because he doesn't want to be with you. You're waiting on him, and he's waiting on you."

"He knows where I live, Olsa. If he wanted to pursue something—"

"Is that how it worked before?" she asked, interrupting him. "Did he pursue you?"

Aren felt himself blushing, but he answered. "No."

"And with those damn maids at the McAllen ranch? Did he pursue any of them?"

Aren thought back to the night in the barn, and the maids with their unbuttoned blouses and inviting eyes. "No."

"He's doing the only thing he knows how to do," she said. "Waiting for you."

"I told him I wouldn't pressure him—"

"Then you'll both go on being lonely and miserable, staring at each other with big, sad calf eyes. You make me sick. Life's too short to waste it on fools like you." She snatched his not-quite empty bowl away from him and put it on the ground for the dogs. "Get out of my kitchen."

Aren didn't try to argue with her. He didn't get up and leave, either. Instead, he thought about what she was telling him.

Was it possible she was right? He'd been so careful to give Deacon space, but what if the man didn't want space? Aren had felt Deacon watching him. He'd felt the silence between them grow heavy and oppressive. Aren had assumed the awkwardness between them was because he had pressured Deacon into sex, but maybe it was actually because Deacon was waiting for Aren to make a move again. In some ways, it fitted.

"What if you're wrong?" he asked.

"I'm not," she said. "He may not know how to ask for what he wants, but he sure as hell knows how to take it once it's offered."

Aren stopped in the barn on his way back to the house, looking for Deacon, although he wasn't sure exactly what he planned to do if he found him there. He wanted to test Olsa's theory, and yet he didn't want to cause trouble. He was more relieved than disappointed to find the barn empty.

Back in the old house — he still couldn't quite think of it as his house — he climbed the stairs to his studio. He'd been avoiding the room and what waited within, just as he'd avoided Deacon. The half-finished painting sat on his easel, and Aren contemplated it.

The skin was wrong. He knew that now. He'd painted Deacon's skin smooth and unblemished. He thought of Deacon's scars as he reached for his paints. The artistic side of his brain took over, mixing colours and attacking the canvas with a fevered excitement, while the other side of his brain thought over Olsa's comments with cool, analytical detachment.

He'd never in his life been as sexually aggressive as he'd been with Deacon. Months of pent-up sexual frustration had led him down a path he'd never had the opportunity to travel before, and when it was over, he'd sat back, reverting to old habits, expecting Deacon to act like all of the boys he'd known before, or like Professor Birmingham. He'd assumed Deacon would come to him if he wanted more. The idea that Deacon might be waiting for him was almost intoxicating. He thought about it all night.

The next day was Sunday, the one day everybody, hands and family alike, had dinner together. He was overly meticulous as he tied his hair back into a ponytail — it was finally long enough to be tied back, although only barely—and knotted his tie. One way or another, he was determined to find out whether or not Olsa was right.

Sunday dinners were held not in the kitchen, but in the Pane's formal dining room. When Aren arrived, he was happy to find the chairs on either side of Deacon were still free. It had only been a few days, and yet it felt like ages since he'd sat next to Deacon. It felt good to walk up and sit down with him, exactly as he would have done before they'd had sex. He noted the surprise on Deacon's face, and he didn't think it was his imagination that Deacon looked pleased.

"How have you been?" Aren asked him, looking pointedly into Deacon's eyes.

Deacon's cheeks started to flush, but he didn't look away. "I'm good."

"It's a beautiful day," Aren said, and even talking about something as mundane as the weather with Deacon felt good.

"It is," Deacon agreed.

"What do you have to do this week?"

"We're leaving tomorrow to check on the Austins. But today, I'm just mending fences in the south pastures."

The south pastures. That meant Aren could easily arrange to see him, and he smiled at the thought of taking his sketchpad out into the bright sunlight and sketching Deacon as he restrung barbed wire. Like he was reading his mind, Deacon asked quietly, "Will I see you there today?"

Aren smiled. "Maybe."

The rest of the hands and family had arrived. They barely fitted at the table, all of them scrunched in shoulder-to-shoulder. The wives were still bringing in dishes of food, and the other hands were talking and joking with each other. Aren glanced around and found that nobody was paying even the slightest bit of attention to him and Deacon. They were in a room full of people, and yet it felt strangely intimate.

Aren looked back at Deacon, who was watching him expectantly. It was easy to move his hand over. Under the table, hidden by the long table cloth, it was so easy to rest his fingertips on Deacon's thigh. He saw the surprise in Deacon's eyes, but Deacon didn't pull away. He held perfectly still.

"I've missed you," Aren said, keeping his tone light.

Deacon's eyes darted away, but only to scan the rest of the table as Aren had done, to make sure nobody was watching them or listening, then he looked back at Aren with a smile. "I've missed you, too."

Aren moved his hand slowly up Deacon's thigh. Deacon's eyes drifted closed, and as Aren's fingers traced slowly higher, Deacon spread his knees, allowing Aren's hand to slide easily between his legs. Aren felt a surge of excitement that seemed to start at the base of his skull. It travelled from his brain, down his spine, straight to his groin. All this time, he'd been waiting for Deacon when all he'd really needed to do was reach out and take him. He slid his hand further up Deacon's thigh, his fingers only a hairsbreadth from the cowboy's groin, and he noted the way Deacon's breath caught in his throat.

"Is this what you want?" Aren asked, his voice a whisper.

Deacon's voice was just as quiet when he answered. "Yes."

"Everybody settle down!" Jeremiah suddenly called from the head of the table, shattering the fragile walls of the silent place where Aren and Deacon had been. "We have a lot of work to do today. The sooner we eat, the sooner we get started."

Aren pulled his hand away, and Deacon turned away without a word. They barely spoke for the rest of the meal, but it didn't matter. Aren had his answer.

Chapter Eighteen

Aren was happy when the meal ended, almost giddy with excitement and pent-up sexual energy. He knew Deacon wouldn't have much time before he had to start work, but he suspected they wouldn't need much time to find a bit of relief together.

Deacon was already headed for the door, and he glanced back at Aren. His cheeks were red, but there was no missing the nervous hope in his eyes. Aren wondered how he'd missed it over the last two weeks. He wondered how he'd looked at Deacon and seen disapproval instead of longing.

Deacon's eyes asked a question—the same question they'd been asking all along—but this time Aren recognised it for what it was. He nodded at Deacon and felt his heart flutter a bit at the broad smile his assent elicited from the big cowboy.

"Deacon, wait up," Jeremiah called. "I need to talk to you."

The disappointment Aren felt was mirrored in Deacon's expression, but there was no arguing with Jeremiah. Deacon stepped out of the way so the rest of the hands and family could get past him out of the door, his gaze glued on Aren.

There was still enough commotion to give them some semblance of privacy. Still, Aren kept his voice low. "I'll be in the barn," he said, and Deacon smiled again.

Once inside the big barn, he went to the stall at the end, which Deacon used as a bedroom of sorts. There was no mattress. Only a pillow, clean straw, and a couple of rough horse blankets. Deacon's clothes hung on pegs on the wall. There was a small, low table. It held a brush and a handful of tools, none of which were familiar to Aren. Although Aren was reluctant to search too thoroughly, a cursory inspection of the rest of the stall revealed nothing that could be used as lubricant.

Aren had been planning nothing more than a quick tryst, but as he sat on a bale of hay waiting for Deacon to arrive, his plan began to evolve. For those brief moments at the table, Deacon had felt like putty in his hands. He'd seen a hint of submission in Deacon's eyes, and it thrilled him. He found himself wanting desperately to explore how far that submission went.

"I'm glad you waited," Deacon said when he finally entered the stall, "but I only have a few minutes."

"That's fine." Aren contemplated Deacon's strong, muscular frame and the bulge that was already forming in the cowboy's pants. He knew Deacon only owned three or four pairs of pants, and about as many shirts. The ones he wore now were his nicest ones, kept aside for dinner with the family. "You're not wearing those to work, right?" Aren asked.

"No."

"Good." Aren stood up and closed the door to their stall. They still wouldn't have total privacy—the walls only came up to Aren's shoulder—but it somehow served to underline the point that they were finally alone. He turned to find Deacon watching him. His expression was exactly as it had been at the dinner table—hopeful, aroused, and completely submissive. "Take off your pants," Aren said.

Deacon smiled at him. "Have to take my boots off first." But he didn't argue. He pulled his boots off, tossing them into the corner. Then he slowly took his pants off. He didn't toss those on the floor. He folded them and placed them on a hay bale before turning back to Aren. His shirt hung down past his hips, although the front of it was caught on his rather impressive erection.

Aren stepped up close to him and began to unbutton his shirt. "We don't have enough time to do this right," he said as he worked his way down the front of Deacon's shirt. "But I'm not letting you hide from me anymore."

"I wasn't the one hiding." Of course that was true. Aren hadn't thought of it as hiding, but he could see now that was exactly how it had looked.

"I was trying to give you space if you wanted it."

"Seemed like you didn't want to see me."

"I woke up in the morning and you were gone. I figured that was your way of telling me you didn't want it to happen again."

"No," Deacon said, looking amused. "That was my way of telling you I had chores to do before breakfast."

"You're forgiven," Aren said, even though it hadn't actually been an apology, and he was pleased when Deacon laughed. Aren undid the bottom button and pushed the shirt backwards off Deacon's shoulders.

"You have to undo the cufflinks," Deacon said.

Aren smiled and shook his head. "Not this time." He pulled the shirt down Deacon's arms, and just as he'd planned, the sleeves turned inside out, but stopped before Deacon's big hands escaped from the cuffs. Aren moved behind him. He pulled Deacon's hands together and used the fabric of the shirt to bind Deacon's hands behind his back. It wouldn't be enough to hold him if he really wanted to get free, but Aren was pretty sure Deacon didn't want to escape anyway.

He walked back in front of Deacon, tracing his fingers down the scar that started at Deacon's collarbone and trailed towards his navel. Deacon's eyes were closed, his breathing heavy, his cock hard and tipped with a bead of moisture.

"You don't get to come right now," Aren said. He leant forwards to tease one of Deacon's nipples, flicking his tongue over the bud of flesh. "You're going to have to wait."

"Then what are you doing here?" Deacon asked.

Aren reached down to cup Deacon's heavy sac in his hand, squeezing gently, and Deacon moaned. "I want you to be thinking about me all day."

"That won't be anything new."

Aren smiled, undeniably pleased by the confession. He slid his fingers backwards, towards Deacon's taint, but his access was blocked by Deacon's muscular thighs. "Spread your legs for me."

Deacon did, widening his stance so that Aren's hand slid easily between his legs, and Aren felt that same bolt of excitement lance down his spine. Deacon's ready compliance made him breathless. He massaged the thick cord of flesh between Deacon's legs. "Has anybody ever done this for you?"

"No," Deacon breathed.

"Wait until you feel my tongue on it," he said, and Deacon moaned.

Aren pulled his hand from between Deacon's legs. He slowly moved around Deacon's muscular, trembling body, trailing his hand over Deacon's hip as he did. "You don't get to jack off today," he said. "I want you feeling desperate all day."

"I'm feeling desperate *now*."

Aren smacked his flank playfully, and noted the groan it elicited from Deacon. "You don't know what desperate is," Aren teased. Deacon's bound hands and the bulk of his shirt hid most of his ass, and Aren crossed slowly behind Deacon until he stood at his other side. His right hand rested on Deacon's firm ass. His left hand fingered his erect nipple. "I want you squirming in your saddle all day." He pinched one of Deacon's nipples, and the cowboy's gasp of pleasure made him moan.

He slid his right hand down Deacon's ass, his fingers probing between his cheeks. He pushed gently when he found what he sought, and he felt Deacon's muscles tighten instinctively. "I won't hurt you," Aren whispered as he nipped at Deacon's shoulder with his teeth. He slid his left hand down Deacon's stomach, skirting his erect penis, and rubbed his fingers back again onto Deacon's taint. "You'll learn to love this," he whispered as he started to move both hands at the same time. He didn't try to gain entrance with the fingers of his right hand. He only rubbed gently, moving in tandem with the fingers between Deacon's legs. "I'll teach you how to relax," he said as he massaged Deacon. "You won't believe how good it can feel."

Deacon made a sound, something close to a whimper. "Please," he said.

"'Please' what?" Aren teased, his fingers still moving together on Deacon's body.

"Please," Deacon said again. "Let me touch you. Or kiss you. Or...*something!*"

His desperation made Aren smile. Aren took a step back, taking both of his hands off Deacon's body, and Deacon moaned in frustration.

"Not yet. Come to my house tonight."

"Aren—"

"Don't forget what I said. No masturbating today."

"You can't leave me like this."

"I can," Aren told him. He moved to stand again in front of Deacon. The unmistakable desire and frustration in Deacon's eyes made his heart race. "Tonight. Say you'll be there."

"I will," Deacon said.

Aren only doubted him a little.

* * * *

Aren returned to his house feeling as if he could fly. The encounter in the barn had left him painfully aroused. He debated masturbating to relieve the pressure but decided that wouldn't be fair. Not after forbidding Deacon the same form of relief. He wondered if Deacon would do as he'd said or not.

He worked on Jeremiah's books for an hour, but the golden sunlight outside seemed to call to him. It was a bright, warm day, the birds sang an invitation, and Aren knew he'd see fewer and fewer such days over the coming weeks. It would be winter before long. His chances to sketch outdoors would be limited.

After some debate, he closed the accounting books. He took his sketchpad, his penknife, and his satchel of pencils and headed for the south pastures.

He knew it was silly to look for Deacon, but he did it anyway. It wasn't hard to find him. He and Garrett were stringing barbed wire between two poles. Garrett waved at him. Deacon didn't seem to know he was there.

Aren settled down in the grass. To the south was an abandoned grain silo, its roof gone and its walls beginning to crumble. The north side of it was covered with crawling vines, and behind it, the sun reflected off the shining ribbon of the river. Aren took out his pencils, and as he sketched, he forgot about Deacon and Garrett. He forgot everything except the strokes needed to bring the picture to life.

His hands flew over the paper. His mind retreated to a place comprised only of lines and edges and colour. He thought vaguely of trying to paint the scene later, but for now, he had only his pencils.

The silo was straight and rigid and hard, but its strength was gone. The vines were alive and moving and seemed so fragile, and yet in time, they would bring the stone silo crumbling to the ground. The grass beyond the silo was an ocean, waves cresting and breaking with the wind, creating a soft, rippling song. The wind itself couldn't be seen, which made it hard to draw. *Like trying to draw a wraith*, Aren thought. Yet it had its place in the picture as well. It had to be shown in the bend of the trees and the trailing of the clouds.

He could smell the grain in the field. He could smell a distant tang of cattle and manure, and the bright freshness of the river. He could have sworn he could smell the sunlight. He tried to pour all of it onto his paper. He tried to make the lead in his fingers take on the smells of the day. He wanted people to see his drawing and be able to feel and smell everything here in front of him. He wanted them to be as lost seeing it as he was drawing it.

The toe of a hard, leather boot nudged his thigh, breaking his reverie. Returning to the real world was shocking. It was like surfacing from a deep pool, or waking suddenly from the deepest slumber. It was disorienting and more than a bit annoying. Aren shook his head and examined the work in his hand. It wasn't bad. Not his best, but decent.

The boot nudged him again, and Aren forced himself to look around. His neck had a kink in it from the awkward way he'd bent over his sketchpad, and he massaged it with one hand as he turned his head from side to side, trying to work the stiffness out. He had no idea how long he'd been drawing. The sun had definitely fallen lower in the sky. The shadows were longer. Garrett was nowhere in sight. Aren shaded his eyes with his hand so he could squint up at Deacon, who towered above him.

"What?" Aren asked.

Against the bright sun, Deacon's face was hidden in shadow, but Aren could hear desperation in his voice when he said, "I sent Garrett back to the barracks."

Aren tried to keep from smiling. His eyes travelled down Deacon's strong, muscular body to the giant bulge at his groin. "So?" he asked.

Deacon moaned. "Don't pretend you don't know what I mean," he said. Before Aren could react, Deacon was on him.

He wasn't rough. He wasn't forceful. He wasn't mean, as so many boys in Aren's past had been. He was gentle yet firm as he pushed Aren back into the grass. He ground himself against Aren's thigh. "Aren, please," he whispered against Aren's neck. "Please don't make me wait any longer. I can't even *think* when I'm like this." He ground against Aren again, harder this time. His hand gripped Aren's ass, squeezing hard. "*Please*," he said again.

"If I get you off now, you won't have any reason to come to my house tonight."

"I will."

"I don't believe you."

Deacon moaned, grinding against him again. "I swear I'll be there."

"That's not enough."

"Then what? Saints, tell me what I need to give you, Aren, before I lose my mind. Please!"

"I want you to do everything I say while you're there."

"I will!"

"No matter what?"

"I swear!"

"If I tell you to suck my cock?"

"I will!"

"If I come in your mouth and tell you to swallow?"

"I will!"

Aren's heart skipped a beat at the thought, but he went on. "If I tie you down and spread your legs—"

"Yes!"

"If I decide to fuck you?"

Only a split second of hesitation. "Yes!" Deacon hissed. "Saints, it scares me, but I swear, Aren, I'll be your slave, if that's what you want. Just please let me come!"

"All right," Aren relented. He reached down and began to unlace Deacon's pants. Deacon lifted his hips to give him room, but based on his breathing, Aren half-expected him to climax before he even touched him. He wrapped his hand around Deacon's big, erect cock. He gripped him hard, pushing his fist down over his tip, feeling a hint of moisture under his foreskin as he stroked. "Now," he said.

That was all it took. Deacon cried out, pressing hard against him, grinding into his fist, his whole body shaking as he came. When he was spent, he collapsed on top of Aren, his breathing hard and heavy in Aren's ear. "Holy Saints, thank you," he whispered.

"You were that wound up, but you didn't jack off?" Aren asked.

"You told me not to."

The confession thrilled him. He'd never dreamt of having so much power over another man. Yet he was equally aware that with such power came a certain responsibility. Aren remembered with painful clarity what it felt like to be used by men who cared a great deal about their own pleasure, but not a bit for his. He vowed he would not be so cruel to Deacon.

Deacon didn't move off him, but one of his large hands groped towards Aren's own erection. Aren pushed it away. It wasn't that he wasn't aroused—he most definitely was—but he found he enjoyed delaying his gratification. "You better not stand me up tonight," Aren said.

"I'll be there," Deacon said. "I swear."

Chapter Nineteen

Deacon wasn't at supper, and Aren was sure the big ranch hand was going to break his vow. Aren went home and waited, his palms growing sweaty and his cock hard. The sun fell. Aren went out to the back and started the generator. The world went dark. And still Deacon wasn't there.

Aren swore at Deacon. He swore at himself. He should have known. Like all the men Aren had known in his life, Deacon had forgotten about him once he'd found his own pleasure. Aren damped the fire. He extinguished the lamps. He went up to his bedroom and began to undress. He was debating the best way to alleviate his own sexual frustration when he was startled by a loud pounding noise.

At first he thought it was the ghost, but only for a second. The knocking was too loud, and it came from the wrong part of the house. There was actually somebody knocking at his front door, and there was only one person it could be.

He went quickly down his stairs and glanced out of the window next to the door. It was too dark to make out the face, but even in the dim light of the half-full moon, Aren recognised the lines of Deacon's muscular body.

"What are you thinking?" he asked as he opened the door to let Deacon in. "It's full dark outside!"

"We got back from the fields late," Deacon said, closing and latching the door behind him. He was wearing his long duster over his ranch clothes. "I had to take care of the horses before I came, but I swore I'd be here."

"But it's dark," Aren said, feeling the words were entirely inadequate. How could Deacon have risked his life like that?

"I didn't want to break my promise."

The weight of his words hit Aren hard. Only ten minutes earlier, he'd been calling Deacon every bad word he could think of. Now, he realised what a fool he had been. How many times did Deacon have to prove he wasn't like the boys from school before Aren stopped expecting him to act like them?

"Thank you," he said.

Deacon's cheeks turned red, but he smiled. "I have to leave early tomorrow. I didn't want to leave without seeing you."

The Austin farm. How could Aren have forgotten? Deacon and Garrett would be setting out to determine whether or not anything was amiss at the farm. Tomorrow night, they'd be staying in a shack that may or not still be standing. Time at the farm once they got there. Another night at the shack on the way home, if they lasted that long. Maybe everybody was fine. Maybe everybody was dead. Anything could happen. The idea that Deacon might not come back at all made Aren's heart race. "Do you have to go?" he asked, stepping closer to Deacon. "Couldn't one of Jeremiah's sons—?"

"No," Deacon said, cutting off Aren's words. It was obvious he didn't share Aren's dread. Deacon was smiling, his cheeks flushed, his eyes begging a question. "I brought you something." He reached into the deep pocket of his duster and pulled out a small bundle. He pushed it into Aren's hands.

Aren looked down at the strange gift in surprise. It was rope, twisted into a small loop and tied around itself, thicker than bailing twine, but thinner than most of what they used on the ranch. Aren's heart started to race as he contemplated the implications of the gift. He felt his cock growing hard. He looked up into Deacon's nervous eyes. When he spoke, Deacon's voice was heavy with arousal. "I really liked what you did in the barn."

Aren felt again the shot of excitement he'd felt at the table and in the barn—the excitement born of finally being allowed to be in control. The excitement of having a man—and not just *any* man either, but *Deacon*, the strongest, most masculine man he'd ever met—submitting to him completely.

"Is this really what you want?" Aren asked, hoping against hope Deacon wouldn't say no.

Deacon's cheeks were even redder than before. "I promised I'd be your slave."

"But is that what you *want?*" Aren asked. He didn't want it to come from some misplaced sense of obligation.

Deacon smiled at him. "It is."

"You want me to tell you what to do?"

"Yes," Deacon said, breathless.

"And you'll do whatever I say?"

Deacon didn't answer, but he didn't have to. Aren could see the man's arousal in his eyes. He noted the way Deacon's breathing was speeding up, just talking about it. He noticed the growing bulge in Deacon's pants.

It made Aren's head spin. His own voice was as husky as Deacon's when he spoke again. "Take off your coat."

He saw the excitement in Deacon's eyes that his gift was being accepted in exactly the way he'd hoped. Deacon hung the duster on one of the hooks by the door. Then he stood in front of Aren, his cheeks flushed with desire, awaiting his next order.

"Get down on your knees." Aren could barely stop himself from moaning with pleasure as Deacon did as he'd been told. Aren stepped closer to him. "Undo my pants," he said.

Deacon's hands shook, but he didn't hesitate. He unlaced the front of Aren's pants, releasing his aching erection.

"Touch me," Aren whispered.

Deacon's rough fingers grazed his tip, and Aren gasped at the pleasure of it. Deacon trailed his fingers down Aren's foreskin to his very root. His fingers stroked Aren's balls. "Stop," Aren said and Deacon did, putting his hands back in his own lap.

"Undo your hair," Aren said.

He saw Deacon's surprise at that, but Deacon didn't hesitate. He pulled his long queue forwards over his shoulder and pulled the leather ties free, dropping them onto the floor as he went. When he was done, he sat docilely with his hands resting in his lap in front of the obvious erection in his pants.

Aren ran his fingers through Deacon's black hair, pushing it all back so it trailed down the cowboy's broad back. His left hand still held the rope, but with his right, he grabbed a handful of hair. "You said earlier you would suck my cock if I told you to."

"Yes."

"Open your mouth," Aren told him, "and prove it."

None of his previous lovers had ever performed this act on him, and Aren knew Deacon had never done it for anybody either. It seemed strangely appropriate that it was a first for them both. Deacon gripped him, his thumb and first finger wrapped around the base of Aren's cock while he palmed Aren's sac. He opened his mouth and slowly sucked Aren's tip inside.

Aren gasped at the sensation. He'd known it would feel good, and yet he was still amazed at just how good. He thrust his hips out without meaning to, pushing himself deeper into Deacon's warm, wet mouth, and felt Deacon's instinctive jerk backwards. He knew from experience how unpleasant it could be to have a cock shoved down your throat too hard or too fast, triggering the gag reflex, and he regretted having lost control. "I'm sorry," he said. He forced himself to still his hips. He resisted the almost overwhelming urge to thrust again into Deacon's waiting mouth.

Deacon looked up at him, unsure, and yet with naked lust still showing in his dark eyes. "I don't mind," he said. "I just wasn't ready."

"I'll be more careful." Aren hooked his hand behind Deacon's neck and pulled him towards his cock.

This time, Deacon used his fingers to slide Aren's foreskin out of the way before sucking his tip into his mouth. The sensation was even more intense that way, and Aren cried out. Deacon's tongue moved in circles around his end, over and over again, and although Aren didn't thrust, he pulled Deacon closer. This time, Deacon was ready for him. Aren's cock slid easily through Deacon's moist lips, deep into his warm mouth. Aren cried out again, and at his feet Deacon moaned. His movements became more frantic as he slid up and down Aren's shaft, swallowing his length again and again.

Aren could easily have come. It would have been so easy to let go then and spend himself into Deacon's sweet mouth. But then he remembered the rope, still gripped tightly in his left hand.

"Stop!" he gasped out, and he used his hand in Deacon's hair to pull him away from his cock.

Deacon looked up at him, his lips red and wet, his breathing hard. "I did it wrong?" he asked.

Nobody had ever cared before whether or not Aren enjoyed what was done to him. It touched some part of him he hadn't quite known existed. "You did everything right," Aren said, smiling at him. "I thought we should go upstairs."

Deacon smiled at him. He stood up and Aren followed him up the stairs, admiring the taut, muscular ass in front of him.

"Take off your clothes," Aren said, when they reached the bedroom. Once he was naked, Deacon turned to him expectantly.

"I want you on your hands and knees," Aren told him. He saw the heartbeat of hesitation, the hint of fear in Deacon's eyes, but then Deacon obeyed.

Aren quickly finished undressing, watching Deacon as he did. Deacon was trembling, whether from fear or desire or both, Aren didn't know.

He was struck once again by how amazing Deacon's body was—heavily muscled, strong and firm. His ass was as muscular as the rest of him. A thin patch of hair grew back from his groin, between his cheeks. It didn't cover the firm globes of his ass. It tapered away at the point where Deacon's cheeks started to curve. It drew Aren's eyes. His fingers longed to stroke those sparse hairs, to follow them to what lay at their centre.

Aren grabbed his jar of salve and knelt behind Deacon. He touched Deacon's back, and Deacon jumped at the contact. "Shh," Aren soothed, putting his other hand on Deacon's scarred back. "Relax." Aren ran his hands down Deacon's sides, past his hips. He gripped his firm buttocks in his hands, spreading his cheeks, eyeing Deacon's entrance. Just looking at that intimate part of him, he could tell how tense he was. He wouldn't have been able to push past his rim.

He brushed the ball of his thumb over Deacon's entrance, and Deacon jumped again.

"Relax," Aren said.

"Will it hurt?" Deacon asked, and his voice shook.

"If I did it right now, yes. It would hurt you. But I won't do that. I'm not going to fuck you tonight."

He actually saw some of the tension leave Deacon's body when he said that. He saw the way he seemed to sag with relief.

"I'm going to touch you, though," Aren said. "I'm going to try to help you relax." He opened the salve and spread some on his thumb. He spread Deacon's cheeks again and began to massage his lubricated thumb in soft circles around his rim. "This can feel so good," he said. "Do you believe me?"

"I think so," Deacon said, although he didn't sound very sure.

"I won't push into you tonight," Aren assured him, as he continued to thumb him. "I won't push in until you're ready. I'll only touch you on the outside. Do you believe me?"

"Yes," Deacon said, and he sounded more confident now.

"Good." His thumb continued its slow circles. "I want you to try to relax."

Deacon nodded, and Aren noted his breathing had changed again. Aren felt sure that arousal was starting to win out over fear. Aren kept his thumb moving, and with his other hand he reached under Deacon's body to grip his cock, which wasn't quite fully erect, and he began to stroke. His own erection was aching for some attention, and yet he had no desire to rush forwards. He kept his hands moving, one on Deacon's cock and one on his rim, and was thrilled when Deacon started to move with him, moaning as he pushed his cock harder through Aren's fist.

"Don't you feel how they're connected?" Aren asked. "Don't you feel like when I touch you here," he pushed harder on Deacon's rim, "you can feel it here?" He squeezed the tip of Deacon's cock, making the big man gasp. "Maybe it's just me," he said as he continued to stroke, "but I feel like they feed each other. Like one always makes the other want it more. See how good it feels?" he asked. "Think about me touching you here" — again he pushed a bit harder against Deacon's rim — "and here." And again he squeezed his cock. "Feel the pleasure go back and forth. Feel the way one wouldn't be the same without the other."

"Yes," Deacon groaned. His rim was becoming softer, becoming more and more inviting as Deacon gave himself to the pleasure. His cock was fully erect again, and he thrust himself through Aren's fist, then back against Aren's other hand, over and over again.

"Someday," Aren said, as his hands continued to move, "after we've both bathed, I'll put my tongue where my thumb is now." He was gratified by the moan his words elicited from Deacon. "You won't believe how fucking good it feels."

"Saints, Aren," Deacon gasped. "It feels good now."

Aren took his hand away from Deacon's ass and was pleased at the way Deacon moaned in frustration. "Don't worry," he said. He scooped more salve onto his fingers and spread it down his own aching shaft. "I'm not done." Deacon looked back over his shoulder at him, and Aren saw the cloud of doubt in his eyes. "I'm not going to fuck you. I said I wouldn't. Not until you're ready." Deacon relaxed again, and he pushed backwards, pushing his ass towards Aren. Aren reached under him again and allowed Deacon to thrust into his fist. He pushed his cock against Deacon's crack. "This is all," he said. "I won't fuck you yet. I'm just going to ride you."

Deacon nodded, panting hard, and Aren started to thrust.

So many times he'd been on his knees for other men but never had he been able to do what he was doing now. He didn't care that he couldn't fuck Deacon for real. He was thrilled just to have Deacon in front of him, to be able to slide his engorged cock up and down the crack of Deacon's ass as his other hand continued to jerk him off.

219

"You have the most amazing body," he said as he fucked himself against Deacon's crack. "You have the most amazing ass."

He stroked Deacon faster, and thrust against him harder. He imagined spreading Deacon's cheeks and driving into him for real.

"It's going to feel so good," he told Deacon as he thrust against him. "It's going to feel so good to fuck you."

Deacon whimpered. His arms seemed to give out, and he fell to his elbows, moaning as Aren continued to stroke him. "I want so much to fuck you. I'll make it good for you, Deacon. I swear I will."

"Aren!"

"Not until you're ready."

"Oh, Saints, Aren, I'm ready now!"

"No. I won't do it until you're begging me for it."

"Aren, I'm going to come soon."

But Aren didn't want to let it end so soon. The idea of spending more time, of drawing their pleasure out as long as they could was too exciting to pass up. "No, you're not," he said, forcing himself to stop grinding against the Deacon's hard muscular ass. He let go of Deacon's cock. "Not yet, you're not."

He pulled away from Deacon and stood up, and Deacon moaned with obvious frustration. "Go get on the bed."

Deacon was breathing hard, and it seemed to take him a moment to make his muscles work, but then he slowly pushed himself up from the floor and did as he was told.

"Sit against the headboard," Aren told him as he retrieved the rope from where he'd dropped it on the floor. "Put the pillows behind you if you want, so you're comfortable."

It was easy to tie Deacon's hands to the posts at the head corners of the bed. There were posts at the foot of the bed, too, but with Deacon sitting against the headboard, his feet didn't reach that far. Aren settled for tying the rope around his ankles and running it down the side of the mattress to tie it to the bed frame. It left Deacon with both his arms and legs spread wide, his back padded comfortably against the headboard, and his cock large and hard between his legs.

Aren climbed onto the bed with the salve. He took his time massaging some onto Deacon's cock, watching the way Deacon's hips tried to buck, and listening to Deacon's frantic moans. He greased the entire shaft, leaving the tip for last. Before he oiled it, he leaned over and licked it, running his tongue under Deacon's foreskin, tasting the salty moisture that had collected there. Deacon gasped and attempted to thrust deeper into Aren's mouth, but he had no leverage and nowhere to go, and he collapsed back against the mattress, panting.

Aren sat up to grin at him. "I don't think I'm going to let you come tonight," he said. "What do you think of that?"

Deacon shook his head. "I don't know if I can last."

"I want you to try."

He moved up on Deacon's body, stopping to tease each of his hard nipples with his tongue. Deacon moaned. Aren ran his tongue up Deacon's chest, over his throat, along his jaw. He stopped finally at his lips. He didn't know why he could suck Deacon's cock, or make Deacon suck his, and yet he was still strangely shy about kissing him.

He finally leaned in, brushing his lips over Deacon's awaiting mouth. Deacon moaned and his lips parted. Although his hands were tied, he was unmistakably aggressive as he kissed Aren back, his tongue pushing into

Aren's mouth. Aren pulled back, gasping for air. As many times as he'd had sex in his life, he still wasn't used the intimacy of a simple kiss.

"Don't you come yet," he panted. He used his hand to position Deacon's cock beneath him, and he slowly sank down onto it.

He'd been fucked by more men than he could count over the years, but none as large as Deacon. He went slowly, just as he'd done the first time, allowing his body time to adapt to the intrusion. Deacon watched him the entire time, his eyes burning. Once his body had relaxed and Deacon's length was buried deep inside him, he began to move up and down, slowly at first, but quickly speeding up.

"Holy Saints," Deacon breathed, "you can't do that too long if you expect me to not come."

"A little longer," Aren gasped. He gripped the headboard on each side of Deacon's head and rode him harder, revelling in the feel of the huge cock pounding against that sweet spot inside him. He looked down at Deacon, at the way his eyes were half-lidded with pleasure, his full lips moist and parted as he panted along with Aren. The hesitation Aren had felt before was gone. He kissed Deacon hard, pushing his tongue into Deacon's mouth as Deacon had done to him. Deacon moaned. He whimpered. He squirmed and bucked underneath him as Aren pillaged his mouth, fucking himself harder onto Deacon's cock.

It felt so good. It felt so good to have every part of his body open to Deacon. It felt good to feel Deacon helpless and compliant underneath him. He kissed him harder, pulling the big man's long hair, grinding hard onto Deacon's big cock.

"Aren," Deacon gasped. "You have to stop."

Aren could hear the desperation in his voice. He was close himself, and he knew Deacon was fighting hard to keep his climax at bay. "Your mouth," he said frantically as he grabbed Deacon's head. "I want your mouth." He pulled himself up quickly, off Deacon's cock. It was an awkward position, and he ended up half-standing and half-kneeling, holding fast to the headboard with one hand and gripping Deacon's head with the other. He drove his cock deep into Deacon's mouth. His restraint from before was gone, and he thrust harder and harder, but Deacon didn't try to pull away. He didn't seem to mind. His moans were as loud as before as Aren fucked his mouth. Aren reached behind himself, sliding his own finger into his wet hole, fingering himself as Aren swallowed his cock whole.

"Holy Saints, I want to fuck you," he panted as he drove into Deacon's mouth. "I want to fuck you so much." He slid a second finger into himself, and his hips moved faster of their own accord, driving in and out of Deacon, in and out of himself. "You're going to beg me to fuck you," he said. He pulled his cock out of Deacon's mouth and looked down into his burning eyes. "Do you believe me?" he asked.

"Yes!" Deacon said. "I'll beg you now if you want."

"Not yet," Aren said. He was still moving his fingers in and out of himself, and Deacon's eyes darted down to the movement.

"Let me," he said, looking back up at Aren. "Untie one hand?"

Aren looked at Deacon's big, strong hand, secured to the bed post, his fingers thick and callused. Just the thought made him want to come. He unknotted the rope as quickly as he could and was thrilled at the way Deacon's finger immediately found his entrance.

"Holy Saints," Aren breathed as Deacon's finger slid tentatively inside. Deacon opened his mouth, stretching towards Aren's cock, and Aren pushed into it, crying out at the pleasure. As good as it felt, having Deacon's fingers fuck him while his warm mouth swallowed his cock, Aren knew it was only the beginning. He reached behind him, grabbing Deacon's wrist. "More," he said, and gasped as he felt a second finger slide into him. Still, Deacon seemed hesitant. His fingertips were barely past Aren's rim. Aren thrust into Deacon's mouth. He used his hand on Deacon's wrist to push his fingers in deep, spreading him wide, touching that wonderfully sensitive spot inside him. "Yes!" Aren yelled.

He came hard, filling Deacon's mouth, thrusting into that warmth as Deacon's fingers filled his ass. His orgasm was the best he'd had in months. Maybe longer. Maybe ever. It left him breathless and trembling. There was not even a hint of the shame or regret that had so often followed his sexual encounters. There was only an enormous feeling of release and relief. "Deacon," he said when he could breathe again. He sank down across Deacon's lap and kissed him hard, tasting his own cum and finding it undeniably erotic. "Holy Saints, that was good."

"Do I have to wait until morning?" Deacon asked. He didn't seem unhappy about it though. He was smiling.

"I haven't decided yet."

Aren unknotted the rope at Deacon's other wrist and was dismayed at the angry red welt he found underneath it. He found the salve and began to gently rub it into the oozing wound. "You should have said something," he said to Deacon. "I didn't mean to hurt you."

Deacon shrugged as he watched Aren work. "I didn't notice."

Maybe that was true, but Aren vowed to himself to do better next time. Even if Deacon didn't mind the pain, it wouldn't do to have him wandering around in front of his men with rope burns on his wrists. If he wrapped Deacon's wrist in cloth first, it would help. He might still have a red mark, but at least the rough rope wouldn't be able to cut into his dark flesh.

Aren was relieved to see that Deacon's ankles weren't as badly chafed. Still, he apologised again.

"It's fine," Deacon told him, pulling him up to the head of the bed. "I ain't complaining."

He lay down, pulling Aren with him. His naked body was hard against Aren's back, his thick, still-erect cock pushing against his ass, but he didn't try to push into Aren as so many men had done before. He sighed happily as he pulled the blanket up over them both. He kissed the back of Aren's neck.

"Aren," he said quietly, "I think I could get used to this."

Aren might have wondered at the strange feeling those words stirred in him.

He might have. If he'd only been a bit more awake.

* * * *

He woke face down on the bed, with a weight against his back and a familiar pressure between his thighs. For a few seconds, Aren thought he was back in school. Some boy who wouldn't speak to him in the light of day was spreading his legs, and although Aren's cock was already growing hard, something in his brain rebelled at the thought.

"Aren, please," a hoarse voice whispered in his ear, and in the blink of an eye, Aren knew where he was. He was in his own bed, in the house that wasn't quite his. The candles had burnt out. Outside, wind howled through the trees, rattling his shutters. The sobbing in the cellar was barely distinguishable. And the weight on his back wasn't some cruel boy from school. The cock asking for entrance didn't belong to somebody who would mock him in the morning. It was Deacon, the man whom Aren suddenly couldn't imagine living without.

"Please," Deacon whispered again. His lips gently kissed the back of Aren's neck.

Even in the dark, it was easy to find the salve on the bedside table. It was easy to reach behind him and rub it on Deacon's erect cock, causing the big cowboy to moan. Then, still face-down on the mattress with Deacon on his back, Aren guided Deacon to his entrance. He pushed backwards and felt Deacon's tip slide easily inside.

"Holy Saints, Aren," Deacon moaned as he pushed farther inside. "You feel so good." His thrusts were long and deliberate, his hands and lips gentle. And even though Deacon was behind him, it reminded Aren of their first night together. Deacon was slow and careful, his hands caressing Aren everywhere. He kissed Aren's neck and his shoulders. He continued to whisper in his ear, telling him he was amazing, he was beautiful, he was perfect. Eventually, one of his hands found Aren's cock, and he stroked Aren as he made love to him.

But through it all, even as the pleasure grew, even as Deacon's thrusts grew more urgent, Aren could only think of one thing—in the morning, Deacon would be leaving, heading into the wild. Aren heard the wind pounding against the windows. He imagined wraiths loose in the night, trying to gain entrance. Brighton and Shay hadn't come back. There was no telling what waited for Deacon at the end of the road.

Deacon moaned, thrusting deep into Aren, crying out as he spent himself. As he did, Aren found himself fighting tears for no reason he could explain.

"Tell me what you want," Deacon said, once he'd caught his breath. He kissed Aren's neck again. "I'll use my hand or my mouth. You can tie me down again if you want."

"No," Aren said.

"Then what?" Deacon asked. "Just tell me."

It was good that it was dark. It was good that Deacon was behind him. It was good that he could hide. "I want you safe," Aren said. "I don't want you to go."

"I have to."

"I know." He was trembling, and he felt Deacon's arms tighten around him. "I want you to come home. Tell me you're coming home."

"Even the wraiths can't keep me away."

Which was exactly what Aren was afraid of.

Chapter Twenty

Deacon was up early the next morning. They wouldn't even get to eat breakfast together. Deacon and Garrett wanted to be on the road as early as possible, in case the trouble they ran into was at the shack. Aren did his best not to let his dread show on his face. He sat in bed, watching Deacon dress, trying to find the right words to say. "Goodbye" seemed so final. "Be safe" seemed too light.

Deacon pulled on his boots. "I have to go," he said.

"Come home," Aren said. "Please."

Deacon smiled. "You worry too much." He leaned over and kissed Aren goodbye, a quick grazing touch of his lips on Aren's forehead. "I'll be back in no time."

Aren didn't go with him to the courtyard, even though he knew most of the BarChi would be there to see them off. He was afraid that in saying goodbye, he would betray himself and his feelings for Deacon there in front of everybody. He might break down and beg Deacon not to go. He might cry as he watched him ride away. Aren didn't want anybody to think he was weak.

He waited, as he always did, until the hands had finished their breakfast before going for his own, and afterwards, he climbed the stairs to his studio. He found it a mess—his paints and brushes scattered on the floor. The picture he'd painted of Deacon was face down in the corner of the room. He sighed and started to clean up the ghost's mess. He was getting used to her little displays of temper. He'd once come home to find all his clothes scattered on his bedroom floor and holes ripped in half of his shirts. He considered himself lucky this time that no real damage had been done.

He had a new canvas ready. He hadn't yet decided what to paint, but as he cleaned up after the ghost, he found himself thinking of Deacon. He thought of the night before—not just the sex, but about Deacon's submission. He thought of Deacon standing naked in front of him, waiting for his instruction. As he put the previous painting back in its place, he examined the scars on the ranch hand's skin. He thought about the scar that should have been there, but wasn't—the BarChi brand.

And suddenly he knew.

He started out unsure, but as so often happened, his art carried him away. His arm moved and the paint flowed, and it seemed not so much that Aren created the picture as that the picture was already there. It was only using Aren to find its way free.

He painted for hours, stopping only once when somebody knocked on his door.

"This is for you," Daisy said, holding a strange stick towards him.

"What is it?" he asked, impatiently. He was still lost in his paints, victim to his muse. He resented her intrusion.

"It's a riding crop," she said.

"Why are you giving it to me?"

She sighed, shoving it into his hands. "Olsa told me to," she said as she turned to leave. "She said you'd need it."

Although Aren had grown used to caring for the horses, he'd never ridden one. He had no intention of riding one any time soon, either. Leave it to Olsa to send him something he had absolutely no use for.

He tossed the crop into his bedroom and went back to his studio. He surrendered himself again to the will of his paints. The picture was taking form — Deacon, the brand, images of the BarChi.

He was finally shaken from his reverie by the supper bell. The hands were about to eat. He thought about his own supper and his heart sank a bit when he realised he'd be eating alone. Still, there was nothing to be done about it.

He stepped back from the canvas to examine what he'd done. He liked it. It was different from anything else he'd ever painted — a bit more abstract. Almost a dreamscape. He thought it was good, but he knew it wasn't finished. He didn't know what exactly was missing. He only knew he couldn't sign his name in the corner yet.

He hated the idea of coming back to his empty house after supper — that was when he knew he'd miss Deacon the most — so he took his sketchpad and pencils with him. There was a new colt in the barn, and Aren hoped to sketch it. He wanted to see if he could capture its clumsy curiosity on paper.

He sighed as he headed out of the door. Sketching a horse seemed like a pitiful replacement for the way he'd have preferred to spend his evening.

"I've been waiting for you, boy," Olsa said as soon as he walked in. His plate of food was already waiting on the table. "I have questions to ask you."

Aren put down his pad and the satchel that held his pencils and penknife. "All right," he said, as he sat down and started to eat. He supposed he'd better not waste any time, in case one of his answers prompted Olsa to snatch his food away.

"Has what's in your cellar been keeping you awake at night?" she asked.

"Not so much anymore. She makes noises. She tries to get out, then she cries. That's about it. I'm getting used to it."

"What about Deacon? Does it keep him awake when he's in your bed?"

Aren felt himself blushing. He didn't bother to ask how she knew that Deacon had spent the night with him. "It seems to spook him a bit," he admitted.

She nodded. "Good."

It seemed like a strange thing for her to say, but Aren didn't have time to ponder it before she asked her next question. "Have you checked the ward we painted?"

"Yes." In truth, he probably checked it far more often than he needed to. "It's fine."

She sighed. "Guess that will do for now."

He thought about that as he ate more of his dinner. The sign on the cellar door seemed to keep the ghost confined. It was similar to the wards over the doors and windows, and yet Olsa and Deacon claimed they no longer kept the wraiths at bay. "Olsa, why is it the ward on the cellar door works, but the wards over the doors don't?"

"Symbols have power," she said, "but only so long as people know."

"You told me that once before, but I still don't understand."

"Give me your paper," she said, holding out her hand. Aren handed her his pad. She opened the tablet and began to turn pages. Many of the sheets were loose from the time the ghost had torn the pad apart. Olsa's blind eyes stared at some point over Aren's head as she went through the sketches. She stopped at each page as if she could see it, and although she wasn't looking down at the paper, she seemed to be looking for one in particular. "Here," she said on about the eighth one. "This one has a mark."

Aren walked around the table to stand next to her, looking down. It was the picture he'd drawn ages before, on the day Deacon let him move into the house. "It's just a bull," he said.

"Bah! Not the drawing. The mark!" And her gnarled finger came down with uncanny accuracy on the corner of page, right where Aren had signed it. It wasn't much. He never signed his full name. Only the letter A, with the second leg stretched longer than the first.

"That's how I sign my work."

"It's a symbol," she said. "To you, it means it's finished. It means it's good. It tells the world, 'I'm proud of this.' That's its power. Now," she flipped to the back of the book, where the pages were empty. "Give me your pencil," she said. Aren pulled one out of his satchel and placed it in her hand. She put the lead to the paper and drew. Her hand was shaky and the lines wavered, but what she drew was simple — a circle with a line within it.

"What is it?" she asked him.

"The BarChi brand."

"Right. You go into town, or any ranch in Oestend, and you make that mark, people know. You put that mark on the cattle, people know it belongs here. You put that mark in a ledger in the store, they know which account to charge. Folks know this mark's for the ranch, so it has power. If you went home to the continent and you put that mark on a cow, what good would it do?"

"None. Nobody knows the brand."

"Right," she said. "Wouldn't matter if you told them it was a brand. Wouldn't matter if you told them about the BarChi. The power'd be gone. To them, this mark's only lines on paper."

"That's what happened with the wards?"

She nodded. "People forgot the meaning behind them."

"But they say the generator uses them to make the net."

"Bah!" She waved her hand at him. "Bull dung. The generator makes noise. It's unnatural. Smells like metal and gears. It's an abomination to them, so they stay away."

"So it *does* help deter them?"

"Sure," she said. "But it's got nothing to do with the wards."

"Could the wards be made to work again?"

"It's too late," she said. "Nobody left who believes. Only me. Deacon, maybe, deep down in his heart, though he won't yet admit it." She shook her head. "We're not enough to protect all of Oestend."

Aren still wasn't sure he understood. He stared down at the symbol on his paper. It was only a brand, right? How could it have power? But looking at it made him think of the painting at his house — the brand, with Deacon in the centre.

Olsa's hand suddenly gripped his arm tightly, more tightly than he would have thought the little old lady could manage. "You've changed it," she said in awe.

"What?" he asked, baffled.

"I can feel it! You painted this!"

"Well, yes, but —"

"What does this symbol mean?" she asked again, pointing at the brand.

"It means the BarChi —"

"Not to Oestend, boy!" she snapped, slamming her hand down on the counter. "To you! What does it mean to you?"

"It means..." He stumbled, embarrassed by his answer. "It means Deacon."

"Take me," she said. "I need to see the painting."

Aren didn't understand, but he knew better than to argue with Olsa. He led her across the grass to his house, up the steps and in the front door, then up the stairs to the spare room he used as his studio. He was holding her arm to guide her, but as soon as they stepped into the room, Olsa shook herself free of him.

She walked into the room, her arms outstretched, moving slowly. He only had two easels, so most of his other paintings sat on the floor, leaning against the wall. "This one isn't done," she said as she passed one. "No mark." She came to the next one. "This one is," she said, but she didn't stop. She moved to the next one. "What is this one?" she asked.

Aren felt his cheeks turning red, but he answered her. "It's Deacon." It was the first painting he'd done, of Deacon in the barn.

"The mark on this one is strong," she said. Then she moved on to the new one.

She stopped in front of it, drawing in her breath. Her sightless eyes looked up over the edge of the canvas, seemingly at the corner of the room, but she held her hands out towards the painting as if she wanted to touch it. "What is it?" she asked.

"It's him again," Aren said, blushing even more.

"What else?"

"The brand," he said.

She sighed in frustration. "Curse you, boy! Stop being embarrassed and tell me all of it!"

"It's the brand," he said, "around the outside, like a frame. Deacon's in the centre. There's barbed wire wrapped around them both, tying them together. There are horses and cattle and the houses around him, too, except small. In the background, like they're part of a dream. Mostly it's just him, and the brand, and the wire, all holding each other in place."

"Aww," she breathed, and he was surprised at the reverence in her voice. "You said once that Deacon was the heart of the ranch."

"Yes, but—"

"You made it true," she said, nodding. Aren didn't know what to say to that, so he held his tongue. She held one hand down towards the bottom right corner, where Aren usually signed his paintings. "There's no mark yet."

"No. It isn't quite done."

"You've changed the way of things," she said in awe. "There have always been many paths, and most of them led to death. But now you're shining light on a new course."

"I'm *what?*" Aren asked. "I don't know what you mean. It's only a painting."

But she seemed not to have heard. She turned to him, and even though her eyes were white, they seemed to bore into him. "Show him this," she said. "When he gets back. He has to see the symbol is him!" She pointed her finger at him. "This is important, boy. Tell me you'll do it."

"All right," Aren said, hoping he sounded more confident than he felt. "I'll show him."

"Make sure that you do," she said. "This could be what saves you both."

* * * *

Shortly before supper on the fourth day, a lone rider appeared at the top of the ridge, leading a whole string of horses behind him. Two men had gone out, but only one was coming home.

Aren felt as if his heart stopped beating. Dread seemed to expand inside his chest, nearly choking off his breath. From a distance, there was no way of knowing which man it was, but as he drew nearer, Aren was able to make out his body shape, the slope of his shoulders, the way he ducked his head against the falling sun.

He felt as if he might sob with relief. Some of the other men had gathered to watch as Deacon rode into the courtyard, and Aren let himself fall back into the shadows by the kitchen door. He didn't want to betray too much by rushing to Deacon's side, or by the sheer relief he knew had to be evident on his face.

Deacon dismounted. Nobody in the courtyard said anything as his eyes made their way around the circle, looking for one man in particular.

"Where's Simon?" he finally asked.

"In the north pasture," Frances told him.

Deacon nodded. He motioned Frances forwards and handed him the reins. He said something to him, too low for Aren to hear. Frances nodded and led the horses towards the barn. "Somebody go find Jeremiah," Deacon said. "Tell him it's important."

"What happened?" one of the men finally asked.

"You'll find out," Deacon said, "but there's other men have the right to hear it before you."

He headed towards the back of the house, where Aren stood, and Aren ducked inside the doorway of the kitchen, so they'd be out of sight of the other men when they greeted each other. Only Olsa was in the kitchen. Her back was to Aren as she stirred whatever was over the fire. She hummed idly, as if she had no clue what was going on.

It was all he could do not to throw himself into Deacon's arms when he walked into the room. He was trembling, and he would have given anything to feel Deacon hold him, to hear Deacon reassure him. But he knew instinctively this wasn't the time. There was a brittleness about Deacon that spoke of being wound too tight. Whatever had happened in the wild had shaken him, and still his job wasn't done. Aren would not make his burden greater by asking for his strength now, when he obviously had so little left to give.

Deacon's eyes landed on him the moment he walked through the door, and he crossed over to Aren, grabbing Aren's shoulders in his big hands. Deacon didn't hug him, but he pulled him close, his fingers digging painfully into Aren's upper arms. He put his face down into Aren's hair, and Aren held very still, trying to determine what Deacon needed from him.

Deacon took a deep breath, and it actually seemed he was drawing strength just from the simple fact that Aren was close. He squared his shoulders again. He stood up straight, suddenly letting Aren go.

And that was it.

He turned to Olsa, who was putting down bowls of stew, and kissed her on the cheek. "Eat now," she said, "before those boys. Jeremiah's on his way."

Deacon sighed heavily as he sat down, and Aren sat next to him as he always did. Olsa gave Aren a bowl, too, although he didn't feel like eating. He stirred the thick stew around and around his bowl while Deacon ate. He wanted to ask questions. He wanted to ask about Garrett. Instead, he waited.

Jeremiah came in a few minutes later. He'd obviously come in a hurry from wherever he'd been, because he was breathing hard.

"Well?" he asked Deacon.

Deacon pushed his half-empty bowl away and, watching him, Aren could tell how hard it was for him to answer. "They're all dead," he finally said, his voice low in the silent room. "Every one of them."

Jeremiah fell heavily into a chair and put his face in his hands. "How?"

"Generator ran dry," Deacon said. "Hadn't been kept up. Gears were all clogged. Windmill wouldn't turn at all. They were running it on coal, but it must've been burning twice the fuel to keep cranking. Engine burnt out."

"Oh, Saints," Jeremiah moaned, putting his head down between his knees. "How many?"

"Zed Austin and his wife. The daughter. Five maids." He hesitated, watching Jeremiah. "Brighton, Shay and their boys."

238

The silence in the room was heavy with grief. Nobody moved. Nobody made a sound except for Jeremiah, who was crying quietly into his hands. But he wasn't giving himself up to grief. Not yet, anyway. Aren suspected he would save that for the privacy of his own room. "Go on," he said to Deacon.

"Farm's a mess. Cattle in the field had chewed it to the dirt. Animals locked in corrals had starved. Horses kicked their way out, but one broke its leg in the process. Had to put her down. Opened the gate for the cattle. Couldn't take the time to herd them to pasture like they needed. Just have to hope they don't go no further than the next patch of grass. Figured it was better than letting them starve. I brought back the BarChi horses that was there, plus a couple of theirs. The rest should be fine in the pasture for a bit." He stopped again, obviously working up the courage to say the rest. "Didn't have time to bury the people," he said. "I know you would have wanted that. But we had to try to fix the generator before dark. Digging the graves would have burnt daylight—"

"I understand," Jeremiah said. "Are they still there?"

Deacon shook his head. "It wasn't pretty. They'd been gone a while. We put them all in the far shed. Used lantern fuel and burnt it down."

Jeremiah nodded, wiping his eyes with the heels of his hands. "That was good thinking." He dropped his hands from his face, but he didn't look up. "And Garrett?" he asked.

Deacon winced, but he answered. "Dead."

Jeremiah nodded again. "Anybody else know?"

"No. Thought you should hear it first."

Jeremiah stood. He walked slowly across the room to where Deacon sat. He put his hand on his shoulder and looked into his eyes. "I'm sorry you had to see all that, son. I know a thing like that can't ever be forgot."

Deacon shrugged, although the gesture didn't seem as casual as normal. It was stiff and awkward and seemed to be more a matter of him having no idea how else to respond.

"I'm grateful you made it home safe," Jeremiah said. Deacon ducked his head as he always did when confronted by anything so personal. "You're family, too, whether you admit it or not. I love you like I love my own sons. I'm glad to have you home."

Deacon didn't speak. The slightest nod of his head was the only indication he'd heard at all, but Jeremiah seemed to take it in stride. He clapped Deacon on the shoulder once. "I have to go tell Dante and Jay."

The silence in the kitchen felt strained and tense. Deacon still stared at the floor. Olsa was watching him closely with her spooky white eyes.

"Tell me what happened, boy," she said suddenly. "I see the confusion. You want to ask but you're afraid of the answers."

"We got there just before supper time," Deacon told her. "Debated how much we could do for the animals. Whether or not we could bury the bodies. There wasn't much time." He shook his head. "Spent the last of the daylight trying to get the generator running. Never could, though. Gears were locked up tight. Jammed in the hub too, I think." He stopped again, taking a deep breath and looking up at Olsa. "We ran out of light."

She leaned across the table, her long wooden spoon in her hand. Her sightless eyes seemed to burn into Deacon. "What happened?" Her manner was strange. It wasn't concern for Deacon or idle curiosity. There was an urgency to her question, a feverish excitement that seemed out of place.

"The wraiths came," Deacon said. "Couldn't see nothing different to know they was there. But it got cold, real fast. Garrett was shivering, then all of a sudden he started gasping. Like he could breathe, but only barely. Turning blue." His voice started to shake and he looked down at the table. "I didn't know what to do. I held him and I talked to him. But it was like his lungs quit holding air." He fell silent. Still Olsa's piercing stare was on him.

Aren had to force himself to breathe. "Why?" he asked Deacon, speaking for the first time since Deacon's homecoming. Deacon looked over at him, his eyes wary. "Why did the wraiths take him but not you?"

"I don't know," Deacon said.

"Liar!" Olsa snapped. Her spoon came down hard on the back of Deacon's hand. "You know why!"

"No, Olsa," he started to say, but she wasn't listening.

She darted around the counter with surprising speed. "Liar!" She smacked him hard across the shoulders with her spoon. "What does it take?" she asked, as she hit him again. "When will you admit it?"

"Olsa, stop!" he said, trying to block her blows, but she was quick and her spoon landed on his other shoulder.

"It's in your blood!" she said. "I've been telling you your whole life, and you refuse to believe."

"There's no way of knowing that Ezriel wasn't my father."

"Bull dung!" She stopped smacking him with the spoon and pointed it at him instead. "I knew the day your momma birthed you that there weren't a drop of Pane blood in you! The mark on her arm would have stopped his seed!"

"Folk tales!"

She smacked him again. "Isn't the fact the wraiths left you proof enough?"

Aren sat watching in stunned silence. Pane blood? Who was Ezriel?

But it seemed there would be no more answers tonight. Deacon stood up from the table. "It don't matter," he said. He walked out of the door and into the courtyard without a backwards glance.

Still Aren sat, staring at Olsa in shock. He wondered if she'd explain. He was about to ask, but she sighed and turned away. "Better get going," she said to him over her shoulder. "He needs you right now more than you need your answers."

Chapter Twenty-One

Aren found Deacon sitting on his porch steps, his hat off and his head in his hands.

"Please don't ask me right now," Deacon said when Aren stopped next to him. "You can have Olsa tell you. I don't care if you know. But I can't tell you right now."

Aren put his hand on Deacon's head, tracing his fingers over his black hair. "All right," he said, and Deacon sighed with relief. Aren was curious, but he'd known even before Deacon spoke that this wasn't the night for him to ask. Deacon had plenty of other things to worry about without also having his lover make demands of him.

Deacon reached up and took Aren's hand. He looked up at him. "You're the only one, Aren."

"What do you mean?"

"The only one not asking me for something every blessed hour of the day."

Aren didn't think that was true. He was sure he relied on Deacon as much as everybody else at the BarChi—

maybe more—but just as it wasn't the time for asking questions, it wasn't the time for arguing, either.

"Come inside," he said.

Deacon nodded, releasing Aren's hand. He picked up his hat and stood up. "I told Frances to bring Simon here."

Aren couldn't help but be disappointed that it wasn't his turn yet, but he understood. Simon and Garrett had been riding together for years. He had a right to hear firsthand what had happened. Simon and Frances arrived a few minutes later. Frances hung back, standing against the wall as if he felt out of place. Simon took the drink Aren offered him and sat down in the wooden chair to face Deacon.

"He's dead?" he asked, without preamble.

Deacon nodded. "Yup."

Simon sighed, rubbing his forehead with his hand. "What happened?"

And so, for the second time in an hour, Deacon told his tale of the Austin ranch—of the starving cattle and the corpse-filled house and the generator that had run dry. His voice was worn and gravelly, and Aren could tell just listening to him that he was exhausted.

"I tried to help him," he finished. "But there was nothing I could do."

Simon nodded. "Anybody else, I might doubt, but I know you'd not let a man die if there was a way to stop it." He swallowed his whisky and sat staring down into the empty glass. He didn't seem to be in shock. He was...resigned. Oestend was a hard place. That was what he'd told Frances, and Aren suspected Simon had known it was only a matter of time before something happened to one of them.

He stood up. "Thanks for telling me before the others," he said.

Deacon only nodded.

Simon put his empty glass down on the table on his way out of the room. Frances, whose glass was still full, left his behind as well. Aren followed them to the door, closing it behind them. He watched through the cloudy glass next to the door as they stopped on the porch. Frances said something to Simon, and Simon nodded. He ducked his head, covering his eyes with his hand, and Frances waited.

They'd been growing closer since Miron's death. Aren had noticed many times the way Frances' eyes seemed to always follow Simon. He wondered if they were lovers. But even as he wondered, he saw Frances reach out to touch Simon. He saw the boy's hesitancy, and the way he stopped short, pulling his hand back before he made contact.

Not lovers. Not yet, at least.

Aren found Deacon pouring more whisky into his glass, studiously not looking at him.

"Are you all right?" Aren asked him.

"I'm alive."

"It must have been awful," Aren said. "All that death."

Deacon was silent for a moment. He kept his back to Aren. He seemed to be studying the wood grain of the table in front of him. "I've seen a lot of death before," he said. "Had men die in my arms before, too. But nothing like Garrett. Knowing it was a wraith—it wasn't that he was injured and bleeding—but a thing. And yet, I couldn't see it. I couldn't touch it. Definitely couldn't fight it." He shook his head. "Seems like there should have been something I could do, besides sit there and watch him die."

"Nobody blames you."

"They should blame me. I blame me."

"There was nothing you could do."

"That ain't the point!" Deacon snapped. "I'm in charge of the men. And I got one killed. Get men killed all the time. It's part of the job, but I'm the one who chooses which men go and which men stay. Lost track of the number of men I've seen die and every one of them was following my orders when he did it." He downed his glass of whisky in one gulp and slammed his empty glass down. "Having everybody tell me it ain't my fault don't make me feel any better."

"People die." Aren thought of the lecture Simon had given Frances after Miron's death. "Sometimes things are just accidents. Like with Frances and the bull."

"Exactly," Deacon said. "Like Frances and the bull. Why do you think I knocked his ass in the dirt?"

It was such a strange comment for him to make. Aren had to stop and wonder, first about why he'd said it, then about the question itself. Why had Deacon done that? To establish discipline? Or was there more to it? Did he somehow think the punishment would make the guilt easier to bear?

And suddenly, Aren knew what to do.

"Deacon," he said, and this time, he didn't say it gently. He took all the sympathy out of his voice. He tried to sound absolutely sure of himself. He needed to be commanding. "I want you to go upstairs and take off your clothes."

Deacon froze. He didn't turn to face Aren. "Don't think I'm really in the mood for sex."

"I didn't say anything about sex, and it's not open for debate. I gave you an order. Go upstairs. Take off your clothes. And wait."

Deacon hesitated and Aren wondered if he'd misjudged. He wished he could see Deacon's face. But then he saw something that was almost as good—he saw the way Deacon's shoulders fell. He saw how the tension suddenly went out of him. Deacon picked up the whisky Frances had left behind and swallowed it, then he set the glass down and walked out of the living room and up the stairs.

Once he was gone, Aren went to the bar and poured himself a drink with shaking hands. He didn't know if what he had planned was a good idea or not, but it was the only plan he had. He slowly drank the whisky, giving Deacon time to undress, giving him time to wonder, and giving himself time to find the resolve he feared he would need.

* * * *

Aren went slowly up to the bedroom. Deacon had done as he was told. He stood in the centre of the room, naked, his head down. He'd unbound his long hair, and it hung around his face. Aren could almost see the mantle of grief and guilt weighing him down. He wanted more than anything to simply comfort him. But Deacon wasn't the type of man who could accept comfort.

Punishment, though. That he could accept. And Aren knew now why Olsa had given him the riding crop.

"Get down on your knees," he said to Deacon, and Deacon did. Aren grabbed the small ottoman from the corner of the room, knocking his pile of laundry off it as he did. He moved it in front of Deacon.

"Bend over it," he said.

Deacon looked troubled. He looked unsure, but he obeyed. He leaned over the ottoman as he was told.

The rope Deacon had brought him the night before he'd left was still on his bedside table, and Aren used it to tie Deacon's wrists to the legs of the ottoman. It was a small piece of furniture. It fitted under Deacon's chest, allowing him to rest on it rather than holding himself up with his arms, but it ended at the bottom of his rib cage, leaving his stomach and groin accessible—a point which Aren made note of for future use. Deacon looked unbelievably sexy bent over the ottoman, his naked ass sticking out at Aren.

But this wasn't about sex.

"You let Garrett die," Aren said as he picked up the riding crop.

"Yes."

"You tried to save him—"

"Yes."

"But you failed."

"Yes."

"Do you think you should be punished?"

Deacon looked up at him in surprise, although he had to crane his neck to do so. It seemed he was only now beginning to see where Aren was going.

"I said, *do you think you should be punished?*" Aren asked.

And he knew he wasn't imagining the relief he saw in Deacon's eyes. "Yes," Deacon said, relaxing onto the ottoman with a sigh. "I want to be punished."

Aren didn't allow himself to hesitate. He brought the crop down on Deacon's back.

It wasn't a hard blow. He pulled it at the last minute despite himself, but he imagined it still had to sting. He heard Deacon's breath hiss out between his teeth. Aren's hand was shaking. Seeing Deacon's gorgeous, naked body bent over the ottoman was undeniably arousing, but Aren wasn't sure how he felt about deliberately causing him pain.

"More?" he asked, wishing his voice didn't shake so much, half-hoping Deacon would say no.

A moment of hesitation, then Deacon said, "Yes."

Aren was glad Deacon couldn't see how his hand shook as he raised the crop. He brought it down on Deacon's back again.

Deacon tensed when the crop hit him, but only a heartbeat later he relaxed. "More," he said and Aren obliged. Red welts were forming on Deacon's back, and Aren began to wonder if the crop had been a very bad idea. "More!"

Aren smacked Deacon with the crop again.

"Blessed Saints," Deacon said. But this time, his voice was different. This time, Aren heard the stress. He heard the way the words strained to hold back the emotion behind them. He could almost feel the weight of what lay on the other side, waiting for the dam to burst.

He hit Deacon again.

"I killed him," Deacon said.

Aren hit him again.

"I let him die!"

Aren hit him again.

"I let all of them die!"

And again.

"Oh, Saints, Aren," Deacon cried and his voice broke. "Why does it have to be me? Why does it *always* have to be me?"

Aren knew now they were getting close. "Because there's nobody else." Aren brought the crop down again.

"I want somebody else to do it!"

Aren's hand had stopped shaking. He was sure, now, and he brought the crop down again.

"I want it to be somebody else's fault."

"There's nobody else." Aren hit him again. "This is *your* job."

"No!" Deacon said, then he burst into tears. "I don't want it anymore!"

Aren hit him again.

"I'm so tired of it always being me."

Aren hit him again, although not quite as hard.

"I don't want men to die because of me."

"They don't," Aren said. He hit Deacon again, although only half as hard as he'd been doing before. "They die because of wraiths." He hit him again. "They die because of bulls." And again. "And they die because they're boys out here trying to be men." Again. "They die because people like the Austins get lazy and let their generator die." He hit him again. "But they *don't* die because of you." He hit him one last time, then stepped back to catch his breath.

Deacon's broad back was a mess of bright red welts. His entire body shook from the force of his sobs. So much grief, Aren wondered how he'd ever held it in at all. For what felt like ages, Aren simply let the man cry. When the flood started to abate, Aren put down the crop. He laid his hand carefully on Deacon's back. He waited, his touch soft and gentle, until he felt Deacon still.

"Men die because of your choices," Aren said, "but they live because of them too." He knelt and began to untie the ropes, freeing Deacon's hands. "You beat them into submission. You force them to respect you. Some of them may hate you for it. But no generator on this ranch will ever run dry. The wraiths can't touch the BarChi. You keep them as safe as they can be in this Saints-forsaken place."

His hands free, Deacon sat back on his heels and covered his face with his hands.

"It's your job, Deacon," he said. "*Somebody* has to do it. And there's nobody else here could do it right. If anybody else tried, even more men would die than do now."

Aren reached out, wanting to comfort Deacon, but found himself a bit distracted by the big cowboy's naked body. He trailed his fingers down Deacon's bare chest.

Deacon dropped his hands and when his gaze met Aren's, there was gratitude in his eyes, but there was something else there, too—a naked hunger that took Aren's breath away. There was something predatory about him.

"Aren," he said, his voice husky and breathless.

It took nothing more than that look to bring Aren's cock to life. He felt the ache of arousal deep in his belly. He was glad he wasn't standing, because his knees were suddenly weak. He closed his eyes, letting the sudden wave of desire carry him under. "Yes," Aren said, not knowing what he meant, not even caring what the question was.

"Oh, Saints," Deacon breathed.

Then he was on him. Aren was overwhelmed by Deacon's strength. In their times together, he'd never used it, but he used it now. He pushed Aren down, crushing his mouth with his own. His hands tore at Aren's clothes. Aren counted it as a blessing that he was able to reach the salve from where he was and spread it on Deacon's hard cock in time, because he wasn't sure Deacon would have stopped. Deacon hooked his elbow behind one of Aren's knees, pulling to angle Aren's hips up, and he pushed in.

Aren cried out, partly from pleasure and partly from pain, and his cry seemed to spur Deacon on. He slammed into Aren hard and fast, driven by something more than lust. There was some primal need that seemed to demand this of him, and Aren had no desire to fight him. It felt good to be fucked by Deacon. It felt good to be *needed* by him. Even though he was the one on his back, even though it was his body being pounded by Deacon's large cock, it felt like control. It felt empowering.

It didn't take either of them long. Deacon's big, rough hand grabbed Aren's cock, pumping hard, and Aren came, crying out as he did. Deacon slammed into him one last time, holding him tight, groaning as he spent himself.

He collapsed on top of Aren, breathing hard. "I'm sorry," he panted into Aren's neck. "Did I hurt you?"

"No." It wasn't exactly true, but pain or not, he'd enjoyed every moment of it, and he wasn't about to give Deacon more reason to feel guilt.

"Aren," Deacon tightened his arms around him and he kissed Aren's neck, suddenly gentle. "Thank you."

"For the riding crop or the sex?"

Deacon laughed. "Both."

"You're welcome." Aren rubbed his hands gently up Deacon's broad back, feeling healed scars and the newly-raised welts against his fingertips. He tangled his fingers into Deacon's thick, black hair. He felt sated and safe. All the fear and tension of worrying about Deacon while he'd been away were gone. The horrible sense of waiting while Deacon dealt with Jeremiah and Simon, of waiting for it to finally be his turn, was gone as well. Deacon was safe. Deacon needed him. Aren felt unbelievably at peace. "I'm glad you're home," he said.

"Why, Aren?" Deacon asked. Aren thought for a minute he was asking why he was glad he was home, but then he went on. "Why does it have to be me?" It wasn't guilt or a need for reassurance. It seemed to be an honest question.

"It takes somebody strong," Aren told him. "And there's nobody here even half as strong as you."

Deacon was still for a moment, thinking about that, then he kissed Aren's cheek. "That's not true," he said, smiling down at Aren. "I can think of one."

Chapter Twenty-Two

They ate breakfast together the next morning as always. Afterwards, Deacon assigned the men to their chores. Deacon had to meet with Jeremiah rather than working himself, which meant the hands were once again two men short. They also had three more horses than usual, so Aren volunteered to muck out the barn. He was still there when Deacon found him two hours later.

"You're slow," Deacon said, leaning on the stall door to watch him.

"I know." Most of the other men could do it faster than him, but it was still one less job they had to do themselves. "What were you discussing with Jeremiah?"

"Deciding when I'd go back," he said.

"To the Austin farm?" Aren asked. The thought filled him with dread. He didn't look at Deacon as he asked the question, for fear Deacon would see how much it bothered him.

"Yup. You gonna be able to keep up on the books for two ranches?"

Aren stopped what he was doing to look up at Deacon. "What do you mean?"

"Brighton was set to inherit the Austin farm, as part of Shay's dowry. Now the whole family's gone. Good land up there. Cattle and horses. Nobody else'll bother to claim it."

"You're saying Jeremiah now owns it, too?"

"Now he has one ranch for each son he's got left. Just have to get the generator going so he can start getting that one back on its feet."

Aren thought about that. He thought about Deacon having to go back. He thought about what might happen if he couldn't get the generator fixed before nightfall.

"Will you tell me now what Olsa meant about the wraiths not taking you?"

Deacon sighed, pushing his hat back to rub his forehead. He looked down at the ground, scuffing his boot in the straw. "It's just folk tales."

"Then tell me the folk tales."

Deacon glanced up at him, smiling. "Should've known you'd say that." Aren laughed as he turned back to his work, and Deacon took a deep breath and started to talk. "The Old People—well, first I should tell you, they don't call themselves that. They're called the Ainuai. And there ain't too many of them left. Olsa's the only full-blood one I know of."

Aren wondered why Deacon didn't count himself, but he didn't want to interrupt. That question would have to wait.

"When the settlers first came, the Ainuai tried to be friends but things went bad fast. Now, you ask any good

Lansteader, he'll tell you nothing happened that hasn't happened in a hundred other places. He'll tell you the Ainuai were uncivilised and naïve. He'll tell you the settlers tried to help them and educate them. Gave them jobs and such. The descendants of the Ainuai will tell you different. They'll say they was all but exterminated. Men was killed. Women taken. Survivors, which was mostly just kids, were put up for auction as slaves. It was a bloody time."

Aren had stopped shovelling, stunned by Deacon's words. "I've never heard any of that."

"'Course you haven't. Don't think those people at your fancy Lanstead school ever stopped to ask the Ainuai how they felt about it."

It made Aren ashamed, even though there was nothing he could have done about any of it. "Go on," he said.

"Well, towards the end, when the warriors was all but gone, the ones who was left got together. And they sang a song to the ancestors. They made marks on their skin to block them from the path to the sacred land. They promised to forsake their souls for the right to take vengeance on their enemy."

"The settlers?"

"Yup."

"So you're telling me the wraiths are actually the damned souls of your ancestors?"

Deacon's cheeks turned red. He ducked his head, pushing his hat down low. "Of Olsa's ancestors, yes."

"And the wraiths don't kill Annia—" He stumbled on the unfamiliar word. His tongue didn't even want to form the sounds.

"The Ainuai," Deacon said. "Right. They don't harm their own."

"And that's why they didn't harm you?"

"I don't know!" Deacon said with obvious annoyance. "Like I said, it's just folk tales!"

"But—"

"My ma was Ainuai. But nobody knows who my father is. No matter what Olsa says. No matter what Jeremiah says. Nobody knows for sure."

"Why else would the wraiths have taken Garrett and left you?"

Deacon shrugged. "No telling. But it ain't the first time it's happened. There've been men caught out in the dark on cattle drives, and some were taken and some weren't, and every one of them was as light-skinned as you."

Aren thought about that. He thought back on the story Simon had told Frances. "Simon said that once Garrett walked right through the night to the outhouse. The men he was with were killed, but he wasn't touched."

"Exactly," Deacon said, seemingly relieved that Aren understood. "Just 'cause they left me once don't mean they'll do it again."

Aren went back to shovelling straw and manure so he'd have an excuse to look away before asking his next question. "Is there any chance somebody else can go?"

"I guess they could," Deacon said, "but I'm the one knows what needs to be done." Aren heard Deacon's footsteps on the floor of the barn as he came up behind him. He wrapped his arms around Aren from behind and buried his face in Aren's neck. "Hey," he said quietly, "when was the last time you had a bath?"

Aren laughed. "Way too long ago. Why? You telling me I need one?"

"I know I do," Deacon said. "There's a great spot in the river on the far side of the south pasture." One of his hands slid down Aren's stomach to graze his groin, and Aren's breath caught. The idea of bathing together was undeniably arousing. "What do you say?"

"Shouldn't I finish this first?"

"Yes," Deacon said. He reached around Aren and tried to take the pitchfork from his hand. "But it'll take you all blessed day."

"You don't need to do my work for me," Aren protested, refusing to let go of the handle. He hated Deacon to think he was weaker than the other men.

"I know I don't," Deacon said as his lips brushed the back of Aren's neck, "but we'll get to the river a lot sooner this way."

Aren laughed despite himself. "Fair point." He let go of the pitchfork and turned to look up at Deacon. "I can meet you there before supper?"

"I'll be there."

Aren didn't mind leaving the barn behind, but as he walked out of the door, he wondered what he'd do in the hours before he was to meet Deacon. He was caught up with Jeremiah's books. He could paint, but he knew there was other work to be done. Garrett had been one of the few hands who did more than his share of the work. Ronin and Simon were the only men who were as good as he had been, and grief had stolen some of Simon's energy. Aren knew the man would find his feet again eventually, but until he did, it felt like they'd lost three hands rather than one.

After the gloom of the barn, the warm sunlight that bathed his face seemed unusually bright. The wind was blowing as it ever did, and the long grass swished and rustled like a song. The breeze came from the south and was warmer than usual. It smelt sweet, and Aren breathed deep, savouring the feeling of liberation that Oestend stirred in him. It still caught him by surprise every so often.

Aren heard laughter and the unmistakable sound of an axe on wood coming from the side of the barn. He had no desire to go back inside on such a glorious day. He rounded the corner to find Ronin and Sawyer chopping wood. Red was probably supposed to be gathering the split pieces and carrying them to the shelter that kept the BarChi's firewood dry. Instead, he was leaning against the side of the barn, watching his brother and Sawyer work.

"Looky here!" Red said when his eyes landed on Aren. "It's the city boy!"

Aren laughed. The twins had been more friendly towards him since the incident with the bull. Ronin was actually polite. Red, on the other hand, liked to goad him, but Aren had realised it was meant to be friendly. He wasn't exactly sure when or why the twins had decided to be nice to him, but he certainly didn't mind.

"You guys need a hand?" Aren asked, eyeing the pile of wood that Red still hadn't carried to the pile.

"Not from you," Sawyer said.

Aren turned to him in surprise, but Ronin laughed. "Don't listen to him, Aren," he said. "He's had his knickers in a knot all blessed day." He turned to look at Sawyer. "What's your problem, anyway?"

Sawyer didn't answer, but Red did. "I think that cow he favours finally kicked him when he tried to sneak up behind her," he said, and he and Ronin laughed. Sawyer's cheeks turned red and his jaw clenched. Aren felt himself blushing at the crude joke and was glad the twins were too engrossed in ribbing Sawyer to notice.

"Not like it's big enough she'd notice when you slipped it in," Ronin said. "Must have been you slapping her on the ass when you came that did it."

Aren's cheeks burnt hotter than before. Red, who was standing next to Aren, was doubled over with laughter. Sawyer drove his axe through a log with a muffled curse, which only caused the twins to laugh harder. Aren tried to will the blush away from his cheeks, wondering if he'd lose what respect he'd managed to earn from Red and Ronin if he simply walked away.

He looked away from Ronin, who was still laughing, and Sawyer, who was still furiously chopping wood, and he saw what nobody else did — Dante, who had just rounded the corner of the barn and was walking up to them, his face livid, and his strides long and determined.

Ronin and Sawyer had their backs to him, but next to Aren, Red said, "Speaking of somebody whose knickers are in a knot."

Ronin and Sawyer barely had time to turn before Dante reached them.

"What's up?" Ronin asked Dante, still smiling.

Dante didn't answer. He raised his right hand and Aren's heart skipped a beat when he saw the gun in it.

Boom!

The barrel of the gun had been a mere inch from Sawyer's forehead. His head jerked back. The back of his skull exploded in a mess of blood and tissue. Next to Aren, Red's face was a mask of surprise as he was splattered with gore. There was a dull thud as Sawyer's lifeless body hit the ground.

"Mother fuck!" Ronin swore. Red was cursing and spitting, trying to wipe the mess from his face and neck.

Deacon rounded the corner of the barn at a run. He stopped short, his eyes quickly taking in the scene—Ronin and Dante standing over the body, Red cursing, and Aren standing in numb shock. "What happened?" Deacon asked. His voice wasn't normal. It was far shakier than usual.

"Same thing that always happens," Dante said. He didn't even look at Deacon. He turned and walked towards the house, the gun at his side.

Deacon took a deep breath as if to steady himself, and Aren wondered if he was the only one who noticed how much the shooting had shaken him.

"Red," Deacon finally said, "all you're doing is making it worse. You'll need water."

Aren glanced at Red and felt his bile rise. The man's face was covered in blood. His attempts to wipe it away had only smeared it further. Aren looked quickly away, willing his stomach to behave. He didn't want to be the one man who retched.

"Ronin," Deacon went on, "start digging the grave."

"You got it, boss."

Red and Ronin walked away, both shaking their heads. Once they were gone, Deacon leant back against the side of the barn. He covered his face with his hands, and as he did, Aren saw how they shook.

"Are you all right?" Aren asked. He was surprised that Sawyer's death would rattle Deacon so much.

"I thought it was going to be you," Deacon said, his voice muffled by his hands. "You walked out of the barn door, then I saw Dante walk by and I heard the shot..." He leaned over and put his hands on his knees, as if he was about to be sick. "I thought for sure I was going to find you lying in the dirt."

"I haven't been rolling with Daisy," Aren said. "He has no reason to hate me."

Deacon laughed shakily, standing up straight again to look at Aren. "You're giving him too much credit. He ain't always rational." He reached out and grabbed Aren's arm to pull him closer. He put his hand behind Aren's neck and put his lips against Aren's forehead. "Blessed Saints," he whispered, "you have no idea how scared I was."

Was it horrible to feel a small rush of joy at Deacon's words while a man lay dead on the ground behind him? Aren wasn't sure.

People were coming from the house. The barn blocked them from sight, but Aren could hear their footsteps against the hard earth as they ran across the courtyard. Deacon apparently heard them, too, because he let Aren go, stepping away from him, turning to face Jay, Daisy and Tama as they came around the corner.

"It's Sawyer," Deacon said, and Aren saw that the big cowboy's eyes were dead on Daisy as he said it. The woman barely flinched.

Tama also turned to look at Daisy, but whether it was disgust or pity or condemnation in her eyes, Aren wasn't sure. She turned quickly away and headed back to the house.

"I sent Ronin to start digging the hole," Deacon said to Jay. "Get done quicker if you help him."

Jay nodded, his gaze still lingering on the body on the ground. "No problem." He turned and followed his wife.

Only Deacon, Aren and Daisy were left. Deacon turned to Aren. "See you before supper?" he asked quietly. "Where we said?"

"Yes," Aren said. He found it hard to believe their conversation about a bath had been only minutes before. It felt as if ages had passed since they'd been standing in the barn together. Aren had no great love for Sawyer, but he'd rarely seen death close up.

"You all right?" Deacon asked him.

Aren shook himself, trying to find his footing. He looked down at the body, only a few feet away. Sawyer's eyes and mouth were both open, a look of mute horror frozen on his face. Although his head lay in a giant pool of blood, from the front there was only a small, red hole to testify to the means of his death.

"Aren?" Deacon asked.

"Yes!" Aren said, tearing his gaze away. He forced himself to look at Deacon. Deacon, who was alive and warm and who had come running for fear it would be Aren he'd find on the ground with the hole in his head. Deacon, who seemed to care about him in a way nobody ever had before. "I'm fine," Aren said, and as he said the words, he knew they were true. "I'll see you at the river."

Deacon hesitated for a moment, watching Aren as if trying to determine whether or not he was lying. Finally, he nodded and walked away.

Aren watched him go. Next to him, he heard a sniffle. He turned to find Daisy looking down at the body. There were tears on her cheeks, but if she was racked by grief or guilt, there was no hint of it in her manner.

"Did you love him?" Aren asked.

Her head snapped up. She looked at him for a moment as if she'd forgotten he was there—as if she had no idea who he was—then she shook her head. "No," she said. "He was a means to an end."

Her cold detachment caused anger to stir in his breast. "To *this* end?" he asked. "Is this what you wanted?"

"Of course not," she said. "I had no reason to want him dead."

"But knowing it could end this way wasn't enough to stop you from fucking him." It was more a statement than a question.

Her gaze on him was level and although she looked sad, there was no apology in it. "Have you ever loved someone who didn't love you back?"

Had he? Aren wasn't sure himself. At one point, he'd thought he loved Dean Birmingham. He'd hoped Dean loved him, too. Now, in hindsight, he wasn't sure he'd been correct on either count. "No," he told her.

"Wait until you have before you judge me."

Chapter Twenty-Three

Sawyer was already in the ground by the time Aren met Deacon for a bath. The river water was too cold to stay in for long, and certainly too cold to allow proper functioning of critical body parts, but despite the horror of the day—or maybe because of it—they had fun. Deacon unbraided his hair and they washed each other as quickly as they could. They should have climbed out of the pool then, but instead they played like boys, dunking each other until they heard the supper bell in the distance, calling them home. They dried off as well as they could while shivering, and finally walked back to the kitchen for supper.

After eating, they went to Aren's house and Aren went upstairs for his comb while Deacon stoked the fire. Aren got on his knees on the cowhide behind Deacon. His own hair had long since dried, but Deacon's thick, black hair was still slightly damp, and Aren combed it until it shone.

"I'll make a mess of it if I try to braid it," he said.

"I'll do it tomorrow." Deacon turned to look at him, his head cocked to one side, seemingly lost in thought. "Don't think I've ever been so scared in my life as I was today," he said finally. Aren felt himself blush. He wasn't sure how to respond, but Deacon wasn't finished yet. "You're really all right?" he asked. "You seemed sort of freaked out at the time."

"I was," Aren said. "I've never seen anyone killed like that before. Only Miron, and there was so much else going on that day..."

"Most men get sick first time."

"It was a close call for a minute there," Aren confessed.

Deacon continued to look at him, his eyes thoughtful. "Can't believe how wrong I was about you when you first got here." He shook his head. "When I picked you up at the inn the first day, I thought, 'This one won't last a month.'"

"I wasn't so sure myself." Aren thought about that night at the inn, how he'd wondered if he'd made a mistake in coming to Oestend. He never wondered anymore. He knew he was finally where he was supposed to be. "You think I'll make it another month?" he teased Deacon.

Deacon smiled. "If you want to, you will. You're damn stubborn." Aren laughed but Deacon's eyes were serious. "You're different now, you know."

"Different how?"

Deacon shrugged. "Lots of ways. You even look different."

"I do?"

Now it was Deacon's turn to laugh. "Don't you have a glass here?"

"No." Mirrors were expensive. He'd long since learnt to shave without one.

Deacon reached over and took Aren's hand. "When you first came here you were pale." He ran his fingertips up Aren's arm, from his wrist to his shoulder, raising goosebumps and making Aren shiver. "Now you're kind of golden." He looked up into Aren's eyes. His cheeks were red, his eyes shy, but he kept talking. "Your hair was sort of not-quite-brown and not-quite-blond." He reached up and ran his fingers through Aren's curls. "Now it's lighter. And when the sun shines on it, it's almost red."

"It is?" Aren asked, reaching up instinctively to feel his hair, as if it would somehow feel any different.

"You were kind of skinny," Deacon went on. "But the ranch has made you strong." His finger brushed over Aren's cheeks. "It's made you beautiful."

Aren didn't feel strong. He certainly didn't feel beautiful. But when he looked into Deacon's eyes, he knew the big ranch hand meant every word he was saying.

"And," Deacon went on, "when you came here, it seemed like you swung back and forth between being sad and being pissed at everyone you saw. But now?" His thumb brushed Aren's lips and Aren smiled. Deacon smiled back. "Now you seem happy."

"I am," Aren said and he meant it. Never in his life had he felt so much joy just waking up each day. "The BarChi makes me happy." *You make me happy.*

He leaned near and brushed his lips over Deacon's and Deacon pulled him close and kissed him, his strong arms wrapping around him and holding him tight. Aren pushed him backwards onto the rug, kissing him harder. He ground himself against Deacon's hard body and was thrilled at the feel of Deacon's cock quickly growing hard against him.

He broke their kiss, breathless already, and looked down into Deacon's dark eyes.

"Do you trust me?" he asked.

"Yes." No hesitation. No hint of doubt in his eyes.

"Would you let me tie you down again?"

Deacon's eyes closed and his breath caught. He moaned, gripping Aren's ass with both hands and grinding his erection against him. When he opened his eyes again, Aren could see naked desire burning in them. "Yes," he said, his voice husky. "*Please.*"

The sheer need Aren heard behind that one word thrilled him. It made his cock ache. It made his heart pound. He rolled off Deacon and stood up. "Let's go upstairs."

They stopped first to start the generator for the night, then Aren followed Deacon up the stairs. Watching Deacon's firm ass in front of him, Aren couldn't help but wonder if tonight he'd be able to fuck him. The idea thrilled him, yet not as much as he'd anticipated. What he really wanted was to tie Deacon down and make him come undone. He wanted to tease him until the big cowboy couldn't stand it anymore. He wanted to make Deacon come so hard he saw stars.

"Get undressed," he told Deacon once they were in the bedroom. He watched as Deacon obeyed. He still found Deacon's body amazing—his dark, scarred skin and hard, bulging muscles. He ran his fingers down Deacon's broad chest.

"Shall I tie you to the bed?" Aren asked, "On your back, like before?"

"Yes," Deacon said.

"Or should I leave you standing and tie you spread eagled at the foot of the bed?"

"Yes," Deacon said again.

"Or should I order you to your knees and tie you over the ottoman like I did the other day?"

And this time, he heard Deacon's sharp intake of breath. It was almost a moan when he answered, "Yes."

Aren used his foot to push the stool in front of Deacon, and Deacon immediately got to his knees.

"Wait," Aren said, before he bent over it. He got to his knees behind Deacon, his stomach against the big man's back. He ran his hands down Deacon's broad shoulders. He caressed his back, feeling the taut muscles under his fingers. He kissed his spine, loving the way Deacon's breathing became heavier as he did. He slid his hand over Deacon's hip, reaching around him to grip his large, hard cock in his hand. Deacon moaned as Aren started to stroke him. With his other hand, he explored Deacon's chest and stomach. "Last as long as you can," he said as he did. "You tell me when you get too close, so I can pull back."

Deacon moaned again, but he nodded.

"Good." He stopped stroking, and smiled when Deacon groaned in frustration. "Don't worry," he said. "I'm not even close to being done."

He stood up again and grabbed the rope, which was still lying on the floor from the last time he'd used it. "Bend over the stool," he said, and Deacon did.

Aren went to his armoire and pulled out an old, black shirt. The ghost had ripped it weeks before, making it useless as anything but a rag. Aren tore strips from it and used them to wrap Deacon's wrists before tying them to the legs of the ottoman. When he'd finished, he moved behind him again. Deacon's ass was a perfect invitation in front of him. Aren's cock strained against his pants as he gripped Deacon's cheeks and spread them wide. He saw the way Deacon's entrance tensed, but he also noted the way his breathing sped up.

Aren leaned over and touched his tongue to the soft flesh between Deacon's legs. He started low, moving slowly up Deacon's crack, and when he reached his entrance, Deacon gasped. He tensed, but Aren kept his tongue moving in slow, soft circles.

"Oh," Deacon said, almost a whimper, and under his tongue, Aren felt the muscles of his rim start to relax.

He kept his tongue moving, teasing around and around Deacon's opening. He couldn't believe how turned on he was. He longed to do more. He wanted to spread Deacon's cheeks and push his tongue deep inside, but he wasn't sure Deacon was ready for that. Instead, he reached between Deacon's legs and started to stroke his cock. The folds of his foreskin were wet, and Aren slid it backwards, brushing Deacon's tip with his fingers. The low moan that escaped Deacon's throat went straight to Aren's groin. He'd told Deacon to last as long as he could, and now Aren found he was the one who might not be able to last.

He pulled away from Deacon and the big cowboy groaned again, in frustration. Aren smacked him playfully on the ass as he stood up and was surprised that his slap caused a moan, too. "Hold on," Aren told him. "I'm not even undressed yet."

"What the blessed hell are you waiting for?" Deacon asked breathlessly, and Aren laughed as he took off his clothes. Only an hour before, he might have felt inadequate next to Deacon, but he found he didn't now. Deacon was right. The ranch had made him strong—not huge and hard like Deacon or Simon or some of the other men—but strong enough. And even if he didn't quite believe he was beautiful, he believed Deacon thought he was. That was more than enough.

"What should I do to you now?" Aren asked.

"Anything," Deacon said. "Everything."

"Should I fuck you?"

"Yes."

"Should I make you suck me?"

"Yes."

"Should I punish you again?"

And just as before, he heard the heartbeat of hesitation as Deacon thought about that, and the quiver of anticipation in his voice as he said, "Yes."

Aren hadn't actually expected that, but he grabbed the crop. It wasn't like before. This was purely sexual, and while it seemed Deacon was asking for pain, Aren didn't want to go too far. He tapped the end of the crop against Deacon's ass and heard Deacon's breath catch. "Yes," he said again, his voice low and husky.

Aren brought the crop down. Not across Deacon's back this time, but across the firm round globes of his ass. Not as hard as he could, by any means, but hard enough that a red mark formed beneath it. Deacon gasped, straining against his ties, then collapsed against the ottoman with a moan. Aren smacked him again.

"Holy Saints," Deacon breathed. He was writhing, squirming, bucking his hips, and Aren knew he was trying to find a way to rub his hard cock against the ottoman.

"Do you like that?" Aren asked him.

"Yes!"

Aren smacked him again.

Deacon gasped, arching his back. He held his breath for just a moment, and when he let it go, it came out a moan.

"It hurts right at first," he said breathlessly, "but then it changes."

Aren smacked him again, and again Deacon's gasp of pain trailed away into a deep-throated moan. He tried again to push his hips towards the ottoman, but he couldn't reach. Aren loved to watch him — the way the muscles in his back bunched and relaxed, and the motion of his ass as he strived to find some release. When he'd used the crop before it had been different, but this time he found it unbelievably arousing.

Aren hit him again.

Deacon arched again at the pain, but his breathing was heavy, his hips still moving as he fought to rub his cock against something. Aren reached down with his free hand and gripped his own cock, gasping at the pleasure of it. As he stroked himself, he hit Deacon with the crop again.

"Aren," Deacon cried, and the sheer desperation in his voice made Aren's legs go weak. He fell to his knees in front of Deacon, grabbing his head, pulling desperately on his hair, and Deacon knew what he wanted. He opened his mouth and Aren drove his cock inside.

He almost came. After the intensity of their foreplay, having Deacon's warm mouth around his aching cock was almost more than he could bear. He held Deacon's head against his pubic bone, frozen with his cock deep inside Deacon's mouth. He forced himself to wait there until the urge to climax abated. He made himself take three deep breaths. When he had control of himself again, he began to thrust into Deacon's mouth. He closed his eyes and gave himself to the sheer relief of that warm, wet heaven. He held on to Deacon's hair. He listened to his lover's laboured breath. His hips moved faster as he drove in and out of Deacon's mouth. He wasn't sure anything had ever felt so good.

A moan from Deacon brought him back from the brink. He forced himself to slow down. He tamed the urgency of his thrusts. He looked down at Deacon's broad, scarred back. He eyed the globes of his ass, now streaked with red welts.

The relief he found in Deacon's mouth was exquisite, but he didn't want to finish quite yet.

"Stop," he said, pulling back, pulling his cock from Deacon's reach.

"Please," Deacon collapsed onto the ottoman and let his head hang down between his bound arms. "Please, please, please…"

Aren ran his hands down Deacon's back. By leaning forwards, resting against Deacon's bowed head, he was able to reach his ass. He ran his finger down Deacon's crack, and Deacon's pleas came faster.

"Please, Aren, please, Aren, please…"

Aren let him go. He pushed himself to his feet, smiling at the moan of frustration it elicited from Deacon. "I need the salve," Aren told him and Deacon moaned.

He found the jar and took it with him as he knelt behind Deacon. He gripped Deacon's cheeks again, spreading them wide, and this time, Deacon didn't tense. Aren leaned over again to tongue him and was thrilled at the way his rim remained soft and inviting. He circled his rim as he'd done before, teasing at his entrance. The sounds Deacon made drove him wild. The fact that somebody so big and so strong could whimper and beg like Deacon was doing turned him on more than he could ever have expected. He lapped at Deacon's body until Deacon gasped out, "Please, Aren, *please!*"

He reached between Deacon's legs and gripped his cock. Deacon's cry was hoarse and breathless. His hips bucked as he instinctively fucked himself into Aren's fist, and as his hips came up and back, Aren let his tongue push past Deacon's rim.

"Awww!" Deacon's cry was more than a moan, less than a scream, undeniably a sound of wanting, of needing, of finally receiving, and Aren took it as an invitation. As Deacon fucked his hips up and down, sliding his cock through Aren's hand, Aren pushed his tongue as deep as he could. He used his free hand to hold Deacon's ass. His thumb pressed against Deacon's rim, opening him wider so his tongue could caress inside. Deacon writhed and squirmed and panted and whimpered in pleasure, and Aren spread him wider still, moaning against his wet flesh as he tried to reach deeper.

"Aren!" Deacon cried.

Aren knew the sound for what it was—a warning, an ultimatum, a confession, all in one—and he stopped, although it took more willpower than he would have thought he had. He let go of Deacon's cock and his ass. He leant back to watch Deacon writhe as he used the back of his hand to wipe his face.

"Aren, please," Deacon begged. "Don't stop don't stop don't stop, oh, Saints, don't stop don't stop…"

He was breathless, shaking, pleading, and it was the greatest sexual rush Aren had ever felt. All of the times he'd come, he'd been fucked, he'd been used, he'd begged for it himself—none of them matched the thrill of being able to reduce Deacon to a state of such base, primal need.

"Aren, please, Aren, please, Aren, please, please, please…"

Aren dipped the first two fingers of his right hand in the salve, oiling them well. He moved again into position behind Deacon, sliding his left hand over Deacon's hip, down his stomach, towards his cock. His slow touch made Deacon squirm. It made his breathless words come even faster than before.

"Arenplease, Arenplease, Arenplease, oh, Saints, pleasepleaseplease..."

Aren gripped Deacon's cock with his left hand, letting his fingers play over his moist foreskin. The oiled fingers of his right hand slid slowly down Deacon's crack.

"Yes!" Deacon gasped, arching his back, pushing his hips back against Aren's hand. "Yes yes yes please please please..."

Aren's fingers found Deacon's rim.

"Yes, Aren, yes, Aren, yes..."

He applied a bit of pressure.

"Yes! Aren, yes, Aren, please, please, please..."

He pushed them inside.

"*Yes!*" Deacon bucked against him, letting Aren's fingers penetrate deeper. Deacon's pleas were replaced by a sharp cry of pleasure. He wanted it so much. Aren knew that, and he revelled in it. His own climax was bearing down on him, a pressure that could not be held at bay much longer.

Deacon had stopped begging, but only because he was too far gone to speak. There was no mistaking the urgency in his breath, the desperation as he strained against his ties, arching his back, pushing his hips back, fucking himself harder and harder onto Aren's slick fingers. His hips pumped, his cock moved through Aren's fist. Aren slid a third finger inside, and Deacon nearly screamed. The thrusting of his hips became frenzied.

He was close. There was no way Aren could hold him back now. He ground his own aching cock against Deacon's ass, pushing against his firm, tanned skin. Aren leant down against Deacon's back, letting the ottoman hold the weight of them both as Deacon bucked and arched and panted underneath him. He was wild, lost in pleasure, and Aren put his lips against Deacon's ear. "Think how good it will feel when I fuck you," he said.

"Aww!" This time, it really was a scream as Deacon finally came. Aren felt Deacon's body spasm around his fingers. He felt Deacon's warm seed spill over his other hand as Deacon shot again and again, and Aren finally let go. He rubbed against Deacon, allowing his own orgasm to crash down over him, losing all sense of everything else as he did.

He couldn't believe how good it felt. He was only rubbing against Deacon's ass—not fucking him, not being sucked by him, not even feeling his strong hand on him. But the sheer pleasure of teasing Deacon, of making him beg, of taking him to the edge and back, made him dizzy. Already, he wanted to do it again. He wanted to see how much further he could go.

When he opened his eyes, he was draped across Deacon's back. The wetness of his cum between them was sticky and growing cold, and Deacon was still trying to catch his breath. Aren pushed himself to his feet, even though his legs still shook. He found a shirt that was already dirty and used it to wipe off his hands and stomach. He knelt next to Deacon and wiped the cum off his back. The ottoman had cum on it too, no doubt, but he'd have to untie Deacon before he could worry about that. He made a mental note put a rag over it next time.

He untied Deacon's hands. Once he was free, Deacon sat back on his knees, rubbing his wrists, looking at Aren with a lazy, sated smile.

"Why didn't you?" Deacon asked.

"Why didn't I what?" Aren asked as he moved into Deacon's arms.

"Why didn't you want to fuck me?"

That was a good question. Aren wasn't sure he knew himself. Being able to fuck another man was something he'd wanted for a long time, and yet now, when it was offered, he found he liked the teasing so much more. It was something unexpected, and he smiled at the realisation that it was yet another thing about him that had been changed by the BarChi. "It's not that I didn't want to," he told Deacon. "But I *really* like hearing you beg."

Deacon smiled as he pulled him close and kissed him. "Any time you want me to beg," he said, "I will."

Chapter Twenty-Four

Their days remained unchanged — breakfast and supper together, evenings in front of the fire — but their nights began to take on a whole new meaning.

For the first time in his life, Aren found himself with a partner who not only gave him free rein, but who longed to surrender himself to Aren's control. Deacon loved submitting. He loved to be tied down, to be forced to beg, to be driven to the point where his need eclipsed all else. And Aren loved being the one who could take him there.

He liked exploring which pleasures Deacon could handle while holding his orgasm at bay, and which things drove him over the brink. The most exciting thing of all was the way small amounts of pain fed in to it. In general, Aren didn't think of Deacon as a masochist. Pain in and of itself meant nothing to him. But when he was aroused, it was different. As his need grew and he lost himself in the pleasure Aren gave him, his response to the pain became more intense. Deacon told him the pain lasted only a second, but behind it would come a rush of pleasure that was almost unbearable in its intensity.

What Aren liked best was to tease Deacon, to make him beg, to give him only as much as he could handle without exploding. He would take Deacon to the edge, ordering him as he did not to come. He would demand that Deacon hold his orgasm at bay. And when he knew that every ounce of Deacon's concentration was centred on holding back, he would use pain to give him that final nudge — his teeth on Deacon's nipple, his fingernails raking his flesh, or a sudden smack with the crop. There would be a mere heartbeat when the pain would hit Deacon, distracting him, making him gasp, drawing his attention away from his impending climax, and in the very next second, the rush of pleasure that always followed would push him over the edge, demolishing his self-control, exploding out of him with a force that often made him scream.

Aren loved making Deacon lose control. He loved watching him come undone. He found that making his lover squirm, reducing him to such a state of primal need, was the greatest aphrodisiac in the world. Knowing he had the power to give so much pleasure was the most intensely erotic thing he'd ever known.

Afterwards, Deacon would pull Aren into his arms. He would kiss him and hold him and whisper in his ear, and sometimes the intensity of his emotions would leave them both as breathless as the sex.

On Deacon's fifth night home, Aren awoke in the night. Next to him, Deacon lay wide awake and staring at the ceiling. In the cellar, the ghost was crying, great heart-wrenching sobs. Aren had long since grown used to the ghost, but he knew Deacon still found her unsettling.

There were two ways Aren could distract his lover from the sounds in the cellar, and since he was still heavy with the sated contentment of their earlier lovemaking, he opted for the second option.

"If I ask you something, will you answer?"

Deacon jumped a bit, obviously having thought Aren asleep, but then he smiled. "If I say 'no', will it stop you?"

"The first time we…" Aren stumbled, feeling his cheeks turn red, trying to decide how to finish his statement.

"Yeah, the *first time*," Deacon laughed. "I know what you mean."

"Well, you said you'd never been with another man—"

"Oh, Saints," Deacon moaned, covering his eyes with his hand, but Aren kept talking.

"You were so upset. I guess I'm surprised you got over being bothered by it so easily."

"You caught me off guard, that's all."

"That's not an answer."

"It ain't?" Deacon asked. "Felt like one to me."

Aren slid his hand across the bed and found Deacon's thigh with his fingers.

"Ouch!" Deacon yelled as Aren pinched him. "What the hell?"

"Should I get the crop?" Aren asked.

"Definitely," Deacon said, smiling. "But that won't make me answer." He was relenting, though. Aren knew him well enough by now to recognise the signs. Deacon sighed. "I wasn't freaked out so much about you being a man as about you being *you*. You're the only friend I got on this Saints-forsaken ranch, and I was sure I'd just ruined everything."

"So you've always liked men?"

"Always." He stopped for a minute, seemingly debating his next words. "I told you how when I was a boy, I lived out in the barn? And how Old Man Pane hated me?"

"You did."

"Well, when I was younger, I started fooling around with another boy. We never did much, but one day Old Man Pane caught us at it in the barn. It hadn't ever occurred to me I was doing anything unusual, but he went nuts. Tanned my ass good. Told me it was unnatural and wrong. See, he'd been alive back when the missionaries were around, talking about the Saints and the sins and what it meant to be holy. 'Course their Saints couldn't do nothing about the wraiths, so people here didn't listen much, and by the time I was growing up, the holy men had given up and gone back to the continent. But Old Man Pane believed that stuff, and he told me no damned boy was going to ruin his ranch with sin." Deacon laughed, a harsh, bitter laugh. "As if I were the only man here ever sinned." He sighed. "Anyway, after that, I started realising most men didn't do what I'd done. And Old Man Pane told me on more than one occasion that if he ever heard about me doing it again, he'd throw me to the wraiths, and I tell you what, he meant it, too." He shook his head. "Well, I guess I liked girls well enough, too, and it didn't seem to be nothing worth dying over. It wasn't like I ever *stopped* liking men, but the older I got, the easier it seemed to ignore them." He laughed. "But I sure couldn't ignore you. Half of me was thinking how getting involved with anybody on the BarChi was a bad idea, and the other half of me couldn't stop wondering what you looked like naked. I was still trying to decide which half to go with and you were already ripping my clothes off and getting down on your knees." He looked over at Aren with a smile. "Dirty way to win an argument, if you ask me."

"Saints, I hadn't had sex in months!" Aren said, laughing.

"You were damn determined."

"I guess I should have given you a chance to say yes or no before I pulled your pants down."

Deacon smiled. "No. I'm glad you didn't wait."

"But there was never anybody else?" Aren asked. "The years I was in boarding school, there was always some boy I was fucking. You lived in the barracks with all those men, and you never had a relationship with any of them?"

He knew immediately it was the question Deacon hadn't wanted him to ask. Deacon closed his eyes, wincing as if the question caused him pain. He covered his face with one hand. "Why you got to know this?" he asked.

They'd gone from laughing to serious so quickly, and Aren found he didn't really want to leave the laughter behind. "I don't," he said. He'd been curious, but he hadn't actually expected the answer to be something so upsetting to Deacon. "You don't have to answer."

Deacon scrubbed his hands over his face, but then went back to looking up at the ceiling. "There was someone," he said, his voice very quiet. "But not like you're thinking. I'd just turned twenty. Old Man Pane had died during the winter before, and Jeremiah'd taken over. He put me in charge of the hands, even though I was only a boy." He laughed sadly. "'Course, I didn't think I was a boy at the time. I thought I was man enough." He shook his head. "There was another boy there." He stopped, and it was a moment before he managed to say the next word. It was only a name.

"Cody."

It was strange how hearing it told Aren so much. On one hand, it seemed to take all of Deacon's strength to say it. He seemed to have to force it out. But at the same time, once it was spoken, there was a sense of relief about him, as if he'd cleared the highest hurdle in his memory.

"He was younger. Only eighteen. And we were young and shy and too nervous to do much." He turned to look at Aren, and Aren was pleased to see that he was smiling. "Not like you," he said, and Aren laughed. "We just kept circling each other, you know?" he said, looking again up at the dark ceiling above. "We both knew what we wanted, and we both knew we'd get there. But there was something so...fun, I guess, about playing the game." He shook his head. "I still remember how it felt to see him walk in the door—like my heart might jump out of me. Like I couldn't breathe and I couldn't stop smiling like a blessed fool.

"Back then, every look meant something. It took so much nerve just to touch him. I remember we were playing cards one time with some of the other hands, and Cody and I'd been watching each other and getting bolder. Just the way he kept smiling at me had me hard and squirming in my chair. When the others weren't looking, he reached over underneath the table and touched my leg." He shook his head again. "That's all it was, but I thought I was going to shoot my load right there at the table." He was still smiling when he said it, but there was a tightness in his voice, a feeling of heartache about him so strong, Aren knew instinctively the smiles were going to end. He slid his hand over and put it on Deacon's arm, and Deacon closed his eyes against what came next.

"I still didn't think of myself as the boss, even though I was. I didn't realise how other men would see it." He stopped, as if going on was more than he could bear. It made Aren ache for him.

"Go on," he said.

"I sent them out one day. We'd just cleared the north pasture and needed to fence it in. I sent them to dig the post holes. Cody and four other men." His voice was getting shakier. "Just past midday, one of them came running back. He was scared, I could tell, and he'd run the whole way so he could barely breathe to talk. But he grabbed me, and he pointed, and he said, 'Cody' and 'help'."

He stopped short, shaking his head. "I think that's what he said. Don't know that I remember for sure. I think I was already running."

He had to cover his face again before he went on. "They beat him so bad. Not just with their fists, either. One of them used a shovel. There was so much blood, I couldn't even see his face, and I remember thinking, 'this can't be him.' He was conscious, but he didn't know much anymore. I held him, and I know I was crying like a babe. He kept calling me Janson—and I don't know who Janson was—but he kept saying, 'do you forgive me?' and so I told him, 'I do. It's fine. You don't have to be sorry anymore.' And it was like that was all he needed to hear, and he kind of smiled. Then he just went away. I could feel the way his life drained right out of him."

He fell silent, lost in his memories, and Aren thought about how devastating it must have been for Deacon to feel as if he'd caused Cody's death. "Did they do it because you were both men?"

"No!" Deacon said, and his voice broke on the word. "You don't listen!" And even though Deacon was lashing out him, Aren couldn't find it in himself to mind. "It was because I was the boss! Whether I sent him herding or digging holes or mucking out stalls didn't matter. Those men thought I was treating him different."

"I'm sorry," Aren said. "I didn't mean to make you go through it again."

Deacon shook his head, wiping his eyes. "I don't really know what happened next. Jeremiah showed up. He sent the hands away and he sent me home. Olsa gave me some kind of tea that knocked me out cold, and when I woke up he was already in the ground. I walked back into the barracks the next day, and those men, those *boys*, were just sitting there, playing poker."

"What did you do?"

"I killed them."

It was such a frank, unapologetic statement. It took Aren a moment to process it. "You what?"

"I pulled my knife out of my boot, and I cut their throats," he said. "Got the first two quick. Third one had time to get up and run, but he didn't get out the door."

"Then what?"

Deacon shrugged, and Aren didn't know if he found it comforting or disturbing that Deacon could talk about killing the men who'd killed Cody with such calm detachment. He might only have been talking about herding cows.

"I moved back to the barn. And I never flirted with another hand again."

Aren lay there in stunned silence. He had only wanted to know more about Deacon's past. He'd never dreamt it would lead to something so horrific.

"I'm sorry," he said again.

Deacon suddenly reached over, taking Aren's hand. "I'm glad you asked. I was mad for a long time, but I think now that I let them win. 'Cause I let myself forget all the good parts. And he deserves that spot in my head more than they do."

"I'm sure he does."

They lay there in silence. Aren knew Deacon was remembering Cody—remembering the wonder and the heart-pounding excitement of first falling in love. He thought about them both, and about the happiness they should have had, for a little longer, at least. He pulled on Deacon's hand, and Deacon took his hint. He moved closer, rolling on top of Aren and looking down into his eyes.

Aren pulled him down and kissed him, soft and gentle. "I can be Cody if you want," he whispered against Deacon's lips. "I don't mind. Just for one night."

Deacon's arms tightened around him. "Maybe a little piece of you," he said. "But mostly I just want you."

Chapter Twenty-Five

The next morning, Deacon languished in bed with him, something he rarely did. He let Aren push him down onto his back, and they made love as if they'd never have another chance. When Aren was spent, he fell into Deacon's arms knowing it was the only place in the world he ever wanted to be. It was a feeling of delicious satisfaction that left him grinning and at ease.

He should have known it was too good to last.

Eventually, they dressed and wandered across the grass. The sun was out, the cool breeze from the north was lively, and Aren thought it might be the most beautiful morning he'd ever seen. They walked in comfortable silence to the kitchen. And that was where Jeremiah found them.

"You ready to go?" he asked Deacon.

Aren had no idea what he was talking about, but Deacon apparently did, because he said, "Yup." Deacon was leaving? Was he headed back to the Austin farm so soon?

"Who's going with you?"

"Just Red. He's practically worthless as a ranch hand if I'm not here to ride his ass. Figured I may as well take him along."

"You going to hire new men to replace to Garrett and Sawyer?"

"Yup."

"Good," Jeremiah said. "Travel safe."

He left only a minute later, and Aren turned to Deacon. "Where are you going?" he asked.

"To town. Didn't I tell you?"

"No!"

"Oh," Deacon said, frowning. Then his face broke into a wicked grin. "You must have been distracting me."

But Aren didn't feel like laughing about it. "When do you leave?"

"Tomorrow morning."

So soon? "Why now?" Aren asked, feeling inexplicably betrayed. "Why you? Why can't somebody else go recruit new men?"

"They could, if that was the only reason I was going, but it ain't."

"Then why?"

"You know I have to go back to the Austin ranch and get that generator running?"

"Yeah. So?"

"So," Deacon said, with slow deliberate patience, "I have to go to town to get the parts."

"Why can't you just have Red do it?"

The slight annoyance in Deacon's eyes was quickly turning to confusion. "Why you so mad?" he asked.

Aren turned to stare down into his bowl. His stomach was tied in knots. He couldn't possibly eat now. He pushed it away. "It's nothing," he said, but he knew he was lying.

The McAllen Ranch. That's why he was mad. It wasn't that Deacon was going into town. It wasn't even that he'd forgotten to mention it. It was that he'd be stopping at the McAllen Ranch, once on the way there and again on the way home, and there was no doubt in Aren's mind what Deacon would be doing while he was there.

"I'm the one who saw the generator," Deacon said. "Gears come in all sizes. Different teeth. Different size holes. I try to tell somebody else what to get, there's a one-in-a-hundred chance they get it right." He pushed his own bowl away, and Aren kept his head down, his gaze on the table in front of him, unable to meet Deacon's eyes. "Why the hell would I send somebody else when I'm the one who knows what I'll need?"

It was a valid point, Aren knew, but he hated it nonetheless.

"You done eating?" Deacon asked.

"Yes." What he'd managed to swallow felt like lead in his gut.

"You coming?" Deacon asked.

"No," Aren said, shaking his head. "You go ahead."

Deacon didn't move. Not at first. Aren could feel his eyes on him. He could feel his utter confusion, but he couldn't face him. After what felt like ages but could only have been seconds, Deacon got up and left the room.

Aren sat there, staring at the table, hating himself for caring so much.

"He can't fix it if you don't tell him what's wrong," Olsa said.

Aren didn't answer. He wasn't in the mood for her eccentric, questionable wisdom. He left the table and he walked away.

He went slowly back to his house. What had started out as a bright morning suddenly felt like a frigid day. He wrapped his jacket tightly about him against the wind and told himself over and over he was a fool. It was only sex. It had nothing to do with him. Expecting Deacon to give up women wasn't only unreasonable, it was downright childish.

No amount of self-reproach made the heart-wrenching feeling of betrayal go away.

He hung his coat on the hook inside the door and walked into the living room to find the floor covered with broken glass. The glasses he kept stacked on the bar had all been swept to the floor and shattered.

"Perfect," he muttered. "Thanks a lot, ghost." At least she'd left his whisky.

Back across the grass he went to borrow a broom and to beg extra glasses from Olsa. Once the mess was cleaned up, he stacked the ones she'd given him on the bar. He stoked his fire. He threw himself into his chair and tried not to feel sorry for himself.

He failed.

After a couple of hours, he admitted self-pity wasn't going to change anything. He made himself get up. He climbed the stairs to his studio and stood staring at the painting on his easel. It was the one of Deacon, inside the brand. Aren still didn't feel it was finished. He examined it for a while, trying to determine what it needed. Eventually, he picked up his brush and he started to paint.

He added a windmill to the background, and the shadow of a bull. He examined the barbed wire, where it dug into Deacon's dark flesh. He used the tip of his penknife to add a finer point to each and every barb. He added a drop of blood.

He wondered if he was part of the wire. Was he one of the barbs, making Deacon bleed, leaving yet another scar on his dark skin?

He intentionally went to dinner late — so late that it was closer to supper. He went ahead of the hands and sat alone at Olsa's counter. She ignored him once she'd served him, humming quietly to herself, coughing from time to time.

He forced himself to chew and swallow, even though it tasted like dirt and left his stomach feeling worse than before. He knew he had to eat or he'd be starving by bedtime. He went back home rather than eating supper with Deacon.

He knew he couldn't avoid him. Having stood him up at supper would only make Deacon more determined to find out what was wrong. As the seconds ticked by, his depression deepened. His dread grew more oppressive. He was afraid to face Deacon, yet he had no choice. Unless he was going to hide in his room, he could not avoid him any longer.

He drank a glass of whisky and waited, but when the inevitable knock came at his door, he knew he wasn't ready.

"You didn't come to supper," Deacon said as soon as Aren opened the door. It wasn't a question. It was more like an accusation.

"I don't feel well," Aren said, which was true in a way, he reasoned. It wasn't exactly a lie.

"Will you quit being ornery and tell me what's wrong?"

"Nothing's wrong," Aren said. He went to the bar and picked up a glass. He didn't pour a drink, though. The thought of more whisky made his stomach turn. He put the glass back.

"I'm sorry I forgot to tell you."

"It doesn't matter."

"Well, something's got you riled up."

If I tell you, you'll think I'm a fool. Aren stood with his arms crossed, staring at the wood grain on top of the bar.

Deacon sighed heavily. "Aren, will you look at me? Please?"

Aren had to take a deep, shaking breath to steady himself. He forced himself to turn around. Deacon's hurt confusion was clear in his eyes, and Aren hoped his own heartache wasn't as plain to see.

"I don't know what you want me to do," Deacon said. "I don't know how any of this works. I wish you'd just tell me why you're mad at me."

"I'm not," Aren said, which was partially true as well. He wasn't angry with Deacon for going into town. He wasn't even angry he'd roll with a maid on the way. What really made him angry was the fact that it made him so angry.

"You're lying," Deacon said.

Aren couldn't face him any longer. He couldn't admit how much it hurt knowing Deacon was going to share himself with somebody else. He could barely admit the entirety of it to himself, let alone to his lover. "Just go!" Aren turned away again. He put his hands on the top of the bar, bracing his weight on it, biting his lip against the lump in his throat, hoping he could keep himself together until Deacon was gone.

"Holy Saints!" Deacon swore in exasperation. Aren heard the scuff of his boots on the wood as he turned to leave, but after three steps towards the door, he stopped and came back. "Aren, I leave for town as soon as the sun's up. I don't want to leave with you angry."

As soon as the sun was up? He wasn't even waiting until after breakfast? "Why so early?" Aren asked, and no matter how hard he tried, he couldn't keep the bitterness from his voice. "You're in such a hurry to reach the McAllens'?"

Deacon's only response was silence, and Aren resisted the urge to turn around and face him. He knew whatever he saw on Deacon's face—whether it was anger or mockery or disgust—he wouldn't be able to bear it.

"So," Deacon said at last, "that's what this is about."

"What?" Aren asked, even though he knew exactly what Deacon meant.

"The McAllen farm," Deacon said, and although Aren had his back to him, he could hear Deacon's heavy footsteps as he crossed the room. "The women."

"No," Aren said. "They have nothing to do with anything." His voice betrayed him, though. He knew he didn't sound convincing.

Deacon's strong arms wrapped around him from behind. "You're lying," he whispered in Aren's ear before flicking his tongue over it.

It made Aren shiver. Being in Deacon's arms and feeling his broad, strong body against his back stirred his blood, but not enough to overcome the heaviness of his heart.

"You want me not to roll with any of the maids?"

Just the image those words brought to mind made Aren's heart clench inside his chest and tears sting behind his eyes. He couldn't help but picture Deacon's hands on some woman. His lips on her throat. He imagined Deacon whispering in her ear, telling her that she was beautiful, that she was perfect, saying all the things he said to Aren when they made love. He pictured the way Deacon looked when he was lost in pleasure, only this time it was a girl who straddled his hips. It was her name he cried as he came.

"It's none of my business," he said, although the words came out a whisper.

"Why isn't it?" Deacon asked. One rough hand pushed Aren's hair off his neck, and Aren felt his warm lips there.

"I can't tell you what to do."

Deacon chuckled throatily against Aren's neck. "You tell me what to do all the time." One strong hand travelled down Aren's stomach to stroke his half-erect cock through his pants. "Have you forgotten how much I like it?"

Aren fought to keep his mind on what he was saying and not on what Deacon was doing with his hands and mouth. "In my bedroom, yes, but this is different."

"How so?"

"It just is."

"That ain't an answer."

He hated that Deacon was pushing him. He hated that he was making him face it. Deacon nipped at his neck, and prodded him again. "Tell me why you can't order me to keep my pants tied."

"I don't own you!" Aren relented. "That's why!"

Deacon froze, his arms still around Aren and his lips still on his neck. Aren wondered if he'd somehow upset him. But only for a moment.

Deacon made a sound against his neck — something that was more growl than moan. "Is that what you think?" he asked. His hand on Aren's groin became more aggressive.

He ground himself against Aren's back. "Because I think you might be wrong. I think you do own me. I think maybe you own every single inch of me."

"No," Aren said. Or tried to, although Deacon's hand and his mouth and his body were quickly robbing him of the ability to think.

Deacon turned him around, his grip strong and his hands rough. His usual gentleness was gone. He pushed hard against Aren, grinding his erection against him, shoving Aren backwards against the bar. He bit at his neck. One of his hands squeezed Aren's ass, making him gasp.

"Do you think I let anybody else tell me what to do?" Deacon asked. His hand moved around to the ties on Aren's pants, ripping them open. "Have you ever seen me take orders from anybody but you?"

"No." Aren's eyes drifted closed. Deacon's hands felt so good. His lips felt so good. His weight as he ground against him felt like heaven.

"You think I've ever let anybody else tie me up?" Deacon asked.

"No," Aren gasped.

Deacon's hand slid inside his pants, gripping his cock hard and pumping it. Aren was sure his knees had stopped working. It was only Deacon's iron grip on him holding him up.

"Do you think I'd let any other man in the world tie me down and whip me with a crop?"

"No."

Deacon growled again. His arm tightened around Aren and he lifted him, shoving him backwards onto the bar, sweeping everything else off it as he did. The glasses Aren had begged from Olsa shattered on the floor. The whisky bottle hit the wooden planks with a thud. Deacon ignored them. He climbed on top of Aren, grinding hard against him, still stroking Aren's cock with his other hand.

"And if they did hit me with a crop, you think I'd beg them to do it again?" he asked, breathless. "You think I'd beg anybody for *anything* the way I beg you each and every night?"

Aren was beyond words. He couldn't think at all. Deacon's hand continued to move on him. His weight was solid and heavy on Aren's body, and it felt unbelievably good. Aren had had men be rough with him before. He'd had men hold him down. But always, it was so they could take. Always, it was their own pleasure they sought and even though Aren had usually been willing, to some extent at least, never had he had a man be so aggressive in order to bestow pleasure upon him. It made him breathless.

"You *do* own me, Aren," Deacon said. "Tell me what to do."

Aren knew exactly what he wanted Deacon to do. He put his hand on Deaconn's head and pushed, and Deacon went where Aren directed, down Aren's body. He moaned when he got to Aren's groin.

Aren's fingers clenched in Deacon's long hair. Deacon's warm mouth closed around him, his tongue caressing his aching erection, and Aren cried out. His back arched, and Deacon began to move up and down Aren's cock. One strong hand pushed between Aren's legs. Aren's pants were still on, only open at the fly, but he felt Deacon's fingers grab him through the thin fabric, squeezing his cheeks, pushing in between. His touch was rough, violent, almost painful, and it tipped Aren over the edge. His orgasm tore through him, taking him by surprise, taking with it all his anger and all his strength. He shot into Deacon's eager throat, again and again, and when he was done, he collapsed back on the bar, breathing hard.

Deacon loomed above him, his lips moist and red and his eyes serious. "Those maids got nothing I need," he said. "I only need you."

Aren had pulled half of Deacon's dark hair out of its queue while Deacon sucked him. He reached up and brushed the loose strands out of Deacon's face. He traced his thumb over his wet lips. "You might change your mind once you're there."

Deacon shook his head. "I won't."

Aren wished he could believe him, but he didn't. It wasn't that he thought Deacon was lying to him — not really — it was only that he didn't expect the big cowboy's resolve to last long when presented with the soft, smooth flesh and open legs of the McAllen maids.

Deacon must have seen the doubt in his face, because he leant down and kissed Aren, his lips gentle. "You could come with me," he said.

That was true. He could. But he'd only be in the way, and the idea of having to fight the maids off without Red knowing, or of watching as Deacon gave in to temptation was too much to bear. "No."

Deacon watched him for a minute, thoughtful, then he broke into a mischievous grin. "Tell you what," he said. "Soon as I get home, I'll come get you and we'll go straight to Olsa. She'll know if I rolled with a maid or not, and you know she won't hold back about it, neither." Aren laughed despite himself, and the smile on Deacon's face became more genuine. "There's nothing they can offer that's worth making you mad," Deacon said. "I mean it."

Aren sighed. "Fine," he relented, wrapping his arms around Deacon's neck. "I believe you." *I think.*

Deacon smiled down at him. "You're done being mad?"

"It seems like I am."

"Hmm…" Deacon nuzzled Aren's neck. "That's too bad. 'Cause I sure wouldn't mind if you took some of that aggression out on me."

"Oh, really?" Aren teased. "Are you saying I should make use of that rope?"

"Mmmm," Deacon said, grinding his erection against Aren's thigh. "I think so."

"And the crop?"

Deacon groaned, grinding against him harder. "Yes, please."

"You broke all my glasses. You'll have to bring me more."

"I will," Deacon said, as breathless now as he'd been before. "Aren, *please.*"

"Fine," Aren said, laughing. He pushed Deacon up off him, although he made sure as he did to caress the large bulge in his lover's pants, just to tease him. "Let's go upstairs." He pushed himself off the table and turned to follow Deacon out of the living room door, but something caught his eye.

There was somebody looking in at the window!

A face! He was sure of it, but when he turned to look again it was already gone.

"Wait!"

Deacon stopped and turned to look at him over his shoulder. "What?"

"I thought I saw something." Aren said, but he was already doubting himself. "Somebody at the window."

"Who?"

"I..." Aren's words stuttered to a halt. *Who?* He had no idea. He hadn't actually seen a face, he realised. He'd only had the impression of one. But it had been a mere glance, a fraction of a second at most as he'd turned past the window. He hadn't truly been looking out of it. Had he imagined it?

"The wind's blowing something fierce today," Deacon said and it was true. It howled outside, battering his shutters, making the tree branches creak. "You probably just saw a tumbleweed or a leaf blowing by. Could even have been a bird."

"A bird," Aren repeated, pondering. It seemed possible and far more likely than the thought that anybody would be at his window when there was less than half an hour left of light.

"Aren," Deacon said, pulling him into his strong arms. "There's nobody there. Please don't make me wait any more. I'll get down on my knees and beg you here and now if that's what you want." He squeezed Aren tight, pushing his erection against Aren's hip. "*Please* come upstairs now."

Aren couldn't help but laugh. He loved the way he could make Deacon desperate. He loved to make him plead. And now that he'd already climaxed himself, it would be easy to spend hours making Deacon squirm, making him beg for more. The thought made Aren's pulse race.

"Go upstairs," he said, making his voice a command.

"What about you?" Deacon asked.

"I'm going to start the generator now so we don't have to stop later."

Deacon groaned against his neck, nipping at his ear. "Good idea."

Aren reached down to squeeze Deacon's groin, loving the deep-throated moan it caused. "You have no idea what you're in for."

Chapter Twenty-Six

Aren didn't go to the courtyard to see Deacon and Red off. They'd said goodbye in bed, Deacon dressed and ready to go, Aren still naked under the sheet.

"Don't you worry about those girls," Deacon teased as he kissed Aren goodbye. "I'll be thinking about you every second of the day."

"You better be." Aren forced himself to smile. He did his best to smother the little voice inside him that still had doubts. "Hurry home."

"Two days there, two days back," Deacon said. "Can't do it any faster than that."

He paused in the bedroom doorway, turning to look back at Aren. His cheeks turned red, and he put his hand on the top of his head, pushing his hat down low — except his hat was still hanging on the hook by the front door.

"Aren," he said, "I..." His words died away. He stared down at the floor.

It made Aren smile. Deacon never did well with sentiments. Whether he'd been going to say, "I'll miss you," or something more, Aren didn't know. But he recognised the effort.

"Don't forget my glasses," Aren said, deciding to let Deacon off the hook rather than watching him squirm.

Deacon looked up at him in surprise. His face broke into a smile. "I'll buy you the best crystal they sell."

And so Aren was able to laugh as Deacon walked out of his door. "Don't bother," he said to the empty room, still smiling. "The ghost will only break them anyway."

He hoped he could keep his spirits up. He hoped he could maintain his optimism and hold on to the trust he'd felt when Deacon was still in the room. He worried that the time spent alone would lead him down a path of doubt.

It turned out he'd have other things to occupy his mind.

* * * *

He was surprised, when he finally wandered over to the house, to find that Olsa wasn't in the kitchen. Tama was there instead. "She's sick," she said. She looked worried.

"How sick?" Aren asked.

"I don't know. I don't know much about fevers."

Aren didn't, either, but some sense of foreboding told him this was a situation he couldn't ignore. "Where is she?"

Tama led him through a hallway, then down a flight of stairs. The basement was cold and Aren found himself thinking how cruel it was that Olsa was confined to the basement.

"We've offered her another room," Tama said, as if reading his mind, "but she says this one is already hers."

Aren could hear Olsa coughing from the hallway. "She seemed fine yesterday," he said.

Tama shrugged. "She's been coughing more and more. Mostly, I think she hides it from Deacon."

"Blessed fools," Aren cursed. Olsa and Deacon both were stubborn to a fault. He knocked gently on the door before going in.

Her room was small and tidy, with several dressers and cupboards. It smelt like something earthy and herbal. It was also dreadfully cold. And in the corner, on a narrow bed, lay Olsa.

She was coughing, and when Aren touched a hand to her forehead, he found it hot, but not overly so. She grabbed his hand, her grip surprisingly strong. "He won't break his promise," she said. "He told you true."

He hoped she was right, but at the same time he knew there was no point in worrying about it. Olsa, on the other hand? He decided it made sense to worry about her.

"It's too cold in here," he said to Tama. "Do you have warming pans?"

"Of course."

"That's what she needs. And more blankets. And..." He tried to think what they'd done for boys at the boarding school. "Make a mixture of lemon juice, warm honey and whisky. That will help with her cough."

Tama shook her head in confusion. "What's lemon juice?"

Aren cursed. He hadn't seen a citrus fruit since leaving the continent. "Use water," he told her. "Water, honey and whisky. Don't get that rotgut from Red either. If there's no good whisky in the house, you can go get mine."

So began Aren's vigil.

He stayed in the chair by her bed all day and all night, giving her the honey mixture. It did seem to cut down on her coughing and although her fever didn't break it didn't seem to get any worse, either.

By the second day, she seemed to be better. Tama brought beef broth with barley in it, and Olsa managed to eat a bit. She coughed less, and she had regained some of her usual orneriness.

"Go home!" she snapped at Aren that evening. "Having you hovering over me won't make me better!"

Although he felt he should stay, his aching back begged otherwise. The idea of another night sleeping in the chair didn't sound appealing. "I'll be back tomorrow morning," he told her.

"I'll be up and ready to take my spoon to you." But she was wrong.

Tama was banging on his door as soon as the sun was up. "She's worse," she said when he opened the door. "Much worse."

Olsa was no longer coughing. She seemed barely conscious, and Aren could tell before he even touched her that her fever was higher than ever. She shivered under the covers, although sweat beaded her brow.

"This is bad," he said to Tama. "I don't know what to do."

"Deacon," Olsa croaked. Her hand clamped down on Aren's wrist, and he noticed her grip was far weaker than it had been two days before. "Need Deacon."

"He's not here," Aren said, taking her hand and holding it between his. "He went to town. He'll be back tomorrow. Just hang on—"

"No." She shook her head. "Not tomorrow. The rain."

Those few words seemed to exhaust her, and she closed her eyes, breathing hard. "Don't worry," Aren told her. "You need to rest. I'll bring Deacon to you as soon as he gets home."

She slept fitfully for most of the day. Shortly before dark, her wrinkled hand found his again. "Aolo'ui," she whispered.

"I'm sorry," Aren said. "I don't know that word."

"Tell Deacon, aolo'ui."

"Oh-lo-hu-ee?"

"Aoilo'ui."

"Ah-lo-hue-eye?" It was frustrating. Their language was so different. The vowel sounds seemed different than any he'd ever heard, somehow longer, and with completely new inflections. No matter how he tried, he couldn't seem to mimic them.

"He'll say it won't work," she said. "Tell him to try."

"I will," he assured her. "But you have to rest."

The next morning, he awoke to thunder. Even down in the basement, in Olsa's tiny room, he heard it. He left her side and wandered upstairs to the kitchen. It was a journey he'd made many times in the previous days, but this time the trip seemed ominous. He could hear a dull roar ahead of him, behind him, all around him.

He made it to the kitchen and stood looking out of the door, stunned and horrified. It was like no rain he'd ever seen. It was a river pouring from the sky. The water barrel on the roof of the barracks was already running over. The courtyard was nearly two inches deep in water. Lightning seemed to crackle constantly and the thunder no longer boomed. It was a steady, low rumble, ever-present, buried just beneath the sound of the driving rain.

"Holy Saints!" Aren said. "What the blessed hell is going on?"

"Monsoon," Daisy said behind him. "We only get them a couple of times a year, but they make up for it when they're here."

"Will it last all day?"

"Not like this," she said. "Another hour or two and it'll die down, but yeah, probably won't stop until around supper."

Aren's heart sank. This was the day Deacon was due home, but he knew there was no way he and Red would force the horses to travel in such weather. He was probably holed up in the McAllen barn. Aren found at that moment that he didn't even care whether or not Deacon had one of the maids for company. All he knew was, Olsa needed him. By the time Deacon made it home, Aren feared it would be too late.

* * * *

By afternoon, the rain had slowed to a drizzle, and Olsa fought for every breath. Aren could hear the rattle deep in her chest.

"Hold on," he begged as he held her hand. "Hold on. Just one more day."

He nearly wept with relief when the sun rose the next morning and Olsa's laboured breathing hadn't stopped. He stayed by her side all morning, but after the dinner bell, he broke his vigil to eat. Afterwards, he went to the barn, where he found Ronin and Frances doing chores. He pulled Frances aside.

"Their horses will be tired," Aren told him. "You have a fresh one ready. As soon as you see him, you run it out to him and tell him to get here as fast as the blessed animal can carry him. Understand?"

"Of course."

"Tell him it's Olsa, and to come straight to her room."

"You got it, boss," Frances said.

Aren was halfway back to Olsa's room before he realised Frances had called him 'boss'. At any other time he might have found it amusing, but now it only served to underline the fact that the real boss wasn't around.

He held on to Olsa's hand over the next few hours. He listened to her breathing as it became even shallower. It felt like an eternity, but finally he heard footsteps running down the stairs.

"He's coming," Tama said, bursting into the room.

"You hear that?" Aren said to Olsa. "He's coming. Don't you die yet!"

He would have known it was Deacon coming down the stairs even if Tama hadn't told him. He knew the weight and the cadence of his footfalls. "What is it?" he asked, coming into her room.

As soon as his eyes landed on her, he moaned. Aren moved quickly out of his way so Deacon could take his chair at her side. "Olsa?" he said, his voice soft. There was no response. He turned to Aren. "How long?"

"Since you left," Aren told him, "but it wasn't this bad until the day before last."

He saw the understanding in Deacon's eyes. If it were the first day, there might be hope, but now it seemed they could only wait for the end.

Deacon turned back to her. He picked up her tiny, withered hand and held it in between his own large ones. "I should have been here sooner," he said. "I should have come through the rain."

"There's no way you could have known," Aren said. "Even if you'd been here, there's nothing you could have done." Even as he said it, though, he found himself thinking about what Olsa had told him. Maybe there *was* something Deacon could do. "She said to tell you, ool-oh-uly." He knew the sounds weren't right, even before Deacon turned to look at him in obvious confusion. "Owl-ole-yu-li," he tried again.

It still wasn't right, but he saw the understanding dawn in Deacon's eyes. "Aolo'ui?"

"Yes!" Aren said with relief.

Deacon shook his head. "It won't work."

"She said you'd say that. She said to try."

Deacon still had her hand between his, and he put his head down on them, breathing deeply. "It won't work," he whispered. "It's folk tales. It can't help."

Aren put his hand on Deacon's back, imagining he could somehow pour strength and belief into Deacon. "Does it hurt to try?"

It took Deacon a moment to answer. He stayed where he was, his head down. Finally, he took a deep breath. He sat up and looked at Olsa.

"Laa'ha ma aolo'ui?" he whispered.

And Olsa heard! Although she hadn't reacted to anything else in two days, there was no doubt she heard his voice. Her head turned towards him. Her eyes didn't open, and she said, "Ai'loma." Her voice wasn't even a whisper, only a tiny, shallow breath, but Deacon sagged with relief. He leaned over and kissed her forehead before jumping up so fast he startled Aren.

Deacon strode to one of the cabinets in Olsa's room and pulled it open. He searched through it, finally pulling out a small bowl and pestle, and a tiny corked bottle. He turned and handed them to Aren.

"Get ash from the hearth," he said. "Not any hearth, either. The one she cooks at." He pointed to the bottle. "Mix in some of that, so it's a paste. Then add enough water to thin it down. It needs to be like paint."

"I will," Aren promised, and rushed to do as he'd been told. He didn't know why Deacon needed paint made from ash, but he didn't care. Anything was better than sitting and watching Olsa die.

When it was done, he took the bowl back to her room. He stopped short in the doorway, in surprise. Deacon was drawing signs on the walls, singing as he did. All around the room, all over the walls, was the same symbol over and over again. It wasn't the same as the wards or the mark on Aren's cellar door, but it was similar—a circle with a strange series of lines inside.

Deacon's song stopped when he saw Aren in the doorway. He put down his chalk and turned to take the bowl of paint. "In the same cabinet, there's a paintbrush," he said.

It didn't take long for Aren to find it. It was a crude brush, made by binding horse tail hairs to a stick. Deacon had brushed her hair off her forehead and unlaced the top of her nightgown, gently pushing it aside to expose the top of her chest.

Deacon took the brush from Aren, and he began to sing again. It was like the song Olsa had sung over his cellar in that it seemed to be only a few words repeated over and over, but Aren knew it wasn't the same song. This one sounded sweeter. And as Deacon sang, he painted. He painted a mark on her forehead, and on the back of each hand, and on her chest. It was the same symbol he'd drawn on the walls of her room.

"Le'ama aolo'ui, eye'nay lao'ola. Le'ama aolo'ui, eye'nay lao'ola. Le'ama aolo'ui, eye'nay lao'ola," Deacon sang, over and over again. Even after the symbols were done, he sang. He sat at her side, holding her hand carefully so as not to disturb the sign he'd painted, and he sang on. Whether he believed it would help or not, Aren didn't know, but he seemed to find strength in having something to do. "Le'ama aolo'ui, eye'nay lao'ola. Le'ama aolo'ui, eye'nay lao'ola."

Aren sat down on the floor. He leant back against the door with a tired sigh, and he drifted off to sleep.

* * * *

Aren awoke an indeterminable time later, when the door he was leaning against opened a crack.

"I'm sorry," Tama whispered. "I thought you could use a break."

"We could," Aren confessed.

He looked over at Olsa and Deacon. Deacon had moved from the chair. He was sitting on the floor next to the bed, his head resting next to Olsa's hand. He was still singing, although his voice was little more than a rasp. "Le'ama aolo'ui, eye'nay lao'ola. Le'ama aolo'ui, eye'nay lao'ola."

Aren stood up, stretching his cramped and aching muscles. His back was killing him. He couldn't even remember what a real bed felt like anymore. Deacon didn't move. He seemed to be half asleep, although his singing went on. "Le'ama aolo'ui, eye'nay lao'ola. Le'ama aolo'ui, eye'nay lao'ola."

Aren moved as quietly as he could to look down on Olsa. Her chest still rose and fell. Not only that, Aren heard no rattle. He put his hand on her forehead. It was warm still, but nothing like it had been before.

It seemed like Deacon's song had worked, but Aren didn't want to assume too much. She'd seemed to get better once before, too.

Aren put his hand gently on Deacon's back, and Deacon's head popped up. His words died away. He looked up at Aren with eyes full of grief. "Is she dead?" he asked.

"No. She's asleep." He reached down and took Deacon's arm, pulling him to his feet. "Come on. Let's go home where we can sleep in a real bed."

"Can't," Deacon said, although his voice was mostly gone. "Dark."

"How do you know?" Aren asked. There were no windows in the basement. Aren had no idea what time it was.

"Generator," Deacon rasped.

Once he listened, he could hear it. He'd grown so used to its incessant whine, he barely noticed it anymore. He looked over at Tama.

"Is there an extra room?"

"Yes," she said. "Upstairs—"

"I won't leave her!"

"Deacon," Aren said, thinking to reason with him, but Tama interrupted him.

"The next room down was Gordon's," she said. "It's closer, but there's only one bed."

"I'll sleep on the floor," Aren said. "It's not like I have the option of going home."

"But—" Deacon started to protest.

"I'll wake you if anything changes," Tama said. "Aren's right. You should sleep."

The fight seemed to have gone out of Deacon. Aren took one of the candles with him, and Deacon allowed himself to be led down the short hallway to the only other room in the basement. It was small, but the bed looked clean. It wasn't as big as Aren's bed at his house, but it was big enough for them both if they didn't move too much.

As soon as the door had closed behind them, Deacon pulled Aren into his arms, holding him tight.

"Thank you for taking care of her."

"I did my best," Aren said as he wrapped his arms around Deacon's waist, letting himself relax against Deacon's broad body. "I'm glad you're home. I was worried you wouldn't make it in time."

Deacon was quiet and when he spoke again, Aren was glad to hear a hint of a smile in his voice. "You're *not* sleeping on the floor."

"No," Aren laughed. "I'm not."

They didn't undress all the way, for fear they'd be needed on short notice, but they took off their shoes and climbed into the bed. Deacon rested his head on Aren's chest, although Aren knew it had to mean his feet were hanging out of the other end. Aren slowly unbraided Deacon's hair and ran his hands through it. He massaged Deacon's temples. He rubbed his back and shoulders until he felt Deacon's muscles soften and his breathing slow.

Deacon sighed sleepily. "I wish I had the strength to rip your clothes off."

Aren laughed. "Tomorrow," he said. "But tonight, you should sleep."

And Deacon did.

Aren woke later to pins and needles in his arm. He knew the sun must be up, because the generator no longer whined. Deacon's back was snug against his stomach, his head lying on Aren's arm, which had caused it to fall asleep.

Despite everything else going on in the world, Aren couldn't help but think how good it felt to push his morning erection against Deacon's muscular backside. He longed to slide his hand down Deacon's stomach, to wake his lover with soft caresses and the gloriously slow torment of a morning orgasm when one's bladder was full as well.

He refrained, though. Not only was the chance of having somebody catch them too great, he also felt Deacon needed sleep more than he needed sex.

Still, Aren couldn't help but hope things would get back to normal soon.

He took care of his morning toilet. He stopped in the kitchen for some biscuits and milk. Just being out of the basement, looking through the kitchen window at the sunlight, felt good.

He was coming back down the stairs when Tama came out of Olsa's room, smiling. "She's awake," she said. "Deacon's with her."

Deacon was again sitting in the chair next to the bed, bent over Olsa's hand as he held it in his own. "I was so scared," he said, his voice still hoarse from the song.

"You did good," she told him. "I could feel your heart singing."

"I thought you were going to die."

"So did I," she said.

Deacon let go of her hand. He scooped her thin body up in his strong arms and rocked her. "Thank the Saints."

"The Saints had nothing to do with it, boy. If you want to thank somebody, you do it the right way."

He held her for a minute, still rocking her, not saying a word. But then he sang. It was a new song. "Sa'ahala nai'alini. Sa'ahala nai'alini."

"You're a good boy," she said. "Now put me down before you break my old bones."

Deacon laughed, letting her rest again back against her pillows. There were tears in his eyes, and he wiped them quickly away.

"Send Tama or one of the women in here to help me. I have to use the privy."

Deacon laughed again. "I will."

"Good. Now go away. You stink like horses and hay and Gordon's lye soap." She waved her hand at him dismissively. "Guess I shouldn't complain. It's the first time you come back from the McAllen's not smelling like cheap perfume and cheaper maids."

Chapter Twenty-Seven

It was a great relief to leave the sickroom and the main house behind. They went to the river and stripped naked and dived into the deep, cold water. It was even colder than before, and they washed as fast they could, then went back to Aren's house, which seemed almost as cold after having nobody in it to light the fire for so many days.

Aren dragged a warm, heavy blanket from the bed while Deacon stoked the fire. Then Deacon pulled him down onto the cowhide rug and they made love in the warmth of the flickering flames. It was slow and gentle, Deacon's callused hands caressing him as he whispered in Aren's ear that he was soft, that he was beautiful, that he was everything he'd ever wanted. Aren wrapped his legs around his lover and let him in, letting him rock them both until they fell breathless and spent into each other's arms.

Aren felt sated and more at peace than he'd been since before Deacon had left, but Deacon was already picking himself up off the floor.

"I have to go," he said. "Been away so long, those lazy hands probably let the place go to hell." He dressed quickly, then stood looking down at Aren. "I'd rather eat here. I'll bring supper back with me," he said.

Aren smiled. "That sounds perfect."

Deacon left and Aren cuddled down under the comforter, cosy in front of the fire, and he fell fast asleep.

* * * *

Things at the BarChi returned to normal. Deacon swore Jay had nearly let the ranch fall apart in his absence. Aren knew it was an exaggeration, but only a small one. Frances confided in him that while some of them had done their best to keep up, a select few of the men were always willing to sit back and let others do the work when Deacon was gone.

Olsa returned to the kitchen. She was doing better, but Aren knew she wasn't as strong as she had once been. He suspected it was only a matter of time before they had to hire somebody to help her. Still, by her fourth day back, she had reverted to snatching Deacon's food away when he did something wrong.

"You'd think she'd be more grateful," Deacon said to Aren that night as they sat in front of the fire with their drinks. "I *did* save her life." He said it jokingly, as if it weren't true.

"You did," Aren said, in earnest.

The smile on Deacon's face faded. "Not really. It was just good timing."

Aren didn't think that was true. He thought Olsa had been saved by the magic of the song and the power of the symbols.

Symbols had power. That's what she'd told him.

He thought suddenly of his painting, and the day she'd made him promise to show it to Deacon.

"Come on," he said, standing up. "I have something to show you."

"Something upstairs?" Deacon asked, grinning wickedly at him.

"Not like that," Aren laughed. "A painting."

"Do I get to show you something afterwards?"

"We'll see." Aren took his hand and pulled him up from his chair. "Only if you behave. Olsa was talking to me a few weeks ago about symbols," he explained as he led Deacon up the stairs, "and she somehow knew I'd painted something with the BarChi brand. She made me bring her to see it—"

"She's blind."

Aren laughed. "You think I don't know that? Anyway, she said it was important. She said you had to see it."

They'd reached the room that was his studio, and he led Deacon inside. The painting that met them when they walked through the door was the first one he'd done of Deacon in the barn.

Deacon stopped short, staring at it in wonder, and Aren felt himself blush. Having somebody look at his art was worse than having them look at him. He felt horribly exposed.

"Is that how I look?" Deacon asked, looking over at him in surprise.

Aren felt himself blush more, but he smiled. "That's how you look to me."

Deacon looked back at the canvas, nodding. "Like the bull," he said, reminding Aren of the day so long ago, when he and Deacon had sat in the grass. "You made me better than I really am."

"No," Aren said. "That makes it sound like a lie."

"But that's not how I look."

"It's more than how you look. It's how I feel when I see you. I try to mix that in. I want other people to look at it and to see you the way I do."

Deacon turned again to look at him. "It's some kind of magic."

"It's just art."

"Same thing," Deacon said. He reached up and brushed his hand over Aren's hair. Aren wasn't sure Deacon had ever looked at him with such tenderness. "Wish I could do it for you," he said. "Wish I had the magic, too, so you could see yourself the way I do."

The sweetness of the sentiment surprised him. Deacon's ability to say so much while saying so little amazed him. It made him smile. He wrapped his arms around Deacon's neck and stood on his toes to kiss him. "You'll have to find some other way to show me."

Deacon made a sound—more than a moan, almost a growl—and pulled Aren hard against him. He kissed his neck. "I'll show you now if you want," he said. "I'll get down on my knees and you can tell me what to do." His big, strong hands moved down Aren's back, and Aren shivered. "Please," Deacon whispered in his ear. "You can tie me up. You can use the crop."

"Oh, Saints," Aren moaned. Every part of his body was responding, and he could feel Deacon's erection hard against his hip, but his sense of obligation nagged at him.

"Wait," Aren said, pulling himself free. "You still haven't seen the one Olsa meant."

"I'll see it later," Deacon said, trying to pull Aren back into his arms.

"No," Aren said, laughing. "It will only take a minute."

He took Deacon's hand and pulled him around to look at the other canvas, and although Deacon groaned in frustration, he followed.

"This is the one she wanted you to see. She said it was important."

The moment Deacon's eyes landed on the canvas, he stopped dead in his tracks, as if in shock. He stood very still, staring at it. He didn't seem to find it flattering or fascinating the way he had the first one. He seemed unnerved by it.

"What do you think?" Aren asked.

Deacon didn't seem to have words. He shook his head, still staring at the painting.

"She said it made the symbol yours, or something like that." He was surprised at Deacon's reaction. The big cowboy looked slightly spooked. "Do you know what she means?"

Deacon shook his head again. "Folk tales," he said, but the casualness of his words was belied by the tremor in his voice.

Aren had expected Deacon to laugh, or to shrug it off, or to ask him questions. He found his strange response unsettling. "Hey," he said, taking Deacon's arm and turning him away from the canvas. "Forget the painting."

Deacon grinned at him, although there was still a shadow of uneasiness in his eyes. He put an arm around Aren's waist and pulled him close. "Is that an order?"

"As a matter of fact, it is."

And for a while, they did forget. Aren went downstairs to start the generator, then they went into the bedroom. Aren ordered Deacon onto his knees. He tied him face down over the ottoman, and before he'd even finished securing the rope Deacon was begging him to fuck him. Aren found it was more fun to tease him. He greased his fingers and pushed them into Deacon, fucking him hard with his hand while Deacon bucked against the ottoman, crying Aren's name. When Aren knew neither of them could hold out much longer, he moved Deacon off the ottoman. He lay him down on his back, with his hands still tied, and he took Deacon's cock into his mouth while shoving his own aching erection deep into Deacon's throat. Deacon could take his full length now without any problem at all, and Aren fucked himself hard into Deacon's mouth while sucking his cock. They moved together, thrusting and grinding and moaning together until they were both spent.

Afterwards, they lay side by side on the bed, staring up at the ceiling. Aren was heavy with sleep, sated and unbelievably content. He was drifting off to sleep when Deacon spoke.

"I feel like that sometimes," he said.

"Hmmm?" Aren asked, unable to even formulate a real response.

But Deacon seemed to know what he meant. "Your painting. Sometimes I feel like that, like I'm tied to this ranch. I think I can even feel that barbed wire digging into my skin. If I pull too hard, it might bleed me dry. Sometimes I hate it."

Aren looked over at Deacon in surprise, but the big cowboy was still staring up at the ceiling. "Why don't you leave?"

"Because everything I love is here, too."

They didn't say anything else and before long Deacon's breathing became heavy and slow. Once Aren knew he was asleep, he slipped quietly out of bed. He tiptoed into the extra room, where the painting sat waiting on the easel. He picked up his tiniest brush, and dipped the tip in paint. He put his mark in the corner.

Symbols had power.

* * * *

Aren did his best not to think about the day when Deacon would leave again, but pretending it wouldn't happen didn't change the facts. The days wore on, and the time for Deacon to leave again was suddenly upon them. The morning before he was to leave, Deacon rose early, as he often did, in order to do chores before breakfast. Aren wandered across the grass later in the morning to meet him.

Aren often wondered if anybody had figured out that Deacon no longer slept in the barn. He wondered if they'd noticed that he went to Aren's house every night after dinner and didn't leave again until morning. He wondered how much trouble it would cause for them when people did start to figure it out. He loved the life he and Deacon were building together in their tiny house. He hoped nothing would threaten the happiness he'd found there.

Just as Aren and Deacon were finishing their breakfast, Jeremiah arrived in the kitchen, looking for Deacon.

"You ready to leave in the morning?" he asked.

"Yup."

Jeremiah stood there for a moment, regarding Deacon with thoughtful eyes. Finally, he walked across the room to stand in front of Deacon. Sitting on the stool at the table, Deacon was a few inches shorter than Jeremiah.

"I want you to be careful," he said. "You're more important than that ranch or any of the cattle on it. Do whatever you need to do to keep yourself safe. You understand?"

Deacon shrugged. "Just got to fix the generator, and we'll all be fine."

"You really think you can do that?"

"Don't see why not."

Jeremiah nodded. He looked up at the ceiling and took a deep breath, as if he had to gather his courage before going on. When he looked back at Deacon, he looked wary but determined, and Aren couldn't help but wonder what he was planning to say that made him so nervous.

"Once the generator's up and running, you come back here. I'll take Dante and some of the hands, and we'll start getting that ranch back on its feet. You can send Jay into town to hire more hands—as many as we have room for between here and the Austin place, as long as Aren says we can afford them."

"Yes, sir," Deacon said.

Another moment of hesitation, and again Aren wondered what he had to say to Deacon that would cause him such anxiety. "I talked to my sons last night," he said at last, "about what's going to happen. Jay doesn't much want to run any ranch. He's not always smart, but he's smart enough to know he doesn't have what it takes to make a ranch work. Tama wants to stay here, and Jay's happy to work where he's needed."

Deacon nodded but said nothing, and Aren thought he looked as confused about where the conversation was headed as Aren was.

"Deacon," Jeremiah said, "this ranch was always supposed to be yours."

"No!" Deacon said, standing up.

Jeremiah put a hand on his shoulder and pushed him back down onto the stool. "Listen to me. For once in your life, son, listen to what I'm saying instead of arguing." Deacon ducked his head, clenching his jaw, but he didn't respond. "This ranch was never supposed to be mine," he said. "You know that. It was supposed to be your daddy's."

"We don't know —"

" —that he was your father," Jeramiah finished for him, in a tone that bespoke how many times they'd had this conversation. "I know. But I'm telling you, it don't matter. This ranch was his, and by rights, that makes it yours. Now, if you don't want it, then say so. But if you're going to persist in saying you somehow don't deserve it, I may have to take you out back and whip you like I did when you was a boy."

Deacon smiled a little at the words, although he didn't look up. "Good luck with that, old man."

Jeremiah laughed. His hand was still on Deacon's shoulder. He stooped a bit, trying to meet Deacon's eyes, but Deacon kept his gaze on the floor. "Nobody knows this ranch like you, son. Nobody loves it like you. You've spent your whole life insisting you aren't Ezriel's son, and yet you're the one who proves over and over you deserve to be his heir. You could have lived in this house once my pa died. Could have had a room and a wife, too, but you were always too proud to claim what you thought wasn't yours."

"It's not mine," Deacon said, his voice quiet. "There's no way of knowing."

Jeremiah shook his head, amused but exasperated. "Son, I don't care whose seed put you in your momma's belly." That statement seemed to reach Deacon as none of the others had. He finally looked up, meeting Jeremiah's eyes. "I've told this to my boys, and although Dante's fit to be tied, I'm sure he'll get over it. The Austin ranch will suit him fine, once he gets settled. As long as I'm alive, you can keep thinking you're nothing more than a glorified ranch hand, but once I'm gone, the BarChi goes to you."

"You have other heirs," Deacon said. "You have grandsons."

"If it worries you so much, you can pass it on to Jay's boys. But until they're grown, or you have a son of your own, the BarChi belong to you." He leant back and crossed his arms to glower at Deacon. "Do I have you convinced?" he asked.

Deacon looked back down at the floor, fidgeting with a fold in the leg of his pants. "I'll think about it."

Jeremiah laughed, shaking his head. "I guess that's good enough for now."

He clapped Deacon on the shoulder before turning to walk out of the door, leaving Deacon, Olsa, and a very stunned Aren in his wake.

"Well," Olsa said to Deacon after he'd gone, "you finally going to claim part of what's yours?"

He sighed, looking up at her in annoyance. "You want me to admit I'm full Ainuai, but you want me to say I'm Ezriel's son, too." He shook his head. "I can't be both."

Smack.

Olsa's wooden spoon landed hard on the back of Deacon's hand and although he winced, he didn't move.

"You *are* both," she said. "You're the only damn fool on this ranch who doesn't see it."

Chapter Twenty-Eight

The day was long, and for Aren, it was torture. Deacon was leaving. That was the one thought that plagued him every moment of the day. He was going into the wild, headed to a place with a generator that didn't work, hoping for the best. He said he could fix it, but what if he couldn't? Deacon didn't trust that his questionable heritage would keep him safe, and as the seconds ticked by, Aren found himself less able to trust it as well.

He wanted to grab Deacon, to hold him, to drag him to his house and tie him to the bed. To force him to stay at home, where he'd be safe. He wanted to stop time, to never let the next dawn come. He imagined going to Deacon and begging him to send somebody else—*anybody* else—in his place. In his daydreams, Deacon kissed him and held him close and agreed to send a ranch hand instead, but in reality, Aren knew the dream was foolish. Deacon was going. There was nothing Aren could do to change it. Deacon would leave, and Aren would have to wait, hoping and praying his lover would make it home. How many days might pass? How many hours would he lie awake, wondering if Deacon was safe? How many days overdue would Deacon be before Jeremiah sent somebody after him? How many nights might Deacon's cold body lie dead at the Austin ranch before anybody else arrived? And how would Aren ever go on without him?

Aren's heart grew heavy. His stomach tied itself in knots. He told himself it would be fine. After all, Deacon said he could fix the generator in time. But as the sun fell in the sky and the generators began their quiet whine for the night, Aren found himself overwhelmed by a terrible sense of foreboding. As they drank their whisky in front of the fire, he found himself choking on a lump in his throat. He could not look at Deacon lest the tears behind his eyes find their way free.

Deacon watched him, obviously confused. He asked more than once if Aren was all right. Aren could only nod. It wasn't until they were upstairs in the bedroom, beginning to undress for bed, that Aren finally made himself speak.

"Who's going with you to the Austin ranch?" he asked.

"Simon and Frances."

That surprised Aren. "You trust Frances now?"

He could tell the question amused Deacon. "'Course I do," he said, laughing. "He's a good man. Had to toughen him up a bit, but that's nothing new." He shrugged. "Frances probably wouldn't have been my first choice, but Simon volunteered to go, and *him* I know I can use. Seems Frances won't let himself be left behind."

That didn't surprise Aren a bit. Although he knew the two weren't lovers, he suspected Frances was very much in love with the older ranch hand. Frances probably felt it was better to die with Simon than to be left behind. It was a sentiment Aren could sympathise with, now more than ever before.

Suddenly, Aren knew what he wanted to do. "Deacon," he said, his voice shaking, "take me with you."

Deacon turned to him in alarm. "What?"

"*Please.*"

"Aren," Deacon said, his voice shaking. "No!"

"Why not?"

"Because..." But he didn't finish his sentence.

Aren knew the reason, though. It was the same reason he'd always been left behind. "You want me to stay behind because you think I'm weak."

"*What?* Aren, that's not it."

"If I was bigger and stronger, like you and Simon —"

"Size has nothing to do with it." Aren didn't believe him and Deacon must have read the disbelief on his face, because he said defensively, "I'm taking Frances!"

"Only because of Simon! Besides, Frances is stronger than me now. You're afraid I'll hold you back, but I won't. I can do whatever you tell me to do. I can keep up. I promise I won't embarrass you! I swear —"

"Aren, it has nothing to do with you embarrassing me. You're not weak! I never said you were. I don't know why you always say that —"

"Then why can't I go with you?"

"Because..." But his words died away again. He seemed to have suddenly run out of courage. He stood there for a moment, his mouth still working but no sound coming out.

"Well?" Aren demanded.

Even with the deep tone of his skin, Aren could see Deacon's cheeks turning red. His mouth snapped shut, and he looked down at the floor, shoving his hands deep into his pockets. Aren knew the signs. They'd reached a point where Deacon wouldn't say any more.

Aren sighed in frustration. He sat down heavily on the bed and put his face in his hands. He was *not* going to cry! Not in front of Deacon.

"Aren?" Deacon said.

"Go away."

But Deacon didn't obey. Aren listened to his footsteps as he crossed the floor to where Aren sat on the bed. Aren lowered his hands and watched as Deacon got onto his knees in front of him. Deacon ducked his head, and Aren saw his broad shoulders rise and fall as he took a deep breath.

"I need to think clear when I'm in the wild," Deacon said. "I need to know I'm making the best decision for everyone involved. If you're there, I won't. Only thing I'd care about is you. I'd throw the others to the wraiths if it came down to it. I'd slit their throats myself if that's what it took to keep you safe. I can't let that happen, Aren. I'm asking you, please, don't put me in that position. 'Cause if I had to choose between them and you, I'd choose you every time."

"You're worried they'll know," Aren said, thinking perhaps he finally understood. "You're worried they'll see what's between us, and they'll think you're weak because of it."

"No!" Deacon said, looking up into Aren's eyes. "I don't care if they know! Any man thinks loving you makes me weak, he can find out the hard way he's wrong!"

Aren's heart skipped a beat at Deacon's words. *You love me?* But he wasn't going to let that distract him. "Then let me come with you."

"No, Aren. You don't understand. When I'm out there, I have to be in charge. Being strong isn't enough. I've got to be stronger than all the rest of them. That's my job — to be *in control.*"

"I know," Aren said, confused as to what it had to do with the topic at hand.

"The thing is, when I'm here with you, in this room, it's different. It's the only time — "

His voice seemed to fail him, and he stopped short, taking another deep breath as if to steady himself. He was trying so hard. Even through his frustration, Aren recognised the effort Deacon was making. Some of his anger at the big cowboy drained away. He reached out with one hand and rested his fingertips on Deacon's head, tracing the course of his dark hair towards his temple. Even with that faint touch, he could feel Deacon trembling. But that soft touch seemed to give Deacon the courage to go on.

"Whether it's here on the ranch, or out in the wild, I always need to be tough. I always need be strong. And I didn't realise till you came along how tired I was. It's like, being their boss is a weight I got to carry with me everywhere I go. And it wears me down, Aren. It wears me out." Deacon took Aren's hands. His own were large and hard with calluses and seemed to envelop Aren's from fingertip to wrist. He stared down at their hands, lying together in Aren's lap, dark skin against pale gold. His fingers stroked the back of Aren's hand. "I need you, Aren. More than I can say. More than you know. I need to know you're here. I need to know you're safe and that you'll be waiting for me when I get home. I can't risk losing you. If I had to hold you and watch the wraiths take you like I did with Garrett..." He stopped, shaking his head as if he couldn't bear to put any more of that thought into words. He put his head down in Aren's lap again, on top of their clasped hands. "Being with you, and the things we do together, when you use the rope and take control, those are the only times I feel like I can breathe. Those are the only times I can't feel the weight. You keep saying you're weak, but I know you're not, Aren, 'cause you're the one who makes me strong." He took a deep, shuddering breath, and Aren felt the dampness of his tears against their entwined fingers. "Be here safe for me, Aren. Please be here waiting. 'Cause I'll need you more than ever when I come home. You're the only one who lets me put down the weight."

How could Aren argue with that? The last thing he wanted was to add to Deacon's load. He bit down on his lip, using the pain to fight back his tears. Right or wrong, weak or strong, he didn't know, but his resolve was gone.

He extracted one of his hands from Deacon's grip and placed it on top of Deacon's head. He could feel him trembling. He could almost feel the effort Deacon was putting into trying to pull himself together.

"You win," he said, although his voice broke on the words. "I'll stay."

Deacon's relief was almost palpable. "Thank the Saints!" he said, putting his arms around Aren's hips and holding him tight, his face buried in Aren's lap. "Thank you."

But relief for Deacon was heartache for Aren. He wished he knew Deacon would be safe. That was the crux of the matter. It wasn't that he particularly wanted to go into the wild with him. It was only that going with him seemed easier than staying behind. It seemed preferable to lying in bed, night after night, hoping and praying that wherever

Deacon was, he was alive and well. He needed to know he'd be coming home.

But what Deacon needed was for him to be strong.

He gripped a handful of Deacon's hair and pulled his head back, forcing him to look up into his eyes. He saw the surprise on Deacon's face, but he also saw the spark of arousal in his eyes.

"Don't you die out there! Don't you dare leave me here alone!" He tried to act strong and sure, but he only partially succeeded. Although his voice was firm, his eyes betrayed him. He felt tears running down his cheeks. "I'm ordering you to come home to me. I don't care what it takes."

"I will," Deacon said. "Don't you doubt it for a second."

Relief and regret fought for dominance in his heart. Aren had never known that so much joy and so much grief could exist in the same moment. He used his grip on Deacon's hair to pull him onto the bed, suddenly desperate to feel his hard, strong body underneath him. He kissed him hard. He tore at Deacon's clothes. His tongue invaded Deacon's warm mouth, and even as he stripped them both naked, as he pushed Deacon back onto the bed, he could not stop his tears. He stopped trying to fight them. He let them run down his cheeks as he spread Deacon's legs and pushed his oiled fingers inside. He cried at the sounds Deacon made, at the way his body writhed underneath him, at the way he called out Aren's name. He cried at the taste of Deacon's sweat and the feel of his flesh and the musky smell of their shared arousal. He cried at the way Deacon touched him, the gentleness of his rough hands and the tender things Deacon whispered in his ear. He nearly sobbed as Deacon begged him to finally claim him.

All the times Deacon had begged him before, Aren hadn't quite known why he'd resisted, but he knew now. This was what was meant to be. This was the moment he'd unknowingly been waiting for. He thrust his way inside his lover. He watched as Deacon's face was transformed by the pleasure of it, and at last Aren's tears were forgotten. He felt the tight, smooth heat of Deacon's body around him, and it was perfection. He revelled in the way they fitted together, at the way every inch of them seemed to be made to serve the other. He felt his heart unclench. His mind became clear.

He loved Deacon with all his heart, and he knew Deacon loved him, too. Not only that, but Deacon truly *needed* him in a way nobody ever had before. If Deacon needed him to be strong, he would be. Aren wanted only to take as much of the burden from him as he could. He wanted to make Deacon's pleasure as great as it could be. He dedicated himself to the thrill of making Deacon squirm, the joy of feeling their bodies move together, the exhilaration of hearing Deacon beg for more. He pushed Deacon's legs into the air and fucked him harder, losing himself in the eroticism of skin against skin.

He did not worry that it might be the last night they ever had. He did not worry that Deacon would not make it home. They were one now. He had to trust that fate would not lead them wrong. He gripped Deacon's swollen cock. He pumped it with his fist as he ravaged Deacon's body. He ordered him to fight his orgasm until he could no longer fight his own and they spent themselves together, crying out in one voice, declaring to the world and the wraiths and everything in existence that they could not be torn apart.

And when it was done, as Aren collapsed onto Deacon's broad chest, trying to catch his breath, all he could do was hope it was true.

They could not be torn apart.

* * * *

That was easy enough to believe in the black of night, but the next day, his courage began to fail.

It was a wet, cold morning. The family and the hands who were to remain behind stood in the courtyard, watching the men pack the last of their things onto their horses. The air was heavy with mist that couldn't quite coalesce into rain, and their breath puffed out in warm, white clouds. The horses seemed to blow steam as they pawed impatiently at the ground. Birds circled overhead and the dogs ran in happy, oblivious circles around them.

Aren was sure his heart was going to break.

He stood apart from the others, gripping his coat closed at the collar with one cold hand. He watched Simon and Frances mount up. Deacon stood on the other side of the courtyard, his back to Aren, talking quietly with Jeremiah. Finally, the men shook hands, and Deacon turned and headed for his horse.

Aren braced himself to watch them leave. He told himself he would be strong. He wouldn't cry. At least, not until he was back in the privacy of his own house.

But Deacon didn't mount his horse. He walked right past it. Aren wondered if he was imagining the way the other men all glanced at each other in confusion.

And there in the courtyard, in front of every single person who called the BarChi home, Deacon walked up to him. He hooked his big, strong hand behind Aren's neck and looked him in the eye.

"I'm coming home to you. Don't you doubt it for a second," he said quietly, repeating his vow from the night before, then he pulled Aren close and kissed him.

It was like their first kiss, soft and gentle, and Aren realised that here, in front of everybody, he really could let go. In the bedroom he had to be strong—he wanted to be strong, for Deacon, because that's what Deacon needed—but here, nobody would expect it of him. He surrendered everything that he was to Deacon's will. He wrapped his arms around Deacon and let his lover hold him tight against his big, muscular body. His lips were cold, but his mouth was warm, and Aren imagined he could open himself wide and feel Deacon's strength pouring into him.

"I love you," he whispered as Deacon released him, before he lost his courage.

Deacon smiled at him. He tilted his head down, resting his forehead against Aren's. "Reason enough to stay alive, just to hear you say those words again." He brushed his lips over Aren's one more time, a quick, soft touch.

Aren feared he'd fall when Deacon let him go. He felt sure he wouldn't be strong enough to stay standing on his own. But when Deacon released him, turning towards his waiting horse, Aren found himself standing straight and still.

Deacon swung himself up into his saddle, ignoring the stunned looks of every person present. He rode out of the courtyard without a backwards glance.

Nobody else moved. They all seemed to be in shock. All, that was, except Frances. Frances smiled at Aren. He reached up and touched the brim of his hat, almost a salute, before turning to Simon. He smacked his friend with the end of his rein, causing Simon to jump.

"What the hell you waiting for?" Frances asked. He kicked his horse into a trot and followed behind Deacon. Simon seemed to suddenly realise he was being left behind. He nudged his horse into motion and followed Deacon and Frances up the hill and out of sight.

Aren released the breath he seemed to have been holding. There was nothing left to do now but wait, and pray, and trust that Deacon would come home.

Aren shook himself out of his reverie and looked around, and as he did, he felt a blush creep up his cheeks.

Every person in the courtyard was watching him.

Some, like the wives, looked shocked. Jeremiah looked surprised, but pleased, too. Some, like Red and Ronin, simply looked amused. When Aren's eyes landed on them, the twins both laughed good-naturedly. Ronin turned and smacked his brother's chest and held his hand out, and Red started digging in his pockets. They'd actually had a wager going, and Aren found himself laughing too.

But then Aren's eyes landed on the last person in the courtyard, and his laughter died. His mouth suddenly went dry.

Dante was staring at him with such naked hatred in his eyes, it made Aren's blood run cold. Some people didn't like seeing two men together. It seemed Dante was one of them.

The crowd in the courtyard was breaking up. Everybody had chores to do and standing around gawking wasn't getting them any nearer to being done.

The wind suddenly seemed colder, the sky less bright. He was alone. His lover and the two men on the BarChi he was closest to were gone. The rest of the hands were civil to him, but none of them were his friends.

Aren pulled his coat more tightly around himself and went back to his empty house.

Chapter Twenty-Nine

Aren spent the morning painting. He painted the sun setting over the Oestend prairie, a tall windmill silhouetted in front of it, but the result was mediocre at best. His heart wasn't in it. After a few hours, he set down his brush. He turned to look at the painting of Deacon in the BarChi brand.

It was the best work he'd ever done. He could see that now. It had taken some time and distance, but the painting evoked a haunted loneliness in him that none of his other paintings did.

Symbols did have power.

He wanted to hang it up. It didn't belong in his studio. He debated putting it in the living room on the mantelpiece, but he wasn't sure he wanted the rare visitors to his house to see something that felt so personal. In the end, he took it into the bedroom and propped it up on top of the armoire. He smiled as he did it, thinking he could at least see Deacon as he fell asleep.

He was startled from his thoughts by a knock on his door. He was surprised when he opened it to find Tama on the other side.

"Am I interrupting something?" she asked.

"Not really." He opened the door wider and moved aside. "Come on in. Have a seat."

He followed her into the living room, where she sat in the chair on the far side of the fireplace—the chair he thought of as Deacon's—and he found himself wondering if it would be bad form to offer a glass of whisky.

"I kept wondering before why you weren't willing to marry either of my sisters." Her cheeks were red and her hands fidgeted in her lap as she spoke, but she was able to meet his eyes. "I guess now I know."

Aren felt his own cheeks turn red as he remembered Deacon kissing him in the courtyard, but he made himself smile. "I guess you do."

"You and Deacon are...?"

She didn't finish her sentence, but it didn't matter. "We are."

She nodded. "I see." She looked down at her lap, where her hands were twisting her apron around and around her fingers. "The thing is, I wondered if you'd consider marrying Alissa anyway?

Just when he thought they'd taken a step forwards, they had to take another step back. "I don't think that's a good idea."

"It wouldn't be a good idea to marry Beth," she said. "I can see that. But I think you still might be happy with Alissa. She could cook and clean and sew for you." She bit her lip, looking down at her lap. "She wouldn't mind about Deacon." She looked up at him again, hopeful. "I think, actually, she might be relieved if she weren't expected to..." She blushed again, apparently unable to finish. "You know."

"You're saying I should marry her even though we'd never actually consummate the marriage?"

Her blush deepened even more, but she nodded. "Yes."

"Why?" he asked. "What is there to be gained for either of us?" Aren was perfectly happy with his life with Deacon. He could see no reason to bring a woman into it at all, regardless of whether or not he was expected to have sex with her.

"My father will pay you a dowry—"

"I don't care about that. I have everything I need already."

She looked down at her lap. He could see her chin trembling as she chewed nervously on her lower lip. He had no idea what he'd do if she started to cry. He decided the best thing to do was to cut through the mountain of manure he was being presented with and get to the facts underneath.

"Tama, why don't you quit trying to convince me that I need a wife, and tell me why you're so anxious to see your sister married?"

She looked up at him, her blue eyes full of tears. "She's my sister."

"So it's only because you want her here, with you?"

"That's part of it, yes."

"And what's the other part?"

She looked down at her lap, wiping her eyes with the heels of her hands. "My father caught her in the barn," she said, so quietly Aren had to strain to hear her.

"Caught her? You mean, with a man? With one of the men from the BarChi?" *Please don't tell me it was with Deacon.*

"No," she said, shaking her head. "Not with a man."

Aren sighed in frustration, rubbing his hands over his eyes as he tried to make sense of what she was saying. He failed. "Then what exactly did he catch her doing?"

"What you think," she said. "Except with a maid."

Aren barely refrained from slapping himself on the forehead. Of course! How could he have been so stupid? Hadn't Olsa hinted at it months ago? And although it had never actually occurred to him there might be women who preferred their own gender, he realised it made as much sense as his own sexual preferences.

"My father's threatening horrible things," she said. "From banishment to things I won't speak of." She shuddered. "Things men have told him will *cure* her."

Aren could only imagine what those things might be. If they were suggested by uneducated men, they were bound to be less than enlightened.

Aren found himself feeling sympathetic. It was far too similar to his own situation. His father had disowned him years before for his indiscreet sexual activities. He'd relied on Professor Birmingham's generosity after that. He'd wanted to believe Dean had taken him in out of love, but deep down, he'd known he was nothing more than a kept boy—an amusing pet who could be disposed of when he'd outlived his use. After four years of the arrangement, the price had become too high and Aren had fled. Still, he had managed to escape to freedom, even if he hadn't quite realised it at the time. As a woman who wasn't attracted to men, Alissa would be committing herself to a very lonely life at the BarChi.

Unless…

"Is she in love with the girl?"

Marie Sexton

Tama shook her head. "I don't think so. Even if she was, the girl must not love her back. She was rather cruel to Alissa afterwards. Anyway, Alissa said my father had already sent Lacy away."

Aren thought back to his night at the McAllen ranch, and the way Alissa had glared at the women as they surrounded Deacon. At the time, he'd thought it was because she was prevented from trying for his attention as well, but he realised now she might have been watching Lacy instead.

"Will you think about it, at least?" Tama asked, interrupting his thoughts.

"I will," he said, and it wasn't exactly a lie. Although he had no intention of marrying her for any reason, he was considering possible solutions.

He thought about it all night, and the more he did, the more he felt it made sense. The next morning, after eating breakfast, he found Jeremiah in his office and presented his plan.

"So you're saying we should hire her to help Olsa?"

"Right," Aren said. "And to take her place once…" Once Olsa was gone, but Aren couldn't bring himself to say that out loud.

Jeremiah shook his head. "Son, you have any idea what kind of trouble it will cause to have a single woman running around this ranch? One woman for all those hands to fight over?"

"I don't think Alissa will be interested in any of the hands," Aren said.

"That don't mean they won't be interested in her."

Aren had already considered that as well. "I know it's a risk, but I think if she's willing to take it, we should be, too. I think as long as Deacon tells them she's to be left

342

alone and leaves no doubt as to the severity of the consequences, she'll be as safe as any of the wives are now."

Jeremiah leant back in his chair as he considered it. "You heard me tell Deacon this is his ranch now?"

"Yes, sir."

"It ain't my decision to make. He's the one you need to convince."

Despite Jeremiah's obvious doubt, Aren didn't think he'd have any trouble convincing Deacon to hire Alissa. The fact she wasn't interested in men worked in her favour, and Aren suspected Deacon would put up with just about anything if it meant helping Olsa.

After leaving Jeremiah's office, he went in search of Tama, thinking to tell her of his idea. He found her in the kitchen. Unfortunately, she wasn't alone. Dante was with her. They were standing close together, holding hands, and although their voices were too low for Aren to catch their words, there was no missing the intimacy between them.

They heard him enter, and they immediately jumped apart.

"I'm sorry," Aren stuttered. "I didn't mean to interrupt."

Tama recovered fastest. "You didn't," she said, giving him a warm smile. "We were only talking."

Aren glanced at Dante, who was glaring at him with open hostility. Aren felt quite sure there'd been more than talking going on. "I wanted to speak with you," Aren told Tama, "but I can come back later—"

"No," she said. "Really, it's fine."

"Right," Dante said, pushing past Aren towards the door. "I have work to do anyway."

Tama watched him go, her eyes full of wary concern. "Don't mind him," she said to Aren, once Dante was gone. "He's upset about the inheritance."

Aren didn't believe her. He remembered hearing Daisy say to Dante, "You'd do it too, if the one you wanted would have you." He hadn't known who Daisy meant at the time, but it was clear now she'd meant Tama.

"What did you need to talk to me about?" Tama asked.

Aren told her of his plan, and his discussion with Jeremiah, and his belief that they'd be able to convince Deacon if they made it clear that Alissa was coming to help Olsa. As he spoke, Tama's eyes filled with tears, and he could see the relief in them.

"I don't know how she'll feel about not being a wife," Aren finished. "She'd be closer to a servant."

"Is there a difference?" Tama asked through her tears.

The answer surprised him. There were only the wives and Olsa at the BarChi, no maids for Aren to hold them up against. It was certainly true that the wives did as much work as anybody. "I don't know," he said honestly. "Is there?"

She closed her eyes and shook her head—not saying no, but as if she could negate having ever made the statement. "I didn't mean that," she said. "Not really." She opened her eyes again to look at him. "Can she stay here, in the house?"

"You understand we still have to clear this with Deacon, but assuming he says yes, then I don't see why she couldn't stay here. There are empty rooms, right?"

She nodded. "Brighton and Shay's, and the one that was their sons'. And if Dante or Jeremiah choose to stay at the Austin ranch, that will make another one. And there's Gordon's old room downstairs, too."

"I can't imagine where else she'd stay," Aren said. "Not in the barracks. I guess she could take Deacon's old stall in the barn." He meant it as a joke, and he was glad when she smiled.

"Thank you," she said.

"Don't thank me yet," he said. "Let's convince Deacon first."

* * * *

The next morning, Aren went to breakfast when he always did, after the hands had eaten, even though it usually meant eating alone. This time, though, he found Tama waiting for him.

"I thought you might like some company," she said, and Aren couldn't deny it was true.

They didn't talk about much. She told him that Jay supported their plan to bring Alissa to the BarChi. She talked of milking the cows and that one of the hens had stopped laying eggs. She told him about a litter of kittens just born to one of the barn cats in the far shed, and how her boys had been searching to find where the mother cat had gone to have her brood. Tama hadn't told them for fear they'd accidentally hurt the babies.

He found that he liked her. She was open and honest and simple—not simple meaning slow or stupid, but simple in that what one saw with her, was everything she was. She didn't try to hide behind her beauty. She didn't flatter him with false praise. She was one hundred per cent genuine, and Aren admired her. He could see why Dante loved her.

After breakfast, he walked back to his house. The story of the kittens had intrigued him, and he wanted to take his sketchpad and pencils and find them. He walked into his house and up the stairs to his studio and felt his heart sink.

The ghost had been there. His paintings were in ruin. Every one of them, including the first one he'd painted of Deacon, had been slit. They lay in a pile on the floor, shreds of canvas hanging from the simple wooden frames, and Aren felt as if they were pieces of his soul, torn apart and trampled by the ghost for no reason he could ever understand. Of all the things she had done—shredding his sketchpad, breaking his penknife, tearing his clothes, smashing glasses—this was by far the worst. It felt personal.

Aren covered his face with his hands, blocking the carnage from his sight. He took a deep breath.

He loved the house. That was foremost in his mind. He loved the freedom, and the privacy. More than anything, he loved that it gave him a place to be with Deacon. It did not matter what the ghost did to him. He wasn't leaving.

It was with a horrible sense of dread that he walked into his bedroom, but when he did, the sorrow in his heart faded just a bit.

The ghost's wrath had all been vented in his studio. The painting of Deacon in the BarChi brand still sat on his armoire, completely intact.

Aren sighed with relief. Somehow, having that one painting spared meant the world to him.

He grabbed his sketchpad and his satchel of pencils and left the house. He left the mess to be dealt with another day.

He found the shed Tama had said held the kittens. It was one of the far outbuildings, one Aren had never had reason to enter before. It held old horse tack, dilapidated furniture, a wash tub with a hole in the bottom, along with a myriad equipment Aren didn't recognise—a bit of everything, it seemed. It was apparently the dumping ground for items that had lost their use and yet still seemed too worthwhile to throw away. It took some searching, but he finally found the cat, curled into a crate in the back corner, her kittens sleeping next to her. He had to shift more crates and some wagon wheels, but he finally made a space on the floor where he could sit.

The mother cat watched him with wary eyes, but when he settled onto the floor and opened his sketchpad, she seemed to decide he was no threat. She stretched lazily, her front legs reaching for the far wall, and closed her eyes. Against her side, the kittens looked like nothing more than little balls of fur.

Aren began to draw.

He'd finished the kittens and the crate, but was still working on the curve of the mother cat's ear when he heard somebody enter the shed. He had no idea how much time had passed.

He was tucked into the corner behind a pile of old saddles, and he couldn't see the door to determine who had entered. He thought maybe it was Tama coming to check on the kittens, or maybe her boys on the hunt for them, but then he heard Daisy say, "Well, say what you want to say."

Aren's heart sank. Whether Daisy was there with Dante or another man, Aren didn't want to hear it, and yet standing up and declaring his presence didn't seem like much of an option either.

"I'm not going."

"Dante, please! This is our chance to start fresh. To have our own ranch. To have a real marriage! We can leave all this behind. Maybe we can have children. Have our own family!"

"No," he said. "I'm staying here."

A stony silence followed, then, "Why?"

"I'm Jeremiah's oldest," he said. "This ranch is supposed to be mine."

"Liar! Tell me the real reason."

Dante didn't answer for the longest time. The silence seemed to stretch on. Aren's nose itched, and his foot was getting pins and needles in it from the awkward way he was sitting on it, but he didn't dare move lest they discover his presence.

"You know why," Dante said at last.

Daisy laughed—a harsh, bitter, angry laugh. "You're pathetic. You're going to stay here just so you can be close to a person who's never going to love you back. Not the way you want, at any rate."

"Say whatever you want. Leave if you want. I could care less."

Daisy's breath hitched, and when she spoke again, her voice was thick with tears. "Why can't you love me?" she asked. "Why can't we go to the Austin ranch together? Why shouldn't we try to make this work?"

"It doesn't matter what you say," he said. "I've made up my mind. I'm not going."

"Well, I'm not staying! I won't sit here and watch you pine after—"

"I don't know why it should matter to you," Dante said, interrupting her. "You can spread your legs for ranch hands here as well as you could there."

There was a crash as something hit the wall of the shed. "I hate you!" Daisy cried. Her voice broke on the words, and she lapsed into sobs which faded away as she turned and ran out of the door.

Dante sighed heavily. "If only that were true."

* * * *

Deacon's return started much as it had the time before. Three men had gone out, but only two appeared at the top of the ridge.

One was small, and Aren knew him immediately to be Frances. It didn't take much longer for him to confirm that Deacon was the other, and he sighed with relief. Still, he steeled himself for what was to come. Deacon would have to talk to Jeremiah, maybe to the men. If it was anything like last time, he would need every ounce of his resolve to get through the rest of the day. Aren would not add to that burden. He vowed to himself he would do everything he could to bolster Deacon's strength rather than deplete it.

He knew, though, as the two men rode into the courtyard, that it was nothing like last time. Both were smiling. Red and Ronin, the only two hands not out in the field, greeted them at the gate, offering to take care of the horses for them, and as Deacon and Frances dismounted, Aren heard Frances say, "He's fine. He's stayed behind to start fixing things up."

Nobody was hurt. Nobody had died. And when Deacon turned to him with a smile, he knew there was no reason to hold himself back. He threw his arms around Deacon's neck and felt Deacon's strong arms wrap around him.

"I told you I'd be back," Deacon said into his ear, and Aren laughed. A week of heartache and worry were gone in the blink of an eye, and he couldn't believe how good it felt. Deacon kissed the side of his head, then pulled back to look at him. "I have to talk to Jeremiah. See you at supper?"

"Yes," Aren said, still smiling. He didn't resent at all that he had to wait his turn. He was just happy Deacon was home, and safe, and without the horrible trauma he'd suffered the last time he'd gone north.

"Good." Deacon started to turn away, but stopped halfway. He looked down at the ground, pushing his hat down low as he often did when he was uncomfortable with something. He turned back and put his hand behind Aren's neck, pulling him close for a moment. His lips brushed Aren's ear, making Aren shiver. "I missed you," he whispered.

Aren closed his eyes as the feeling those words stirred rushed through him. They made him giddy. He felt so light, he imagined he might float away. Even after Deacon had let him go, Aren wondered at the sheer joy those simple words gave him. Deacon has missed him.

"I missed you, too," he said, even though Deacon had long since walked away.

That night, Tama met them in the kitchen for supper. She was nervous. She kept wringing her hands together. Deacon was clearly confused as to why she was there, but as they ate supper, Aren told him about Alissa. As he expected, Deacon started out sceptical. Aren thought the man's eyes might pop out of his head when he told him that Alissa favoured women. Deacon's cheeks turned red, and his eyes shifted to the side, and Aren knew he was imagining what two women might do together.

"I don't see why she would be different than any of the other wives," Aren said. "She won't be encouraging them. It would only be an issue if one of them forced himself on her, but as long as they know how severe the consequences will be, I doubt they would. They've never raped any of the wives, right?" He turned to Tama. "Have they ever caused you trouble?"

"Nothing serious," she said. "Nothing that wasn't stopped by one of the other men threatening to string them from the nearest tree."

"See?" Aren said, turning back to Deacon. "She'll be as safe as any of the wives are now."

"I suppose that's a fair point," Deacon said.

"And I think Olsa could use the help," Aren said. They all looked over at Olsa, who had her back to them as she kneaded dough on the countertop.

"Olsa?" Deacon asked. "What do you think?"

"I don't need any damn help," she said with a stubbornness that made both men smile. "But leaving that girl with her daddy and that foul sister of hers would be downright cruel."

Deacon sighed heavily, looking at Tama with resignation. "Jay leaves for town the day after tomorrow," he said. "Guess it's easy enough for him to bring the girl back with him."

"Thank you!" Tama squealed. She threw her arms around Deacon's neck, and Aren almost laughed at the alarm on the man's face.

"You're welcome," Deacon said, pushing her gently off him and turning away. "No need to get hysterical."

She smiled at him, and Aren laughed at Deacon's discomfort, but the next second she was hugging Aren, and Deacon was laughing at him instead.

"Thank you," she said.

Aren patted her awkwardly on the back, glaring over her shoulder at Deacon, who was still laughing. "You're welcome," he said, and was relieved when she suddenly let him go.

"I have to go tell Jay," she said, rushing from the room.

"Blessed Saints," Deacon swore after she'd gone, shaking his head. "I won't be doing her any more favours if that's the kind of thanks I get."

They walked back across the grass to Aren's house. They still had two or three hours before nightfall, and normally they spent at least some of that time talking before going upstairs, but it became clear as soon as they walked into the house that Deacon had no desire to wait. He grabbed Aren and pulled him into his arms and kissed him.

It was strange. His kiss was urgent, yet hesitant. Deacon gripped him hard, pulling Aren hard against his body, and yet his hands didn't stray anywhere else. He broke their kiss, his breathing heavy.

"Aren," he said, and he sounded desperate. The word was almost a question, and yet Aren wasn't sure exactly what it was he was asking.

"Come upstairs," Aren said, and Deacon smiled in return.

Aren led him up the stairs, but as they passed the door to his studio, Deacon stopped short. "What happened?" he asked.

Aren looked into the room. He'd cleaned up some of what the ghost had done, but he hadn't known what to do with the ruined paintings. He couldn't fix them, but he couldn't bring himself to throw them onto the trash pile either. They sat on his easels, and on the floor leaning against the wall, their tattered pieces hanging pitifully from the wooden frames.

"The ghost," Aren said.

Deacon looked at him, his eyes wide with alarm. "It can't be."

"Forget it," Aren said, taking Deacon's hand and pulling him to the bedroom. Deacon's kiss had stirred desires far more intriguing than anything his torn paintings had to offer.

Deacon's distraction lasted only for a moment. Aren pulled him into the bedroom and kissed him, unbuttoning Deacon's shirt as he did. Deacon held him tight, kissing him hungrily as Aren began to undress him, but Deacon never reached to remove any of Aren's clothes.

Aren wasn't sure what to think of Deacon's reluctance. On one hand, there was no doubt the big cowboy was turned on. His moans and the urgency of his kisses would have told Aren that if the giant erection that ground against Aren's hip wasn't enough. But Aren didn't understand the way Deacon seemed to be holding something back.

"What's wrong?" he finally asked.

Deacon gripped Aren's shoulders hard. He leant down and put his forehead against Aren's. "There are two ways we can do this." His voice shook, and Aren recognised the desperation in it. "There's the way I know you deserve after I been away. The way I think it should be the first night I'm home. But there's the other way..."

Aren smiled, comprehension finally dawning. "The way you *need*?"

Deacon's fingers clenched tighter, digging painfully into Aren's flesh. "Please."

Aren kissed him first, gently, acknowledging the sacrifice Deacon thought he was asking him to make, but Aren didn't see it that way. Yes, they could make love, slow and gentle while Deacon whispered in his ear. Aren loved the way Deacon made him feel cherished and beautiful when they did that. But he didn't mind waiting for it, because more than anything, what he loved was knowing that Deacon needed him. He loved being able to give him something nobody else could. He loved that by tying him up, by pushing him down, by making him beg, he was giving Deacon the strength he needed to go on the next day.

He stepped back from Deacon, out of arm's reach. "Take off your clothes," he said, and he saw the relief on Deacon's face. He watched Deacon undress, contemplating how best to give them each what they wanted.

When the last of his clothes had been tossed away, Aren led him to the foot of the bed. "Spread your legs," he said. Deacon had to spread them wide in order for Aren to tie his ankles to the legs of the bed. Deacon was taller than him, but making him spread his legs so far brought him lower, which would make it much easier for Aren to fuck him if he so desired. Deacon's front was towards the bed, his groin a few inches above the mattress.

"Grab onto the posts," Aren told him, and Deacon obeyed.

Aren had the black strips of cloth ripped from his old shirt, and he used them to wrap Deacon's wrists before securing them to the bedposts with the rope. When he was finished, he sat back to look at his lover. Deacon looked amazing, tied spread eagled to the bed, his cock hard and heavy between his legs. Aren wrapped one arm around his neck and kissed him, stroking Deacon's erection with his other hand. He couldn't decide what to do to Deacon. The possibilities were too many—fuck him, or be fucked by him, suck him, or be sucked by him, use the crop on his back, use his own fingers to penetrate him. He wanted to do it all, and he moaned against Deacon's lips as he considered his options.

First, though, he had to get rid of his own clothes. He let Deacon go, smiling at the groan of frustration he elicited. He was just standing up to pull his shirt off when somebody knocked on his front door.

"You're not going to answer that, are you?" Deacon asked.

He sounded so desperate, and it made Aren feel wickedly devious. "I think I am," he said. "You stand here and think about all the things I might do when I get back."

Deacon groaned again, and Aren laughed as he went down the stairs to answer the door. He made sure his shirt was covering his groin before he opened it. It turned out to be Frances on the other side.

Frances was smiling, the wind blowing his sandy blond hair. "Can I come in?" he asked.

Aren thought of Deacon, tied up in the bedroom. He wondered how long he could leave him there and have it still be erotic rather than simply uncomfortable. "Sure," he said, stepping aside so Frances could come inside. "Do you want a drink?" He asked the question from habit as much as anything, and he was a bit relieved when Frances shook his head.

"No," he said. "I don't know if Deacon told you or not, but I'm leaving tomorrow. Going back up north to help Simon. I only came back to get our things. I wanted to say goodbye."

Aren hadn't quite realised that Frances and Simon were leaving the BarChi for good. The thought made him a bit sad. "I'll miss you," he said.

Frances smiled, and Aren found himself thinking how much the boy had changed since the accident with Miron. He was more sure of himself. He was confident without being cocky. He was still quiet, but he'd developed a subtle humour that seemed to keep both him and Simon smiling. "I wanted to thank you," Frances said, "for being my friend when there was nobody else."

"You're welcome." Aren had reached out to Frances because he'd known how it felt to have nobody to turn to. Yet now, they'd both found other people. Aren had Deacon, and Frances had Simon. "Do you love him?" Aren asked.

Frances blushed, looking down at the floor, which was an answer in and of itself.

"Does he love you?" Aren asked.

Frances shrugged. He shook his head, looking up at Aren. "Not like you mean," he said. "But I think he needs me, and I guess that's enough."

"I can understand that." Although Aren wondered how long Frances could live with 'enough'.

Frances smiled at him, cocking his head to the side. The slight bend in his nose made him look less innocent, more rakish. He stepped closer to Aren so he was standing only an inch or two away. His eyes were playful. "You turned me down once before," he said, "and I'm glad. But I wondered if now, you might change your mind."

Aren felt himself blush as Frances' meaning dawned on him. He wondered how different things might have been if it had been *this* Frances who had offered himself so many months before, rather than the Frances who was broken and scared. "I'm no longer in a position to accept your offer," Aren said.

Frances was still smiling at him. "Because of Deacon?"

"Because of Deacon."

Frances stepped back a bit, giving Aren more room. "Figured it couldn't hurt to ask." He ran his fingers through his hair and laughed nervously. "Saints, Aren. It's been a blessed long time! And looks like not much chance anytime in the near future, either."

"Not with Simon?" Aren asked.

"I wish!" Frances said, shaking his head. "He's not like us." He smiled again at Aren. "I'd be happy to find anybody right now who was willing."

Aren thought suddenly of Deacon, still tied to his bed upstairs, and he felt himself smile. "Wait here," he said. He didn't wait for Frances to respond, but ran quickly up the stairs and into the bedroom.

"Holy Saints," Deacon swore when he walked into the room. "You're killing me here! Who was at the door?"

"Frances."

"What did he want?"

Aren didn't answer as he climbed onto the bed. He put his arms around Deacon's neck and looked into his eyes. "Do you trust me?" he asked.

"You got me naked and tied to your bed," Deacon said, smiling. "What do you think?"

"I want to try something new," Aren said. "Something we haven't done before." He saw the curiosity in Deacon's eyes. Aren ran his hand down Deacon's chest and wrapped his fingers around Deacon's cock. His erection had gone down as he'd waited, but it responded readily to Aren's touch. "Do you trust me?" Aren asked again.

"Yes."

Aren grabbed the largest strip of black cloth and used it to blindfold Deacon, tying it behind his head. "I'll be right back," he said when he was finished. "Wait here."

"Where the blessed hell you think I'm going?" Deacon asked, and Aren laughed as he walked back out of the door and down the stairs to where Frances waited.

"Come on," he said, taking Frances' hand. "Come upstairs with me."

Frances' cheeks immediately turned red, but he smiled. "What about Deacon?" he asked as Aren led him up the stairs. "Last thing I want is to have him mad at me."

"He won't be," Aren told him. He stopped at his bedroom door and turned to look at Frances. He could see the arousal in the boy's eyes, eager anticipation clearly written on his face. "Promise me you'll follow my lead."

"I'll promise anything you want. Long as you don't change your mind now."

Aren stopped before opening the door, struck suddenly by a memory — the memory of being blindfolded and tied to a table in Dean's study. The memory of Dean bringing other men into the room without asking Aren first. Aren had never known who they were. He'd never even known for sure how many of them there were. They'd used him in every conceivable way, and on some level, Aren had enjoyed every minute of it. He'd climaxed more than once. But later had come the shame, and the regret, and the anger Dean had waved away with a flick of his manicured hand.

Was what he was about to do to Deacon any different?

Yes.

It *was* different. He was sure of it, just as he was sure the Oestend wind would sing through the night. Dean hadn't cared about humiliating Aren. He'd laughed when Aren asked with some embarrassment the next day if the other men were professors, too. And although Aren had enjoyed the sex, it hadn't been because they'd gone to any effort to make it good for him. They'd used him for their own pleasure. Any pleasure he'd managed to find was a product of his own body, and his own mind.

What he had planned for Deacon was something else entirely. There would be no shame involved. He wanted to give pleasure, not take it.

Aren opened the door and led Frances in. As soon as the boy's eyes landed on Deacon, he stopped dead in his tracks. Deacon's back was to them. His muscles were taut and accentuated by the lamplight. He looked unbelievably erotic tied to the bed, with his long dark hair hanging loose down his back. "Holy Saints," Frances breathed.

Deacon jumped. "Aren?" he asked, his voice suspicious.

Aren went to him. He climbed onto the bed as he'd done before so he could face Deacon, even though the blindfold prevented him from making eye contact.

"You trust me, right?"

"I trust *you*," Deacon hissed. "Nobody else."

"It's Frances," Aren said. "And he won't do anything without my permission."

"That ain't the point! I can't have him see me like this!"

"You *can*. He's leaving tomorrow. You're not his boss anymore."

"What about the other men?" Deacon asked, his teeth clenched.

"Do you really think he'd tell anybody?" Aren asked. "What would he possibly have to gain by doing such a thing?"

Deacon seemed to think about that for a moment, and Aren saw the tension go out of him. He sighed. There was still suspicion in his voice when he asked, "Why did you bring him up here?"

"Because he's going to help me," Aren said. He put one arm around Deacon's neck. He kissed him, and with his other hand, he grazed Deacon's half-engorged cock. "We're going to work together," he whispered as he kissed Deacon again. He ran his fingers over Deacon's foreskin, causing him to moan.

"Are you going to let him fuck me?"

"No," Aren said, and even with the blindfold, he sensed Deacon's relief. "I might let him do other things, though," he said. "I might have you do things for him." Deacon's breath caught, and Aren continued to stroke his lover's cock, which was fully erect again. He flicked his tongue over Deacon's lips. "I think we'll use your mouth," Aren said, because he knew it turned Deacon on to be used in that way. "We'll use our hands." He nipped at Deacon's lips. "I might fuck you," he said, "or just use my fingers." Deacon whimpered, straining against the ropes that bound his wrists. "Don't worry about anything," Aren said. "Just relax. I'll make it good. I'll take care of you. Let me show you something new." Deacon moaned again, thrusting his hips out, pushing his cock through Aren's hand. "Do you trust me?" Aren asked again.

Deacon went limp in his bonds, breathing hard, and even before Deacon spoke, Aren recognised it for what it was—a surrender. "Yes," Deacon said, and the word came out a groan.

Aren smiled as he kissed his lover one more time. "Oh, honey. We're going to make you feel so, *so* good!"

Chapter Thirty

Aren climbed off the bed and quickly stripped out of his clothes. Frances watched him, his eyes occasionally darting over to where Deacon stood, bound to the bed. The boy's eyes were wide, his cheeks flushed, his pants tented over the bulge at his groin.

Aren went and stood behind him, pushing up against his back, and he heard Frances' breathing speed up. He looked over Frances' shoulder at Deacon. "Isn't he gorgeous?" he asked quietly.

Frances nodded. "Amazing," he said, his voice thick with arousal.

"Don't you want to touch him?" Aren asked. Frances nodded again, but he didn't move. Aren reached around Frances' waist and unbuttoned his shirt. The boy held perfectly still as Aren pulled it backwards off his shoulders. On Frances' right shoulder blade was a familiar symbol, the BarChi brand. It was beginning to heal but still looked tender and pink. Aren guessed the brand was less than two weeks old.

He reached around Frances again and began to untie the boy's pants. Frances pushed his hips out, thrusting his groin towards Aren's hand, but Aren didn't caress him. He merely opened the boy's pants to free his erection. "Take them off," he said.

Frances hurried to do his bidding, and Aren bit back a laugh at the boy's eagerness. When he was naked, Aren stood next to him and whispered in his ear, "You don't have to let him fuck you." Frances looked at him in confusion, and Aren smiled. He'd understand when he saw how large Deacon was. "Come on," Aren said. He took Frances' hand and led him over to Deacon.

Frances eyed the big man in front of him. His excitement was obvious in his eyes, but there was a cautious wariness there too. He didn't move. Aren smiled at the boy's hesitation, but he was glad for it, too. There was no doubt in Aren's mind that Frances would follow his lead.

Aren stood behind Frances again, allowing his erection to push against France's small, firm ass. He took Frances' right wrist and guided his hand up to Deacon's back.

Deacon jumped when Frances' fingertips made contact, and Frances jumped too, pulling his hand away.

"Shhh," Aren soothed, taking the boy's wrist and moving his hand again to Deacon's back. "We're all here for the same thing," he said. "Nobody needs to be afraid." He let go of Frances' wrist, and Frances slowly ran his hand down Deacon's back, then back up. He traced Deacon's scars with his fingertips.

Aren watched Frances' pale hand move on Deacon's dark skin. As he did, he stroked Frances' hip. He kissed the boy's shoulder and the back of his neck. Aren wanted to find the perfect line between making things good for Frances, too, but not giving more of himself to the boy than he felt he should.

Frances' hand moved lower. He caressed Deacon's hip, and Deacon's breath sped up in response.

"Do you know who's touching you?" Aren asked quietly.

"Frances," Deacon said.

"How can you tell?"

"Your hands are softer."

Aren smiled. He liked that Deacon knew his touch so well.

He was still behind Frances, and he pushed the boy closer. He pushed him up against Deacon's back, and both men moaned. Aren ground against Frances, causing Frances to grind against Deacon, and all three of them drew breath together.

Aren put his right hand over Frances' where it lay on Deacon's hip. He guided it slowly around, across Deacon's stomach, to Deacon's thick, hard cock. He wrapped both of their fingers around it, and Deacon gasped.

"Holy Saints, he's big," Frances breathed as Aren began to guide his hand up and down Deacon's shaft. "Now I know why you said what you did."

Aren kept Frances' hand moving on Deacon's cock. "Keep going," he whispered in Frances' ear as he released his grip. "Go around to his front."

Frances did, climbing around Deacon's right side and onto the bed in front of him. Aren moved to Deacon's left side. He could see Frances was still stroking Deacon with one hand. His other hand caressed Deacon's side. Deacon's head was thrown back, his breathing becoming fast and heavy.

Frances glanced at Aren before leaning over to touch his tongue to Deacon's nipple. He looked at Aren again, confirming that what he was doing was acceptable, and Aren smiled at him. It was clearly all the encouragement he needed. He shut his eyes, closing his mouth over Deacon's nipple, sucking it between his lips as he continued to stroke Deacon's cock, and Deacon moaned.

Aren ran his right hand down Deacon's back and between his legs, moving his fingers slowly down Deacon's crack. He closed his mouth around Deacon's other nipple, and was gratified by the sounds it elicited from Deacon. He found Deacon's entrance. His fingers weren't oiled, so he didn't push in, but he massaged Deacon's rim as he bit lightly at Deacon's skin.

Deacon's arms jerked against the ties that bound him, and Aren smiled against Deacon's dark flesh. With his left hand, he reached down. Frances was still stroking Deacon, his hand low on the man's shaft. Aren wrapped his hand around Deacon's crown, and they stroked together. Deacon whimpered. He tried to thrust his hips, to push into their hands, but he had no leverage, and he fell limp against his ties, moaning as Aren and Frances stroked him. Aren moved up to Deacon's lips, although it meant removing his other hand from Deacon's crack. He wrapped his right arm around Deacon's neck, keeping himself off to one side so he didn't interfere with what Frances was doing. He flicked his tongue over Deacon's lower lip, and Deacon's lips parted. He opened up for Aren, leaning in to the kiss, moaning against Aren's mouth as Aren kissed him and stroked him, as Frances continued to tease the big man's nipple. They were all breathing hard. Every moan from Deacon seemed to trigger one from Frances as well. Aren kissed his lover harder, tightening his grip on Deacon's shaft.

"Aren!" Deacon gasped against Aren's lips, and Aren knew it was a warning.

Aren released Deacon's cock, pushing Frances' hand away from it, too. Frances took his hint, although he continued to caress Deacon's body as he kissed his chest. Aren pulled back and eyed Deacon's soft, moist lips. "I think I may have to make you work a bit," he said to Deacon. "Earn your keep."

Deacon moaned again. He strained against the rope that held his wrists. "Yes," he moaned, his voice a mere whisper. "Aren, please."

Aren moved away from him, grabbing Frances as he did, pulling him away from Deacon, too. Frances looked at him with fevered eyes, his lips moist, his breathing heavy. Aren guided him to his feet. He stood behind him again, pushing against his back, urging him closer to Deacon. He guided the boy's hands to the canopy frame above them and Frances took his hint and grabbed hold. Aren pushed harder against Frances' back, grinding against his backside, granting himself the tiniest bit of release as he did, the first real touch on his own cock. With his right hand, he reached around Frances. He hooked his hand behind Deacon's head.

Deacon knew what that meant. He opened his mouth, and Aren guided Frances' cock into it.

He thought for a minute the boy was going to come right then. Frances cried out. He tensed, thrusting his hips forwards, thrusting his cock deep into Deacon's mouth. He froze there, and Aren waited, but then Frances took a deep, shaking breath. "Holy Saints, that feels good," he breathed.

"Keep going," Aren said as he released his grip on Deacon's head and stepped back, away from Frances. He watched as Frances started to thrust. "Don't come yet."

Frances made a sound—not quite confirmation, not quite protest—but he was too lost in pleasure to do anything else.

Aren went to the bedside table and grabbed the salve. They were getting low, and he smiled as he thought about having to ask Olsa for more. He spread some on the fingers of one hand and stepped up behind Frances. "Don't come," he warned again. Then he slowly pushed his fingers into Frances.

The boy cried out, and Deacon, who seemed as lost in the pleasure he was giving as Frances was in receiving, moaned in response.

"Aren!" Frances cried, and Aren recognised the desperation in his voice. Aren used his other hand to grab Deacon's hair, pulling him off Frances' cock, and both men groaned in frustration. "Not yet," Aren whispered in Frances' ear. He moved his fingers in and out while Frances panted and moaned. Aren was careful not to touch the sensitive spot deep inside the boy. He didn't want to trigger an orgasm. He was only getting Frances ready.

He slowly removed his fingers, and Frances sighed. He was still hanging on to the frame of the canopy, trying to catch his breath. Aren nudged him gently to the side, and used his hand in Deacon's hair to turn Deacon's head towards him, towards his own groin. Deacon moaned and buried his nose in Aren's hair.

"Aren," he said quietly. He put his tongue out, on the base of Aren's shaft, and licked up to his crown.

"How do you know it's me?" Aren asked.

"I know the way you smell," Deacon said. His tongue moved again up Aren's length. "I love the way you smell."

Aren had meant to make Deacon do for him what he'd done for Frances, but his lover's words triggered something in him that was more tender. He dropped to his knees and kissed Deacon hard. As he did, he reached down and began to stroke Deacon's cock. Deacon gasped, arching his back, throwing his head back even though it meant breaking their kiss. "Aren," he breathed. "More, more, more..."

"Soon," Aren said, smiling at Deacon's impatience. He moved off the bed and went to stand behind Deacon. He looked up at Frances who was smiling down at him, having finally caught his breath. "You're going to suck Frances again," Aren whispered in Deacon's ear. "Would you like that?"

"Yes," Deacon said.

"If I untie one hand, you can use your fingers on him."

"Yes."

"And I'm going to use my hands on you."

Deacon groaned, a sound that came from deep within his chest. "Yes."

"Frances won't last long," Aren whispered. "You don't get to come when he does."

"I won't."

"Good." Aren reached up with one hand and grabbed Frances' cock, guiding it to Deacon's mouth. Frances' eyes drifted shut as Deacon sucked him in. He began to thrust, slower than before. "Good," Aren said again, nipping at Deacon's shoulder. He ran his hands down Deacon's sides to his hips, then forwards over his stomach. Deacon moaned and his breathing sped up as Aren's hands neared his cock.

"I'm going to fuck you later," Aren said in his ear, keeping his voice low so Frances would be less likely to hear. "But not yet." Deacon whimpered, but could say nothing with Frances' cock still moving in and out of his mouth. "For now, I'll give you this." He wrapped his hand around Deacon's cock.

Deacon moaned again, and for a minute, Aren lost himself to the simple pleasure of stroking his lover, feeling his thick cock moving in and out of his hand. He ground his own erection against Deacon's firm ass. He nipped at his shoulder.

Above him, he could hear Frances' breath growing ragged. Deacon's moans were becoming more urgent. Aren let go of Deacon long enough to reach up and untie one of his hands. As soon as Deacon's hand was free, Aren moved back to where he'd been, stroking Deacon while grinding against him from behind. Frances' eyes were closed, but they snapped open when he felt Deacon touch him. He slowed, his eyes wide as he looked down at Aren. He was breathing hard, but he stopped thrusting, allowing Deacon, who was still blindfolded, to find his entrance.

Aren couldn't see from where he was, but he knew the instant Deacon's fingers pushed inside. Frances' back arched as he hung on to the canopy frame above him. "Oh, Saints, yes!" he moaned, and his words seemed to trigger a greater arousal in Deacon as well. Deacon's hand began to move, Frances' hips began to thrust harder and faster, forwards into Deacon's mouth, backwards onto Deacon's hand. They were panting, their breathing almost in sync, and Aren tightened his grip on Deacon's cock. He ground hard against him from behind. He revelled in the feeling of having both men submit to him, of being able to give each of them something they needed. Aren dug the fingers of his free hand into Deacon's side, scratching his flesh. He bit harder on Deacon's shoulder as he ground against him, as he stroked him harder and faster, moving his hand to the tempo of the ragged breaths of his lover and the man whose cock was deep in Deacon's mouth, the man who Deacon's fingers fucked faster and harder than before. He lost himself in the rhythm of their breathing, the motion of their thrusts, the guttural urgency of their moans, until suddenly Frances cried out.

Aren stopped stroking Deacon, for fear Frances' orgasm would trigger Deacon's, too, but he held him as Frances thrust again into Deacon's mouth. Deacon's hand drew him in deeper, and Frances yelled out again as he spent himself in Deacon's mouth.

Frances pulled out of Deacon's mouth, and as soon as he did, Deacon started to talk. "Aren," he said, "Aren, Aren, Aren, Aren..."

It was only his name, but Aren knew it for what it was. Deacon was begging him for more. He wouldn't let himself plead in front of Frances the way he normally did, but his need compelled him to say something.

"Shhh," Aren soothed. He took Deacon's hand and tied it back to the bedpost. He grabbed the salve off the bed and spread more on his own fingers. Frances, who had collapsed backwards onto the bed looking unbelievably relieved, watched him with a sated smile on his face. "We're not finished yet," Aren said to Deacon.

Aren put his slick fingertips against Deacon's rim. He pushed, just barely.

Deacon's body bucked. He strained against his bonds.
He arched his back, trying to push his hips back, trying to
push himself further onto Aren's fingers.

Aren pulled out, and Deacon moaned. He went limp
against the ropes, sagging. "Aren," he panted, "Aren,
Aren, Aren…"

Aren didn't grant Deacon what he wanted right away.
As Frances watched them, Aren continued to tease his
lover, barely pushing in, then pulling out, drawing their
pleasure out as long as he could. He wanted to make it
last. He also wanted to give Frances time to recover and
join back in if he so desired. The boy was young, Aren
thought with a smile. If any of them could do it, it would
be him.

Besides, more than anything, Aren loved teasing
Deacon. He continued to caress him and kiss him, but he
never went all the way. He made sure to give Deacon a
little less than he longed for, less than he needed, making
the big man buck and squirm, until he was nearly frantic.

"Aren," he cried out. "Please!"

Aren smiled. He kept his fingertips firmly on Deacon's
entrance, rubbing in slow, sensuous circles. He reached
around with his other hand to grip Deacon's cock. Then,
very, very slowly, he pushed his fingers past Deacon's
rim, sliding them deep inside. Deacon whimpered. He
writhed. He groaned. He pulled against his ropes. Aren
kept his fingers moving, in and out, in and out. He kept
his other hand moving up and down Deacon's shaft.

Frances, whose cock was growing hard again, watched
them with half-lidded eyes. He crawled across the bed. He
got to his knees in front of Deacon. He ran his hands up
Deacon's sides. He eyed Deacon's face and his lips, and
Aren wondered how Deacon would respond if Frances

kissed him. But Frances seemed to decide against it. Instead, he began to kiss Deacon's neck and his chest. He let his hands wander over the big man's chest and sides.

Aren continued his motions with both hands, fucking Deacon from behind with one while stroking his cock with the other. He ground his own aching erection against Deacon's hip, biting his lip to fight back his own impending climax.

He felt Frances' small, callused hand on his, and Aren let Frances take over stroking Deacon. Aren concentrated on moving his fingers in and out of Deacon, grinding himself against Deacon's hip as he did. He watched as Frances kissed his way down Deacon's chest to where he held Deacon's big cock in his hand. He saw the way Frances eyed it, debating. Aren could tell just by watching the boy that he'd never sucked a man's cock before.

Frances pulled Deacon's foreskin back. He put his head down and touched the very tip of his tongue to the end of Deacon's shaft.

Deacon bucked, gasping, and Frances looked up at him, his eyes burning. The boy was stretched out on his stomach, and Aren noticed the way his hips ground into the bed. He heard Frances moan. Frances pushed his hips down again as he bent his head back to Deacon's waiting cock. He put his tongue out again, flicking it over Deacon's crown, and Deacon moaned again, pulling against the ropes.

"Yes," he whispered. "Yes yes yes yes..."

That seemed to be all the encouragement Frances needed. The boy opened his mouth and took Deacon's tip in, and Deacon cried out, his voice hoarse and husky with need. Frances began to move up and down—he couldn't take in more than half of Deacon's length—but he made up for it with sheer enthusiasm. He attacked Deacon's erection, sucking it, pumping the base of it with his fist as he humped his own hips against the bed. The boy was moving faster and faster, his thrusts against the bed becoming more urgent as he sucked Deacon.

Aren sped up, moving his fingers faster in and out of Deacon, watching as Frances sucked Deacon's cock. Frances and Deacon were lost again in the pleasure, and Aren let himself get lost, too, grinding against Deacon's firm hip. Their moans began to overlap. Their ragged breathing fell into sync. He pushed harder against Deacon's smooth flesh as he pushed a third finger inside.

"Aren!" Deacon cried. "I can't, I can't, I can't…"

Aren's own arousal was peaking. He couldn't hold his own orgasm at bay much longer, let alone Deacon's.

"Not until my cock is in you," he said. Deacon moaned in response, pulling on his ropes, biting his lip in what Aren knew was an attempt to distract himself from the pleasure.

Aren moved into position behind Deacon. His own cock was rock hard, almost painful with the need for release. He pulled his fingers out of Deacon. He used his hands to spread him wide, to open him up, and he slowly pushed his cock inside.

"Awww!" Deacon cried out, pulling harder against his bonds as Aren started to thrust. The bedposts creaked from the strain as Deacon's muscles tensed. Aren thrust harder. He watched Frances' hips humping against the bed. He heard Deacon's low, desperate cry. He felt the weight behind it, the pressure of Deacon's orgasm bearing down on them all.

He reached around Deacon. He grabbed hold of his nipple with one hand. And he squeezed.

Hard.

Deacon gasped, sucking in his breath as the pain hit him, then his back arched and he screamed. His body tightened around Aren's cock, and Aren came with him, pumping into Deacon's body as his lover cried out again from the force of his release.

His orgasm was quick but unbelievably intense, and Aren collapsed against Deacon's back, holding himself up only by his grip on Deacon's body. Deacon was limp in his bonds, his sides heaving as he fought to catch his breath. Aren forced his knees to work. He made himself stand up on legs that were wobbly from his own climax. He looked around Deacon's body at where Frances lay on the bed. The boy obviously hadn't been able to swallow Deacon's cum. He had apparently pulled away and used his fist instead. There was cum on his hand, in his hair, on the sheets, on his cheek. He let go of Deacon and sat up, breathing hard, but smiling ear to ear. He looked down at the sticky wetness on his own groin, where he'd climaxed again. He grinned up at Aren.

"I made a mess of your bed."

Aren burst out laughing. "You're forgiven," he said. He turned to look at Deacon, who was smiling, still trying to catch his breath. He wanted to untie him, but he found that now, after they were all spent, he wanted his lover to himself. After being tied up, Deacon was always tender with him. That was when Aren felt the most cherished. It was a moment he didn't want to share.

He looked over at Frances, trying to decide what to say, but to his surprise, Frances was smiling at him, already getting off the bed. "I'll go downstairs," he said.

"I'm sorry," Aren started to say, but he stopped when Frances burst out laughing.

"Holy Saints, Aren, you sure don't owe me any apologies." He smiled at Aren again as he picked his pants up off the floor. "I'll drink your whisky. You take your time."

When he was gone, Aren untied Deacon's legs, and the big cowboy moaned, more from pain than from pleasure, as he straightened back up to his full height.

"I'm sorry," Aren said again, and Deacon laughed, just as Frances had done.

"You don't owe me any apologies, either."

But suddenly, Aren wasn't so sure. He remembered the shame he'd felt as Dean Birmingham had untied him so many months before. He remembered fighting back tears as he lay there, cum from at least three men running down his legs. He remembered how humiliated he'd felt that some of it was his own. He didn't want that for Deacon.

Aren climbed onto the bed. Deacon's hands were still tied but being able to stand all the way up had given him some slack. Aren knelt in front of him. His hands shook as he slowly pushed the blindfold off Deacon's eyes. He was afraid of what he'd see in them. When Deacon's gaze met his, Aren's doubts seemed to shrink, but they didn't disappear. Deacon looked as he always did after sex—happy, sated, relaxed. And as he looked at Aren, Aren saw also the tenderness he'd grown used to seeing in Deacon's eyes.

"What's the matter?" Deacon asked immediately.

"Did I do wrong?" Aren asked, his voice shaking.

"No," Deacon said. "You never do."

Aren reached up and untied one wrist. "I don't want you to feel ashamed."

"Why would I?"

Aren moved to the other hand. "Do you regret letting me tell you what to do? Do you hate me for bringing Frances in?"

Deacon was looking at him with puzzlement in his eyes. "Not one bit." With both hands free, he reached for Aren, pulling him into his arms, holding him tight against his body. "Here in this room, you're in charge," he said, "I'll do anything you say. I'll follow any order you give me."

Aren felt a lump in his throat, although he couldn't have said exactly why. "Tell me you love me."

Deacon smiled. He pushed Aren backwards onto the bed, still holding him tight. His hands moved on Aren's skin, petting him, soothing him, reassuring him. "I do love you," he said. "More than you know. More than I can say. More than anything else in the world." He kissed Aren's neck and his jaw. He caressed him. "I love you more than I ever thought possible. I don't know how I ever lived without you. I hope I never have to live without you again."

Aren felt tears running down his cheeks. His entire body was trembling, and Deacon held him tighter. "I don't regret one second of my time in this room with you, and I don't want you to regret any of it, either. You make me what I am. You make me strong. You're perfect, and you're beautiful, and I love you. And I need you. And I depend on you. And there's nothing in this world I wouldn't do just to see you smile."

Aren drew a deep, shaking breath. He felt the world grow steady and solid again around him. Deacon looked down at him. He gently wiped away Aren's tears, concern and love and a hint of confusion in his eyes.

Aren didn't blame him for being confused. He was glad Deacon wasn't asking for an explanation for Aren's sudden loss of control, because he wasn't sure he had one to give. But Deacon's reassurances had steadied him. He hadn't made a mistake by bringing Frances into their bed. He had wanted to make Deacon feel good, to give him as much pleasure as he could, to give him the release he knew Deacon so desperately needed, and he realised he had succeeded. His sudden and irrational fear that he'd shamed his lover was nothing but a ghost of his own past.

He was safe, and he was strong, and he was cherished, and there was nothing wrong in the world. He wrapped his arms around Deacon's neck and smiled up at him.

"I love you, too."

They finally dressed and walked downstairs, where Frances waited. The sun was falling low in the sky. It would be time to start the generator soon.

"I should go." Frances held out his hand to Deacon. "Thank you," he said, then he seemed to stumble. His cheeks turned an alarming shade of red. "Not for *this*. I mean, for before. For everything."

Deacon laughed as he shook Frances' hand. "Sorry about your nose."

Frances touched the tiny bend in it. He smiled. "I'm not." He turned to Aren, stepping up close to him, but then he stopped short, glancing over Aren's shoulder at Deacon.

"Don't mind me," Deacon said.

Frances smiled. He put his arms around Aren's waist, and he kissed him. It was soft, and hesitant. It was pleasant, but it was nothing like when Deacon kissed him. It didn't trigger arousal in him the way Deacon's kisses did. Frances parted his lips, leaning in to deepen the kiss, and Aren was about to pull away when a familiar, solid presence leaned against his back. Aren felt Deacon's lips on the back of his neck. One of Deacon's hands slid down Aren's stomach, cupping his groin. Deacon wrapped his other arm around them both, pulling Frances tighter against Aren's body.

Suddenly, every nerve in Aren's body was on fire. Deacon was against his back, nibbling on his neck and caressing him, and Frances was at his front, kissing him urgently, and Aren's knees suddenly felt as if they wouldn't hold him anymore. He heard himself moan.

Frances suddenly broke their kiss. He was breathless, his cheeks flushed, his lips moist. He glanced over Aren's shoulder at Deacon. "Another night?" he asked.

"Definitely," Deacon said. "Next time, we'll make Aren scream."

Chapter Thirty-One

"Son of a bitch!"

Aren awoke with a start. There was something terribly, terribly wrong. Aren knew it. He sensed it. His heart began to race, and yet his sleep-addled brain couldn't quite focus on what it was.

Next to him, Deacon was sitting straight up in bed. "*Son of a bitch!*" Deacon swore again. He jumped out of bed and pulled on his pants. "It can't be," he said. "I checked it. It was fine! It was only last week. It can't—"

"What's going on?" Aren asked.

"The generator," Deacon said as he pulled a shirt on over his head.

Then it hit Aren what was wrong—the low, chronic whine of the generator was gone. There was only the wind outside, and a strange, eerie silence. Aren's heart began to pound in his chest.

"What do we do?" he asked, getting out of bed and reaching for his own clothes.

"'We' don't do anything. You stay here. I'm going to check on it."

"But you'll have to go outside—"

"Aren, if Olsa's right, they won't take me. Whatever's wrong with it, I should be able to fix fast. You stay here." He grabbed Aren's shoulders and kissed him on the forehead. "Keep the door closed," he said. "You'll be fine."

But Aren heard the tremor in his voice. He saw the hint of panic in Deacon's eyes before he turned away.

No matter how brave he tried to sound, Deacon was scared—and that frightened Aren more than the wraiths.

Deacon left, closing the bedroom door behind him, and Aren paced. His heart pounded as he waited for the sound of the generator starting again, but it never came. What if Olsa was wrong? What if the wraiths could take Deacon? What if they had taken him already?

Aren paced some more, wishing he had his pocket watch. He had no idea how much time had passed. It felt like hours but might have been only minutes.

He paced the length of the small room again and again, growing more nervous with each step. He began to count seconds. When he reached sixty, he started again. By his seventh time through, he was beginning to panic. When he reached nine, he grabbed his pants, pulling them on as quickly as he could.

Something was wrong. Something had happened. He had to find Deacon.

He was reaching for the doorknob when Deacon burst into the room. He slammed the door shut and leaned against it, breathing hard. He leaned over and put his hands on his knees, and Aren could see that he was shaking.

The generator still wasn't running.

"Deacon?" Aren asked, willing his heart to stop pounding, willing his voice to sound normal instead of squeaky and scared. "What's wrong?"

"Somebody did this, Aren," Deacon said. "Somebody sawed through the cable. I checked it just last week, and it was fine. There's no way it could have worn through in that amount of time. They must've sawed most of the way through and left just enough that it would run for a bit but would wear through quick."

"You're saying somebody sabotaged it?"

Deacon looked up at him. "That ain't all. The ward on the cellar door's ruined, too. Whoever it was must have used a shovel or a hoe or an axe and scraped some of the paint away."

"I just checked it the other night," Aren said.

"Me, too." Deacon stood up finally, looking gravely at Aren.

The wind battered against the windows. Aren felt himself shiver. The gravity of their situation was beginning to become mind-numbingly clear. "Is there any way to fix it?" he asked.

Deacon shook his head. "Not without a new cable."

"Coal?" Aren asked. "There's a bucket outside, under the porch to stay dry—"

But Deacon was already shaking his head. "Not the windmill that's busted. Cable runs the engine. Coal or wind, I can't make it work without another one."

"Is there one anywhere on the ranch?"

"Only in the other generators, and they're bigger. Even if we could get over there to take one, it wouldn't work."

Aren hugged his arms around himself. He took a deep breath. Panic wouldn't help them. He needed to be calm.

"Should we try to make it to the house?"

Deacon shook his head. "We'd never make it."

"What do we do?" Aren asked again.

"Best bet is to keep the doors closed," Deacon said. "Hope the wards will hold. Hope for the best." He crossed over to Aren and pulled him into his arms, holding him tight. "We'll be fine," he said. "Just have to get through until morning."

They were brave words, but even Deacon didn't sound like he believed them.

* * * *

Deacon took the comforter off the bed and settled on the floor, leaning back against the bed so they could see the door, although Aren wasn't sure what they were watching for. Wraiths couldn't be seen.

Deacon reached up and took Aren's hand, pulling him to the floor. Aren settled between Deacon's legs. He leant back against him, and Deacon wrapped the blanket around them both. With his lover's broad chest behind him and his strong arms holding him tight, it was hard to believe anything could touch him.

"I have to tell you about my parents," Deacon said quietly into his ear. "I should have told you sooner."

"You weren't ready."

"I was being a fool. I put you in danger."

"How?"

"Listen," Deacon said. He shifted his weight, allowing Aren to cuddle closer. "You've heard Jeremiah mention Ezriel?"

"Yes. He says he was your father."

"Maybe," he said. "Maybe not. Ezriel was the eldest brother. More than ten years older than Jeremiah actually, and by a different wife. He was supposed to inherit this ranch. He's the one who built this house."

There was a screech outside—the wind, maybe, or something more, and Aren shivered. Deacon wrapped the blanket more tightly around them. "He got married young, and he and his wife lived out here for ten years, but she never got with child. Jeremiah was getting to the age where he was getting offers of dowries from other families. And that was bad for Ezriel."

"Why?"

"Old Man Pane decided that instead of splitting his ranch in two, he'd give it to whichever son had an heir first."

"Why?" Aren asked again.

Behind him, he felt Deacon shrug. "Olsa says he was starting to see that Ezriel was lazy, and Jeremiah wasn't. Or maybe he wanted to light a fire under Ezriel's ass. Maybe he thought it made more sense to pass it to somebody who already had an heir of his own. I can't say. But about that time, Jeremiah got married, and Ezriel knew it was only a matter of time before that wife of his had a baby. So he went to town, and he got himself a new wife."

"Wasn't he already married?"

"He was, but guess he didn't love her too much, and the feeling must have been mutual, 'cause as soon as he came home with his new woman, his first wife packed up and left."

"And his new wife was your mother?"

It took Deacon a moment to answer. It was cold in the room. Aren wondered if the fire in the downstairs hearth had gone out. He huddled closer to Deacon, trying to steal his warmth.

"You remember the platform in town?" Deacon finally asked, his voice low.

"Yes. You said they used it to auction off slaves."

"That's where he found my mother."

"You mean...?"

"He bought her. I guess someone had found a shack of Ainuai hiding in the mountains, and they killed the men—or so they thought—and dragged the women into town to sell."

"Holy Saints," Aren said, shivering again. "That's awful."

"If you ask Olsa, she'll say it ain't much different from dowries, but that's neither here nor there. Ezriel brought her back here. And it caused a stir, because this was right at the end of the slave trade, and some people thought it was wrong. I think Olsa had a right fit. But Old Man Pane didn't much mind, so Ezriel kept her here."

"In this house?"

"Yes," Deacon said, his voice shaking. "Jeremiah told me later that he locked her in the cellar at first, until she agreed not to run away. After that, I guess she was compliant enough. Her family was dead. She didn't have anywhere else to go. And Olsa was here, so I guess she settled in. And whether she was allowing Ezriel what he thought was his, or whether he was just taking, I don't know. But it seemed Ezriel was happy enough, bragging that he was bound to be a daddy soon."

"That's disgusting."

"I know it. About that time, they had a new hand show up, too. His name was Uly, and he was dark like me."

"Ainuai?"

"Right. And Old Man Pane thought that was lucky, 'cause he didn't have to pay him too much. Ainuai couldn't ask for full wages. They figured they were lucky not to be up on that auction block like my ma had been. So things here at the BarChi went back to normal until about a year later, when I was born."

"Olsa said she knew as soon as she saw you that you weren't Ezriel's son."

"Apparently that's what Ezriel thought, too. He walked right out of the room. Grabbed his gun on the way. Walked right up to Uly and shot him dead."

"Holy Saints," Aren whispered again. He couldn't believe how cold the room was getting. He couldn't stop shivering.

"This was before the generators," Deacon said. "It was right as the wards were starting to fail. That night, after Ezriel was asleep, my ma put me in my crib. She went downstairs and opened all the doors. Then she went down to that cellar. She took the gun Ezriel had used on Uly, and she used it to kill herself."

"The wraiths took Ezriel?"

"They did. But that's not the end of the story. Or it is, but there's part that I left out. See, once my ma and Uly were dead, Olsa sang their death songs, but she said she knew it didn't take. That was when she thought to check for marks. And she found two on each of them. They had each others' marks on their arms. Olsa said those scars were old."

"What does that mean?"

"Means they were married, before my ma was sold. Probably he followed her here to be with her. The other sign—Uly's had been there a while, but my ma's was fresh, carved into her chest just before she died."

"What sign?"

"The sign to keep her from passing into the sacred land."

"She became a wraith?" He wished he could just get warm. He wished they could go downstairs and sit by the fire.

"She did, but she did it wrong. She should have been outside. That way, she'd have been out there with the others. She did it inside walls, and maybe she sang the song wrong, too. I don't know. But now she's trapped." He was quiet for a minute, then said, his voice quieter, "That's her down in your cellar. She's been stuck there since she died."

"Your m—m—mom?" He was shivering so hard now, it was hard to talk. "M—m—maybe you should try reasoning with her?"

It was a bad attempt at a joke, and Deacon snorted. "It don't really work like that," he said. "There ain't that much of her left. The longer they're wraiths, the more they forget."

Aren thought about that, shivering harder. Something wasn't adding up, although it took him a moment to put his finger on it. "W—w—wait," he said, fighting to keep his teeth from chattering. "But if she's a wr—wraith, she should only have c—c—caused trouble at n—night."

"She did only cause trouble at night. That's what I'm trying to explain. All that other stuff—your paintings, and things being broken when you were gone—it had to be somebody else."

Who? That was what Aren tried to ask, but he couldn't make himself speak.

"Aren?" Deacon asked.

So cold, Aren thought. He was going numb. He felt like he couldn't quite breathe.

"Aren?" Deacon said again, and Aren could hear the fear in his voice. Deacon pushed him away, turning him around in his strong arms so that he could look at him.

No, Aren tried to say. *You're the only thing keeping me warm.*

"Oh, Saints, Aren!" Deacon cried. His hands gripped Aren's shoulders, and he shook him hard. "No, no, no!"

It was getting harder to breathe. No matter how he tried, he couldn't seem to get enough air to fill his lungs. They burnt.

"Aren!"

It's fine. Just have to stay warm. I need you to keep me warm.

"Aren, don't you go," Deacon said, suddenly pulling him close and hugging him tight. "I can't lose you. I don't know what to do."

The wraiths have come.

He found he didn't care too much. He knew he didn't want to leave the BarChi, or Deacon, but the feeling seemed remote. It was a faded memory.

Deacon was sobbing now, holding Aren close. "He's mine, he's mine," he cried, rocking Aren as he'd rocked Olsa. "Take me. Take me instead, or take us both. Don't take him and leave me. He's mine! Don't—"

He stopped short, suddenly pulling away to look down at Aren. Aren felt the loss of his body heat like a blow to the gut. He gasped harder, fighting to breathe.

"That's it!" Deacon looked up at the painting on the armoire, of him inside the brand, then back down at Aren. "I'll be right back," he said. "Don't you give up!"

Don't leave! I'm so cold!

Deacon's footsteps seemed to pound on the floorboards as he ran from the room. It seemed to Aren he was part of the house. He could feel the path of Deacon's boots as he ran into Aren's studio and back to the bedroom where Aren lay gasping on the floor. Deacon pulled his shirt off and knelt by Aren's side. "Please let this work, please let this work, please let this work," he said over and over again. Aren felt Deacon take his hand, although it seemed his hand was somehow very, very far away. Deacon pressed something into it. He lifted Aren's hand. Aren was starting to see spots. The room was becoming distorted and dark, but he recognised what was in his hand—it was his penknife. Deacon's hand was wrapped around his, and he pushed the point into his own bare chest.

"Make your mark," he said, "like on your paintings."

Aren's hand shook. He was so weak.

"Please, Aren," Deacon begged. "Make it big."

Then he ducked his head, and he started to sing.

It was an Ainuai song. Aren couldn't understand the words, although they made a beautiful pattern in his mind, repeating over and over. "Ailua ma'ana nai'i roha'ala. Ailua ma'ana nai'i roha'ala. Ailua ma'ana nai'i roha'ala." Aren summoned every last bit of his strength. He pushed the knife into Deacon's chest and made his mark.

It was poorly done. His hand shook. The lines wavered. The knife started to slip from his fingers, but Deacon's hand closed over his, helping him carve the last line.

"Ailua ma'ana nai'i roha'ala. Ailua ma'ana nai'i roha'ala," Deacon continued to sing.

Aren couldn't see anymore. He couldn't breathe. He closed his eyes. He just wanted it to end. If it weren't for the horrible coldness, he'd feel nothing. He almost felt nothing already. Then...

Something.

A tick. An itch. A tingle on his chest that wasn't quite right, followed by a hint of warmth. It flowed over his chest, down his side. It lasted only a second. Almost as soon as it had begun, the warmth faded.

There was only cold.

"Ailua ma'ana nai'i roha'ala. Ailua ma'ana nai'i roha'ala."

He was dying. He knew that now. The wraiths were taking him. This was what Garrett had gone through. Garrett had died in Deacon's arms, too.

"Ailua ma'ana nai'i roha'ala. Ailua ma'ana nai'i roha'ala."

He wondered what would happen now. He wondered if Deacon would go on living in the house. He wondered if he'd take a wife.

"Ailua ma'ana nai'i roha'ala. Ailua ma'ana nai'i roha'ala."

Something pressed against his lips. Something warm and soft and heartbreakingly familiar. Even from the distant place where he now dwelt, he recognised the feel and the taste of Deacon's kiss.

Then blessed air!

Aren choked. He gasped. The warmth that finally filled his lungs burnt like fire, but he could breathe!

"Aren!" Deacon cried in relief, pulling him into his arms. "Thank the Sain—" He stopped. He seemed to choke on the words. Then, as Aren breathed hard, as his fingers and toes began to tingle with new warmth, as the fog cleared and his vision returned, Deacon rocked him in his arms, and he sang. "Sa'ahala nai'alini. Sa'ahala nai'alini."

Aren knew that song. He'd heard it before, the day Olsa had almost died.

It was the song of thanks.

* * * *

"I still don't understand," Aren said some time later. They'd moved downstairs, in front of the fire, and Deacon had slammed a healthy measure of whisky before pushing a glass into Aren's hand as well. After that, he didn't seem inclined to let Aren get more than two feet away from him.

"What don't you understand?" Deacon asked.

"If it wasn't the ghost — the *wraith* — then who was it?"

Deacon ducked his head, his cheeks turning red. And Aren suddenly realised he knew the answer.

"Dante," he said. He thought back to what Deacon had told him a few weeks before. "You said Old Man Pane caught you in the barn with another boy. You didn't say a ranch hand. You said another *boy*. The only boys on this ranch were you and Jeremiah's sons."

Deacon nodded. "Old Man Pane tanned my ass, but he never thought I was worth much anyway. But Dante was his oldest grandson and the one he loved most, and it hurt him to find us like that. It hurt Dante a lot to suddenly have his granddad refuse to look at him." He rubbed his eyes, and Aren thought he'd rarely seen him look so tired. "Dante hated me after that."

"It wasn't your fault, I'm sure."

"Well, yes and no. I sure didn't force him to be in that barn with me. He was willing enough. But I think it was easier to blame me and try to win his place back in his granddaddy's heart. And once Old Man Pane was gone, Jeremiah arranged for Daisy. I thought he'd be happy, but he never was."

"Did he ever try to get you back?"

"He came to me once, not long after Cody died. He was drunk, and he told me how he couldn't never make things work with Daisy. Not with women much in general." He glanced up at Aren. "He's more like you than me. He told me he was sorry. He told me he still loved me—that he'd always loved me..."

"But you didn't love him back?"

"Not by then. Maybe I thought I did when we was boys, but he'd been damn unpleasant to me in the years that followed. Then to come to me right after Cody died? I could barely stand to look at him, I was so mad."

Aren had heard the expression that love and hate were two sides of the same coin, but never before had he fully understood it. "All this time, I thought it was Tama he was in love with."

Deacon laughed, a short, humourless sound. "I wish. They're friends. I think Tama understands him better than most."

"You think he's the one who sabotaged the generator?"

"Can't imagine it would be anybody else," Deacon said, and Aren had to agree with him.

Aren started to reach for Deacon, but the pain in his chest caused him to stop short. He looked down at himself, pulling the blanket Deacon had wrapped around him aside to see the mark that was scabbing over. It was the BarChi brand, and inside it, the A he signed his paintings with. Despite being scared, Deacon had made the mark small and neat. The corresponding mark on his own chest wasn't nearly as pretty. Aren's A was too big, slightly askew, the lines wobbly, but inside it, Deacon had carved the BarChi brand.

"What does it mean?" he asked.

Deacon ducked his head, his cheeks turning red. "It means we're married. Not legally, I mean, but according to the Ainuai."

"And that saved me?"

"They won't take me," he said, "and they won't take what's mine."

Aren was almost afraid to ask his next question, but he did. "Could you have saved Garrett this way?"

To his surprise, Deacon laughed. "No. The ancestors will know if you try to lie. They would've known I was trying to cheat them." He blushed again, but he didn't look away. "They would've known I didn't love him."

Aren looked again at the mark on his chest. "It's going to be a wicked scar," he said. "I might actually look tough."

Deacon laughed, reaching out to pull Aren into his arms. "You are tough." He pushed Aren's hair out of the way and looked down into his eyes. "I have a confession to make, though." His eyes still had laughter in them, but Aren saw a shadow pass through them as he remembered what had happened only a few hours before. "I was so scared. I wasn't thinking right. I sang the song the way Olsa taught me when I was a boy."

"What's wrong with that?" Aren asked.

"I called you a woman. I claimed you as my wife."

Aren laughed. "Saints, I don't care! If it was good enough for your ancestors, it's good enough for me!" Deacon kissed his neck and as he did, Aren thought about everything Deacon had told him before the wraiths had almost taken him. "So, Jeremiah wanted you to be Ezriel's son. And Olsa wanted you to be Uly's. And instead of choosing between them, you refused them both."

Deacon stopped kissing his neck. He pulled back to look down at him, his eyes thoughtful. "Can't say I ever thought of it like that, but I guess that's right enough."

"How did you think of it?"

"Jeremiah wanted me to be Ezriel's heir. Olsa wanted me to be a descendant of the Ainuai." He shrugged. "I can't be both."

"Obviously you can," Aren said, "because you are."

Chapter Thirty-Two

Aren woke an indeterminable time later to the sound of a door slamming. It took him a moment to get his bearings. He was on the rug in his living room. The sun was up. The fire had burnt out. The wound on his chest throbbed.

Deacon was gone.

Aren looked out of the window and saw him, already halfway across the grass to the main house and walking with a steady determination that bespoke danger.

This can't be good.

Aren rushed upstairs, tearing his room apart in an effort to find pants before realising he already had them on from the night before. He found his shirt and hurriedly pulled on his shoes. He sprinted after Deacon, catching him just as he reached the main house.

"What are you doing?" Aren panted.

"Going to kill Dante."

"*What?* Deacon, no!" He tried to grab Deacon, to pull him back, but Deacon turned and roughly pushed him away.

"Aren, stay out of it!"

Deacon walked into the kitchen, and Aren followed. The hands were eating, and as they entered, all eyes turned their way. Aren bit back his protests, ducking his head. Even now, he would not question Deacon in front of his men. He followed him out of the kitchen, into the hallway that led to the dining room.

"Deacon, wait!" He kept his voice low, but he reached out and grabbed Deacon's arm. "Please, don't do anything you might regret later!"

Deacon turned on him. He grabbed Aren's shoulders and pushed him back against the wall. He looked down into Aren's eyes. He wasn't mad, Aren realised. He was scared. "Do you have any idea how close you came to dying last night?" he asked, his voice unsteady. He shook his head. "I can't take a chance he'll try again, Aren. Your life means more to me than his."

"What about Jeremiah?" Aren asked. "What about the ranch?"

Deacon shook his head again. "I don't know," he said. "I guess we're about to find out." He leant down and kissed Aren's forehead. "I love you, Aren. But don't you dare get in my way."

There was nothing Aren could do but follow Deacon as he burst into the Pane's dining room.

"Tama, Daisy," Deacon said as he walked into the room, "take the boys out of here."

Neither Tama or Daisy moved. In fact, nobody moved. They all stared at Deacon in mute shock and confusion. Only Jeremiah seemed able to respond.

"What the hell is going on, Deacon?" he asked.

Deacon didn't answer. He walked straight up to Dante. He grabbed him by his shirt and pulled him from his chair, slamming him into the corner. "Did you think I wouldn't know it was you?" he asked, holding him against the wall. "Did you honestly think it would change anything?"

Dante's eyes were huge. His voice shook when he answered. "What was me?" he asked. "What did I do?"

"Don't pretend like you don't know!"

"But I don't—"

"Deacon!" Tama said, standing up from the table. "Why don't you calm down? Let Dante go and tell us what's wrong."

Deacon didn't let go of Dante, but he turned to look at Tama over his shoulder. "Unless you want those boys of yours to see something they'll never be able to forget, I suggest you get them out of the blessed room like I told you."

The blood drained from Tama's face. Next to her, Daisy's hand flew to her mouth, her eyes wide.

"Girls," Jeremiah said, finally standing up from the table, "I think you should do as Deacon said."

The two boys, who were only four or five years old, were starting to cry and Tama turned to them quickly, hushing them gently, grabbing Daisy's arm as she did and pulling the other woman out of her chair. "Come on, boys," she said. "Everything's all right. Let's go down to the kitchen and see if Olsa will give you some of her cheese."

Daisy seemed to have finally come to her senses. She took the hand of the smallest boy, and she and Tama herded them out of the room. The rest of them—Deacon,

Dante, Aren, Jeremiah and Jay—stood frozen in place. Once the women were gone, Jeremiah turned to where Deacon still held Dante in the corner.

"Deacon." Jeremiah's voice was quiet, but with the unmistakable weight of authority. "Let go of my son."

Deacon did, but he didn't do it gently. He slammed Dante backwards into the wall as he let him go. "If those boys hadn't been in the room, you'd be dead already, you son of a bitch."

Dante held his hands up in front of him, his eyes still wide with fear and confusion. "Deacon, I don't know what—"

"*Don't lie to me!*" Deacon yelled.

Dante winced, but he didn't break. "Tell me what you think I did."

"Were you trying to kill us both, or just get rid of Aren?" Deacon asked.

Dante glanced towards Aren and, for the first time, Aren saw a hint of panic in his eyes. For the first time, he thought he saw comprehension. "Kill?" Dante asked, his voice shaky. "I never tried to *kill* anybody!"

"Are you telling me it wasn't you?" Deacon asked. "Sneaking into the house during the day? Breaking things? Destroying Aren's paintings? Are you trying to tell me that wasn't you?"

Tama stumbled alone back into the room. She stopped short next to Aren, her hand over her mouth and her eyes wide. Dante glanced at her. His cheeks started to turn red. He turned back to Dante. "All right," he said. "Yes, that was me, but—"

"Bastard!" Deacon yelled. He lunged for Dante again, grabbing his lapels and slamming him against the wall. Jay and Jeremiah both moved closer, obviously unsure whether they should interfere or not. "Why did you do it?" Deacon asked.

Dante glanced towards Aren before answering. "I wanted to scare him," he said. "That's all. I thought the house would scare him away, but when it didn't..." His words trailed away, and he turned back to Deacon. "I only wanted him to leave the ranch," he said, his voice quieter.

"And when he didn't run, you decided to sabotage our generator instead?"

Dante's mouth fell open. He stared at Deacon, his eyes wide and uncomprehending. He looked shocked. And surprised. It was an expression that couldn't be faked, and Aren felt the first hint of doubt in the back of his mind.

"Deacon," Jeremiah said, moving closer. He was close enough he could have grabbed Deacon and attempted to pull him away, but he didn't try. "What is this?" he asked.

"He destroyed our generator! And he ruined the ward on the cellar door!"

"No!" Dante said. "No, I didn't!"

"*Liar!*"

"Deacon, I would never do anything to put you in danger."

"Then who was it?" Deacon yelled. "If not you, then who?"

"*It was me.*"

The voice came from behind Aren, and everybody in the room turned as one to look towards it. Daisy stood in the doorway. Her cheeks were red, but her head was held high, her arms straight at her sides.

"Oh, no," Tama moaned, backing up against the wall, her hands over her mouth.

"Daisy!" Dante said. "How could you?"

Deacon had relaxed his grip on Dante, although he still held him against the wall. "Why?" he asked Daisy.

"Don't stand there and pretend like you don't know!" she said. "All these years, I've watched him pine for you. He's *my* husband, but *you're* the only one he ever wanted! Always watching you and waiting for you to notice. It was your name he'd say in his sleep. The few times he was drunk enough to find his way between my legs, I'd lie there knowing he was thinking of you as he did it!"

Dante's cheeks were red with shame, and he pushed Deacon away. Deacon let him go. Dante buried his face in his hands, and despite everything, Aren felt a sudden rush of pity for him.

Nobody else was looking at him, though. Everybody else was staring at Daisy. "You think it's *my* fault?" Deacon asked. "You think I ever asked for any of it?"

"I don't care whose fault it is," she said. "If it weren't for you, I'd have a real husband. If it weren't for you, we'd be leaving this Saints-blessed ranch and starting a family up north. Instead, I'm stuck here, watching the man I love be in love with you!"

"Daisy," Jeremiah said, but Aren never learnt what Jeremiah planned to say.

She raised her right hand from behind her skirt. Jeremiah's gun was in it. She pointed it straight at Deacon. "I hate you!" she said.

Aren had just enough time to grab for her hand, knocking her aim downwards before she pulled the trigger.

The sound was deafening in the small room. Tama screamed. Aren wrenched the gun from her hand and it fell to the floor, clattering dully on the wooden planks. Deacon crossed the room in three fast strides and punched her in the face. It wasn't quite a full punch. It was nothing like when he'd punched Red or Frances, but it was enough to knock her down onto the floor.

She held her hand over her bleeding lip and glared up at him. "Go ahead!" she said. "Prove what a tough man you are by beating me up! That's how you always do it, isn't it?"

"Deacon!" Jay shouted. "Dad's hit!"

They all turned back to the other end of the room. Jeremiah was sitting on the floor, leaning against the wall. Jay was next to him, pushing down hard on his leg. Blood welled up between his fingers. On Jeremiah's other side, Dante looked up at Deacon. "Help him," he said.

As always, in a moment of crisis it was Deacon they turned to to solve their problems. And as always, Deacon did what needed to be done.

"Aren, help me," Deacon said as he moved to Jeremiah's side. Aren went to the man's other side, and between them, they helped Jeremiah to his feet, half-dragging and half-carrying him from the room.

"Dante, you and Jay take Daisy. Lock her up or tie her up or cut her fucking throat. I don't care which. Just make sure she can't do any more damage. Tama, do we have morphine now?"

"Yes," Tama said, her voice shaking. "We bought some after Miron."

"Go get it. Tell Olsa whatever else she has, we'll need it. Bring clean cloths and bandages and some water. And any kind of strong alcohol you can find. A sharp knife. And whatever you'll need to sew the wound when we're done."

Nobody argued. Everybody jumped to follow his orders.

Aren and Deacon awkwardly manoeuvred Jeremiah down the hall. Their progress was unbearably slow. "We'll never get him up the stairs to his bedroom," Deacon said. They took him instead to the living room, where they laid him on the couch. His face was white, his teeth clenched. "How you doing, old man?" Deacon asked.

"Hurts like all hell," Jeremiah said.

Tama arrived with her arms full. She dumped most of her burden onto the table by the door and held a cup out to Deacon. "Drink this," Deacon said, and he helped hold Jeremiah up while he drained the cup.

"Aren," Deacon said, "wash your hands as good as you can. Have Tama pour the alcohol on them."

"Why?" Aren asked as Tama came to him with a bottle of whisky, a bowl and some towels.

"You have to get the bullet out of his thigh."

"What?" Aren asked, as his heart began to pound. "I don't know how to —"

"Aren, look!" Deacon grabbed Aren's wrist. He held Aren's hand up, and his own hand palm to palm with it. With the heels of their hands touching, Aren's fingers ended at the knuckle below Deacon's fingertips. Next to Deacon's thick, callused fingers, Aren's hand looked small and dainty. Aren looked up into Deacon's eyes. There was no mistaking the desperation he saw there. "It'll hurt him a lot less if you do it," Deacon said.

"All right." Although he was still wasn't sure he could. The thought of it made his heart race with fear.

Tama poured the whisky into a large bowl. Aren noticed her hands were shaking and her face was ashen. "I'm not good with blood," she told him. "I'll have to leave the room while you do it."

Aren washed his hands in the alcohol, and as he did, Deacon knelt down next to Jeremiah's bleeding leg. "This is bound to be awkward for us both," he said, "but we've got to get those pants off."

"I always knew you was that way," Jeremiah said. Deacon laughed, and Aren supposed it was a good sign that they could still joke.

Jeremiah unlaced his pants. Once the fly was open, Deacon grabbed them and ripped them down the leg, exposing Jeremiah's thigh.

"You ready?" Deacon asked Jeremiah.

"Not yet," Jeremiah said, and Aren breathed a mental sigh of relief. "Give the morphine a bit more time to kick in. Wait for my sons so they can help hold me down. You won't be able to do it on your own."

Aren dried his hands, willing them to stop shaking. Tama handed him a knife. Her face had gone from grey to slightly green. It was clear she wasn't going to last much longer in the room with them. "The sharpest we have," she said. "I already washed it."

"What do I need it for?" he asked, feeling that he should know, but unable to make his brain work.

Tama didn't answer. She clamped her hand over her mouth and ran for the door.

"You'll have to cut his leg," Deacon said as he came to stand in front of Aren. "Bullet just makes a tiny hole. Even with your small fingers, you'll have to make the opening wider."

Aren looked down at the knife in horror. He felt his bile rise. He was sure he was going to be sick. He heard Jay and Dante come into the room behind him. Couldn't one of them do it?

"Aren," Deacon said, taking Aren's face in his hands, forcing Aren to look into his eyes. "The rest of us will have to hold him down. It has to be you. You can do this. I know you can."

"I'm scared," Aren said.

"So am I."

Those three tiny words hit Aren hard. Deacon was scared, too. Of course he was. Jeremiah was the only father he'd ever known, no matter that he wasn't actually his father at all. Aren looked around the room and realised that every person there was scared, Jeremiah himself probably most of all. Somehow, the knowledge calmed him.

"All right," he said, looking back at Deacon. "I'm ready."

They moved Jeremiah to the floor so they could more easily hold him down. Aren knelt next to his leg. It was a mess of blood. He could barely tell where the entrance was at all. He used a clean rag and some whisky to wipe away the blood until he found its source.

Deacon had been right. The hole was surprisingly small. Aren was able to slide his finger down into it. He had to push hard to reach the bullet. Jeremiah screamed, and the men holding him strained to keep him from moving. Aren pushed deeper and was able to feel the metal against the tip of his finger. There was no way to grab it though, or to manoeuvre it back up the opening it had made.

He pulled his finger back out and picked up the knife, debating the best way to proceed.

"The muscles go up and down," Deacon said. "Probably best to cut that direction, rather than across them."

Aren had no idea if that actually mattered or not, but he had no reason to argue with it either.

He was never sure afterwards how he'd done it. Somehow, he made the cut. He slid his fingers into Jeremiah's open thigh, and as the man screamed, fighting against the men who held him down, Aren pulled the bullet out of his flesh.

"Who's going to sew it?" he asked, looking up at the others.

They all looked at each other, apparently having not thought that far ahead.

"Shay always did it," Jay said, but of course Shay was dead.

"Can't trust Daisy," Dante said. "And Tama can't stand the blood."

They all looked at Aren, and he was about to say he'd never sewn anything in his life when Tama came into the room. She was positively green, and she kept her eyes averted as she inched into the room, holding a small bowl out to them. "Olsa says don't sew it. She says better if it can drain. She says pack this in and bandage it. She says…"

Jay jumped up and managed to grab the bowl from her before she ran from the room, retching. Jay shook his head. "You'd think after all these years, she'd be used to it."

"Go clean up," Deacon said to Aren, gently pushing him out of the way. "Jay and I can do the rest."

Aren sat back, sighing in relief. Deacon smiled over at him. "You did good," he said quietly, and Aren couldn't help but smile back at him. At least, he smiled until he saw Dante watching them, grief and jealousy etched on his face.

Aren went to the kitchen. The hands had been sent outside. Aren could hear them buzzing in the courtyard, no doubt wondering what had happened. He was extremely relieved to not have to face them.

Olsa worked the pump for him as he washed the blood from his hands.

"Did he sing the nai'i?" she asked.

Aren didn't know if that was the song Deacon had sung or not. He pulled the collar of his shirt aside. He took her hand and placed it on the mark on his chest.

"Symbols have power," he said.

She looked up at him with her sightless eyes and smiled. "Such a smart boy."

* * * *

When his hands were clean, Aren went back down the hall towards the living room. The door was still closed. Only Dante had emerged. He sat in a chair against the wall, his head in his hands. He glanced up at Aren, and Aren saw that his eyes were red. His cheeks were wet with tears.

"I never meant you any harm. I just..." His words trailed away and he shook his head.

"You just wanted him for yourself," Aren said.

Dante looked up at him. "I did." Behind him, Aren heard the door open and close again. A glance over his shoulder revealed that it was Deacon. Dante looked down at the floor, apparently unable to face the man he loved.

"Daisy can't stay here," Deacon said.

"I know. Jay's taking her with him tomorrow when he goes into town. What she does from there is her own problem."

"What about you?" Deacon asked.

Dante looked up, over Aren's shoulder at Deacon. His eyes were so full of shame, and yet, behind it all, Aren saw a hint of hope. For the second time that morning, Aren found himself feeling sorry for the man.

"We used to dream when we were boys about the day this ranch would be ours," Dante said to Deacon. "You always said you didn't want to own it, and that meant it would pass to me, and we talked about how we'd work it together. That's how it was supposed to be. The BarChi is ours, Deacon. That's all I ever wanted — to run this ranch with you."

"If you'd said that to me twelve years ago, or ten, or even eight, it might have meant something," Deacon said. "But the time when we could have made that work is long since passed."

That spark of hope started to waver, drowned by the tears that filled Dante's eyes. "We could try," he said, his voice barely a whisper.

Deacon didn't respond, but when Aren turned to look at him, he could see the answer on his lover's face. Dante's plea obviously stirred pity in him, but there was no love in his eyes.

"I think you should go north," Deacon said. "Take over the Austin ranch. Make it your own."

"But—"

"The BarChi is *mine*," Deacon said.

"I could help you—"

"Stop!" Deacon said. He stepped up next to Aren, taking his hand as he looked down at Dante. "I got all the help I need."

Dante's face seemed to crumple. He put his head in his hands. Deacon didn't say another word. He used his grip on Aren's hand to pull him past where Dante sat and down the hall.

Dante's shoulders shook with silent sobs as they passed. Watching him, Aren felt no anger or resentment. He felt only sympathy. "I'm sorry," he said to Dante as Deacon pulled him towards the door.

He wasn't sure if Dante heard him or not. He wasn't sure if it mattered, anyway.

Deacon took him to the kitchen. Its warmth and brightness stood in stark contrast against the backdrop of the morning's events. The room smelt of honey and porridge and Aren realised suddenly how hungry he was. It was far past the time when he normally ate.

"Bet you're glad now I made you learn the nai'i," Olsa said to Deacon.

He smiled at her, then gently wrapped his arm around her waist and hugged her. He kissed her on the cheek. "I am."

"Ungrateful brat," she said fondly, pushing him away. "There's something else you need to do."

Deacon sighed again, his cheeks turning red. "I know. There's one more song we need to sing."

* * * *

The rest of the day passed in a flurry of work. Frances left for the Austin ranch and Dante went with him, as did Calin and Aubry. The hands who were left behind had plenty to do, and Aren did his best to help them. Jeremiah still swore the BarChi belonged to Deacon, and for the first time, Deacon seemed to agree.

Jay and Deacon went over the generator again, but there was nothing to be done until Jay came back from town with a new cable.

"Coal won't work," Aren said. "I guess we sleep somewhere else until he gets back?"

Deacon laughed at him. "It don't matter. The wraiths can't touch you now."

That evening, after supper, Olsa walked with Deacon and Aren across the grass to their house. Deacon carried a shovel. Aren followed them up the porch steps, through the front door and down the short hallway to the pantry. The ruined ward greeted them. Somehow, Aren had forgotten about the ghost — *the wraith*, he corrected himself — in the cellar.

"Will you repaint the ward?" he asked.

Deacon shook his head as he reached down and unlatched the door. "Something better." He grabbed the handle and swung it open. Aren instinctively took a step backwards, running into the wall behind him. "Don't worry," Deacon said to him. "She can't hurt you now. Can't do anything in the daytime, even if you didn't have that mark on you."

He went down into the cellar, and Aren made himself walk to the edge and look down.

It was a cellar like any other. There was nothing to hint at the horror it had seen. The floor was dirt. The walls were lined with empty shelves.

Olsa reached over and grabbed Aren's arm. "Help me down," she said.

"Down into the cellar?" Aren asked, horrified at the thought of trying to get her down the rickety ladder and back up again.

"Don't be a fool," she said, to Aren's relief. "I just need to sit down." With his support, she sat on the wooden floor with her feet hanging through the cellar door.

"Part of the problem is the dirt floor," she said. "Can't use paint. Can't use chalk. Deacon will have to dig to make the mark. You sit there and keep quiet while we sing."

"What exactly are you going to do?" Aren asked.

Deacon looked up at him from the cellar floor. "We're going to make an opening into the spirit world so she can pass. Put her at peace."

Aren looked at Olsa in surprise, then back at Deacon. "You mean, you could have done that all along?"

Deacon shook his head. "It wouldn't have worked if I'd done it," he said.

"Because you didn't believe?"

"Exactly."

Aren looked at Olsa. "But *you* did. You could have done it."

"'Course I could have. But then somebody else would have claimed this house long ago, and it didn't belong to them. Every path that led where I wanted to go ended with him living in this house with his wife." She shrugged. "Didn't know till you got here the wife part wasn't exactly right. Still, it served my purpose to leave the wraith here until Deacon was ready to claim what was his."

"What about all the other wraiths?" Aren asked. "Can't you put them at peace, too? Then nobody would need the generators."

He knew before he'd finished asking the question, though, that the answer was no. Both of them were shaking their heads, but it was Olsa who explained.

"Have to know the right spot," she said. "The exact place they died. I put Uly at peace long ago. But the rest of them?" She shrugged. "We'd have to walk the lengths of Oestend, sing the song over every inch of land."

"Can't be done," Deacon said. "Oestend will have to deal with the wraiths." He smiled up at Aren. "But we won't have to deal with my ma after today."

Aren went into the living room and poured himself a drink. He took it back into the pantry where he sat against the wall, out of the way. He watched. And listened.

Olsa and Deacon both sang. Down in the cellar, Deacon slowly dug a mark into the dirt floor. It took them more than an hour, but even Aren knew when the change happened. The chill that had ever been present in the pantry suddenly abated. The air suddenly seemed cleaner.

The ghost was gone.

"Olsa's a little bit evil," Aren said that night as they climbed into bed.

Deacon laughed as he pulled Aren tightly against him. "You only now figuring that out? All this time I thought you was smart."

"People died because of her," Aren said. "Because she left the wraith here when she could have put it at peace."

Deacon was quiet for a long time, and Aren feared he'd upset him, but he finally sighed and answered. "You got to think about how long Olsa's been alive. How much death she's seen. Every Ainuai she ever knew was killed or sold as a slave. She saw everything that mattered to her forgotten — the songs, the history, the truth of what the settlers had done. She lost her husband. She lost her sons. The only person she had was me, and I was busy being a blessed fool." He shrugged. "People die in Oestend every day. Guess she figured trading a few more against her hope was worth it."

"Do you think it was?"

"I do now." Deacon's arms tightened around Aren. His lips brushed the back of Aren's neck. "There's nothing in this world I wouldn't sacrifice to keep you safe."

"No sacrifices tonight," Aren sighed. "I'd rather sleep."

And so it was that on his first night in an un-haunted house, as the wind howled outside and beat against the shuttered windows of his room, Aren Montrell slept soundly in his bed. He had found his place—in the far, dusty reaches of the Oestend prairie, on a cattle ranch called the BarChi, in the strong, warm arms of the man he loved—and it was the only place in the world he wanted to be.

About the Author

Marie Sexton lives in Colorado. She's a fan of just about anything that involves muscular young men piling on top of each other. In particular, she loves the Denver Broncos and enjoys going to the games with her husband. Her imaginary friends often tag along. Marie has one daughter, two cats, and one dog, all of whom seem bent on destroying what remains of her sanity. She loves them anyway.

Marie Sexton loves to hear from readers. You can find her contact information, website details and author profile page at http://www.total-e-bound.com.

Total-E-Bound Publishing

www.total-e-bound.com

Take a look at our exciting range of literagasmic™
erotic romance titles and discover pure quality
at Total-E-Bound.